Matthew Thom...
Before & After, ...
sheep. He insisted on publication that he had
nothing personal against sheep. He'd like to now
point out that he also has nothing personal
against the Shadow Government and alien
manipulators ruthlessly running our lives for their
own benefits. Matthew Thomas lives somewhere
in England, exact whereabouts unknown.

Matthew Thomas is a pseudonym.

Frank wants to know YOUR conspiracy theories.
Mail him at: Insane_Frank42@hotmail.com

BY MATTHEW THOMAS

Before & After
Terror Firma

Voyager

MATTHEW THOMAS

Terror Firma

HarperCollins*Publishers*

Voyager
An Imprint of HarperCollins*Publishers*
77–85 Fulham Palace Road,
Hammersmith, London w6 8jb

www.voyager-books.com

A Voyager paperback original 2001
1 3 5 7 9 8 6 4 2

Copyright © Matthew Thomas 2000

The Author asserts the moral right to
be identified as the author of this work

ISBN 0-00-710022-1

Set in Goudy Old Style by
Rowland Phototypesetting Ltd
Bury St Edmunds, Suffolk

Printed and bound in Great Britain by
Clays Ltd, St Ives plc

'There are two secrets to the successful clandestine management of human affairs. One, never let on all you know.'

Becker, MJ13

For Lisa and Dan

1. All Good Kings
Must Come to an End

Present day, somewhere, South Pacific

Elvis knew his days were numbered.

Over the past few hectic weeks he'd noticed a number of disturbing trends – a sharp decline in his ongoing manifestation schedule and a steady increase in his already abundant food allowance. They'd upped the steroid dosage too; he was feeling younger than he had for years. Last Tuesday he'd caught himself gyrating his pelvis while pitch-forking a specially prepared 'King'-sized sausage from the weekly beach barbie. He hadn't even known he was doing it. Worse, he'd grabbed John Lennon's guitar as he led the evening campfire singalong and told him to quit with that hippy shit and play somethin' rockin'.

But the implications of what were behind these changes were less palatable that the triple cheese-burger with extra gherkins he'd polished off for breakfast. There was no escaping the conclusion that his time on The Island was coming to an end. He could tell by the way his strange guards watched him that the moment for one last final mission was at hand. And they wouldn't be bothered about stepping on his blue suede shoes, not even ramming their steel toe-capped jack-boots down his throat for that matter – their dull dead dark eyes held no pity, and no understanding as far as he could tell. Elvis felt certain this would be a come-back tour without an encore. He wouldn't be returning from this gig – a final deadly road-trip to end them all.

This knowledge stirred little emotion in his straining

drug-drenched heart, apart perhaps from a sense of weary relief. There was only so much of The Island you could take without losing what was left of your sanity – and he'd lounged in this hellishly opulent five-star prison for the best part of thirty years. After the first decade the rejuvenation treatments and brain-washing began to take their toll. So a big part of him – which meant all of him, because all parts of him were big – would look forward to the onset of the warm smothering blackness he knew would accompany his final sortie.

He didn't have to look forward for long. As the sun reached its zenith over the crystal-shimmering lagoon the King watched the black triangular craft, all sleek lines and eye-watering inhuman curves, skim towards him with unnatural speed. It didn't so much glide over the waves as bully them into submission – splicing the whining air-molecules with a low-pitched electromagnetic hum. Then he saw others approach suddenly, right across the horizon, winking out of nothingness. He had seen many different types of such runabouts in his time – ridden in quite a few on his short bewildering trips back to civilization – but he'd never seen such a density of air-traffic as currently hovered over their lush tropical atoll. They were all there; the usual triangles and glowing orbs, plus the ones disguised to look like clouds – even some of the old steam-powered saucers that were crashed on purpose to mislead those Air Force suckers.

Leading the formation was the black triangle. It had his name on it, he knew. He felt it in his waters. And his waters, though frequent, were never wrong. He was as certain of this fact as he was that Jimmy and Janice should stay off the nose candy – those kids could play when they put their half-fried minds to it. But there was no time for idle speculation. Slowly, the craft set down at the edge of the shallow lapping waves and a black gangway glided across the water and onto the sand.

He barely had time to finish his drink. As was customary, few of the other inmates who were scattered along the stretch of bone-white sand paid much attention to the diminutive pilots. You kept your profile low as a limbo dancer while these guys were around. Twenty yards away a wider-than-he-was-tall former media mogul lolled on a double deckchair reading a newspaper, occasionally shaking his head with knowing contempt and letting out a subterranean chuckle – standards had obviously dropped since he'd taken his involuntary swan-dive off his yacht. But as the craft's pilots marched past he buried his sunburnt face in his paper, seemingly enthralled with the small print. If only his former employees had done the same with their pension schemes.

All too soon the newcomers halted at Elvis's spot in the sand and reached out their spindly three-fingered hands. The King didn't wait for them to resort to the lethal force he knew they had at their disposal. With weary resignation he shoe-horned his enormous frame from his badly warped sun-lounger and stooped to kiss his quietly sobbing companion goodbye.

Norma might have seen better days, but her eyes still held some of their innocent, sultry charm. And now they were filling with tears. Elvis was touched. Involuntarily, his top lip curled back, and his beefy loins set off on a frightening frequency all their own.

'Aha-haau. Don't cry little chickadee. Say goodbye to mah rebel Jim for me. And tell the Princess I'll save the last song for her.'

There was no time for more elaborate goodbyes, not even regrets that he'd turned down Norma's last offer to 'love him tender' – at their age no amount of lubrication could prevent it becoming an all-too painful literal truth. She'd get over him just like she'd got over all the others.

Sadly, Elvis turned to follow his dead-eyed captors towards the craft.

At least he'd be free of the evil Warden who oversaw their stretch. If he closed his watery eyes he could see her contemptuous sneer – so different from that of the sweet innocent she'd been switched for in public life. It was a supreme irony that he trudged past the demure original right now, as she sat in her swimsuit thumbing through a copy of *Horse and Hounds*, blissfully unaware of the depraved machinations of the genetically modified doppelganger who had usurped her throne.

Just how the inhabitants of The Island fitted into the Warden's schemes Elvis could only guess at, but it was unlikely they were going to be used for anything as mundane as entertaining the troops. Very little of what he did know made sense, but then he'd long suspected that was part of the plan.

The King was just glad he wouldn't be around to see it happen. He only wished he could say the same for the rest of the poor deceived human race.

2. Foiled Again

Present day, central Nevada, USA

The unmarked military trucks raced through the starry night as if chased by all the demons of Hell. Huge off-road tyres churned the dusty trackway into a hurricane of debris as they tore through tumbleweed and over the mummified remains of ancient cacti. But on this crisp desert evening these trucks weren't the quarry in some devilish game of cat and mouse – they were the hunters. In fact, if their trackers were correct, their prey lay smouldering just over the next rise.

In the back of the lead vehicle Captain Cyrus Free-mantle, US Special Forces, briefed his elite team of Air Force Black Berets. 'OK men, I want a nice clean dispersal, just like we practised. This is *not* a drill. We have ourselves a Case Red situation so trespassers *will not* be prosecuted – if you do your jobs they won't live long enough to get to a court of law. Do I make myself clear?'

The curt nods from his squad told him all he needed to know. These men were hand-picked veterans, fanatic-ally loyal to him personally; the sort who would, if it were in the country's interest, gladly shoot their grandmothers – and enjoy it.

As one they removed safety catches from their machine pistols and lowered NBC warfare gas-masks – not strictly necessary but they scared the shit out of your enemy.

With a screech of brakes the trucks skidded to a halt atop the first ridgeline. Freemantle lifted the canvas awn-ing and focused his image-intensifying goggles on the dried streambed beneath. The gully was clearly visible as a dark slash across his green, phosphorescent field of view.

Within seconds, he'd located the target: a beacon of white heat amidst the encroaching darkness.

He tutted to himself. 'For super-intelligent beings they seem real fond of crashing.'

With a resigned shake of his head, Freemantle refocused his night scope. Against all the odds, one of the little bug-eyed incompetents had survived the carnage. It had clambered out of the wreckage and was now jerking around like some inbred at a hoe-down. In doing so it was in no way aided by the large satchel it cradled in its fragile arms. The trail of faintly glowing green blood it left as it stumbled from cactus to cactus hinted that perhaps all was not as it should be. The creature might not have been as dead as its hapless co-pilots but it was pretty close.

'Looks like we've got ourselves a live one, people. Move!' But before Freemantle could turn back to his men he felt the blood freeze in his veins. Something else was moving in the valley, and moving fast. Instantly, the scope homed in on the intruder.

There was no denying he was human, a realization which for a fraction of a second made Freemantle panic. Then, almost instantaneously, professionalism kicked in and he started shouting again.

'WE HAVE A HOSTILE WITHIN THE PER-IMETER! Terminate with extreeeeeme prejudice! I want this bastard rattling like maracas when we slap him on the slab. Where the hell are the choppers? Johnson, get me Control on comms – *now*!'

As his troops sprang into action, Freemantle stayed glued to the viewfinder. Down in the gully some hippie freeloader was attempting to piss on the Captain's parade, and Freemantle intended to pre-emptively yank shut his zipper.

But for now he had to content himself with watching proceedings as if on some sickly green video game. If their uninvited guest was allowed to escape, Freemantle was under no illusions as to the reality of the consequences. Tantalizingly beyond his reach the contest unfolded at breath-taking speed.

Adroitly, the troopers raced to take firing positions, as a hundred yards away the newcomer continued his headlong charge towards the UFO. Showing an unnerving talent for tactical movement he made full use of every twig of available cover, as if it were second nature to him. Finally, his way clear, he hurdled a line of low scrub and threw himself at their target. Freemantle's gritty jawline hung open as he watched the stranger tackle the alien with the full weight of one wiry shoulder. No sooner had they gone down, they were off again, the survivor hefted upright in a fireman's lift.

Momentarily, the kidnapper regained his breath; his hot face standing out clearly against the cool desert landscape. It was now that Freemantle got his second nasty shock of the evening – with a startled gasp the Captain recognized him.

The intruder seemed to pause for a second, spotting something else on the ground for the first time. Bending at the knee he lifted the large satchel the creature had been carrying and was off again, running a jinking course as the first bullets impacted around him. Diving for the dried streambed, he disappeared from view as a hail of fire flew over him.

'Cut him off. He's getting away!' But by this stage it was far too late. In the confused darkness his troops set about riddling anything that moved with bullets. As most of the moving was being done by a platoon of overdrilled psychopaths attempting not to get shot, the results were depressingly familiar.

One by one empty magazines slipped from lifeless fingers until only a few of his men were left standing. Calmly, the communications technician informed Freemantle that air support was on its way, and that his boss was riding in the lead chopper. Silently, Freemantle reflected that today was turning into a *very bad*. They all started off as a *less than satisfactory*, because that's how life went. You don't expect miracles, you're not disappointed when they unmiraculously fail to turn up. Occasionally, a day would rise to the dizzying heights of an *OK, but don't get too excited*. Usually they stayed stable, and that's how Cyrus liked it. But today was a *very bad* and heading for an *I'm not going to talk about it* which was worst of all.

'What's going on?' came the Colonel's gruff voice from the radio. 'Thought we heard shooting. Hope you ain't using coyotes for target practice again.'

Freemantle took a deep breath. 'Sir, we have a security breach at the incident site. Request an immediate thermal scan of the terrain beyond our position. Whoever's out there won't get far.'

When it came, the Colonel's reply was full of suppressed menace. 'Better not, son, for your sake. We'll get the infra-red scope on the sucker in no time flat.'

As Freemantle silently crossed all of his available fingers and toes, the helicopters thundered overhead.

Half a mile down-range the kidnapper halted. He had no time to reflect on his monumental good fortune. As he'd discovered in the jungles of South East Asia and the deserts of the Persian Gulf, you made your own luck in this business. The best way to manufacture such a slippery commodity was through lavish amounts of patience, meticulous planning and armaments. With regard to the first of those virtues he'd spent months awaiting an opportunity like this – camped out in this alternately scorching and freezing desert, with nothing but his binoculars and service rucksack for company as he scanned the vast empty skies. With regard to the second, he quickly dropped his unnatural load and peeled off his rucksack. Stuffed just inside the camouflaged canvas sack was twenty metres of catering grade aluminium Bakofoil. Working quickly, he swathed the semiconscious alien in the stuff. With regard to the third, well, he was fond of explosives and would use them if necessary. But for the moment he contented himself with a swift kick to the alien's head, saying: 'How's this for a turnaround, you sneaky grey bastard? One of us abducting one of you for a change?'

Then he hastily stuffed the creature under a nearby thorn-bush and turned his attention to his own survival. Now came the tricky part. In practice he'd got it down to thirty seconds flat, but whether it was the excitement of doing it for real, or the thought of his former colleagues bearing down on him like a pack of hounds, he now managed it in half that time.

Soon the desert's diverse fauna had a new addition: a six-foot silver caterpillar wriggling its way under a convenient tangle of tumbleweed. Until the first wave had passed him by all he could do was wait, lying perfectly still, his ears straining to count the number of rotor blades they'd sent to find him.

Twenty minutes later, aboard the unmarked Black-Ops helicopter gunship that hovered overhead like some diabolical nocturnal insect, Freemantle's superior was in a state one step beyond apoplexy and immediately adjacent to an embolism. After failing to find so much as a hot-dog over the sort of distance even the fastest man could cover on foot, he had proceeded to administer to Captain Freemantle the sort of ear-bashing normally reserved for British heavyweight boxers.

As he listened, crippled by embarrassment and shame, Freemantle silently made himself a solemn oath. It was the sort of oath best made in deserted crypts at midnight, with candles made from boiled-down choir-boys and pentagrams of virgins' blood daubed on the floor in case of misfire. He knew exactly who had got him into this career-threatening mess, he knew just how the renegade's burnt-out fried egg of a brain worked, and as far as he was concerned this knowledge gave him a crucial edge. As the Colonel ranted on, Freemantle began to marinade in the vitriol of his planned revenge.

'You're gonna have to answer to some very influential people over this, Freemantle, do you hear me? *Very* influential. When it gets out you've mislaid a visitor, security agencies you ain't even heard of are gonna be queuing up to mince your manhood! Freemantle, you there? ... *Freemaaaaantle!*'

But the Captain had already embarked on a personal blitzkrieg all his own. Brandishing his combat knife, he went charging off into the gloom shrieking like a banshee with toothache.

A hundred metres to his rear, weighed down by a cargo never meant to walk this Earth, and discarding tinfoil like a born-again Christmas turkey, Frank was too busy running for his life in the opposite direction to care.

3. Invasion

Present day, somewhere far above North America

The vast alien mother ship slid silently through the interstellar void. Round about it the *de rigueur* invincible space armada jostled for position as it plunged towards the small defenceless disc of Earth.

Or perhaps not. From behind an insignificant, and conveniently placed, asteroid a handful of single-seat fighters swooped to the rescue. Crewed by pilots representing the full ethnic and sexual diversity of their home planet, this brave band of warriors charged to almost certain death. Sportingly, the aliens held back the myriad of wonder-weapons their ancient civilization was no doubt able to deploy, instead launching swarms of their own tiny fighters. These craft, bearing an uncanny resemblance to various Earth insects, were piloted by the most clumsy and ham-tentacled of their species. Those that made it out of the vast hangar doors without crashing engaged the Earthlings in a swarming battle of instant death. Even so, due to the sheer numbers of alien craft, the humans faced an uphill struggle. Today was no day to be without their hotshot ace pilot.

Aboard the alien Emperor's personal star-barge Captain Troy Meteor, Hero of the Earth Defence Force and Olympic Low-G Fencing Champion, stood tied to an over-endowed and scantily clad cheerleader. It had been a tough break getting captured the way he had. Odds of 9000–1 were not usually a problem, but then Troy knew all about tough breaks, just like he knew all about 'War is hell', Officer's Club banter and YMCA gymnasium showers.

The alien commander squatted in a vat of bubbling indigo goo atop an unholy dais. 'So you see, our plans are quite simple,' it croaked like a multi-hued perversion of a tobacco company's research-lab beagle. 'Even though our two races developed light-years apart, changes in the radiation signature of our sun mean we can obtain sustenance from one source and one source only.'

'But why are you telling me all this?' muttered Meteor darkly, trying hard to make it look like he was attempting to free his hands, but all the while touching-up the cheerleader's bottom. 'If I escape I'll know every detail of your conniving scheme.'

Bringing forth his ceremonial gorging straw the Emperor cackled. 'It matters not, my simian-based friend, for very soon, via your nasal cavity, I shall have sucked out what passes for your brain!'

Half way down aisle C, Dave yanked the lightweight plastic headphones from his aching ears and shook his head in stupefied disbelief. How was his fledgling science ever to be taken seriously when they continued to churn out this Troy Meteor shit? It was enough to make him weep. Beckoning a glassy-eyed stewardess, Dave ordered himself a stiff drink and made yet another effort to read the in-flight magazine.

But it was no use. The text that made up the thirty pages of glossy advertising copy was completely unreadable for anyone with a mental age higher than their shoe size. The words seemed to slip under Dave's conscious brain only to be sucked into the subconscious box marked FOR-GET FOREVER. With a weary sigh, he settled back in his economy seat and did what he always did at times like this. He thought of Kate.

He had asked her to come with him, but he had done it with that same air of hopeless, optimistic resignation that he asked her to do anything – go to a movie, share a curry, or on those rare occasions when copious amounts of lager got the better of his natural timidity, let him get inside her knickers. The answer to the last of these, as always, was no. A movie and curry were OK, but hot gusset action wasn't the sort of thing best friends did.

'But what if I meet a stunning Californian babe and we fall madly in love – what will you do then?' he'd asked her.

'Then I'll look forward to the wedding and pray you name your first trans-Atlantic toddler after me. But if that's the biggest risk I'm running letting you go on your own, fine. It's not even a proper holiday. If you expect a girl to put up with two weeks of emotional blackmail, the least you can do is throw in a beach and a gallon of pina colada.' Then she'd paused, looked at him searchingly, sadly maybe, and said: 'Does everything you ever do have to be tied in with that ridiculous magazine?'

He'd been hurt, as he always was. The 'ridiculous magazine', as Kate insisted on calling it, was Dave's pride and joy: none other than the internationally renowned *ScUFODIN Monthly* – the official journal of the Scientific UFO Discovery and Information Network. And the international renown bit was no idle boast, either; only last month Dave had received an enthusiastic letter from Belgium.

Kate steadfastly refused to acknowledge the journalistic worth of the magazine Dave edited. 'It's written by cranks, for cranks,' she said.

'And where does that leave me?'

'Lovable but misguided? Your letters page reads like the visitors' book of a care-in-the-community drop-in centre.'

It was hard to disagree with this particular point in her otherwise unfounded argument. All of his formal education had trained him for a career in science, viewing the world as a rational and logical place. Inevitably enough he often found himself at odds with the New Age and conspiracy theory wings of the movement. He did his best to keep things on an even keel, but it *was* an uphill battle – like trying to catch a monsoon in a thimble. As an editor who largely relied on the contributions of his readers Dave was at the mercy of the zealots. By the time he'd cut out pieces on 'Holes at the Poles', Flat Earth Society propaganda and 'I've had sex with an alien who looked like Helena Bonham-Carter' abduction stories from the live-at-home-with-my-mum boys, his heavyweight magazine was regularly reduced to a flyweight pamphlet.

And then there was the question of funding. For a journal that at best sold a few thousand copies, and was then universally consigned to a dentist's waiting room in Aberdeen or the bottom of budgie cages, Dave was never short of operating cash. It wasn't as if he ever had to go cap in hand to the magazine's publicity-shy owners. Where it all came from was a mystery. Accounting had never been one of Dave's strong points, but even he found himself a little uneasy at times over the prodigious quantities of cash that came pouring through the magazine's bank account.

As far as he could make out, most of it was simply given to him, though by whom and for what was harder to pin down. No doubt some came from wealthy and elderly benefactors, humoured in their final years and at least glad to have a ready source of emergency toilet paper. But who on Earth were 'The Institute for Meteorological Advancement' and the 'The International Council of Illuminanti'? One month, when Dave took a stand in the interests of scientific integrity and devoted the entire issue to real testable theories, the mystery funding dried up. Dave was no financial whiz-kid but he knew not to rock a boat that didn't even have a keel. Not wanting to incur the wrath of his normally dormant publishers, next month the lunatic fringe returned with a vengeance. And so did the money.

So, truly scientific investigation of the UFO phenomena was currently at a low ebb, lower even than Dave's love life – and as tides went that particular ocean surge was so far down the beach you could smell the rotting seaweed and had to step over the occasional surfer dying of toxic shock. But with Kate steadfastly declining his amorous advances, constantly maintaining that she wanted them to remain 'just best friends', for better or worse, ScUFODIN Monthly remained the real partner in Dave's life.

An overly cheerful mechanical voice, asking him to fasten his seatbelt, brought Dave back to the present with a bump. He was meant to be putting all that behind him on this trip of a lifetime, but as Kate was so fond of saying, 'You don't just bring your work home with you, you sleep with it. If you were female, you'd have its babies.'

When he came down to it he had to admit she was right about the motives for his journey. Sure enough, he was claiming it as holiday, the first he'd had in three years as editor. But in his rare moments of self-honesty Dave knew there was only one reason he was visiting Nevada, and it wasn't because he liked one-arm bandits or dancing girls with ostrich feathers sprouting from their pants. Well, OK leave in the last bit, but really this was a pilgrimage he'd wanted to make all his life. A holy journey you had to do once in a lifetime. Even though his personal desert Mecca was enshrined in triple-thickness security fences, antipersonnel minefields and luminous day-glo signs reading PROPERTY OF UNITED STATES AIR FORCE, TRESPASSERS WILL BE SHOT WITH BIG GUNS he'd be there to worship at the first opportunity.

Ten minutes later, with a cheerful smile and an optimistic swagger, he stepped off the plane at Las Vegas International Airport and gazed up at the star-filled desert sky. Kate or no Kate, while he was here, he knew he was going to have one hell of a time.

4. Revelations

*February 1969, somewhere deep
beneath North America*

The politician stepped onto the circular pedestal and self-consciously smoothed back his sweat-laced hair. One trouser leg was rolled up to the knee, revealing a pallid vein-riddled lower leg. Around him the intense darkness pressed in from all sides. When the beam of white light flooded in from above he squinted through heavy-browed eyes, his weighty jowls quivering as he searched for figures in the blackness beyond. Shortly, the sort of computerized voice that was much in fashion before computers had very much to say gave its verdict.

'*Subject confirmed as Richard Millhouse Nixon. Thirty-seventh President of the United States, and Chairman of the Committee of 300.*' From a rather tinny loudspeaker somewhere far above drifted the first few bars of 'Hail to the Chief'. It was hard to escape the feeling it had done this many times before.

The new President tentatively stepped down and shielded his eyes from the glare. Nothing moved, apart from a small vein at the side of his temple. Then, accompanied only by a faint whiff of sweat, which Nixon quickly realized was his own, a dark figure stepped from the shadows. The newcomer's voice was like gallows-yard gravel ground under an executioner's heel, yet as smooth and cultured as an upper-cut from an Oxford Don.

'Can't be too careful these days, Mr Chairman. Traitors where you least expect.' There was no doubt which of his guest's titles afforded the most respect.

The Commander-in-Chief offered a half-hearted salute,

then thought better of it and turned it into a cheerless wave. 'Well no, I guess not. Reds . . . and worse shades, everywhere. You must be . . .'

'They call me Becker. Some call me worse things, but when the enemies of justice hate your guts you know you're doing something right. You can roll down that trouser leg too – we don't pander to mysticism down here.'

His guest looked to be in two minds. 'I thought you Committee boys were sticklers for tradition?'

Becker's eyes held the faintest trace of annoyance. 'We don't stand on ceremony, as long as it doesn't stand on us. I suspect you've been misled by some of your senior partners. Would you walk this way, please.'

They stepped onto a conveyor belt which whisked them off down a seemingly endless corridor of smooth walls and no doors. The leader of the Free World took the chance to study his companion. He was a big man, wearing an impeccably tailored black suit cut in the 'organization man' style of the early fifties. In his big grizzled hand he held a dark and sinister package. At his wrist was some sort of complex flashing electrical device. Though his craggy features were cast in shadow, somehow his eyes seemed darker still.

Small talk was neither of their specialities, though nervously the President felt an urge to try. 'Quite a facility you have here. Good to know the public's tax dollars aren't all wasted, even the ones we don't account for.'

The Dark Man looked back coldly at his nominal superior. Then, after a heart-stopping instant, his broad face creased into a mirthless smile which got no nearer his eyes than Lee Harvey Oswald's bullets had to JFK. 'We know you're one of us, sir. Those who took you this far will ensure you stay in power. The Committee will back you to the hilt, and beyond – as long as you fulfil your role.'

At this assurance the President grinned his dumbest vote-catching grin. As was his custom, Becker didn't. Further conversation was now clearly inappropriate.

Dark and silent minutes passed, until at last the walkway glided to a halt before a huge and featureless wall.

'The time has come for you to learn what all who hold your high office must know – I speak not of the Presidency but your other, more fundamental brief. Beyond this wall is our organization's most closely guarded secret, hidden even from the likes of yourself – one of our most promising associate members. It's my opinion that if this information ever leaks out the bedrock on which the Committee's power rests will crumble. Unfortunately, not all your colleagues share my views. I have reason to worry about their motives. Prepare yourself.'

The President looked on agog, an expression he was practised at, as Becker fiddled with the device strapped to his wrist. Slowly and steadily a section of the vast wall slid away before them.

What gradually appeared was the interior of a hall the size of an aircraft hangar. The first thing to strike Nixon as odd was the small grassy hill rising from the floor not twenty yards from where he stood. Larger than the infamous Texan 'grassy knoll', it was nevertheless similar enough to touch off a spark of guilty panic in the President's underemployed heart.

That was the first odd thing. Then everything else struck him at once. In the middle distance grew anaemic-looking trees. Overhead, great banks of spotlights produced a sunlike glare. Far away, a snatch of bird-song that warbled for a moment then died off then repeated – tinny and false, clearly recorded. But these details were mere bit-players in the rich pageant of unreason that unfolded before his eyes. Atop the hill was a ramshackle old house with wooden walls which had seen better days, though where, when and how was another matter. The chimney would have embarrassed Pisa's leaning tower. Windows were untidily boarded up. Along its front stretched a tumble-down porch ringed by a crumbling rail. Finally, scattered around this strange scene lounged half a dozen scruffy little children.

But Nixon's eyes were drawn inexorably back to the dusty bare-dirt driveway, and what was suspended above it. Parked up on blocks sat a battered thirty-foot metallic saucer, the type which would have embarrassed even the most short-sighted B-movie special-effects supremo.

The President was about to ask what sort of insane practical joke this was when he took a closer look at one of the children who had now turned at his approach. It stared back at him through huge almond-shaped black eyes set in a featureless grey face. He checked the others again. They were all the same. *These weren't children, they were . . . they were . . .* When the thing that was staring at the President saw his shock, it sprang into jerky action. Seeing this, the others followed suit.

From beneath rag-torn dungarees and hopelessly stained gingham frocks they produced an assortment of musical instruments out of nowhere and got down to work. Banjos and home-made double-bass were much in evidence. It looked like the Walton family had got into a fight with a nuclear reactor and lost. With a quick glance around to see that all were ready, the creatures started to play what appeared to be a rehearsed song. Except that it was a song which had no rhythm, no timing and no tune.

A grim-faced Becker turned to his guest. 'The Visitors like to greet their new "Big Pink Chief" with this tra-ditional cultural display. They maintain they've brought it all the way from their home planet, though personally I have my doubts.'

He coolly continued to study Nixon's open-mouthed, goggle-eyed face. 'Best to show polite disdain, that way it doesn't go on for too long. Eisenhower made the mistake of looking impressed and they kept it up all day. We had to shoot three of them to make 'em stop.'

If anything, the wild revels seemed to be growing in intensity. Two of the more sprightly aliens grasped each other's slender arms and did a fair impression of a Highland jig, the blonde pigtails of a wigged 'female' twirling as it spun. Perched at the rear, granpaw-alien's harmonica playing became so frenzied he fell off his rocking-chair, though it didn't seem to bother him much. Meanwhile the hand-clapper-and-stomper at the front put his foot through a rotten board.

Nixon looked on aghast. 'But they're . . .'

'Idiots. I know sir. Cosmic trailer-park grey scum. Call them what you will. It seems the universe is full of hill-billies. Our top minds have been trying to figure it out for the past twenty-two years.'

'Twenty-two years! It's been going on that long?'

Becker shrugged. 'Maybe longer.'

Taking it in, Nixon forced himself to adopt a bit of composure. 'So, these top minds of ours – what did they conclude?'

For the first time Becker displayed a modicum of unease. 'At present we have only non-positive results to show for considerable endeavour.'

'Meaning we've got jackshit.'

In the darkness next to him Nixon's host gave the faintest shake of his head.

Like many before him the President looked perplexed. 'But how did they get here? It makes no sense. We spend billions on our space programme, employing the best Nazis money can buy, and it's all we can do to launch a monkey round the moon. Then these space freaks turn up and show us how primitive we really are. It's beyond reason . . . And, frankly, it's not fair.'

The Dark Man looked about to say something, wavered, then decided to go for it. 'There is one possibility – a malignant theory that slowly and painfully extends its tentacles of proof by the day. But I have to warn you, Mr Chairman, the rest of the Committee are reluctant to look at my evidence in a rational manner. The policies they pursue might even unwittingly aid whoever is behind these extraterrestrial aberrations.'

'God in heaven, speak English, man. What're you talking about?'

If Becker was offended by this outburst, he didn't show it. 'It's long been calculated that our uneducated brethren would not cope well with the sudden undeniable proof of alien existence. Our most covert think-tanks tell us this knowledge would cause a paradigm shift from which the human race might never recover – a shock so great it could break us as a race. But for whoever's behind this scheme even that does not seem enough. It's as if they want to rub our under-evolved noses in it. I believe we are the victims of . . . a manipulation. What better way to scupper humanity's infatuation with science and technology, to cast us back into a dark age of unreason and superstition, than by showing us another darker path offering better results? Someone or something wants to make us paranoid and superstitious, and they'll go to almost any lengths to do so.'

Nixon squinted at the man again. He wasn't sure he liked him. 'Let me get this straight . . . You think this isn't it? You think there's more, that someone's hurling brain-dead aliens from the sky at us to make the poor old human race *feel* bad? What sort of half-assed theory is that?'

Becker drew himself up to his full impressive height. 'The Committee must end their policy of encouraging conspiracy theories and paranoia – it will play directly into our opponents' hands. There's even talk of leaking information on our grey friends – doctored of course to make it appear we have the situation under control. Sir, I need your help to convince the Committee they're wrong.'

Nixon looked at him, puzzled. 'Why should I do that, if I don't believe you either?'

Becker judged it a good time to give him the evidence. 'Read this, Mr President.' He handed over the package he'd held throughout their meeting – a thick blue folder. '*Read* it, sir. And try not to weep.'

5. 'Mr Frosty' is One of Them

Present day, Tonopah, northern Nevada

Frank pressed himself flat against the damp wall of his shabby apartment, further crumpling the ancient Che Guevara poster in the process. He knew from careful experimentation that in this position he couldn't be seen from the street below, though he could peer behind the tattered tinfoil-lined curtains at the frenetic street scene beneath.

The van was back again, two minutes thirty-seven seconds earlier than the day before. So they were varying their routine, trying to catch him out, but he could see through their shallow games. The operative was apparently busy serving a fast-growing line of eager children, handing them towering ice-cream cones and pocketing their payment, no doubt every cent going to swell the black-budget coffers that bankrolled the insidious Shadow Government. That in itself was a give-away. The real 'Mr Frosty' never gave more than two scoops. What a shit-kicking amateur!

As Frank had been taught during his days with the ill-fated Michigan Militia, the best form of camouflage was often to be seen but ignored. 'The human scarecrow approach,' his crazed Boer weapons instructor called it. Once Frank had pointed out that trying to teach him anything about military field-craft was like teaching a Federal employee how to waste taxes (which he'd done by ambushing the South African as he took a thigh-trembling dump into a plastic bag in the bushes behind their firing range), they'd instructed the class together. What Frank had been able to pass on from his dimly remembered days in the military had served the band of flabby-bellied, flabby-brained fanatics well – but in the long run it had done them little good. After Waco and Oklahoma City their troop had been busted faster than you could say 'One World Government'.

But that had been in better days, before this intense harassment began, before the United Nations funded Gestapo had started bombarding his head with voices and flashbacks – some of them most disturbing. It seemed at times he was being made to remember details of his former life. It seemed microwave energy was good for more than just heating waffles and frying the brains of gullible mobile-phone users.

Whichever government black-ops coven was behind this current mission, they knew what they were about. For a split second Frank experienced a rare iota of panic; he was up against some frighteningly clever opponents. Slowly, using a little-known Zen technique picked up in the jungles of Vietnam, he re-levelled his inner karma. This was undoubtedly part of an ongoing routine surveillance – if they knew he had the merchandise he would have been taken out by now.

Frank pulled himself away from the window and loped across his cluttered flat, made all the worse by his preparations for imminent departure. He'd deal with 'Mr Frosty' when he was good and ready. Even Frank admitted that as far as manifestations went of the International Papist/Masonic plot to elevate the Queen of England to a position of world power, enslaving humanity in the process, old 'Two Scoops Freddy' was hardly the most deadly component. Recently he'd heard rumours of something big brewing in the Far East – some fiendish consumer device which would finally tip the balance in the Illuminantis' favour – though how and when he had no clue. What was certain was that in the coming struggle Frank was going to need every weapon he could get his badly blistered trigger-finger to.

Rubbing puffy red-rimmed eyes, Frank pushed aside a mound of *ScUFODIN Monthly* magazines and copies of badly printed pamphlets (*Kennedy – The Denture Suicide Hypothesis*), to kneel down besides his battered VCR. After thumbing the well-worn eject button he slipped the cassette into its lurid rental-store case. The lengths the Military-Industrial-Entertainment Complex would go to influence the minds of the public never ceased to amaze him. What Troy Meteor lacked in subtlety he more than made up for in xenophobic gung-ho. Frank had noted all the passages containing subliminal messages, not that they were needed – this particular piece of anti-alien propaganda laid it on pretty thick – negotiations must have taken a turn for the worse since *ET*. It had been a long night of constant freeze-framing, but well worth the risk to his already tattered sanity. In time, Frank's findings would be passed on to the relevant groups fighting the imposition of the New World Order.

In moments of doubt he wondered if it was worth it. Would they ever be free from the corrosive tentacles sprouting from the cancerous institutions of the state? At times it almost seemed a hopeless fight. The forces stacked against the brave few champions of liberty were insurmountable. What was needed was a victory that would shake the world to its very foundations – with that thought Frank allowed himself a knowing smile.

Feeling a terrible thirst, he made his way over the jaundiced lino to his prehistoric fridge. He'd given up drinking the bottled water; they could get to that as easily as the tap supply. Beer was now his only hope.

Tearing at the ring-pull he did his best to ignore the sickly-sweet smell that spilled from the chiller-cabinet. Wedged inside, his slowly putrefying houseguest looked back at him with big oval, black eyes, its three-fingered hands still clutching the bulging hieroglyph-covered satchel. Frank undid the oddly shaped latch and slipped out the large blue folder marked *MJ13 – Property of the Committee*.

With a sardonic grin he mused that the disinformation started on the very cover. That its contents were entirely true he had no doubt, but if this document really *was* known to the Shadow Government, then its author was in very deep trouble indeed. It read quite differently from any official report Frank had ever seen. During his time in the Service several of his officers had kept similar journals. They had invariably been scrawled in dog-eared notebooks, in the brief shattered minutes before last lights, or in the odd disjointed moments of spare time that a military career afforded. None had been neatly typed and housed in an armour-plated folder that seemed to warp space-time with its very gravitas. The thought of some junior officer carting this tome around on active service, in the hope of one day being hailed as a syphilis-free Ernest Hemingway, couldn't help but make Frank chuckle.

Besides, few government reports were written in the first person. Randomly Frank thumbed to a page and began to read.

After what happened to Apollo 11 there was no way we could go back to the moon. We had been warned off in no uncertain terms. Of course the great unwashed never got to know. A twenty-second transmission delay and 'solar interference' saw to that.

'Twelve' was ready to go and on the launch pad, but we pulled the astronauts and launched the empty ship instead – possibly the most expensive Fourth of July rocket to go up in history. My heart was heavy to think what my department could have done with the funds – got another Committee member to the top of the Kremlin perhaps, but then first time around that had caused more trouble than it solved. Uncle Joe went soft on us when it mattered.

Thirteen was a nice touch if I do say so myself. By then we were better prepared to properly stage the event – the entire production went down like clockwork. Not having to film the surface sequences made it less of a headache, and the fact that the 'mission' was a 'near disaster' meant that no one suspected a set-up. The simplest plans are always best.

One day I knew the story would make a good old-fashioned heart-warming patriotic film, we'd keep that one up our sleeve until we needed it most. Our Hollywood contacts were proving increasingly skilful at influencing mob psychology, and would only get better as the years progressed.

Needless to say, the later ops were an entire fabrication. Golf on the moon – I ask you! Filming them wasn't cheap, but far less expensive than actually firing those Jet Jocks off into space. Our unofficial funding was given some modicum of support when the billions of dollars officially earmarked for the space programme were diverted to our cause.

If he hadn't been such an arrogant son-of-a-bitch Frank could almost have grown to like the document's shady author – a true professional in his chosen field. But Frank didn't have to read far from any point in the manuscript to be reminded just what an insidiously evil, hard-assed bastard this guy was – the sort of faceless bureaucrat who usurped his nation's power to weave his own personal web of lies and deceit, all the while, no doubt, believing himself to be a patriot.

Frank would nail him. Frank would nail them all soon enough, and he'd especially nail 'Mr Frosty'. His secret weapon, in this most secret of black wars, currently gazed back at him lifelessly from his fridge.

'Not long now, good buddy,' Frank said, taking the first sip of beer as he closed the file. 'You're my grey ace in the hole.'

6. Publication

West Virginia, USA

At his remote mountain retreat high in the Appalachian wilderness Becker's personal phone was ringing. He was much older now than he had been on that fateful night many years before when he'd initiated that wide-eyed fool Nixon into the darkest secrets of the Committee, but even carrying his advanced years Becker moved nimbly for a big man. There was more than one telephone receiver on his cluttered writing desk, but it wasn't hard to know which one to answer.

One phone was so black it seemed to create its own gravity-field. A series of flashing lights along its extended surface indicated sophisticated scrambling circuits were in operation. It connected Becker to the Executive Section's Head of Communications in a bunker deep under DC. It didn't ring often – Becker's underlings knew better than to disturb him when he was at the cabin. On the few occasions there had been call to answer it a superpower had been toppled or a pope had been shot.

The second phone was a translucent red. When it rang and flashed insanely it could only mean one thing, and it wasn't that Gotham City needed Batman to pop a rolled-up sock down his tights. It could only mean the saintly head-of-state of Becker's own 'Great Nation' had got himself into very hot water and needed bailing out. After all, everyone needed a legitimate day job, if nothing else to keep those IRS bloodsuckers off your back. What a waste of his talents, Becker often pondered, to be reduced to buying off two-bit whores and arranging 'accidents' for jewellery-encrusted pimps. Of late this second phone had done more ringing than the first. But today wasn't to be its day.

The third telephone was shaped like Mickey Mouse. There was no good reason why this should be so, but some things were beyond explanation, as Becker knew only too well. Of the three it rang least often, but when it did the thing more than made up for it. The whole plastic mouse would vibrate and wobble, its receiver-holding arm pumping away like a body-builder. When Becker had first purchased the cabin, to allow himself to escape the tortured freneticism of his double working-life, he'd discovered the monstrosity in a box of junk pushed to the back of an outhouse. In a fit of whimsy, the sort that can only descend over a man under the mind-buckling pressure that he experienced every day, Becker had made it his own personal phone.

Today Mickey looked like he was having an epileptic fit. His eerily electric voice screamed, 'IT'S FOR YOU! IT'S FOR YOU!' Becker reached for the bright yellow handset in disgust, as much to put the radar-eared rodent out of his misery as to answer the call.

But when the caller introduced herself, the Dark Man's face lightened considerably – it was an editor from Karl Popf Stein, the major New York publishing house whose address he knew only too well. Two months earlier Becker had sent her a very special package. But as the conversation progressed, the look of hope slipped from Becker's face, badly staining his shirt in the process.

'Look, Mr Decker. Time for a bit of honesty, I think. There's no call for this sort of fiction anymore. The public don't go for this heavy-handed the world's in peril stuff. They want fluff, and I doubt very much you can do fluff. So please, stop harassing this office or I'll be forced to call in the authorities. Your hysterical e-mails are giving our server a nervous breakdown.'

Becker's face began to exude the sort of infrared radiation which had been known to cause men to spontaneously combust. This was too much to take, coming no doubt from someone who was a dope-smoking English Lit major, who probably wet her unbleached Nicaraguan-cotton panties at the first sign of a parking ticket.

'It's . . . not . . . fiction,' he just about managed to stammer. 'That manuscript covers my experiences running the Secret Government's Black Operations Programme. It details why "what happens" *happens*. It's all explained – from what really went on at Pear Harbor to the lies behind alien abduction. From the Gulf War to "daytime chat shows". It's political dynamite. Have you got any idea what a risk I'm taking just sending it to you!'

She cut him off mid stride. 'Quite frankly the only risk involved must have been to the poor Federal Mail employee who delivered it to our door – quite a tome, isn't it. It needs severe pruning. I suggest you get yourself a ruler and a red pen and starting with the first line, get cutting. Then keep cutting all the way to the end.'

Darkest despair gripped Becker, as his cultured voice reached a thunderous new intensity. 'But it's all true! Don't you recognize the blockbuster of the century when you read it? This book lays the secrets of the world bare and breathless, like a big-haired White House intern – one who's just had done to her what you can do to your competitors.'

The editor sounded wary, perhaps suspicious of being further sucked in by the madman down the line. 'But why would an individual in your position bare his soul like this? If half of what you say is true you must be crazier than if it isn't.'

Becker couldn't believe some people's cynicism. The words tumbled forth in an avalanche that had been building for years. 'Have you even bothered to read my conclusion on the last page? There's a paralysis at the very top of our leadership. A reluctance to face facts. We can't rule out the possibility that someone high up on the Committee has an agenda all their own!'

'I'm afraid I didn't get that far. I found your claim that the Vietnam protest movement was all part of some vast CIA mind-control experiment alarming and offensive. I was part of that movement and I can assure you that CIA agents did not supply any of the LSD I took. I suppose you'll be claiming they were sleeping with us next to monitor our responses.'

Becker could only make strangled wheezing noises as the editor continued. He didn't know whether to be impressed by her insight or appalled by her lack of vision.

'And as for your prediction that "The Subversive Power undermining the Committee will soon up the stakes by staging ever-more irrational and paranoia-inducing events," well, I found that simply bizarre. What is this "final killer blow prior to harvesting" you are forever alluding to? Our Science Fiction department might be interested, but we certainly couldn't publish it as a biography, we'd be the laughing stock of the publishing world – and believe me that's a hard-fought title. I suppose what I'm trying to say is please stop phoning us every day, you're wasting our time and yours. I'd recommend a shrink but I don't want to hurt him.'

Before Becker could respond the line went dead. His rage was frightening to behold. Mickey went flying through a window, braining a passing skunk as it ploughed into the needle-covered forest floor.

Slowly, and with many choice curses in several different languages, Becker got his reeling emotions back under control. When he was his normal Antarctic self he picked up the black phone and dialled a very special number. Half a mile beneath the Pentagon a four-star Air Force General sprang to his feet and saluted when he heard his master's voice.

'Start me a war. It doesn't have to be big, but make it

bloody and make it soon. Our friend in Baghdad is due another spanking.'

Perhaps sensing this wasn't the best time to be the bearer of bad news, there was a note of agitation in the General's voice. 'That might not be a problem for long, sir – you haven't heard the news from Urgistan? But there's something even more urgent you should know. There's been a Case Red incident in Nevada.'

Instantly Becker's mood changed. 'You know the drill, we've been through it enough times in the past.'

'I'm afraid it's different this time, sir. Some other agency beat us to the draw. One of the Visitors was abducted, along with certain papers of yours they had in their possession.'

The telephone line went ominously quiet. 'What sort of . . . personal papers?'

'We don't as of yet know. But somehow, before the Visitors went AWOL from their holding area at the Mesa Facility, they broke into your personal apartment and rifled through your things. We have surveillance footage of them exiting the base carrying a large blue book. Image enhancement can just make out the letters "MJ" embossed on the cover. We ran checks but there's no record of it being an official file. Sir? Are you still there, sir?'

The receiver slipped from Becker's grasp. With a sob of rage he reflected that publication of his manuscript might not be a problem in the near future. The harm it would cause if it were done in the wrong way made him shiver.

7. Strange Harvest

Somerset, UK

Kate Jennings prided herself on her open mind, cool professional objectivity and the control she exercised over her career, but this job was beginning to get under her skin. There was something about it that made her brain itch, as if a thousand locusts were dancing on her scalp.

'Maybe you should go through it again from the top, Mr Smith,' she said.

The subject of her interview didn't seem any more comfortable. The young man glanced around the untidy farmhouse kitchen as if expecting to be pounced on at any moment. 'It was like I said to your researcher on the phone – not of this Earth.'

Kate tried hard to appreciate his guarded country ways for what they were – a charming aspect of rural life that would not survive the building of one more motorway but even that was beginning to irritate her now. 'Start again – slowly from the beginning, and I'll just turn on my tape recorder, this time without you getting upset.'

The young farmer looked at her oddly for a second. 'There's no need to patronize me, Miss Jennings. Just because I don't live within gobbing range of a tube station and dodge hordes of muggers each time I go to work, to push bits of paper from one side of a desk to another, doesn't mean I don't know which way to sit on a lavatory. We have traffic jams and dog-shit pavements in the country too, you know. If you saw what I saw I'm sure you'd get "a little bit upset".'

Kate sighed wearily. 'Look, I'm sorry. I've had a long

day. Rest assured I'd very much appreciate any information you could give me for the show. Please go on.'

OK, she admitted to herself, a daytime true-life confession programme wasn't what she'd thought she'd end up working on when she got into TV journalism, but *Panorama* wasn't hiring at the moment. It didn't mean the team of dedicated researchers she headed had no intention of doing a thorough job.

The worried-looking Mr Smith coughed weakly and began again. 'Like I said, it all started last May eve. It was a beautifully clear spring evening, not a cloud in the sky. There'd been a meteor shower earlier but nothing else of note.

'I'd just brought the cows in from the top field when Ned, my hired hand, points up to the southern sky and brings my attention to a bright light hovering in the far distance. Didn't think much of it at the time, probably one of them new military planes they're always testing up at the secret air base on the heath. But now I know it was the beginning of a nightmare that would come to haunt my family far worse even than that unpleasantness with Aunt Betty and the prize bullock from down Yeovil way.'

Kate leaned forward intently, determined to get some sense from her subject this time. The young farmer continued.

'Anyway, me and Ned returned to the farmhouse without giving it a second thought. Just as we were entering for our tea Ned says, "Look, it's still there, Smithy." I told him to forget it before I gave him a sheep-dip shampoo. But all through tea Ned kept looking out the window, muttering to himself that it was coming closer, and something about "the CIA messing with his mind". Not much there to mess with, but there you go. After pudding, Ned was on his way. The funny thing was, as I saw him off, I could have sworn the light was nearer, though it was most likely my imagination.

'After that me and the missis put the kids to bed. Little Gretchen said she wanted a story, so I read her one about a load of elves carting off a bitchy princess until some mad King paid the ransom. By then I was pretty tired myself, so I got my head down too. Don't suppose you townies have an inkling what time cows set their alarms in the morning.'

Don't suppose you have an inkling what time my neighbours get back from clubbing, thought Kate, but managed to look suitably unsure of herself.

'All seemed normal enough till just past midnight. Tell the truth I had a funny dream about two nuns locked in a greengrocers, but that's not the confession you're looking for, is it? Anyway, come the witching hour I was awakened by a bright light hovering above the house. My first thought was that the roof was alight, but I could hear no sound apart from a low-pitched humming. The other thing that convinced me it weren't a fire was its colour. It was the brightest white light you'd ever seen, not red like from flames, but tinged with blue as if from a welding torch. It seemed to be inside the attic. Shafts of light were streaming down the chimney and up through the cracks in the floorboards. I half expected a strange urge to build a copy of Glastonbury Tor in my front room, but oddly enough none came.

'Now you might think any right-minded individual would be pretty keen to discover what had landed on his house, but not me. I was overcome with a strange lethargy. Dead casual, I got out of bed and wandered downstairs as if I didn't have a care in the world. Didn't stop to wake the wife. Didn't stop to fetch the kids. Just plodded off as if this was a regular occurrence.

'By the time I'd reached the back door the light had moved on. It seemed to have landed a hundred yards away in one of my arable fields, behind a line of trees. So I opened the back door and trekked towards it.

'Now I've seen some pretty peculiar things in my time – a Ministry vet trying to explain to Twelve-Gauge Trev why all his cattle had to be slaughtered at cost price, that hunt-saboteur ravaged by fox-hounds last winter – but they were nothing compared to the debauched scene that met my eyes on that foul night.

'The thing was as big as a barn. And not one of those cheap prefabricated modern monstrosities neither. This was like something from the days when they really knew how to build an outhouse, not that you'd want to keep your hay in this perversion against God and nature – not unless you were completely insane, that is.'

Kate lowered the levels on her mini tape-recorder as she tried to ignore the mindless cackling her host had broken into. 'Do you think you can describe the craft?'

Mr Smith composed himself. 'It was all silver looking, and shaped like a giant saucer. Hovering over my cornfield it was, just hanging in the air. Beneath it the crop was bent out of shape, as if by some sort of vortex. But that's not all, see. There was this row of bright windows about half-way up the thing, and inside its occupants were doing a strange cosmic jig. Though if it's dancing that tickles your fancy it wouldn't have been those inside that caught your eye – no indeed. Between me and the ship was another group of them, and what they were doing was disgusting.'

Kate looked on seriously, intent on confirming this crucial point.

'Morris dancing!' stated her host as he barely suppressed a shiver. 'Though no internationally recognized or authenticated routine was this. If the lads at the Amalgamated Federation of Traditional Country Stick Banging had seen *them* they would have had a fit – that's if they hadn't run screaming from the vicinity before a "hey" had even been "nonny nonned".'

Kate leaned forward as the farmer regained his breath.

'And the Maypole, Mr Smith, can you tell me about that one more time?'

The young man winced. 'Well, they were prancing about a sorry perversion of that traditionally wholesome symbol of English village life, though it was decorated in a fashion that makes me shudder. Atop its crown sat the head of my prize Guernsey milker, Daisy. All down its length were draped her still steaming innards. As the small grey pixies danced about its base they waved other bits of her in the air. Pig's bladders are what we normally use, though it is customary to remove them from inside the pig first. Sickening it was, though at the time I just stood transfixed and stared.'

'So what happened next?'

'One of the little grey elves broke off from the pagan rite and skipped towards me. Led me by the hand it did, up into the belly of the saucer, into a dazzling bright light. That's where I met . . . *her*.'

His voice dropped by several poignant octaves at that single menacing word. '*Her*, Mr Smith?' Kate enquired.

'Yes, *her*. Though no human woman was she. Tall, blonde, and with eyes like two burning sapphires. Not one word did she speak, but it were clear enough what she craved. Wanted me to perform . . . *acts* upon her.'

'What sort of acts?'

Smith looked hesitant. 'Strange . . . unnatural *acts*. The sort of perverted bedroom antics that no decent man should be asked to contemplate – not even if he marries a girl from Swindon.'

'And that's when you blacked out?'

Her host slowly shook his head. 'Not quite. She pushed some sort of wriggling creature onto me forehead. Like a multi-legged small puppy, it was. The thing seemed to feed on my mental juices, sucking them out as if it needed them to grow. That's when I finally blacked out. From what little I do remember that was a blessed mercy. Woke

38

up the next morning in the empty field with nothing but Daisy's mangled carcass and a screaming headache for company. But if only that were all. Had to forgo marital obligations for the best part of a month, such was me groinal discomfort.'

Kate tried to look sympathetic but failed. It wasn't so much that she found this hard to believe, but rather the story seemed to strike some deep-rooted chord, a suppressed race memory best left untwanged. It wasn't even as if the climactic top-self conclusion was the end of the matter. 'So tell me about your second visitors.'

Smith took a deep breath. 'Well, not much happened for a week or two, then things *really* started getting strange. The first day I'd felt well enough to go back to work I was having me tea when there was a banging at the door. Hurrying to answer it I found these three strangers dressed in black glaring back at me. Kitted out real odd, they were, – old-fashioned dark suits and hats to match. One of them was carrying a small black box. But the strangest thing about them was they were all wearing make-up, and none too subtly applied at that. They had white foundation smeared on good and thick, and each bore bright red lipstick too. Their eyes were hidden behind horn-rimmed shades.

'Now as folks round here will tell you, I'm a bloke who likes his privacy. "That Smithy loves his privacy," they say. When intimidating strangers come calling, as a rule, I'm more likely to send them packing with two barrels of buckshot than offer tea and drop scones. But on this occasion that's just what I done. I'd lost my innate belligerence.'

'What did they want?'

'That's just it. Nothing as such. Just asked me lots of silly questions. The one with the box was silent throughout; just stood there staring at me and holding his contraption as if it were some sort of gift. One of the others seemed fascinated by my TV. Asked me how it worked, then shut up after that. Their leader did most of the talking.'

'What sort of questions did he ask?'

Smith looked genuinely baffled. 'Mostly stuff about my nightly visitation. But not the obvious things, nothing to do with the craft, or the Morris dancers, or what I thought they were doing, just . . . *odd* things. He seemed obsessed with knowing if I had any physical scars to show for my adventures. Not so much a scarring, I told him, more of a soreness to be quite frank. Even to this day I have to be careful if I sit down at the wrong angle, and the sight of my dairy herd's pendulous udders can spark off an excitement that leaves me doubled up in pain. Needless to say Mrs Smith ain't as impressed as she used to be.'

The young farmer looked suddenly crestfallen down at his feet as Kate pushed. 'And that's when they made their threats?'

The farmer nodded. 'Yeah, all suddenly the mood turned real nasty. Once they'd convinced themselves I bore no lasting marks they crowded round all threatening. The leader told me that if I ever mentioned their visit, or my enforced night of passion, *terrible things* would happen to me. After the *terrible things* that had already happened I was in no mood to argue. Then he handed me these.'

He showed Kate a selection of gaudy promotional fliers for what looked like a New Age mystic religion. The organization claimed to be able to make sense of the most bizarre psychic experiences – new recruits were always welcome. She wasn't certain but she felt sure she'd heard of the Cult of Planet Love somewhere before.

Tearing her eyes from the strangely compelling, almost hypnotic symbols on the covers, she refocused on her subject. 'But you feel able to talk about your ordeal now?'

'Too bloody right,' said Mr Smith, jumping to his feet and barely wincing in pain. 'If their sort comes calling again I'll be ready for them with my gun. I just . . . wasn't ready at the time, that's all.'

Kate stopped her tape recorder and sighed wearily. She had never heard the term 'Men in Black', but she had a close personal friend who knew only too much about them.

8. Aurora Bored-Me-Senseless

The star-speckled sky arched above Dave's head like God's very own dandruff-covered blanket. For the briefest of seconds he suffered a stomach-churning attack of vertigo, his reeling senses telling him he was falling headlong into the infinity of endless night.

With a jolt that almost threw him off balance Dave came crashing back to earth. The piece of earth he came crashing back to was a small patch of rocky desert, beside a dusty highway, eighty miles north of Las Vegas, Nevada. The wilderness around him was very still and very quiet, but he was not alone. Nearby a motley assortment of individuals from every walk and some stumbles of life stood silently, just as Dave did, peering up at the moonless night sky. They had only one thing in common. Hope shone from all their eyes like the light from a flickering candle flame.

Dave stood at a very special spot. This sandy roadside verge was the nearest an unauthorized civilian (and when it came to matters like these there wasn't really any other sort) could get to the Mecca, St Peter's, Wailing Wall and 74 Station Road, Aberdeen of Ufology. Twenty yards away, down the gently sloping desert, a double razor-wire fence stretched off as far as the eye could see in both directions. The signs were evenly spaced: 'USE OF DEADLY FORCE PERMITTED'. The signs were there for one very good reason. Over the jagged ridge on the horizon lay the top-secret US Air Force base known as 'Dreamland', or Area 51.

This facility was so secret that officially it didn't even exist – it said so in all the tourist brochures, books, magazines, films, TV shows and pamphlets that had been published on the matter over the past forty years. In the nearby one-stop town of Rachel you could buy a T-shirt that told you much the same thing. As far as secrets went 'Dreamland' was about as well kept as Colonel Gaddafi's hair.

Area 51. Some claimed that forty-two levels beneath the burning desert there lay a junkyard full of crashed alien craft. Others claimed that the very aliens themselves were housed here, their brains picked over by the sort of government scientist who giggled a lot and hadn't learned to shave. But tonight Dave and the others weren't here to speculate, they were here for the show. And as regular as an atomic clock, they weren't to be disappointed.

At eight-thirty precisely the first lights glided serenely above the horizon. They must have been more than ten miles away but against the translucent indigo sky they stood out like nuns in a whorehouse. As if on cue, a barely audible sigh rose from the congregation. Deferentially, camcorders were raised in unison as the nightly act of worship began.

The display was much the same as it ever was. For thirty minutes the lights bobbed and weaved, dived and swooped. It mattered not that the event was caught on over twenty cameras, the tapes of 'assorted coloured lights dancing in the sky' had been seen many times on TV before. It took much more to impress a cynical public these days.

Shortly, Dave was conscious of a figure standing closer to him than the others. 'Mighty fine sight,' said the new-comer, not taking his eyes from the display for a second. 'Makes you proud to be American.'

Dave looked his companion up and down. He was the sort of middle-aged man who had been fit once, but pizza and Miller Lite had taken their toll. Covering his broad belly was a T-shirt depicting an Arab terrorist cowering beneath a cruise missile. '*Go On – Make My Day*' begged the caption.

'Name's Ray,' he beamed holding out a vast hand that could have easily encased both of Dave's. 'Fifty-eight combat missions over Nam and not a hint of post-traumatic stress disorder.'

Dave nodded meekly. 'Dave. Twenty-six copies of *ScUFODIN Monthly*, and no trace of a book deal yet. Actually I'm not American, I'm on holiday from the UK.' Instantly he was wondering if this was further into conversation than he wanted to get.

'Ah – England!' his new friend gushed. 'We can always rely on you guys to back us up. Winston Churchill and Margaret Thatcher – now they were leaders with real balls, but this new guy of yours makes them look like pussies. Not like the wet farts we have leading us over here.'

Dave correctly surmised that he should direct the conversation away from politics. 'So, have you been interested in UFOs for long?'

Ray chuckled good-naturedly. 'Oh, they ain't no flying saucers, boy. That there's good old Yankee know-how driving those babies. If I was twenty years younger I'd take a shot at piloting one myself.'

'So you think they're just the latest military hardware? If that's the case why is your government so secretive about them? Why not show them off to the world's press to help deter aggression?'

Ray looked pityingly at Dave. 'They ain't just any sort of aircraft. They're the very latest in super-secret stealth technology recon birds. If everyone knows we've got them, what's the point in having a stealth plane?'

Dave looked thoughtful for a long while. 'If it's a super-secret high-tech stealth plane, why is it doing an aerial jig above the horizon and flashing like a traffic light having a nervous breakdown in front of twenty cameras?'

Ray looked confused, an expression which seemed to suite his fat red face. 'Why . . . they gotta test fly them.

Can't just send them into combat without putting them through their paces first.'

'Quite,' muttered Dave, rapidly losing patience. 'But if it is a secret military craft why do they have to test it in quite such a public manner? It doesn't make any sense to test a secret stealth plane in front of a bunch of snap-happy tourists.'

'But they ain't,' growled Ray, a new edge in his voice. 'This here's the Free World's most secure covert base. Ain't nothing comes in or out of there that the Powers That Be don't want to. We're privileged to get a sneak preview. Next time you see those babies they'll be on the Six O'Clock News beating the hell outa Saddam.'

Dave pondered this long and hard. 'Perhaps you're right. *Ain't nothing comes in or out of there that they don't want to.*' With that he turned on the soft desert sand and traipsed back to his waiting hire-car. He felt the display he'd just witnessed lacked just one thing – a large glowing sign projected onto the low clouds reading 'Your Tax Dollars At Work'. Perhaps it could be subtitled 'Return to your homes, and your 92 channels of home-shopping cable TV, safe in the knowledge that we have it all under control.'

It had been Dave's long and burning ambition to see Area 51 in person, but now that he had, he couldn't help but wonder what was going on at Areas 52 and 53.

*   *   *

When he returned to his motel, despite the late hour, Dave was sufficiently stirred by his thoughts to do a spot of research. In fact, as long as it involved sitting at a desk with a nice weak cup of tea, it never took very much to spur him into a flurry of investigation. As long as he had a nice cosy library full of books, or better still a microfilm reader packed with ancient newspaper cuttings, Dave was in his element. Actually getting out into the field to collect hard evidence was a far less appealing prospect. On this road trip, however, all he had with him was his laptop, and that meant, in order find what he was looking for, Dave was going to have to use the internet. The very thought sent a shiver down his spine.

Dave had been slow to jump on the internet bandwagon; as a result it had almost run over him. It was only a glorified version of teletext after all – with just a bit more on it. Now there *was* a medium which had never been fully exploited. Dave's rational, scientific soul was deeply troubled by the way that pinnacle of 1970s technology had been superseded by its younger, flashier cousin. About the only thing you could get on the Net which you couldn't conceivably receive via Ceefax was hard-core pornography – and that was hardly much of a recommendation. It still made Dave fume to think about it – the ultimate triumph of form over content. Dave was not a man to be drawn in by what he saw as incessant hype, quite the reverse in fact. If he saw what he thought was a fad he'd do his best to ignore it. He liked to think he was above the fickle meanderings of the common herd. Lots of Dave's acquaintances liked to think he was a bit of a sad weirdo.

But in the last year even Dave had had to screw up his pride and establish an on-line presence. His beloved magazine would not have been taken seriously unless he had done. Against his better judgement **www. scufodin.org** had been born. Fortunately the setting up of the site had not had to break the bank. Dave's friend Chris was more than happy to build it for nothing more than all the tea he could drink and his own weight in chocolate hob-nobs. Nice one, Chris, milk with two sugars, isn't it.

It an attempt to 'do it properly' Dave had conducted a rigorous scientific analysis of what the world-wide-wacko had to offer. His conclusions left him deeply troubled.

What had Dave *most* bothered about it, especially the bits he was prone to visit, was, not to put too fine a point on it, the unmitigated amount of pure, unadulterated crap there was sloshing about. Was there something about the very medium which brought out the crank in everybody? Reading some of the conspiracy sites it was hard to escape that worrying conclusion.

I ask you – that the English Royal Family was behind a global plot to usurp political power through its communist-riddled puppet, the United Nations . . . what sort of brain-dead paranoid gun-nut dreamt up crap like that? Or that somewhere in the South Pacific there was an island populated by genetically engineered versions of apparently 'dead' celebrities, which some shady organization was using to manipulate the masses in a campaign to spread hysteria and irrationalism. Just where did they get it from? Some people (some Americans, Dave thought smugly) just weren't right in the head. Why did they allow net access in mental asylums, after all?

Things only got worse when Dave began to interact with the cyberspace community. There seemed to be something about messages posted on newsgroups or bulletin boards which led normally sane, polite people to take them completely the wrong way, no matter how many ;) or :) you inserted. It was almost as if they thought you were laughing at them. There was also the bizarre and completely inexplicable tendency for all trans-Atlantic communications to deteriorate onto two-way rants on one highly contentious subject – that one great napalm-fuelled flame-war to end them all.

Dave's earnest postings to a software discussion forum regarding the perceived inadequacies in Nanosoft's latest word processor (Why was it slower on his new 1200 MHz Cray clone than Write Perfect V.1 had been on his 286?) would be met with a barrage of nationalistic vitriol. If American software was so poor, why didn't he use the British alternative? As patiently as he was able, Dave would point out it was far from easy getting hold of an operational BBC model B these days, let alone the software to use it. His reasoned response would not matter, however, as all too soon the discussion would mutate into the same one it always did whenever Brits and Yanks started getting a bit shirty. Somehow the subject would metamorphose into gun-control, or rather the lack of it.

'How can you guys in England be truly free when your government doesn't allow you to carry guns?'

Dave would take many hours poring over his answer, conducting lengthy background reading to help make his point.

'If you truly believe you live under a clandestinely oppressive regime do you really think a Kalashnikov and a landmine-strewn patio is the best solution? Aren't you playing them at their own game? Surely the tactics employed by individual citizens must reflect our own strengths and abilities. Through the spread of know-ledge and information we can conduct a peaceable campaign to bring any such travesty to the attention of all right-thinking citizens, thereby halting any dastardly schemes in their tracks.'

This was what he'd mean to write. What he'd actually post would be:

'You're a smelly poo. And you smell of poo.
So there. Poo-off you smelly poo.
Vietnam, hahaha.'

Of course the exchange could only go downhill from there. With the remorseless, blood-boiling belligerence of the World-Wide-Whine the reply would be posted.

'Geeze. If it wasn't for the US and its citizens' skill with guns you guys would be ruled by a gang of mad, emotionally repressed militaristic right-wing Germans right now. Drop dead and rot, commie-loving scum!'

There was not really any answer to this, apart from to ask if the irate colonial had ever heard of Buckingham Palace – but this would just add more fuel to a fire that hardly needed it.

Dave would honestly try his best to bring a modicum of rationality to the debate, but it would be too much for him in the end, such was brain-numbing effect of 'newsgroup rage'. Dave had even begun to wonder if there was some subtle undertone to the very medium which reduced reasoned, lucid discussion to the level of the school yard. But no, that was paranoid nonsense, wasn't it – almost the sort of thing you'd read on the internet, in fact. When you took into account that the whole thing had initially been set up by the US military to help them survive a nuclear war, it got you to thinking . . .

As so often in the past, on this evening Dave's research didn't so much hit a brick wall as get subsumed into the bland mass of meaningless drivel he found at every turn. As the internet proved all too conclusively, quantity in no way made up for quality when it was information you were after. All the web seemed good for was reinforcing a whole battery of previously conceived misconceptions, strengthening and hammering them home.

More confused and bewildered than ever, Dave fell asleep slumped over his keyboard – the slowly accumulating pool of dribble moulding his moist cheeks to the contours of the harsh plastic keys. When he woke the next day it took nearly an hour of careful massage to coax his face back into its world-weary and slightly less rectangular form.

9. If You Tolerate This Your CD Collection Will Be Next

Not far from where Kate had conducted her interview with farmer Smith, a swampy field just outside Glastonbury was packed with people, just as it always was at this time of year.

But the crowds of bleary-eyed festival-goers weren't solely here for the music. Judging by the mud, and the queues for the toilets, they weren't here for their health either. There existed third-world refugee camps with better sanitary conditions than these. But at least the victims of mankind's latest war weren't crowded out by gaudily tie-dyed stalls manned by grey-haired hippies trying to sell everything from Abduction Survival Kits and King Arthur radio clock alarms to Make Quorn Edible recipe books. There was more crystal in this quiet Somerset town than all the chandeliers in the Versailles Hall of Mirrors put together, but fortunately there wasn't a delegation of high-level Germans getting stitched up nearby. The 'Glastonbury Experience' was designed to cater for far more than just the anally-retentive masochistic music fan, it was ingeniously crafted to appeal to people wishing to make a 'lifestyle choice'.

And what a choice it was. The masses of combat-trouser-clad off-duty estate agents and junior management consultants were there for the dope. If they'd wanted music they had perfectly good CD players in their Audis and BMWs clogging the huge car parks nearby. They were doing something far more profound than simply having a boogie – they were making a stand against the relentless drive of consumerism, and they thought £49.95[1] a head to do so was a bit of a bargain.

Some went with the loud intention of dropping a few 'e's. But the only letter these frustrated public-school boys had ever dropped were 'h's, in a sad attempt to sound more working class.

The admission was a particular bargain this year, though the organizers didn't realize that yet. If they had known the identity of that year's mystery gate-crasher they could have safely trebled the prices, and still sold out ten times over. Lounging in their distant Tuscan villas, value for money had been the last thing in mind – but then soon enough, so too would be mere profit.

As the latest mumbling, moody three-piece band to crawl from the mean streets of Newport left the stage, safe in the knowledge that if you're Welsh and grew up in a terraced house no one would ever accuse you of being pretentious, the next act was warming up ready to go on. But this performer wasn't limbering up backstage. No mineral-water-equipped green room hung with nubile groupies was temporary home to this show-biz heavy weight, just as he wasn't to be flown in last minute on a private luxury jet. The anxious stage manager didn't know it yet, but the next visitor was zooming in from much further afield, both in space and time.

Accompanied by a bone-shaking electrical hum, a perfectly triangular black craft slowly descended through the veil of low grey cloud. It came to rest hovering two hundred feet above the sea of upturned awe-struck faces, bath-

---

[1] Losing a potential additional 4p on every ticket sold, but this tactic had been carefully and cunningly thought out. What this price-point policy, in accordance with the very latest marketing theories, said was: *No, we don't think you're stupid enough to imagine there's a difference between 49.99 and 50, but we're banking on you being seduced by that saving of 5p. We're not satisfied selling you an overpriced concert ticket, with the honour of suffering diarrhoea in a draughty chemical toilet thrown in for free, we intend to patronize you first, too. Card number and expiry date please, you gullible fuckwit.*

ing them in the single baleful yellow light that shone from its keel like an unblinking evil eye. Without a sound the ship effortlessly glided further forward, stopping to float directly over the deserted stage.

The golden light pulsated for a moment, then a single radiant figure slowly descended through the glowing column, as if suspended by an unseen wire.

If the crowd had been speechless before, soon they were hypnotized by the man hunched statue-still up on stage. He wore a spotless white jump-suit, flared cuffs glittering sequin-laced under the eerie light. Behind his lavishly coiffured head stretched an arching radar-dish collar. His bloated top lip was curled in a famous uncontemptuous sneer, as he pressed it hard against a rhinestone-encrusted radio-mike; his other jewel-heavy hand thrust back and up behind him in a quivering stance. The wrap-around shades he wore would have done a welder or an over-sensitive vampire proud.

If this was a publicity stunt then it was well worth the admission fee alone. This was the best Elvis impersonator anyone had ever seen, and he certainly knew how to make an entrance. The sideburns were a touch too long and curly, and shot through with grey if truth be told, but every other detail was spot on. Authentically enough he didn't seem to have missed too many meals lately – what a commendable touch of professionalism in this slapdash age.

Elvis didn't move his ostentatiously bowed head from where it was hunched over the mike. He had the voice down pat too – a harmonious Dixie drawl wrapped up in a diamond-studded velvet glove.

'I'd just like to tell y'all, I don't eat meat no more – not since the military started pumping it full of filthy GM hormones. This next number goes out to all those reformed meat-eaters out there – and by that I don't mean hamburger lovers, you dig?' He formed his upturned hand into a Churchillian victory salute, 'Viva Lost Vegans, everywhere.'

The King then broke into a stirring rendition of one of his best-loved numbers. Accompanied by an unseen orchestra, which seemed to blare out from the black ship above, he tore through 'Always On My Mind', singing not just to the audience but the entire human race. Any doubts that he was the real thing evaporated the moment he opened his mouth. When he pleaded with them to 'give me one more chance to keep you satisfied' the crowd would have hit the roof, if there'd been a roof to hit.

When the noise had subsided to a mere deafening roar, Elvis held up a shaky hand for silence. 'Where've ya been, ya Highness?' yelled an impatient reveller from the crowd's rippling front row.

One of the King's trembling trouser legs started wobbling of its own accord, generating a terrific breeze as it did so. 'Well, howdy there, li'l pardner. Been staying up at the government-run heartbreak hotel, but now I've come back to you folks for good – aha huuuu.'

The crowd erupted into ecstatic screaming delight. Elvis held up a calming hand once again. A fistful of glittering jewellery sparkled amidst the golden light.

'First I've got some news to tell ya. Don't figure y'all like it much.'

As one the crowd fell silent. Elvis continued in his lilting sing-song voice.

'I ain't been gone of my own free will. Been a prisoner dancing to a dishonest warden's very own jailhouse rock. For all those long years I been gone, I was held hostage by darkly sinister forces. Yes folks, there's a conspiracy going on behind your backs, perpetrated by your evil governments and the corrupt politicians who spin you their cynical lies.'

There was a howl of incredulous rage, plus some shouts for further songs by some of the less politically-aware festival goers. But this crowd was far from dubious of the great man's claims, there were plenty here today well capable of believing what he told, many who were completely unsurprised by it in fact – and didn't the unseen puppeteers just know it.

'Those same good ole boys who got to Kennedy, well they got to me too. Kidnapped me from my very own john. Well now I'm here in Engle-land for the very first time, ready to start my come-back tour. Gonna be some show!'

Meanwhile a single unmarked helicopter had come to hover above the crowd. Those camped beneath it felt the brutal effects of its rotor down-wash – tents and teepees flattening beneath its steady thumping force; but its turbines gave off no sound. As it hung there like a spiteful wasp Elvis continued his heart-felt manifesto.

'Hard to believe, I know, but there's more to their depraved schemings than just my heinous incarceration. Your governments have kidnapped others too – but not just men and women like you and me. They've got hangars full of crashed space-aliens – little peace-loving grey brothers who mean to do us no harm. Help me to set them free!'

Those unlucky few beneath the suspicious black chopper clearly saw a hatch swing open in the side of its smoked-glass cockpit. Those not wrapped up in the King's astonishing revelations watched as a long gun barrel protruded from this hole. Their screams of warning were lost in the crowd's angry roar.

As was the single crack of high-powered rifle fire.

'ALIENS GOOD, GOVERNMENTS BAD . . .' Elvis led the steadily rising chant, or at least he did until his vaporized brains sprayed backwards across the stage in an ever-widening cloud.

The first the masses knew of the hit was when they saw their idol's arms jerk forward in an oddly familiar motion, and the condensing cranial matter reform to perform a brief come-back tour of its own as it trickled down the garish display at the back of the set – every detail caught on the giant-sized screens either side of the stage. There was a second of stunned silence, then a massive and strangely resigned moan rose up from the throng.

Somehow managing to look scared for its life, the black triangle beamed up Elvis's remains the same way they had come down and beat a hasty retreat up into the clouds. The hovering black chopper went after it in hot pursuit.

That was when the riot began.

When the official forces of government arrived, in the shape of the hard-pressed British police, they had to use tear-gas and electric cattle-prods to disperse the baying crowd. But their efforts to engineer a peaceful conclusion were to no avail. In a quest for instant retribution the surging hordes went on the rampage down Glastonbury's sleepy main street; their target, any symbol of the heartless Establishment brave or foolish enough to stand in their way.

A corner-shop post office, three Tourist Information Centres and twelve New Age bookshops paid the ultimate price for being in the wrong place at the wrong time.

They said the pall of choking incense, given off by a thousand burning jostsicks, hung over the deserted town for generations to come.

They were right.

10. Containment

The hospital ward was packed with the sort of hi-tech equipment which could have made the most hardened gadget-freak go weak at the knees – that's if the strangely lifeless air and epilepsy-inducing lighting didn't get to him first. However, overcrowding was not likely to become a problem in the near future; this ward contained just one very special patient, but then this was one very special hospital.

Like many of its more conventional counterparts it was of a multi-storey construction, but that's where the similarity ended. While the traditional direction to build a hospital was upwards, this one delved into the bowels of the earth like an overly zealous intern given his first taste of surgery and a very sharp laser scalpel.

Three levels up from the current floor, and nearly twenty years back in time, the bright boys who ministered to the Shadow Government had discovered a general cure for every form of cancer under the sun. Their discovery hadn't made the evening news.

Market forces precluded its release – which was to say there were still way too many tax-funded research dollars sloshing around the Cancer Cure Industry for the pharmaceutical conglomerates to let this particular cat out of the bag just yet. On the surface, capitalism might have relied on competition to drive its stuttering heart – not so the cosy tight-lipped gaggle of cartels which gerrymandered this shady world. As long as everyone kept quiet, all could prosper. You scratch my back, I'll watch yours.

Like so many other groundbreaking discoveries, the wonder drugs had been locked away in the deepest, darkest vaults; along with the common-cold remedies, everlasting

57

light-bulbs and high-calorie foodstuffs which could have solved the world hunger crisis before you could say 'Do ya want fries with that?' There were now so many prototype water-driven engines on the 42nd floor they were fast running out of space to store them. That fossilized dinosaur steam engine was going to have to be moved.

These miracles of modern technology were not for general consumption,[1] they had been created for the benefit of the all-powerful ruling elite – first by benefiting them directly, and then by benefiting their bank accounts. The Illuminanti had paid for the R&D, why shouldn't they have sole usage until comprehensive strategies for full exploitation could be formed? When your timescale ran to centuries a few decades here or there made no difference. This was an organization which could afford to take the longest view. The Committee had a duty to see the profits and power of its descendants maximized – it was only fair after all.

Some of the real money-spinners, wisely held back by their forefathers, were only now being hatched into profitable schemes. A bio-technology bonanza was in the offing and for once it would have nothing to do with overexposure to pesticides. As soon as the public could be manoeuvred into accepting animal transplantation as a matter of course, and not a cause for Luddite revulsion, the real profits would start rolling in. A fresh killing was patiently waiting to be made, and this beast had blood-shot rolled-back eyes.

Years before, those woolly-minded do-gooders voted

---

[1] These days it isn't only angst-ridden poets in fluffy white shirts who die of TB. With the help of virulent new strains resistant to those tried and tested (i.e. cheap, out-of-patent) drugs, almost anyone can receive the benefits of the ultimate creative muse. All over the globe this old favourite was making a comeback as the most efficient regulator of the urban poor, not to mention a most efficient filler of drug corporations' bank accounts. Potent new strains require potent new cures, which in turn require potent research grants and tax incentives.

into power had allowed themselves to be bullied by a superstitious, small-minded public into banning the sale of human organs – something about it being 'immoral'. Hypocrites and killjoys, the lot of them, the Committee had concluded. Well, that distant setback was about to be avenged.

Pig hearts had one big advantage over human ones, pulled from the dwindling supply of public-spirited accident victims. Cute little porkers reared in labs could have their vital organs ripped out to be legally sold at $12,000 a pop – so much better for the balance sheet than printing more of those fiddly donor cards. It was a loophole which would allow the drug firms their final slice of the lucrative Transplant Organ Pie.[1]

Even the other 99.9% of the valiant animal could be put to profitable use. Slap it in a pitta bread, drench it in chilli sauce and no one would ever be the wiser – a sustainable income stream from waste products. This was what the Project's Para-Accountants and Ninja-Management Consultants liked to call a 'win-win' situation. Which was a rather better situation than the secret hospital's only current patient was presently in.

This particular invalid wasn't lucky enough to be a member of the Committee of 300 – he was an expendable minion, but one with a crucial tale to tell. If he could tell it all.

All told, Captain Freemantle had seen better days. And judging by the look of intense frustration splashed across his weathered features, so too had the lumbering figure towering above him.

Nearby a nervous surgeon eyed Becker with considerable disdain, as only a member of his profession could hope to get away with and live to tell the tale.

---

[1] Not to be confused with the Donor Kebab. As in: 'I wish I could donate my stomach to science. Pass me a fresh bucket please.'

'You know that this dosage will probably kill him? This much babble-juice will not sit happily will the medication we've used to stabilize his condition.'

The Dark Man fixed the surgeon with a stare that had brought slack-jawed presidents to their knees, and reduced more than one pope to a blubbering wreck.

'This is a matter of planetary security. Have you heard what went on in England? Daily the Opposition ups the stakes – we might not have much time left. He's only a grunt, he knew the risks when he took his oath, just like you and me. Do your duty, so that he can do his.'

With a heavy sigh the surgeon uncapped a syringe and flicked its large-bore needle. He had watched the news reports from across the pond – there could have been few humans who hadn't. As to the significance of what he'd seen he was currently reserving judgement; better stick to what he knew. With practised ease he found a vein and administered the dose.

Freemantle went rigid from head to toe. For a moment Becker thought rigor mortis must have set in with exceptional speed, but then, with a convulsion that nearly shook their subterranean bunker, the captain's eyes snapped open and the words flooded forth.

His rantings wouldn't have made sense to an outsider. Fortunately Becker was about as much of an insider as you could get without actually becoming inside out. He had also come prepared. Holding a small dictaphone as close to Freemantle as his rabid saliva-flecked monologue would allow, Becker recorded every word for posterity and for the next chapter of his voluminous memoirs.

When the tirade had run its course the surgeon looked bemused. 'Machu Picchu. That's the Inca capital in the Andes, isn't it?

But when he turned to question Becker further he was faced only by a furiously swinging door.

11. Assault

For no obvious reason, suddenly Frank was alert.

Nothing had changed in the dingy third-floor apartment, but like a US Marine's genitals on his first trip ashore in Manila, the hairs on the back of McIntyre's neck had become instantly erect. The TV news still blared in the corner – a hectic report about a military take-over in some tin-pot Central Asian republic. The bowl of Coco Puffs still hovered above Frank's heroically stained T-shirt,[1] the spoonful of the same choc-flavoured corn-based breakfast cereal still suspended precariously half-way to his lips.

But something was different.

Some unknown set of relays had clicked inside Frank's head. The highly tuned sixth sense which had saved his skin on countless occasions had kicked in again. So Frank McIntyre, Master Sergeant US Special Forces (ret), was in danger, but (as he reflected with a detached professional confidence) as of that instant not half as much danger as the other guy.

Just who that 'other guy' might be didn't bother him at this stage. Frank hadn't stopped to consider who had been wearing the Vietcong-issue pyjamas, or enquire after the health of the balaclava-swathed terrorists. The personalities behind the Federal Marshals' badges hadn't entered into the equation. He'd simply seen them as enemies, obstacles to his continued existence – and now there were other 'obstacles' crowding in on him. Frank was an equal

---

[1] 'LIVE FREE and BUY! I've visited Preacher Jack's Old-Time Trading Post and Ammunition Store: Free Wyoming's foremost survivalist retail outlet. Discounts available with NRA membership cards. (No Queers, Papists or UN Stooges.)'

opportunities killing machine, as free with his political allegiances as he was with his ammunition.

That was another good point. His Heckler & Koch sub-machine gun was tucked safely under the bed – no way to reach that now. The laser sight was a toy, but one that gave him and the drivers of the big eighteen-wheel semis that thundered beneath his window constant amusement. Frank owned a fine collection of handguns, but his Colt automatic was shut in his desk draw. His .345 Smith & Wesson Magnum was, as usual, taped to the inside of the toilet cistern. With bitter irony he reflected that he was currently equidistant from all his carefully placed hardware.

If he was going to leave with his guest when the fun started he was going to have to move very fast indeed. Abandoning his guns was not a happy thought, but he knew the deadliest weapon of all was carried with him. The United Nations had never tried to ban it, nor had it been the subject of arms limitation talks, yet its facility to unleash unrivalled mayhem and slaughter was impossible to match. It was the twin handful of pink-grey blancmange that quivered between Frank's ears, and what's more it was currently working overtime.

For the briefest of seconds he contemplated leaving the contents of his fridge undisturbed. No way, hosayovich. His uncommunicative guest represented the chance of several million lifetimes. He had no doubt it was the thing in his chiller cabinet 'they' were after. It was too much of a coincidence to hope his former employers wanted a chat for anything less. They also wanted to take him alive. Otherwise he'd already be dead. Frank knew how these guys operated – he'd all but written the manual himself. But knowing he was wanted for interrogation gave him a slender advantage, and right now he needed all the help he could get.

These thoughts went through Frank's head in a split

second. He didn't have to think about them, the act of knowing he'd been compromised and analysing the tactical situation happened so fast as to be instantaneous. How would he plan it if he were commanding the assault? First off he'd place a sniper team in the derelict warehouse across the street. Secondly, he'd put a back-up squad at the bottom of the fire escape, to rush up when the main team hit the front door. He'd make sure he had every detail planned three ways in advance. But the time for preparation was at an end, now it was time for action.

Slowly, Frank lowered his bowl and made a careful show of appearing relaxed. The surveillance spooks would have him scoped at that very moment; his every move carefully analysed for signs of stress. As Frank got up and stretched, from the corner of the room, the confessional TV show presenter pointed out the problems faced by single-parent-transvestite households. There was a careful line Frank had to tread between haste and circumspection. Too fast and he risked letting on he knew of the raid, too slow and he'd be yesterday's enchiladas before you could say 'justifiable force'. As nonchalantly as he was able he headed for the kitchen, as if to fetch a morning beer.

His speed/stealth quandary was resolved for him. Before he'd gone three steps with low-battery flatness his musical doorbell creaked to life. When the first bars of 'Do You Know the Way to San José?' had trailed away, a carefully measured voice (too quick) called out, 'Floral delivery for Mr McIntyre. I need your signature.'

The image of fifteen black berets, spread-eagled along the threadbare hallway, shotguns and battering rams at the ready, one reading from a carefully prepared script, sprung alarmingly to mind and refused to go away. That settled things. Speed was of the essence, and he'd have to leave by the window. Painful, but not half as painful as getting shot.

'Coming,' Frank called in a none-too-convincing effort

to buy time, as he ducked into the kitchen. He knew that wouldn't stall them for long, but at least he was hidden from view in the pokey windowless room.

Working quickly, he bundled his decaying guest from the fridge, removing its satchel as he did so. Checking the inhuman buckle he securely fastened the bulging sack around his neck. The document it contained was most definitely leaving with him. Next, he jammed the alien under one sinewy arm and tucked its legs up into his armpit. This way he was able to carry the feather-light carcass with surprising ease.

Now came the minor matter of making his escape. Talented and trained he might have been, but Frank held no illusions as to his chances. With a softly spoken 'Hail Mary' he crawled back into the living room. He had the makings of a plan. It wasn't good, but it was painfully simple – with the emphasis very much on the painful part.

Stealthily he backed up against one damp mould-encrusted wall. Next to him the apartment's main window overlooked the busy street below. Luckily they hadn't stopped the traffic going past, otherwise his embryonic plan would have fallen in tatters at his sneaker-clad feet. A loud crash from the hallway's front door told him that the 'delivery man' really wanted to give him those flowers. Sure enough tear-gas soon followed.

The full-length window next to him opened out onto a small balcony, the apartment's single redeeming feature. With an impressive shower of glass Frank kicked his way through it and was onto the veranda in a tobacco-stained flash. Instantly a high-velocity '*whoosh*' came racing in from the building across the street. A split second later a black-flighted crossbow-bolt embedded itself in the rail scant inches from his elbow. Frank recognized the lethal projectile before it had stopped twanging; he had used them himself on more than one occasion. But this was no time to stand around admiring the view. It was just as well that out of the corner of his twitching eye he spotted just what he was after. Up at the intersection a big eighteen-wheel road-transporter rounded the corner and ponderously accelerated down the main street beneath him.

With recklessness born of desperation Frank threw himself from the balcony, his unearthly passenger grasped tightly for dear life. For a stomach-churning second he thought he'd gone too soon, and would slam into the dusty roadway in the vehicle's path. But then, as if in slow motion, the hissing juggernaut arrived beneath him. A bone-crunching impact later and Frank was attached like a limpet to the container section's boxy flank.

One arm grasped the canvas-covered top as the other clung to the alien with grim determination. The bulk of the transporter now shielded Frank from the tactical position across the street. Shortly his pursuers were firing more than just arrows. Within seconds the gaudy awning was peppered with the gaping exit wounds of automatic fire. Soon the barrage was augmented from his rear, as the assault-team joined the party from the balcony above. Frank's flaring nostrils filled with the evil smell of cordite, dragged along amidst the turbulent airflow of the truck's lengthening wake.

The vehicle thundered on, the driver either unaware of the hail of bullets or more likely terrified out of his wits. Frank decided he could hardly blame him. Remorselessly he began the slow process of clambering up on top of the hurtling juggernaut.

By now they were well clear of the apartment block and quickly leaving the crackle of gunfire behind them. Frank judged he was in more danger of being thrown off than of getting hit by a lucky long-range shot. There was a nasty moment as they sped around a corner, the highlight of which saw Frank clinging on by mere fingernails, his glassy-eyed companion grasped desperately by the other hand – spread-eagled like a bony grey starfish – but as they slalomed through the crowded streets the centrifugal forces flung them both back into the body of the careering lorry.

Grimly Frank hauled himself along the length of the tarpaulin. When he reached the container's leading edge he had good reason to thank the gods of chance once more. In front of him, across the metre-wide gap that separated the cab from its articulated container section, the driver's window lay open.

With a superhuman effort Frank swung his posthumous passenger in a wide arc and in through the open window. Seconds later Frank followed his mouldy companion through the opening.

The driver was looking more than a trifle alarmed, as well he might. Yelling at the top of his prodigious lungs he wrestled with the lifeless freeze-dried alien, simultaneously struggling to steer the big vehicle with his enormous belly. Frank's wide-eyed arrival did nothing to calm him.

'Get the fuck out of my cab!' he screamed, scant moments before Frank's fist undid $900 of careful dental bridgework.

'Mmmmrrrph!' the driver spluttered, spitting like a pop-corn machine, as Frank unlatched the door and bundled him from the cab.

The ex-commando had no time for remorse, not that he would have fallen victim to such an emotion anyway. All his nerve-endings had long since been cauterized by the searing heat of battle. This was a shooting war now and the occasional civilian was bound to get hurt. Frank was neither stimulated nor disturbed by this certainty, he merely accepted it as matter-of-factly as he'd accept the readout on a laser range-finder. Besides, it was the forces of 'law and order' which had fired the first shots – he knew from bitter experience they would be no more careful with the lives of the electorate than they had to be.

But there was another good reason why Frank had no time to feel guilty. With testicle-tightening certainty the thought came crashing home that, along with a semi-mummified extra-terrestrial, he was suddenly in control of a decidedly out-of-control juggernaut. The very act of not crashing was going to be a major achievement in itself, never mind the slightly more complex issue of safely bringing the vehicle under control and escaping his omniscient pursuers.

Either side of the highway the city limits gave way to desert at a shuddering pace. This fact at least brought a partial improvement; Frank was no longer in danger of taking half a city block with him on his final death charge. Unfortunately the petering-out of civilization had another, less welcome effect – the road surface over which they flew was no longer capable of sustaining such a speed. When Frank hit the first series of potholes the truck seemed to buck from under him like a Saigon call-girl he'd once known. Stamping on the brakes did little to improve matters, merely sparking off the sort of skid that could have brought tears to the Michelin Man's eyes.

Ahead the road ran up a gentle gradient which did little to bleed off the frightening momentum. Worse was to follow. As the highway plunged over the far side it veered to the left. The wheels barely touching the ground, there was no way Frank could steer his mount around this bend. But it wasn't just a large sandy hill that blocked his path. Half way up the rise a towering advertising hoarding for 'Yoke Cola – *as real as you'll want to get!*' blocked their path. Across it, a scantily-clad young lady frolicked on a deserted beach, red lips clasped around the distinctly shaped bottle.

Seconds later the hoarding no longer blocked Frank's path, because the juggernaut had slammed through it, to embed itself cab-deep in the dusty slope beyond.

Moments before impact Frank had buckled himself into the cab's elaborate strapping system. He was fortunate this truck was a luxury top-of-the-range model. It was fitted with the sort of safety features which could have done spacecraft proud. The gel-filled air-bag offered the ultimate in protection, but also the ultimate in subliminal advertising – being carefully designed to maximize customer exposure to the brand logo at a moment of maximum stress and susceptibility. Frank was saved from serious injury, but left with a peculiar everlasting urge to purchase Ford motor vehicles for the remainder of his unnatural life. Unbeknownst to him his terrified mind had been subjected to some of the most effective and subtle advertising yet known to man.[1]

Admittedly there were strange-coloured shapes dancing before his eyes, and far off in the distance he could have sworn he heard an ice-cream van jingle, but there was nothing new in that. A few scratches and scrapes, and tomorrow some seriously impressive bruising, was all he was going to have to show for his morning's adventure. Unfortunately the same could not be said for the alien.

Amidst the general mayhem the cab's glove compartment had sprung open – somehow the creature's bulbous cranium had got wedged inside. On impact its head had been clasped firmly in this vice-like grip, while its frail body was free to snap wildly around. A fearful whiplash had resulted that by rights should have decapitated the poor creature. If it had been a horse it would have almost certainly been shot by now to put it out of its misery – that's if it hadn't already been long dead of course.

Grabbing the satchel and prising the tenderized alien from its resting place, Frank jumped out into the clear

---

[1] Even more effective than the compelling 1990s campaign by the MIEC to enslave the masses to mobile phone use. Conducted over decades, through a combination of cultural familiarization ('Star Trek' communicators), electromagnetic long-distant brainwashing (those relay transmitters don't just 'boost the signal'), and cynically blatant association with a well-known TV show depicting the uncovering of the One World Shadow Government. Who needs an ID card when everyone carries a transponder and their very own number-of-the-beast?

morning air. Clambering out of the gaping hole cut in the towering young lady's blossoming left breast, he surveyed the swathe of destruction cut through cacti and tumbleweed alike. Briefly he paused, experiencing a terrible and sudden desire for a fizzy sugar-filled caramel-based drink, but he shook it from his mind with iron military discipline.

Gulping past the pain of his itching throat, Frank checked his ponderous load and began trekking off into the baking desert. It was going to be a blazingly hot day, but he had a lot of ground to cover by nightfall. He was going to have to find a more controllable transport if he was to put sufficient distance between himself and his pursuers.

12. The Jimmy Maxwell Show

The studio audience had been whipped up into a frenzy of anticipation. For Kate Jennings, standing off in one darkened wing watching the recording on a monitor, the transformation never ceased to be a surreal and slightly scary experience. No matter how many true-life confessionals she worked on it was always a little alarming just how easily a group of otherwise sane human beings could be agitated into a baying mob; each herd-member impatient for the moment they could sink their fangs into the carnival of human misfortune paraded before them. What had, until half an hour before, been nothing more than a studio full of perfectly normal Britons, united admittedly in the fact that they had nothing better to do than attend the recording of a daytime TV show, was no longer a pretty sight. Each individual's identity and inhibitions was lost in the anonymity of the pack.

It wasn't as if the techniques Kate's show used were particularly sophisticated. The procession of hadn't-been comedians and enthusiastic young floor-assistants were not what instantly sprung to mind when you thought of subtle weapons of psychological warfare. But they were all that was needed.

A more informative and depressing insight into the darker reaches of the human psyche you'd be hard pressed to find – and the show hadn't even begun yet. With the first bars of the terminally cheerful theme tune, Kate knew the unnaturally orange host couldn't be far behind.

Kate wasn't to be disappointed. As the 'Applause' lights flashed their strident instruction, Jimmy Maxwell sprung from an alcove and bounded down the audience aisle stairs leaping, slapping hands with the people and whooping with every breath. Britain's favourite daytime TV celeb might have had the body and face of a middle-aged angel, but put him in front of a tight-lipped guest and he'd rip their tale from them like his career depended on it – which it did. He was undeniably the biggest fish in a small pond, but Maxwell had agents working round the clock to facilitate the move he craved. There was only so far you could take this format in the closeted and provincial TV backwater that was the UK. North America beckoned, like a cut-price whore offering twice as many bangs for the buck. It was rumoured that a major Hollywood producer had flown in today to watch him perform.

Unlike his hair Jimmy Maxwell's appeal was harder to pin down. His voice retained just enough of a regional accent to smack of the exotic, setting the pulses of the housebound ladies of the Home Counties aflutter with hints of the mysterious hinterlands beyond the Stockbroker Belt. His strange mixture of Cockney-Scouse-Brooklyn was as distinctive as his cantilevered hair and trademark grey suit. Ever since the groundbreaking 'I Married My Stalker' episode last season the British public couldn't get enough of him. Between two fingers he currently held a radio microphone like a magician's wand.

'Welcome, ladies and gentlemen, to this our hundredth show, and what a show we have for you today. In a moment we'll be meeting our first guests, but first a word on our topic today – meaningful relationships within a loving family group and how hard it can be to maintain those traditional values in today's hectic world.'

Jimmy cast an indulgent glance over his besotted audience, and ran a manicured hand over his spotless silk tie. He was a self-made man, and worshipped his creation.

'It's easy for us to judge the lives of others and to form snapshot opinions on their lifestyles, especially if those lifestyles differ from our own. At this point I'd like to ask you all to come to today's show with an open mind and a forgiving heart, and the awareness that we all follow different lanes down the long and pot-holed motorway of life.'

It was all Kate could do to fight back the waves of nausea that shuddered through her body. These opening speeches reassured the harried station execs that they were paying for a worthwhile piece of informative public service broadcasting, and not half an hour of bandwagon-jumping emotional warfare that dragged the lowest common denominator down to previously unheard of depths. Jimmy's monologues served as a convenient counter to the show's myriad critics, but it was hard not to be cynical when you knew what was to come. You almost had to admire the cheek of the man for his ability to blurt them out with a cheddary grin smeared across his tea-stain coloured face. Amidst his adoring audience Jimmy hardly paused for breath.

'With those thoughts in mind let's meet our first guest. Come on out, Lucinda!'

The stage was mocked up to give the appearance of a well-to-do family lounge, though no such room Kate was aware of sported six different cameras, enough lighting to beckon down a jumbo jet and a barely restrained audience seated within easy abuse-hurling range. Five chairs formed a stark line across the sumptuous red carpet, chosen that way so as not to show the blood. Behind the carefully polished potted plants a series of painted-on windows looked out over an idyllic view of rolling downland. Onto this surreal tableau bounced the first victim.

Lucinda didn't look the type to get embroiled in the sort of tale this show thrived on, but then that was always half the appeal. She was a little bunny-rabbit of a girl, one who took the word 'wholesome' into entirely new territory – where she rode metaphorical ponies through dewy meadows and won blue ribbons in gymkhanas. Her sweater was as tight as her bottom and as rosy as her smile.

72

Maxwell barely gave her time to settle in. 'Welcome, my dear. Why don't you start by telling us why you're here today?'

Lucinda was only too eager to oblige. 'Hi Jimmy. I'm here to tell you about my wonderful family. We're so close and loving that I just want all the world to share what we're doing right.' At that instant two small boxes appeared in the corners of Kate's monitor. One showed a head and shoulders close-up of a well-dressed middle-aged couple, beaming in a slightly forced manner from ear to ear; the other, a vacantly handsome young man with an unreadable expression splashed across his pallid features.

'That's a very worthy sentiment,' said Jimmy, with the first hint of a smile breaking across his chiselled jaw-line. 'Let's just make this clear, you come from a perfectly ordinary, middle-class family from a leafy London suburb. Is that right?'

'That's right,' said Lucy a little self-consciously. 'Though we do have a second home in the Dordogne – helps Daddy with his wine import business.'

Jimmy's smile widened. Kate could see he was going to enjoy this more than usual. 'Why don't you tell us all about the people who make up this ideal group.'

Lucinda leaned forward in her chair. 'Well, there's Mummy and Daddy, or Edward and Virginia as they're known to their friends. They're the best parents a girl could wish for. There've always been there for me, but have let me know from an early age I've the freedom to discover life's wonders for myself. That freedom ensured I didn't once go off the rails like some girls did.'

Jimmy's eyes lit up, his voice chokingly eager. 'What do you mean by "going off the rails" exactly?'

Lucy dimpled and looked demure. 'Well, you know, "boy trouble". I knew some girls at finishing-school who got into all sorts of bother. Some of them were even expelled and had to attend the local comprehensive.'

'Shocking,' agreed Jimmy. 'But these days you're completely sorted out in the "boy department", I understand?'

'That's right. I've known Toby since we met at Jemima's, that's his older sister's, coming out ball. He's perfect, we're getting married next spring.'

Jimmy looked pleased with himself. 'Well, you know, Lucy, we've got a surprise for you today. Toby, your loving fiancé, is actually backstage. Let's hear it, ladies and gentlemen, for Toby!'

Onto the stage shuffled the sad and stooped figure Kate had seen in the 'picture in picture' shot. His eyes were downcast as he mounted the short flight of steps, barely acknowledging his bride-to-be as she made a brave attempt at a one-way hug. Lucy looked genuinely surprised and more than a little bewildered by her boyfriend's stand-offish behaviour.

Jimmy began pacing back and forth amidst the highly expectant congregation. 'Welcome, Toby, take a seat. Let's not draw this out any longer than we have to. Why don't you tell the lovely Lucy why you're here today.'

Toby's eyes never left his highly polished shoes as he mumbled, 'Lucinda, I've got something I have to tell you.'

Lucinda looked on with growing incomprehension, as Jimmy pressed for the kill. 'Why don't you share it with us, Toby? You'll feel better once you've got it off your chest.'

Toby cast a furtive glance over the audience of strangers that he knew would soon turn against him, then retreated behind his ponderous fringe. 'This isn't easy for me to say, but I've been having an affair behind your back.'

Even though they had known what was coming, the audience let out a collective gasp which seemed to suck the air out of the room. Kate felt her eardrums bulge outwards as, up on stage, Lucy put her dainty hands to her mouth and turned an ashen shade.

Jimmy wanted more. 'That's not all you have to tell

Lucinda, is it, Toby? "Behind her back" is a more fitting phrase in this case than in most others. Why don't you tell us who this liaison has been with?'

Through some strange compulsion not to let his tormentors down, Toby carried on, barely suppressing a self-conscious smile. 'Sorry, Lucy, but I've been sleeping with your mum.'

Another gasp from the audience. Kate could have sworn it was getting harder to breathe. She saw on the monitor beside her that the Director had playfully cut back to a shot of Lucy's smiling parents, still waiting in the green room, oblivious to events on stage.

That raised another point that had always left her baffled. Why the hell did people agree to come on this sort of show? If you were invited to be a guest of Jimmy Maxwell, along with several members of your immediate family, for no *obvious* reason, surely even the most inept viewer would realize it was not to be given 'good news'.

Meanwhile, as usual, events onstage did not leave much time for sober reflection. Jimmy was playing the crowd for all he was worth, and at last count that was quite a bit.

'Well, I'm sure you can guess who we've got back stage, can't you folks? They haven't heard what's happened to this point, but there's plenty of time to correct that right now. Come on out, Eddy and Ginny!'

Half the audience broke into spontaneous cheers, while the other half set up a chorus of boos which would have made an ugly sister feel at home. To her credit Lucinda wasted no time in getting her retaliation in first.

'BITCH!' she screamed, as she threw herself at her bewildered mother.

As the burly security guards peeled her off her reeling parents, Jimmy felt the need to bring them up to speed on recent developments. 'Welcome, Eddy and Virginia. Toby has just been telling us about your very close and special relationship.'

'Mummy' went as white as one of her suspiciously stained bed-sheets. 'Oh my God!' she gasped, sinking to her chair.

'What on earth is all this about?' demanded 'Daddy', as he comforted his wailing daughter.

Jimmy smirked. 'Seems Toby and Ginny have been indulging in a spot of the old double-divan boogie-woogie. Virginia by name, but not, apparently, by nature.'

The audience loved that, this was even better than Maxwell's infamous 'I'm a Fat Transvestite Bisexual Who Sleeps Around' show. There had been crowds in the Roman Colosseum which had given Christian rookie lion-tamers an easier time. Eddy looked on aghast at his wife. 'Is this true, Virginia?'

It was all Ginny could do to nod her head. 'It was him,' she stammered, pointing a trembling finger in Toby's direction. 'He had me under some sort of hypnotic spell. I couldn't say no to his depraved demands.'

All eyes turned to young Toby. Lucy stared at her former fiancé for a second along with everyone else, then made a heroic effort to break from her minder to tear his throat out. The crowd loved that too. There was a spontaneous standing ovation for the plucky young woman, who all knew had been done a great and terrible wrong.

Jimmy stepped up to the stage, a life-raft of tolerance amidst the ocean of chaos. 'Now, now. Why don't we all calm down and talk about this like sensible adults? But first I'd like to welcome a very special mystery guest. None of you knew she was coming tonight, but please put your hands together for Toby's sister Jemima!'

The make-up and costume departments had obviously gone to town on Jemima. She looked like an extra from a certain sort of continental film that found favour with a late-night audience on Channel 5. As the heavily mascara-ed young woman oozed onto the stage she had 'femme fatal' written all over her.

'Hello, uncle Eddy,' said Jemima with *come to bed* eyes, and a *let's stay there* smile. 'Remember me?'

Edward's brow furrowed. 'Uh, I don't see what relevance she has to this discussion.'

'Oh really,' sneered Jimmy. 'I think she might have every relevance. Ever accused any kettles of being overly on the dark side?'

'Edward! You never did?' sobbed Virginia, as she cowered under her daughter's continued stream of abuse.

'He most certainly did, Virginia,' said Jemima in the sort of husky baritone which could have melted pack-ice. 'And may I take this opportunity to compliment you on your choice of husband, or Rock Steady Eddy as I used to call him. No need for Viagra there.'

'Rock steady Eddy' sank to the floor with his head in his hands and began to tremble. An over-excited member of the audience let out a half-hearted 'whoop', then stopped when they realized no one else was joining in. It was strange how, even in these trans-Atlantic times, some traditional elements did not transfer well across the pond.

Jimmy took the time to seat himself next to Toby's chair. 'Well, young man, you and your sister seem to be the catalyst for all this mess. Do you have any sort of excuse to explain your appalling behaviour?'

Toby looked like he was about to burst into tears. 'I'd just like to say, Jimmy, that I'm the real victim here. If I hadn't have got involved with that cult none of this would have happened.'

'Victims, victims everywhere!' exclaimed Jimmy. 'Seems that if you're not a victim these days then there must be something wrong with you. Better make a note, gotta be a show in that. What cult are you talking about, son?'

Toby looked more than a trifle embarrassed. 'They latched onto me when I was at my lowest ebb. They're called the Temple of Planet Love. I didn't even become a full member, just attended one of their missionary sessions.

They treated me like I was special . . . but that was before they started doing things to my mind, giving me strange pills to take. Before they attached me to that living machine.' Toby rubbed his forehead and looked distraught. 'I don't remember much else, but when they turfed me out I was prepared to shag anything that moved, and quite a lot that didn't.'

'Thanks very much!' screamed Virginia, still busily lunging for her husband.

Toby continued. 'After a while the effects died off. That was when I came to my senses, but it was too late. Jemima wasn't so lucky, they got to her too. Seems they still have.'

Jimmy looked disgusted. 'So not only did you debase your own body, but you dragged your poor innocent sister down into the pit of moral despair with you – that's appalling. I hope you're ashamed of yourself.'

Over the cheering and applause, Jemima could just be heard to say, 'Less of the *innocent*, if you don't mind. What are you doing after the show, big boy?'

But Jimmy had more important things on his mind. He looked directly into a conveniently placed camera. 'Interestingly enough, folks, in just a few days time, in a special one-off show, we focus on these goofy oriental nut-cases themselves. If you didn't already know it, the Temple of Planet Love is the whacky UFO cult that's been hitting the headlines, as well as the nation's bed-sheets, of late. If it's not exactly "free love" they preach then at least they offer very competitive credit terms. Don't forget to make a date with us, and them, on our Alien Abduction Extravaganza!'

Off in one dark corner Kate looked on, her sense of shame at being involved in this horrific farce mounting by the minute. Whatever else today proved it at least laid to rest that favourite tabloid rumour, that Maxwell's guests were fakes. Real actors were not this good. This family's story was so outlandish that it could only be true. But the circus wasn't over yet. Much to her disgust Kate's intrepid team of researchers had unearthed one more precious nugget of information – and Jimmy was too much of a pro to let it slip. Jogging down the stage he returned to where Lucinda was pinned to the floor by two burly bouncers.

'How do you feel right now, Lucy?' He rammed his mike in her livid face.

'How do you think I feel, you fucking moron? I've just found out my boyfriend's been banging my mum, and my father's a pervert *doing it* to a whore half his age. I'm more than a little PISSED OFF!'

Jimmy was unfazed, he'd heard much worse in his time. 'Want to tell the world your own sordid secret?'

Lucinda's eyes held a reckless abandon. 'Why not. OK, Toby, I want you to know that it's not only Daddy who's been seeing your sister. She's more of a man between the sheets than you ever were, hypnotic mind control or not! If you took Viagra you'd just get taller.'

The audience exploded into a maelstrom of ecstatic delight. Jimmy sensed the time was right to wrap up proceedings.

'Toby, do you have anything else to say to Lucy and your sister at this stage?'

'Er, yes I do actually. I've always felt I was a lesbian trapped inside a man's body. Next time you get it together, can I watch?'

This didn't so much add fuel to the fire as napalm the entire lot. Lucy's lunge to separate Toby from his testicles was the cue for Virginia to take a swipe at her unforgiven husband, who meanwhile saw his chance to hurl a chair at the sultry Jemima, who had done more than her share to jack-knife the applecart of family peace. The overworked studio hands did their best 'United Nations Peace-Keepers' impersonations and, despite the absence of blue berets and kevlar armour, just like their impersonatees abjectly failed to maintain order.

Whatever had become of the famously English *stiff upper lip*, wondered Kate.

Doggedly the bouncers rushed to separate the warring factions, and the camera cut back to a radiant Jimmy Maxwell, well pleased another segment had concluded so successfully.

'That's all we have time for today, folks,' he beamed as the theme tune started up. 'But remember, it's a complex world we inhabit, and things are often not what they first seem. Society would be a better place if we all stopped being so judgmental and were less keen to poke our noses into our neighbour's affairs – even when they are as juicy as this one! With that thought in mind, I'll see you all next time for our Flying Saucer Special, where we'll be elaborating on some of the themes explored today. Don't miss it for this, or any other world! Take care of yourselves and our sponsors. Goodbye!'

As the titles rolled the camera pulled back to reveal a studio in turmoil. The audience were on their feet, cheering on their selected faction, as each group slugged it out with Security in their desperation to get to grips with each other.

Mercifully off stage, Kate put her head in her hands and, not for the first time, pondered the worth of this career. The conclusions she came to did not make for a happy frame of mind. Fortunately it wasn't the only option open to her. Steeling herself she reached for her note-pad and began to scribble rapidly – she had an important report to file, but it wasn't destined to be read by Maxwell.

13. Cabal

Like an arms-dealer's smile, the conference table was needlessly large and over-polished. To address a member sitting on the far side a delegate would have needed a loudhailer and considerable patience to overcome the pitifully slow speed of sound. So perhaps it was just as well that in front of each exceptionally plush leather bucket-seat, rising up through the reflective mahogany surface, was the sort of computer terminal not seen since the *Starship Enterprise* had boldly gone on and on.

Stalkish microphones were linked to each device, tand hrough them to a ring of loudspeakers carefully hidden in the darkness beyond the bowl of soft mellow light that spilled from the room's impressive centrepiece. Above the table hung an ancient sigil of perturbing design. It was a solid marble pyramid, each carved block picked out on its sloping sides. Two thirds of the way to its glistening summit an orb of dewy radiance cast its baleful light upon the room. Few who entered the chamber could look upon it without experiencing the first gropings of the clammy fingers of insanity. Few who got this far had all that far to go.

More conventional note-keeping equipment was readily to hand at each seat. Genetically-engineered notepads and nuclear-powered pens were laid out with pedantic neatness at each place setting. Next to each sat a clear glass of a fizzy black liquid.

There was surprisingly little communication between the participants as they took their places. These men were not the kind prone to idle banter. For some the journey here had been long and hard. For others the journey back would be harder still.

One by one the twelve members of the Inner Circle of the Committee made their reports. It had been a busy six months. One major civil war had been ended and another begun. In both cases their remorseless agenda had been advanced. On four continents six problematic politicians had been eliminated; three by the standard-issue sexual-pantomime media frenzy, two by assassin's bullet, and one by far more Semtex than was strictly necessary. In central Africa another Armageddon plague had been released, as much to foster a healthy paranoia amidst the Western public as to boost pharmaceutical share prices. The coup in Urgistan was a minor hiccup, but nothing that couldn't be quickly nullified.

The members of the Inner Circle of the Committee of 300 were a diverse group, a gang of boardroom thugs and back-stairs crypto-Nazis, linked only by their membership of this exclusive club. They were the owners of the dark satanic mills, the project managers of hate, guardians of the Status Quo.[1] This was the twitching nervous-system of the Military-Industrial-Entertainment Complex, and it was overdue a major fit. Its members were the powers behind the thrones, and in some cases on them.

National dress was much in evidence around the dim hall – at least the national dress of the capitalist World State. Seven attendees were smartly suited middle-aged men, the sort of captains of industry who commanded very big ships, and in one case several stealth bombers. Two were Japanese, but they represented the only splash of ethnic colour on an otherwise pallid, grey-white face. Amidst them the Vatican's top dog winced and fidgeted

---

[1] Responsible for the publication of all their albums.

– the shoes of the fisherman were tight these days, and didn't half pinch his toes.

Next, in more traditional garb, came three wise men from the East – the bubbling, mad, bad and dangerous-to-know Middle East in fact. But they hadn't brought gold, frankincense, or even a whiff of myrrh in their radar-absorbent executive stealth jets. What they did bring to the table was oil, oil and more oil. Between them they commanded four-fifths of the planet's petroleum production, and judging by the state of their skin in the humid, tense bunker most of it was seeping through their pores at that very moment. They had good reason to sweat. At MIT there was a cold-fusion lab they very badly wanted shutting down – with terminal force if necessary. Despite their common goals the three were seated equidistantly around the table. More than one world war had kicked off thanks to misunderstandings in gatherings such as this. Past Chairmen had discovered to their cost that it never did to be too careful.

The final member stood out from the rest in more ways than one. She'd held her post for fifteen years, ever since the previous incumbent had regrettably fallen off his yacht. Despite what the press had been told, this had not been down to a slippery deck and one-too-many G&Ts. He had rubbed the wrong people up the wrong way – always a fatal move when those people were sat in this room.

The figurative leader before the reluctant swimmer had doubled as America's Head of State – not a happy combination as it turned out. A carefully staged break-in and the threat of impeachment later, and he had gone as quietly as his insane tape-recorded ramblings would allow. The Committee had learned an important lesson with him: no more career politicians, their power was illusionary at best and too easily swayed by the pathetic whim of the great unwashed. The *real* power in the world was gathered here today, like pus in a festering wound. And at its centre sat a malevolent yet inconspicuous foreign body.

OPEC's leading light was just ending off a rambling rhetorical monologue, on the satanic evils encased in the atom, when the Chairman felt the need to interject. She wasn't the first of her line to hold this post, for her power was very much a family affair – as was her perfectly formed accent. She spoke the Queen's English, as well she might.

'Yes, thank you, Yashif. One takes your point.' Reaching for a glass of fizzy black liquid she paused to address the haughty corporate head seated next to her. 'This cola, Bertram, I trust it's not the mind-altering kind you feed to the masses?'

The Corporate Man looked shocked. 'Of course not, Ma'am. These days we've far more effective means of market penetration. Read the Abduction-Scenario Report and see for yourself. The stuff *we* drink is as pure as new snow.'

'Not as pure as the glowing snow lying outside these devil-built reactors, I hope,' muttered the Arab delegate, clearly heard over the elaborate sound system. The others chose to ignore this slight to Madame Chairman's power; not so the lady in question. She had an unnaturally long memory for insults and an infinite appetite for revenge. But that could wait. Revenge was a dish best served cold, and she was colder than most. The Chairman felt the need move the discussion along, before they were side-tracked any further.

'Now to more pressing business. I trust you are all aware that Operation Madcap is ready to begin? Potentially a most profitable endeavour for us all. The funds for the campaign are available and the production lines spool up as we speak. The merchandise will soon fill the warehouses. One simply requires the formality of an authorizing vote, then selected agents can be instructed to get the party going.'

She'd get no dissent on this one. Too many round the table had fingers rammed in this particular pie to take them out and lick just yet. The voting console before her lit up pure green, signifying unanimous assent.

'Good, we can proceed. But now to a less happy task. It has come to One's attention that our Executive Section has been conducting an operation to recover certain . . . items that have fallen into the wrong hands. I've taken the liberty of summoning the head of that section to account for his actions. I know that some of you have reservations regarding his motives in this matter. Shall we call him to state his case?'

A scattered affirmative rumble ran around the room. The Chairman thumbed a console switch. 'You may enter now, Mr Becker.'

The Dark Man looked defiant as he strode purposefully through a pair of vast sliding doors. The faces of his superiors were lost in shadow, but he knew each of them by voice, as well as reputation.

The CEO of the world's biggest aerospace corporation came straight to the point. 'There's been a serious leak from your department. We're going to hold you personally responsible, Becker. You're not going to weasel your way out of this one, like you did that Jamestown fiasco.'

The intelligence chief snorted. 'If it's blame you're looking to apportion may I remind you the Visitors escaped in one of the back-engineered craft *your* corporation were testing at the Nevada site. If your craft hadn't been so easy to shoot down we'd be in a lot more trouble than we're in right now.'

The aerospace CEO looked ready to explode. It was left to the Chairman to raise a restraining hand. 'Now, gentlemen, let's not descend into fruitless bickering. Why do you both assume this leak to be a bad thing?'

The newcomer shifted his weight, while marvelling at Old World aristocratic eccentricity. 'Ma'am, there has been a serious breach of security, that I admit. We are currently mounting operations to recover the remainder of the crashed material. They have not gone smoothly to date, but you have my assurance our resources will tighten to crush the saboteurs in due course.'

One of the sheiks chipped in from the shadows, his accent as thick as the tension-filled air. Few noticed the knowing glance he exchanged with Madame Chairman; Becker wasn't one of them. 'Why do we need to recover this material? Why not simply debunk it as we have done so successfully in the past? Remember the fake autopsy footage?'

For the briefest instant Becker showed the first signs of stress. 'In this case the evidence will be impossible to refute. If it gets into the public domain the truth of our Visitors' presence will be in the open once and for all. We all know what that could do to the public's fragile state of mind.'

The head of a major entertainment conglomerate had to disagree. 'You haven't been keeping up with our latest research. Hard physical evidence has leaked before; we've even released it ourselves to help further our aims. On each occasion the majority haven't given it a moment's credence, while those few paranoids who *do* believe our lies help bolster our hold on power.'

Madame Chairman nodded with an inscrutable smile that sent an icy shiver down Becker's spine. His face, however, showed no sign of such emotion. 'This time things are different. Events have quickly spiralled out of control, almost as if an exterior force were aiding the terrorists as they fled. I have proof that . . .'

The Chairman interrupted him impatiently. 'This is most worrying, Becker. There are rumours that your concern for the retrieval stretches to a personal matter. Can you assure us that nothing of the sort clouds your judgement?'

Becker fixed her with the sort of frosty stare which could have triggered an ice age.[1] 'It is my professional opinion, Ma'am, that the dangerous lunatics who have the creature must be stopped at any cost. And stop them I will. But this situation highlights an issue I feel duty bound to bring to your attention once again.

'I grow increasingly alarmed at the unintended results of Unified Conspiracy Theory. I fear our willingness to spread paranoia and irrationalism could turn out to be disastrously counterproductive. Already some unknown player seems to match us in an undesired duet. Whoever initiated the Glastonbury operation, it certainly wasn't me. I have some very unusual satellite photos of the South Pacific you all must see.'

Madame Chairman had heard enough. She held up a restraining hand and shut her eyes in disgust. Did Becker imagine it, or was she showing the first imperceptible signs of distress?

'Yes, yes,' hastened the aerospace CEO. 'We're all aware of your pet theories, Becker. But I find it hard to believe that we are playing into the hands of some unseen enemy. Our efforts to engender a widespread belief in conspiracies have been most effective. As long as the public think we know more than we do, they're more likely to let us get on with running the show. No one seriously expects their leaders to be honest and open anymore. As long as we make the airlines run on time, and TV drip feeds them a constant stream of mindless crap, the rank-and-file scum live happily in their cosseted world.'

Becker looked at him as if he were a small child who'd recently overpopulated his nappy. 'I'm not arguing with

---

[1] But not as effectively as the Committee's last-ditch 'Doomsday Weapon', housed in central Greenland – control of which was forever being sought (for 'testing' purposes only) by the power generation lobby. Not even they knew the device was currently working overtime in a hopeless struggle to counteract the effects of global warming.

the success of the policy, I myself have been instrumental in making it so. What concerns me is the mood of apathetic irrationalism that has spread like wildfire throughout the lower orders. We're not simply making them believe we are cleverer than we really are, we're making them believe *everything*. Hasn't it ever crossed your mind that we might have been set up for a very long fall? Our dim-witted charges are ripe for the plucking, but not for harvesting by us.'

Now it was the turn of the Chairman herself to fix him with a frigid stare. 'One summoned you here, Becker, to answer for your actions, not to bore us with your own ungrounded fears. You're blowing this incident up out of all proportion. After all, it's only one dead Grey. Learn to "let it go". One *orders* you not to try to retrieve this material, Becker – its exposure can't possibly do us harm.'

Becker's jaw twitched for a moment, then was still. 'Very well, Madame Chairman, as you wish. Are there any other duties you require me to perform, to help me fill my empty days?'

She gazed at him with open contempt. 'As a matter of fact, there are. You know what must be done in Urgistan, we're due another war. The case file is in your in-tray. See the plan is initiated by the end of the week.' The aerospace CEO nodded to their leader his heart-felt respects. Madame Chairman acknowledged him graciously with a smile.

'You may go, Becker. Let us draw a line under this matter, once and for all. Is One *understood*?'

Becker nodded and smiled his sweetest alligator smile, all the while promising himself this was not the end by a long way. He was well used to his theories being ridiculed, but this time the reaction of his superiors went further still. Some other force was at play. For the moment he'd bide his time, tamely following orders – well, some of them at least; meanwhile he'd remain vigilant, forever searching for the final confirmation he craved.

Much later, as he boarded his personal black-operations helicopter, Becker played back the meeting in his head. Perhaps it wasn't only him who was following a personal agenda all his own. But surely such tainted corruption couldn't reach to such lofty heights?

14. Mail

Dave sat in the shabby motel room, staring at his laptop computer screen, sipping warm flat beer, seriously considering suicide.

In truth he didn't 'seriously consider suicide'. He didn't have the bottle to do anything that would have annoyed his mum that much. Flirting with suicide was just the sort of thing he liked to think he did from time to time, a bit like cleaning the fridge or having sex with another person present. It fitted his perception of himself as a tragic hero. But it was getting harder to dodge the inescapable conclusion that he had the first part of that ambition down pat, while the second eluded him like the smallest piece of soap in a very big and cloudy bath.

His and Kate's love was not doomed to failure because of some unbridgeable class divide, nor an incurable fatal illness; it was doomed because one half of it wasn't really interested in shagging the other. But that didn't stop Dave's gothic daydreams continuing to roll on and on in a grainy black and white film noir.

When he had been a teenager Dave had been heavily influenced by a certain type of eighties band; the sort that wore baggy black jumpers, stuck daffodils down their pants and wrote morose songs about their girlfriends getting flattened by JCBs. Listening to this kind of music hadn't made Dave feel any better about himself, it had just convinced him that somewhere, someone with a silly haircut was more depressed than he was. This would help for a while, until he began thinking that – at that very moment – the apparently dour mop-haired waif was no doubt hammering his sports car around LA as he siphoned champagne from a groupie's navel and snorted cocaine through a rolled-up royalty cheque which could have kept Hendrix in purple haze long enough for him to be reclassified as a new type of meteorological phenomenon. This sure knowledge tended to throw the pop star's professional depression into stark contrast with Dave's purely amateur, yet far more profound, melancholy state.

So Dave had come to the painful conclusion that there was only one thing more depressing that being young, sensitive and celibate; that was to be young, sensitive, celibate and listening to a mopey record. This horrendous state of affairs was in no way mitigated by his perception that everyone else on the surface of the planet was humping away like it was going out of fashion, including the dewy-eyed singer – who was currently droning on about how tough life was, coming from his home town and being unemployed – unless of course you happened to be in a chart-topping band, in which case it was much, much worse.

Back then Dave had only one refuge from this heady mix of sixth-form poetry and synth-based pop. Taking a copy of *Busting Out All Over – Underwear for the Larger Lady*, he'd retire to his room, if not exactly to spank the monkey then at least to give it a jolly stern talking to. Thankfully these days he had more meaning to his life, or at least that's what he tried to tell himself. The pages of *ScUFODIN Magazine* would wait for no man, not even if he was the victim of unrequited love and what Dave was fast coming to believe was a vast and awesomely subtle hoax that made a mockery of his entire working life. In the absence of a suitably morbid record, or any mail-order catalogues for that matter, Dave got back down to work.

Currently he was attempting to type up an account of the previous night's UFO event, if you could go so far as to call it that. It was a tried and trusted routine he always performed after one of his 'encounters', as he liked to call them. Best get it down while it was still fresh in his mind.

But it wasn't just the infuriating vagueness of last night's incident which had him depressed. Dave was no stranger to the intense feeling of anticlimax which often followed a sighting – this went deeper than that. He had often reflected how UFO watching was much like being in the infantry in time of war; ninety-nine per cent stupefying boredom, one per cent shirt-drenching panic. After any fleeting high came an equally dramatic and far less fleeting low. The growing suspicion that someone, somewhere, in a darkened room, wanted it that way didn't help in the slightest.

With a heavy sigh Dave concluded that this depression, like most of his others, could be traced back to a far less mysterious source. For the ninth time that day he checked his email to see if Kate still cared whether he lived or died. The answer on this occasion was no different from his previous eight attempts to will his incoming mail prompter to go 'ping'. Not for the first time that day he re-read her last message.

Dear Dave,

Hope you're enjoying yourself as much as I know you are able. Have you met any other Californian beach babes yet? I do like a spring wedding.

All hell's broken loose back home. Have you heard the news of what went on at Glastonbury? It's all people are talking about over here.

All hell's broken loose at work too. After one of the most nauseating shows I can remember we've started researching a special one-off to go out in just a few days time. Word's come down from the very top that we have to be on-air ASAP. It's to be the usual format, Mr Sunbed-Tan and a studio full of 'real people' queuing up to have their insanity beamed out for all the world to see. But this time, the subject matter will interest you. We're getting an audience together of folks who claim they've seen flying saucers. You know, 'I'm having an alien's love-child,' that sort of thing, all the stuff you're into.

Went over to the west country the other day to interview a farmer with a funny tale. I'll pass on the details when you get back. Perhaps you can line me up some other cranks to swell the ranks. You must know a few? It's appalling that my 'career' has come to this. Thinking of you as I scan the appointments pages.

Love K

x

P.S. Give me a chance to reply, why don't you. Some of us do have better things to do than sit in front of a computer all day typing emails – even if we aren't on holiday.

When he finished it Dave re-read it a second time. It was hard to focus on her sudden interest in Ufology, or the latest rock-and-roll PR stunts, with such a clear subtext underpinning her every word. Was it his imagination or were there signs of a subtly increased level of affection tucked in there? Of course she always ended with 'Love K', though this time he got the sense she'd wanted to say much, much more.

But wait a minute, she had only signed off with a single lower-case 'x'. All last week she'd used capitals, and on Wednesday she'd used three. Dutifully Dave got out the small notebook he carried with him everywhere and entered this month's total email kisses. At home he had a wall-planner solely devoted to graphically charting the perceived fluctuations in her affection; it would be filled in on his return.

It was at this moment that Dave concluded, not for the first time, that he was a very sad individual indeed. Yet if he could recognize that fact, didn't that mean he wasn't so sad after all? Or, alternately, all the sadder for being unable to do anything about it? Catching himself before he could slip into one of his all too unproductive bouts of doubt and self-loathing, of which this was just the relatively mild first stage, he composed another reply to the woman of his dreams. The fact that he'd sent three now without response didn't deter him for an instant.

Dear Kate,

As you know, the trip so far has been a resounding success. Obviously I can't go into details over an open channel, but I know you'll be enthralled when I show you my snaps of Area 51. The up-coming show on 'The Phenomena' sounds good – glad to see you've finally taken an interest. Perhaps you can get me tickets.

The people over here are so friendly I've hardly had a moment to myself. Despite the impression I might have given in my last note, I'm just friends with April and Nadine. I'm meeting them both for drinks later. Who knows where we'll end up – probably back in their jacuzzi again. Gosh, they wear me out.

Gotta run, I'm giving a speech to the Nevada State Saucer Convention. I'll have to write it in the limo they'll send to pick me up.

Love as always, see you soon,

Dave

He didn't put any 'x's' on the end of his mail. Despite the overwhelming emotions he felt for Kate, Dave couldn't bring himself to remind them both of it at every opportunity – there was only so much his fragile ego could take. She knew how he felt about her, and he had no desire to appear as desperate as he actually was.

Dave felt no guilt over the little white lies he told to spice up the trip, Kate would see through them immediately. What was important was that Kate knew she hadn't entirely crushed his heroically indomitable spirit.

Dave was startled by the melodic chimes which signified incoming mail. For one second he thought it might be from her – wasn't she getting eager? But when he saw the address his heart sank. It was undoubtedly junk-mail advertising some sordid anatomically-minded site. Who had ever heard of Alien@Outerspace.org anyway? Already filling with righteous indignation, he clicked open the message and read it, waiting to be incensed. He wasn't to be disappointed.

Greetings Earthling,

I am an Alien. Hard to believe I know, but in this case completely true.

If you want to meet up, I shall be at the Hungry Dog Diner, at the junction of Lincoln and Twelfth Street, for the next two hours. It's not far from your motel – get back to the main street and walk three blocks west. When you arrive my companion will make himself known to you.

I need your help. Please come quickly, and be sure to come alone.

Yours,

An exotic Friend.

Dave snorted in disgust. Another feeble practical joke. He was reminded of the wave of obviously faked photographs his magazine had been sent over the previous month, and of that ridiculous Glastonbury stunt – the lengths some hoaxers were prepared to go to made him shudder. Advanced alien civilizations no more used email to communicate with mankind than they used crop circles or thirteenth-century Mayan tomb carvings, despite what some of Dave's esteemed colleagues might think. That some spotty thirteen-year-old hacker had obtained details of his personal account was only slightly less preposterous than the notion that aliens resort to 3D Martian landscape graffiti to get their message across.

When it came to his life's work Dave had a very poor sense of humour. He'd met enough cranks in his time to take his privacy just as seriously as he took his UFOs. They'd be at the diner all right – hunched in some dingy corner, sniggering into their crusty keyboard laptop. He meant to find the individual responsible and give them a very stiff lecture on responsibility in this wired world. After all, he was a busy man. Or at least he would be if the Nevada State Saucer Convention ever actually phoned.

Even so, despite his best efforts Dave couldn't help a tiny buzz of intense hope charging through his veins. There was always the million-to-one chance that this tip-off was genuine. If he didn't check it out he'd never know for sure. After all, it wasn't as if he had anything better to do. Grabbing his shades and wallet, Dave hurried to the door.

15. Rendezvous

Frank looked up from his cheeseburger and checked the highway one more time. Good – no ice-cream vans, and none of the equally ubiquitous black stretch-limousines with the tinted windows, which the clandestine forces of government used when they were undercover and attempting to be discreet.

He'd cruised down Sunset Strip earlier that day in his stolen vehicle, experiencing a perplexing mixture of numb amazement and dim recognition. He *knew* this town, but he didn't think he'd ever lived here, or even come to visit before. Driving past the casinos and the theme-park-sized hotels he'd been struck by their splendour, but also by their monotonous familiarity.

Frank was reminded yet again of the one central fact of his existence – there were huge chunks of his life which remained forever off limits to his straining memory. Over and above the fact that he'd once served in a very special military unit, the rest was just a blur. These days he accepted his black patches the same way he accepted the ever-present mutterings in his head. It was that just at moments like this, when some small detail sparked a flash of recollection – like the shape of a building, or the smell of gasoline from across the street – it became hardest to bear. The voices didn't help. Though the upside of being a paranoid schizophrenic was at least you always had some-one to talk to, even if the conversations weren't up to much. The one claiming to be God which told him to go out and kill prostitutes was rather worrying, but he kept it well under control. He'd got the better of them and knew he'd beat these memory lapses too. He swore he'd beat them; he would do if it killed him.

At long last his aimless journey had taken him to the less opulent side of town. He didn't know where he was going, just that he was fleeing his former flat and the uninvited guests he'd left many tired miles behind. The dull rumble from the trunk reminded him why they'd come a-calling.

When he spotted the run-down diner he experienced a maddening sense of déjà vu, all over again. He was sure he'd been here before, just as he was sure the short-order chef was a huge shovel-handed New Yorker with Marine Corps tattoos plastered up each arm. It wasn't until he'd almost drawn level with the establishment that he realized he hadn't eaten since his cereal that morning had been so rudely interrupted. His rumbling stomach had the final say in the matter. Swerving across two lanes of late-afternoon traffic he hung a left into the half-empty car park.

That had been more than two hours ago. In that time Frank had consumed four cheeseburgers, exchanging several wary nods of recognition with the sweat-laced kitchen-hand through the cluttered serving hatch.

For Frank this was a familiarly maddening experience. But you couldn't just go up to folks who seemed to recognize you to ask 'Where do you know me from?' – it got you funny looks at the very least. For the time being Frank contented himself with the thought that their acquaintance must date back to some chance encounter before his army service came to an abrupt and painful end. He didn't know for sure, but he felt certain he'd been happier then, with the warm companionship of comrades-in-arms to pull him through. He'd been alone so long now he'd almost forgotten what friendship meant.

Maybe he *was* going crazy. Carefully, he checked his hands for the first signs of palm-hair, just like the old wives' tales advised. Outside in the trunk of his battered vehicle what was undoubtedly the find of the century was slowly rotting – so why was he suddenly so assailed by doubt? Maybe he should hire a room and buy some whisky and pills to end it all. Was this war really worth the fight?

Slowly Frank rubbed his throbbing temples. What he needed most of all was a confidant; someone to remind him, after he'd gazed upon his insane find, or read that terrible book, that this *was* real after all and his mind hadn't entirely slipped its gears. He also had problems of a more practical nature – like what to do next. Grand strategy had never been his area of expertise, the nitty-gritty of combat was his speciality. Frank needed an accomplice he could trust. He rocked slowly back and forth in his seat until his head sank so low it was scant inches above his plate. Closing his eyes he did something he hadn't done for years: Frank prayed for guidance, for some sign that his struggle wouldn't be in vain.

The sound of the bell above the doorway brought him sharply back to his senses – Frank couldn't allow his survival instincts to let up for an instant. That was when he got his first clear look at the clean-cut young man who strode in like someone with a very definite mission in mind. But to be more precise it *wasn't* the first time Frank had spotted him; he'd seen that face many times before, and that was why he now sat bolt upright in his chair. The newcomer had the sunburnt, gormless look of a tourist about him, but also the determined body language of a man searching for something he very badly needed to find.

There was no question how Frank recognized him. Not three days ago he'd read his carefully chosen words, and studied the small grainy picture above his magazine's editorial – that was how he knew those serious, bookish features. Frank might have considered Dave to be hopelessly naïve in his conclusions, but there was no denying the young man produced a thorough and well-researched magazine, most of the time devoid of the usual mystic crap. For the moment, Frank was too shocked to appreciate his good fortune.

Pieces of half-chewed cheeseburger cascading down his tie-dyed T-shirt, he lurched to his feet and staggered towards the man he already felt he knew. Frank regretted not having tried religion sooner – he could appreciate what folks saw in it now. It seemed his fervent prayers had been answered.

*   *   *

For his part Dave saw the sad perversion of a human being stumble towards him far too late to do anything about it. For one horrible moment he thought the wild-eyed freak was going to pull a gun and demand money. Either that or beg the price of a cup of coffee.

'You . . . you came so quickly.' The vagrant croaked.

Dave spoke with some venom.

'Of course I came quickly. When someone reaches me that way I always want to hear how they did it. You're party to information not available to the general public and I'd like to keep it that way. I hope you know how sensitive we are to such things.'

Frank stared back at him with mounting admiration, and not a little awe. How could this man be so blasé about his breathtaking telepathic powers? He must take them for granted, just like any other individual's ability to read or write. And here he was asking Frank how he'd done it – the clairvoyant elite had obviously guarded its secrets jealously.

Frank lightly tapped the grubby side of his head, just below his tattered bandanna. 'Don't worry, chum, your secret's safe with me. We'll say no more about it. What's important is that you came.'

'Just make sure it doesn't happen again,' Dave muttered. He looked the unkempt interloper up and down and came to a rapid but eerily perceptive conclusion. Just like Upton Park, this bloke was only two stops short of Barking. He was perhaps the most wizened man Dave had ever seen. His face had that 'lived in' look. Dave got the distinct impression he'd been round the block so many times he'd lapped people twice his age. Old before his time, perhaps, but he was hale and hearty like a seasoned tiger. His taut skin was like tea-stained leather, his wiry beard could have comfortably housed a family of voles. He was as thin as a rake, but well corded with sinuous muscle from head to toe. Very slowly, as if speaking to the inmate of an asylum for the terminally inane, Dave spelled out every word for the crazed stranger. 'How – did – you – recognize – my – face?'

For a moment Frank thought he was missing some subtle code hidden in his new friend's speech, before realizing the question was meant literally. The wide sweeping motion the young man made before his features helped get his point across. Bemused but respectful, Frank answered him in kind.

'From – your – magazine. *ScUFODIN – Monthly*.'

As Dave nodded with dubious appreciation, Frank realized he'd have to break this strange cycle of communication, otherwise they'd be here all day. As subtly as he was able he led Dave by the elbow to a secluded corner booth.

'Look, Dave . . .'

'Oh, it's "Dave" now, is it? Just because you know everything about me doesn't give you the right to become so familiar.'

Frank peered at him oddly for a moment. 'Look, dude, we don't have time to jerk about. I've obtained certain items that you *will* want to see. I think it's what we've been waiting for all this time.'

For a moment Dave thought he was trying to sell him drugs, then he remembered this crank's interest in the magazine and for the briefest of instants his eyes were ignited by a fleeting spark.

'Might these *items* be linked to my particular field of expertise? Something *ScUFODIN* could use?' He could see from the way the stranger's face lit up that he did indeed have something he might use. The young man reserved judgement on its value until he saw the evidence for himself.

The collection of yellow teeth on display hinted at the older man's frame of mind. 'Oh – I think we can safely say it will interest you, Dave. I'd stake my entire Uzi collection on it. Name's Frank by the way.'

He offered his hand, which Dave took rather tentatively. The bewilderingly complex handshake almost powdered his bone. Dave's wince of pain was replaced by a weary, sceptical look.

'You'll forgive me if I'm suspicious. The magazine gets calls from cranks all the time.'

Frank let that one pass. He was well used to the scorn of his peers. For a second he faced up to his perennial dilemma, was Dave an ally or a carefully delivered plant? Frank's paranoia engaged in a brief skirmish with his rational judgement, which for once landed a knock-out blow.

Cautiously, the grizzled man got to his feet. 'Come with me, Dave. I'll show you what I've found.'

*   *   *

With a growing sense of unease Dave followed Frank out of the diner and down the sun-baked steps. The day was a real scorcher, the sort of monotonously oppressive afternoon that served to remind the residents of Las Vegas they inhabited one of the world's hottest deserts, and not just the hedonistic oasis of roulette tables and scantily clad dancing girls it sometimes appeared to be.

Self-consciously Dave put on his replica designer sunglasses, to shield the worst of the glare. Frank put on aviator shades, but for a subtly different reason: he now suspected he'd once been based close to this town, no doubt a favourite R&R destination for battle-fatigued men of his former unit. You never knew when a chance encounter could spell disaster.

Frank turned sharply to face his nervous companion.

'You say you're up for adventure; well, kiddo, this is the point of no return. When you cross the go line you're part of the team – no backing down, no begging off. We see this thing through to the end. Probably both our ends if you want the truth – comprendee voos?'

Dave stared back at him for a long while. He couldn't see Frank's eyes through his mirrored shades but he didn't need to; he could sense the manic zeal which burned behind them, hotter than the blistering asphalt beneath their feet. Dave was no stranger to strongly held beliefs, his magazine had plenty of readers whose passions ran just as high – but precious few could match this crank's blazing intensity. Whether it was the effects of the sun, or the slightly dodgy burger he'd eaten the night before, Dave came to an unaccustomedly swift decision.

He saw himself at a crossroads. The rational part of his brain was telling him to run screaming in the opposite direction, to rush home to his safe existence with his magazine and his familiar friends. The loony before him was way too committed to be anything other than a dangerous psychotic. But then Dave thought again about Kate, and the gentle, friendly scorn she always showed for his beliefs. If there was a one-in-a-million chance of proving her wrong Dave was willing to take it. Besides, he was sick of safe. Safe was his problem.

'Count me in,' he said, with rare edge to his voice. He might have had private doubts but there was something about Frank which sucked you along in his wake, like the whirlpool of a slowly sinking ship, maybe, but irresistible nonetheless.

The older man nodded curtly, then led Dave to the battered orange VW camper-van which served as the nerve centre of his campaign to topple the all-pervasive New World Order. The sunlight blazed through the multi-coloured *Surfing Is Living* sticker on the back window, creating rainbows of verdant light on the hideous psyche-delic interior.

'Nice and inconspicuous,' muttered Dave, all but grow-ing dizzy with the accelerating sense of unreality.

'I didn't have time to be choosy,' said Frank with an ominous lack of sarcasm.

Dave got the distinct impression his new friend hadn't selected the vehicle from a used car lot, obtaining a gener-ous trade-in on his old model as he did so. The scratched paintwork around the door lock and double surf boards still on the roofrack only added to his suspicions. Frank didn't give him long to ponder the local penalties for being an accessory to grand-theft-auto.

'OK Lash Larou, looks like you're onside. Suppose I'd better show you what we've got. Jump in and saddle up.'

They drove in silence for the best part of an hour, the suburban sprawl on the edge of town giving way to open desert with remarkable speed. When they were well clear of any signs of civilization Frank pulled onto a dusty track that Dave could barely see, and led them off along a bumpy rutted road. Five bone-jarring minutes later they crested a low ridge and free-wheeled down into an isolated gully. Frank brought then to rest in a desolate natural amphi-theatre devoid even of cacti or tumbleweed. Dave was hot, frustrated and more than a little scared. He lost no time in getting straight down to the point.

'So where is this earth-shattering proof you spoke of? The only evidence you've shown me so far is that you're a fan of my magazine. Rare though that may be, it's hardly a cause for these cloak and dagger antics. I'm a busy man, Mr MacIntyre. I hope you're not wasting my time.'

Dave was regretting it before the words were out of his mouth. Apart from being patently untrue, what was he going to do to this madman even if he was wasting his time? He got the nasty feeling he was more likely to have things done to *him*. Nervously, Dave shifted on his day-glo plastic chair, vainly trying not to make it sound like he was breaking wind.

Frank gave him a strange look, a heady cocktail of hilarious bemusement mixed with simmering pent-up rage. Where he was about to shove the stuffed olive, Dave didn't want to speculate, but he felt certain it would leave him shaken, not stirred. When Frank spoke his voice seemed on the verge of breaking up. 'This is far enough. The merchandise is in the trunk.'

Smoothly the sun-bleached veteran slipped down from the driver's seat and made his way to the rear of the van. Without much hope, but with an evil crick in his neck and a spinal column which knew how a xylophone must feel, Dave got down and followed him.

Frank carefully scanned the low hills all around them. Once he was sure they weren't being watched he put his hand to his brow and scanned the skies above – he seemed to spend an inordinate amount of time doing so. Slowly he checked the big diving-watch he wore on his corded bony wrist. 'Good,' he muttered under his breath. 'Big Bird 4 should be below the horizon for another sixteen minutes.'

Dave watched him with mounting disbelief, not really sure whether to laugh or cry, or check himself for bugs. It seemed Frank's paranoia didn't so much chart new territories as discover whole new continents.

Then, perhaps most disturbingly of all, the ex-commando got down on all fours and put his ear to the ground for the best part of a minute. He peered up at Dave with one bulging red-rimmed eye.

'CIA spy tunnels everywhere, can't be too careful,' he

said by way of explanation, lurching to his feet and dusting off his hands as if it tainted his leathery skin. 'They riddle all of North America. Don't believe any of the crap they peddle about the San Andreas Fault – it's all down to tunnelling which got out of hand.'

Dave reflected that while it might be impossible to be *too careful*, it was frighteningly easy to lapse into an insanity which would have made a shithouse rat gag with disbelief. But there was no time to call for the men in white coats. Without further ceremony Frank opened the vehicle's boot.

The first thing that hit Dave was the smell. It was not of this world, or any other he wanted to visit. When he'd fought back the nausea, and mopped away the tears of pain from beneath his shades, Dave peered into the compartment's darkest recess. It took an age for eyes to adjust to gloom, but when they did he got the shock of his life. Staring back at him from the blackness, with huge dead eyes, was the epitome of the stereotypical Grey alien.

'Is it real?' He just about managed to stammer, whilst trying hard not to breath through his nose.

'Of course it's real!' Frank sounded quite hurt. 'Pulled it from the burning wreckage myself less than a week ago. Not to mention from under the noses of a Black Government retrieval team.' Frank did a poor impression of Dave's Home Counties accent. ''*Is it real*, he asks! When it walks like a duck, quacks like a duck, and leaves a trail of duck-crap half a mile long, it's a fucking duck, all right? Either that or a pigeon with one hell of an identity crisis.'

Dave found it hard to disagree. And this conclusion wasn't entirely down to his suspicion that contradicting Frank could be dangerous to his health. The carcass certainly looked the part, and smelt it too. Tentatively he reached out a finger and poked the foul-smelling thing. The grey flesh gave way sickeningly beneath his touch, like decomposing meat left to rot in an unventilated out-house.

Whatever it was, it was all too biological in nature.

'But how do you know you haven't been set up – that this isn't some shabby hoax to bring you into the open?'

Frank reached through the van's open side window and pulled out a large battered folder. Food stains and coffee rings smeared its pale blue cover. The document's well-thumbed pages hinted at careful and prolonged study. What looked suspiciously like a bullet hole punctuated the stencilled lettering spelling out its high, narrow title; *MJ13 – Property of the Committee*.

'Because of this.' Frank cradled the folder lovingly against his chest, tapping its cover with one tobacco-stained finger.

'It could turn out to be more important than our grey friend in there. Here's your conspiracy theory, Mr Sceptic – perhaps the only one you'll ever need. If we blow the lid on this baby we've got it made. It's the next best thing to our grey chums landing on the White House lawn and taking a crap.'

In retrospect what Dave said next didn't seem like such a good idea, but he was having an uncharacteristically reckless day, so why stop now? 'As luck would have it I've got a friend who works in TV. She's a top investigative journalist. I was in school with her, and I trust her totally.'

Frank eyed Dave warily as he handed over the blue file. 'Then you'll need to study this. Read it, wiener-boy.'

*   *   *

As the battered camper van rolled along, Dave turned to the opening page, to the section optimistically marked 'Summary'. Sheepishly he began to read.

Once you've accepted that JFK was a 42nd Level Genetically Engineered Freemason Hybrid, unleashed upon an unsuspecting Earth by the Watchers to start World War III and propagate his tainted seed, much of the later half of the twentieth century begins to make sense. Any other attempt to explain events, without recourse to Unified Conspiracy Theory(R) is doomed to failure. It is my humble duty to record the truth here and now, for the first and only time.

Dave snapped the big file shut. He knew just where this document was heading and he didn't like it one little bit. He had read this sort of thing countless times before – in just about every UFO magazine competing with his own beloved, sane and rational *ScUFODIN*. He knew from bitter experience that this way lay madness – but also increased sales figures and appearances on TV. It was a tribute to his integrity that he'd never ambled down this way himself. It would be a bitter pill indeed if it turned out to be true.

Frank sensed his partner's agitation. 'Don't give up on it yet, Davey boy. I bet you ain't even got to the bit about your Royal Family yet? It'll make you wish they *were* just a bunch of emotionally repressed Krauts.'

It took a moment for Dave to get his voice back under control. 'No, I haven't. And I don't intend to either. The bloke who wrote it certainly seems to think a lot of himself – writes like he's got his head stuck up his arse.'

Frank's face became a battleground of conflicting emotion, as if he struggled to remember some long-forgotten fact. 'Yeah, he did always talk like he'd swallowed a dictionary – or at least he did until that last mission . . .'

Frank's features twisted in a violent spasm, his loss of composure almost taking them off the road. When his screams had subsided, and Dave had prised his own fingernails from the dashboard, the younger man stared at the human wreck who was his newest friend for quite a while.

'Er – do you mind telling me exactly where we're going? That's if we make it that far.'

As Dave had read, Frank had driven them back to the freeway. Currently they were heading out further into the desert, as if with an urgent plane to catch.

The jaded vet didn't take his eyes off the road. 'Your return ticket to the UK – you won't be needing that. I figure we *should* take a trip to your homeland, but I'll be making the flight arrangements myself. Know a man in LA who owes me more favours than I can remember.'

Dave's doubts returned in a flash. 'Is that going to be as easy as you think? I don't get the impression it will be straightforward getting our decomposing companion through Health and Immigration. Last time I looked there was no channel for Rotting Aliens. I think it might cause a scene.'

Frank shrugged his bony shoulders. 'Not easy, but a darn sight easier than getting him on TV over here. The Black Government's got Hollywood and the networks sewn up tighter than a shark's butt at forty fathoms. I figure England and this Kate should offer a smoother ride.'

Dave tried not to think about Kate offering any sort of ride; he could do without such distractions now. 'I thought this conspiracy was an international affair. Isn't the British government just as corrupt as yours?'

Frank let out a mirthless laugh. 'Oh, they're as corrupt all right. In fact in their own way your ruling classes have been at it longer than anyone realizes. It's just that . . . your guys aren't as *good* at it as Uncle Sam. No offence, pal, but your MI6 makes even the French look professional.'

Dave's eyes narrowed with confusion. 'And that's a *bad thing*, is it?'

Frank shook his ragged grey head. 'Bad for them, good for us. Mitterrand's guys were only trying to bug the *Rainbow Warrior* back in '85. They couldn't have been less subtle if they'd worn stripy shirts and berets, and made their get-away on onion-draped cycles. A faint whiff of garlic would have gone down well too. Idiots perhaps, but they could still teach MI6 a thing or two.'

Dave didn't know whether to feel proud or offended at his countrymen's lack of sinister competence. 'What about James Bond?'

Frank's giggle was on the point of getting manic. 'Think about it, will you. If you need to resort to that, you're already sunk without a trace.'

Dave concluded that he still had much to learn about the murky world Frank seemed to inhabit. If he was to become a committed student he cradled perhaps the greatest reference work in his white-knuckled hands. *MJ13* drew him back to its dim pages like a helpless iron filing to a powerful magnet. As Dave turned to the next section a small piece of deformed metal slid down the binding and fell to the dusty floor.

'Caseless 9mm dum-dums,' said Frank by way of explanation. Dave didn't get the impression he was joking. 'Standard issue black-ops ammo. About as ethical as screwing your granny and selling the offspring for medical experiments. Not that the cowboys who fired it are likely to give a damn. They used to keep us more pumped full of drugs than any East German volleyball team I ever heard of.'

'You telling me you were in some sort of covert version of the SAS?'

Frank scoffed. 'A bit like them, yeah. But those guys spend more time writing books than they do kicking butt these days. When we hit Tehran in 1980 to get the hostages out the one thing we did *not* have was a platoon of literary agents along for the ride.'

Dave snorted. He'd avidly read more than one 'Kill and Tell' epic in his time. 'Perhaps that's just as well. Didn't you get toasted on that mission?'

Slowly Frank shook his head. 'The entire gig was black-ops from start to finish. The real objective was to get

Reagan in the White House, an objective in which we were completely successful. Got a pretty medal pinned on me for that gig.'

Dave's brow furrowed in concentration. 'I think I see. The shady elite clique you worked for wanted a reliable Commie-hater running the show and signing the arms contracts. I bet good ole "Bomb-First-Ask-Permission-Later" Ronnie was high up in the club himself.'

Frank gave a hollow chuckle. 'Look, I was just a grunt. I wasn't party to the strategy, tactics was my bag. But from what I've read,' he gestured to the big blue file, 'nothing could be further from the truth. Seems the tortured gyrations of our "elected representatives" are nothing but some freakish vaudeville show, stage managed at every beat. Check out the next chapter.'

With a growing desperation, Dave read on.

You probably think of them as the people who make the decisions, the reassuringly familiar faces on the Six O'Clock News; the democratically elected leaders that you chose to shoulder the onerous burden of running our sane and rational world. I'm afraid I have some bad news for you.

The real power resides in a deeper, darker place, a place far older than the Senates, Parliaments or Chambers of Deputies that are in reality nothing more than a hollow and ephemeral façade. The real power slumbers in the same location it always has; in the bank-vaults and the boardrooms of the richest corporations, and in the intertwined genes of a handful of 'families' who run these giant institutions. The real wielders of power are far more retiring and publicity-shy, as they slowly but remorselessly whittle away to carve the very pillars of the establishment behind which they cower.

If voting changed anything, they'd abolish it. But totalitarian oppression has been tried, in some places more recently than others. If it didn't work for controlling uneducated Russian peasants, it's unlikely to work on the perfumed, pampered, overeducated urban masses who chatter away in blissful ignorance, as an illusionary fantasy of fairness and honesty is spun around them. Something more sophisticated is needed to keep you in your place.

The most efficient way to subdue a population is to make them *believe* that they're free as they construct the chains that bind them. Throw them the rag-doll of political debate and allow them to waste their energies tearing their apparent leaders to pieces. Free speech counts for little when those with the true final say don't give a damn what they hear from below, and didn't need your vote to get there in the first place. If the democratic illusion hadn't been born kicking and screaming, my masters would have had to invent it.

The one good thing you can say about 'Democracy' is that you get the politicians you deserve, ineffectual and irrelevant though they are. This state of affairs gives the Committee of 300 the perfect cover to maintain the greatest political confidence trick in the history of mankind. They're not interested in freedom, least of all equality; they simply want a society that produces hordes of servile worker-drones, and more importantly still, herds of compliantly eager consumers.

But if only it was simply money which drove them on.

My wide-ranging investigations have revealed a darker motive driving the Committee's highest echelons. Its rank and file are as deceived and manipulated as the downtrodden masses to whom I now speak. Feckless and servile though you may be, you, gentle reader, offer mankind's last, worst hope for a final desperate salvation. You will forgive me if I don't hold my breath in anticipation of your success.

I am sorry to say that my entire professional life has been dedicated to unwittingly furthering the dark conspiracy against which you now must struggle. In the pages of this manuscript I intend to lay it bare. Study it well, you will surely need all the help you can get if we are not to be enslaved by an even darker master.

Wearily Dave clamped the document shut. Whoever this guy was, he certainly had a rare knack for inspiring perverse motivation. The whole thing read like some sort of black propaganda. Many of Dave's more paranoid colleagues were forever mindful of plants and hoaxes – was that what this file was? Frank seemed too unpredictable a tool to be part of any planned deception.

There was a long and bumpy road ahead until they reached Kate's studio door – if they ever did. Dave concluded he was going to have to ration his intake of MJ13 if he was going to keep his sanity intact until the journey's end. As the first bleak uncaring stars began to twinkle above the empty desert, the spluttering orange camper van sped on into the night.

16. Hypemeister Extraordinaire

London, UK

Marshall Swift was a man of his word. His particular word was 'bullshit'.

To any other individual this would have been an insult of the highest order, but to Marshall it was the greatest compliment he could be paid – and over the years he had been paid quite a few, some by people who actually meant them. 'Saccharin Swift', as he was famed within the industry, was in the advertising business.

But this simple statement didn't tell the whole story, didn't even get past *'Once upon a ti . . .'* in fact. To say Marshall Swift was 'in' the advertising industry was akin to claiming Henry Ford had been a car mechanic. Swift was a superstar of PR, a marketing mogul of mammoth proportions, a god-like individual who strode across the bumpy playing fields of commerce like a blue-balled copy-writing colossus.

As far as the UK was concerned Marshall *was* the ad industry, at least since a series of ruthless takeovers and savage mergers had swallowed up the competition whole, or swept it screaming from the blood-drenched floor. All this while he was still young enough to enjoy sticking his exquisitely hand-made boot in. But his growing empire covered more than just the frivolous never-never-land of broadcast commercials. He had started in the no less hollow world of public relations – nursing the fragile egos of petulant pop stars and wily celebrities alike. He was marketing consultant to the Vatican, lavishly paid from its bulging vaults with funds the source of which he helped obscure. Media manipulation was his game, and he played it with skill, cunning and a disregard for the rules of fair play which would have made an American golf team blush.

Marshall's parent company, Swiftsure PR, ran the most prestigious accounts itself, farming out minor contracts to a gaggle of baying subsidiaries. International clients as big as Yoke-Cola and Nanosoft Computers retained Swiftsure itself to handle all their European publicity needs, and their needs were more than a match for most.

The man himself liked to maintain a hands-on approach. Marshall had been personally responsible for the launch of 'The Big N's' flagship software product, MovieOS™ – an operating system years in development, long hyped as the answer to every computer user's needs, yet needlessly complex and slow – completely useless from any practical point of view. What it was capable of doing, however, was turning a humble desktop PC into one of those strange machines only ever found in films or on TV – the ones with lots of BIG FLASHING warning messages and letters that printed out o . n . e . a . t . a . t . i . m . e in a pulsating hi-tech green script. For decades these features had only existed beyond the trans-dimensional barrier that was the silver screen – now they were available to spotty teenagers hunched double over sticky keyboards all over every land. Progress marched on.

Despite its obvious drawbacks, thanks to Marshall's magical spinning touch, MovieOS was currently selling by the truck-load, along with trolley-fulls of the razor-blades, underarm deodorants and jam doughnuts people would need while trying to install it. This happy state of affairs proved beyond any shadow of a doubt that, reinforced with the right marketing package, in their continuous age-old struggle, 'form' could beat the living crap out of 'substance' any day of the week. For some reason he could not quite put his chubby finger on, Marshall was inordinately proud of this particular blinding success.

But he had plenty of other notches on his mobile phone

case, plenty of other strings to his quivering bow-tie. Marshall had been the man who first put classical music to a car ad, the first to have it driven past a field of burning corn. He had been the brains behind the legendary campaign for the 'self-toasting waffle' – the single greatest leap forward in the snack confectionery industry since the advent of the 'moist cake-bar'. He was a man of many visions, nearly all of them obscene. If pressed on the point he would have concluded 'banal' was a new sort of tropical fruit yoghurt.

Swift had sold everything from tampons to cigarettes in his time, mourning the passing of that most aspirational of products longer than he'd mourned the deaths of some family members – but he knew when to give up a hopeless fight. There was plenty of new opportunities on his glittering event-horizon, plenty more chances for him to ply his amoral trade. If he didn't do it someone else would, so why shouldn't it be him who got paid? He intended to help sell heroin when it was legalized, and what's more he'd sell it well.

Amongst the many proud exhibits in Marshall's own hallowed corner of the Marketing Bullshit Hall of Fame stood perhaps his most enduring legacy: a lovingly crafted, perfectly weighted phrase that summed him up succinctly, perhaps he'd have it inscribed on his tomb, 'Ribbed for *her* pleasure,' it read, in glowing day-glo letters.

One of Marshall's favourite sayings (and he had quite a few) was that there existed 'Lies, damn lies, statistics, and fizzy-drink commercials.' In this at least there was a grain of truth.

When you bought a Yoke-Cola, at the behest of Swiftsure plc, you weren't just purchasing an overpriced sugar solution, you were making a lifestyle choice. You weren't just quenching your thirst, plus helping to keep poverty-stricken dentists in a job, you were making a personal statement about the individual you were, and the one you wanted to be.

Even if the choices you made led you to believe you weren't buying into the ruthless world of turbo-charged consumerism, man or woman, girl or boy, Marshall still had you by the balls. He had pioneered the concept of the 'imageless' product. In these cynical days, being image*less* was the best image to have of all.

'I'm not the type of sado-geek who needs a badge of identity to make me sexy,' thought the hordes of earnest young consumers for whom the opposite was plainly true. Being seen to not need an image was a much-sought-after status, for which the big boys were willing to pay and pay – especially if the image you'd most recently possessed was that of a testicle-tingling military dictator.

Which brought Marshall neatly back to his most recent personal assignment – its victorious end-game currently playing out before his eyes on his wide-screen office TV. Outside the steps of the Old Bailey a fragile-looking former South American despot was being escorted to a waiting limousine by an army of Metropolitan Police. The smaller group of furious human rights protesters were valiantly attempting to lynch the clearly confused old man in a final hopeless quest for revenge, if not legal justice. But just like their pathetic attempts to slur him in the media's myopic eyes, by raking up such irrelevancies as his record while in office, their efforts were to be in vain. They had locked horns with a PR beast completely beyond their capability.

With a mirthless chuckle Marshall reached for the remote control and turned off the set with a flourish. Thanks to his efforts, General Ricochet had got off scott-free, and would soon be boarding a private plane to somewhere tax-free and hot – all thoughts of extradition back to his impoverished, justice-starved homeland as far from the minds of Home Office officials as was any trace of guilt. Remarkable what just the right amount of spin could do.

Gazing out from his fortified glass tower overlooking the Thames, Marshall sank into a rare bout of introspection. What those filthy protesters polluting London's streets, plus those camped outside the Senator's rented Surrey mansion, failed to realize was that profit created its own morality. Those with access to the means to pay carried a ready store of instant virtue in their bulging wallets. That was simply the way the world was made. Marshall hadn't set the rules, he just embraced them; and he was as good at the high-stakes game of political spin as they came – a virtual Pele on the uneven field of news manipulation.

Thanks to his skills Marshall stayed a busy man. That's why when his PA informed him, over the office's elaborate speaker-phone system, that he had an unscheduled visitor whose name she could not divulge, it threatened to melt even his normally glacial façade.

'What do you mean, *can't divulge*? We're an ad agency, not MI5.'

The sudden frenzied behaviour of his desktop terminal wasn't helping matters either. Perhaps it hadn't been such a good idea to convert all office systems to MovieOS, record-breaking sales figures or not.

The PA was silent for a long moment, as if pondering the accuracy of his last statement. She was paid a small fortune to mollycoddle the great man, but was it really worth it to get involved in the sort of covert intrigue this visit was no doubt a part of?

'Sir, I think you *will* want to see her. She says standing out in the lobby is a security risk, and I must say I tend to agree with her. No one knows she's here – for the moment at least.'

Marshall's reply contained several choice Anglo-Saxon expletives, as he simultaneously tried to press every button on his keyboard in an attempt to reset his PC.

The entire screen of the integrated terminal was currently taken up by a large flashing message reading: WARNING – UNSCHEDULED VISITOR ALERT, as an endless stream of scrolling numbers raced past in the background for no apparent reason. MovieOS might have given you the sense you were taking part in the very latest Hollywood action blockbuster epic, but it was also a pain in the arse.[1] And now the speaker-phone had shut down in sympathy.

Giving up in disgust he reverted to a more tried and tested form of communication. 'Send her in then!' he shouted through to the next office at the top of his voice.

His PA left her glass-walled annex and stepped out into the spacious lobby. Cheltenham Secretarial College (renamed East Gloucestershire University of Business Administration) had in no way prepared her for moments such as this.

'You can go in now, er – Your Majesty.'

The visitor all but barged past, declaring in a frosty tone, 'One *appreciates* such co-operation.'

When Marshall stood face to face with the new arrival he experienced a good deal of his PA's agitation, though he did a better job of hiding it. This was indeed someone you didn't keep waiting if you could help it. Marshall had a strange urge to bow or curtsey. In the end he performed something horribly in between.

'Let's cut the formalities, shall we,' said his guest, unzipping her biking leathers to reveal a low-cut vest-top not really in keeping with a lady of such age. 'To tell the truth they do have a tendency to get on One's tits after a while. One hopes very much you're going to be a man with whom One can do business.' She lay her full-face crash-helmet on his aircraft-carrier of a desk.

---

[1] 'ass' – Compulsory North American spelling always in effect. To learn how to disable this feature turn to page 23.92 Appendix 67b (subsection 128) {part ii][(next to the bit about haddock)

Marshall could only nod dumbly, blurting out the first thought that entered his spinning head. 'You're not at all like you appear on . . .'

'On the stamps?' she finished for him, with an unnervingly knowing smile.

The adman blushed despite himself. This meeting was not going well at all. He'd always imagined knighthoods were bestowed through the post, not delivered by person. 'Actually I was going to say on TV, but I didn't just mean the way you look.'

'One feels that One has been somewhat misunderstood over the years.'

Now Marshall was on firmer ground. 'And you want me to help put that right? We can throw a few ideas into the wok and see if it spits . . .'

She studied him closely for a moment, giving Marshall an uncomfortable urge to loosen his tie. 'It's not One's image that is of concern. I'm here in my capacity as head of an influential organization. We want our agenda to be more widely known. This is perhaps the biggest PR job mankind has ever known, and we want you to take the contract.'

Play it cool, play it cool, raced through Marshall's reeling mind a million times a second. 'I'm flattered by your intriguing offer, um – Ma'am,' this was an increasingly surreal experience, 'but I'm afraid I've got a lot on my plate just now. I had a visit yesterday from the head of one of the world's biggest . . .'

'Toy manufacturers,' she finished for him once again.

Christ, that was an annoying habit.

'One knows all about that particular deal. The product he wants you to help sell is fascinating, don't you think, and significant in a way that will be made clear in good time – but not today I think.'

Marshall looked confused. 'What's his connection to you?'

His guest dismissively waved her hand. 'The CEO you met yesterday sits on our Committee too. He wished to check you out himself before we showed our hand.'

Marshall's eyes narrowed. 'So who else is on this *Committee*? You'll be telling me you've got my clients in the Vatican onboard next!'

There was a pregnant pause before his guest went on. 'Perceptive of you . . . You have been doing business with some of them for years – the largest corporations on the planet. We've been grooming you your entire career; when you've helped us there's a special place in our hierarchy for you.'

Marshall was somewhat taken aback. The thought that his meteoric rise had been down to anything other than his own talent had never occurred to him. He was, however, intrigued. 'Perhaps you should tell me more about the brief.'

His visitor took a deep and confident breath. 'There exists a conspiracy at the very highest level of world affairs to make the public believe in conspiracy theories. When this fact is widely known the masses will be, by definition, victims of that conspiracy – the Unified Conspiracy Theory we call it. I work for the forces behind this plan.'

Marshall looked stunned, as well he might. With an air of growing unreality he asked the one question he knew must come first. But it was nothing to do with motives or reasons; Marshall was too much a pro for that. 'So why are you telling me this, when this scheme has remained secret for so long – why now?'

His visitor locked him with her strangely compelling stare. 'Because you are the very best at what you do. We need the very best. We want you to help us spin our plan. The time of awakening is almost at hand.'

If Marshall had been shocked before now he was speechless, though not for the reason anyone else might have thought. Of course he had known he was good, but to be told by none other than the Nation's Head of State he was the best ranked at least a stick-on gold star on his wall-planner.

Unaware that Marshall needed no further inducement, his guest went on. 'Our motives will be made clear in good time. Let one just say that mankind stands on the brink of its finest hour. When the masses know the truth about . . . everything, they'll be more than prepared to sanction what must follow. Now, Mr Swift, will you respond to this ultimate challenge One has lain twitching at your feet?'

Marshall studied the unerringly familiar face in front of him, attempting in vain to penetrate those inscrutable alien eyes. There was undoubtedly more to this than his guest was letting on. Still, if he was going to take her 'Committee' on as clients he might as well start to win her over with his dazzling personality. Leaning forward he graced her with his best disarming smile.

'Yes, of course Your Majesty. By the way, nice tattoos.'

17. Awakening

Urgistan, Western Himalayas

'By all the gods, can it be true?'

General Noroco stood in the chaotic midst of the Republic of Urgistan's Military High Command Centre, or as it had been known up until that afternoon Honest Jubal's Backpacker Café and Second Hand Rug Emporium. The building had been commandeered for the common good that very day, on the basis that it was one of the few in the capital possessing all the accoutrements necessary for the running of high-tempo military operations – put another way, it had a telephone and cappuccino machine. The indignant proprietor had been packed off along with his wailing family, with the half-sincere promise that 'nothing was going to be blown up' in the foreseeable future.

Across the cluttered map-table Urgistan's freshly appointed head of state faced his most trusted lieutenant. Then again perhaps this individual was more of a shady corporal. Yajik was not a military man by profession but he had seen *The Great Escape* all the way through more than once. By the standards of the forces Noroco had at his disposal this made him a formidable soldier of Napoleonic proportions.

'I'm afraid there's no escaping it, Your Worshipfulness,' Yajik mumbled deferentially, tugging on one of his few remaining clumps of hair as if it was an embarrassing parasite he'd rather get rid of.

Noroco shot him a glance full of suppressed venom. Urgistan's newly installed leader was going to have a tough time breaking his people out of their subservient habits – presidential decrees or not.

Urgistan could safely be described as a tin-pot country, that's if someone hadn't stripped the tin off its roof years ago and sold it to raise cash for a new outhouse. Perhaps that wasn't entirely fair. Urgistan had never had a 'roof' of any kind. It was totally devoid of natural resources. Never a big nation, there were European royal families which had larger lawns, and it was getting smaller. Both China and India had for centuries been shaving off slices like it was some high-altitude salami. In its defence, Urgistan had two claims to fame.

Firstly, it was one of the highest nations on earth, nestling in the Western Himalayas like an agoraphobic yak. Secondly, it was also one of the poorest; so poor in fact that not even the World Bank would lend it money, such was the unlikelihood of it seeing any in return.

But these meagre features were about to be put to shame, if reports from the high Kara-Kuri range were to believed. This brooding escarpment of eternal ice and snow was strung along the Tibetan frontier like a jagged row of shattered teeth. If it's true that all communities must have a band of outsiders to poke fun at, some abject group of no-hopers that can always raise a laugh, then the inhabitants of the Kara-Kuri filled that role in Urgistan.

'Two Kara-Kuris walk into a bar' was the start of many a witty tale in the capital's trendiest barber-shops and opium dens. The Urgistanis might live in abject poverty, but at least they weren't mad like those loonies with perpetual frostbite who kept yetis for pets – or at least that's what the more cosmopolitan lowland Urgis liked to believe. But that hellish place was no longer such a laughing matter. It seemed an ancient evil not seen for a thousand generations had once again risen to haunt that accursed land.

'The villagers are sure of what they saw?' Noroco asked his deputy, a look of sick foreboding on his chiselled face.

'There can be no doubt, sir. The ancient tales have

come alive. The hills are full of demons and our doom has come as punishment for what we did to the rightful king.'

Noroco, a man who tolerated medieval mumbo-jumbo as readily as he tolerated toenails in a spring role, pinned his underling to the cracked plaster wall with his muscular forearm in one lightning motion.

'We'll have none of that defeatist talk as long as I'm in charge. That wet-fish of a monarch was a slave to those very creatures from the day he dropped between his mother's bloody thighs – just as were all his corrupt line. They protected their foul dens and kept us from wiping them out while they still slept. Now it's reveille time, and those things have got out of their glacier the wrong side, and no mistake. We did for him, and now we'll do for his abhorrent masters too.'

Yajik was slightly less scared of the 'Hill Witches' than he was of his commanding officer. Twenty years of British service as a senior NCO in the Queen's Gurkha Rifles had given Noroco the air of a man who *would be* obeyed, otherwise you *would be* sweeping up your teeth. He'd broken more than one chinless officer cadet in his time and he'd gladly do it again if, gods forbid, he ever found himself on the other side to his former employers.

'I want the 5th Mobile Division moved into position to monitor the situation and quell the tribesmen's panic. Is that understood?'

Yajik looked pained as he slid down the wall to his shaking feet. Behind him a poster of a tennis player scratching her bum would never be quite the same again. 'I'd afraid that's not possible, sir. Your brother-in-law's truck needs a new carburettor, the 5th Mobile is the 5th Immobile until it's repaired.'

Noroco spat in outrage on the dusty sawdust-coated floor. 'Then we have no hope of containing this menace on our own. We must have outside help.'

Simple as a slug he might have been, but Yajik could see a gaping flaw in his master's plan. 'They'll never believe us, sir. I can barely believe it myself, and I was brought up with the old tales. My granny used to tell them while we huddled round the winter fires, the wind howling outside. But I never gave the stories much credence – just ghost tales told to scare the young and feeble-minded. Until now, that is . . .'

Noroco slapped his rambling companion hard across the face. Despite provocation which would have tried a saint it was the first time he'd resorted to violence since taking charge of his superstitious people.

'Don't you think I know that, fool? But they'll have to believe us when they know the severity of this threat. Pass me the telephone. Thank heaven I still have contacts amongst the British military. They'll send men and planes. Trust me, we're in safe hands from now on.'

18. Briefing

White House, Washington, DC

Becker strode purposefully to his seat in the conference chamber and readied his carefully prepared papers. The other attendees at this highest of high-power meetings were already at their places – the President wearing the same semi-detached expression he wore whenever the discussion focused on anything deeper than the *Sports Illustrated Swimsuit Edition*, the military men around him wearing their campaign ribbons, hard won after long struggles to reach the summit of the Pentagon's greasy flagpole of success. It was clear they gave out more than just Purple Hearts for bravely risking multiple paper-cuts, whilst deciding which multinational got the contract to supply the combat troops' self-toasting waffles.

But Becker was a man on his own heroic mission this morning. When he caught the eye of the Head of the Joint Chiefs of Staff there passed between them a silent acknowledgement. It was nothing as indiscreet as a nod or a wink, rather the gaze swapped by two men who knew they served a common cause. The General was one of the few present who would not be surprised by Becker's regular weekly briefing. As a senior member of the Committee, and an influential Washington insider, the Head of the Joint Chiefs had spent long hours with the Dark Man planning their tactics for this engagement. Both hoped the carefully staged ambush would prove victorious – they knew it could make or break their shadowy second careers, possibly even their lives.

The usual herd of hangers-on in attendance would pose little threat. They were the usual breed of civic parasite

– the surviving spawn of a chaotic hothouse evolution, spanning countless may-fly generations, that unfailingly produced creatures optimized at sucking the blood from the anaemic body politic in the most efficient way. They were the cancerous barnacles fastened to the seat-of-power's vast behind, the embarrassing fluff clinging to the old and threadbare sweater of the Presidency. Becker reserved for them his best metaphors, along with a gallon of contempt in a special chamber of his black and festering heart.

However, these jabbering bureaucrats did serve one purpose, and serve it well. As far as the Committee was concerned they provided the perfect cover – a ready-made pantomime cast to entertain the masses with their ludicrous cavortings and petty indiscretions. Since the troubled birth of modern democracy the real action had slipped off-stage, while the wide-eyed audience were mesmerized by the prancing clowns upon it. Becker despised them, but he was also realistic enough to recognize they were needed. And they were about to unwittingly play their part yet again.

Sure enough, here came perhaps the greatest grinning ringmaster of them all. As was his custom, and in a sad attempt to stamp his authority on proceedings, the President tapped a big cigar on the polished mahogany table and got down to business.

'Right, Bob, what have you got for me today?'

It was an annoying habit, but Becker had been called worse things by chief executives in his time. In thirty years of his official 'day job' as head of the most secret of secret intelligence agencies (the one which kept tabs on those amateurs in the CIA and FBI) he'd often needed to tell incumbents of the Oval Office news they'd rather not hear – he'd had to virtually strangle Nixon with those damned tapes to get him to resign. Of course, sometimes the opposite was also true; it had been his bureau which informed

Kennedy the Russians were bluffing back in '63, while the rest of the Washington security community was collectively filling its diapers because of a few damp fire-crackers down in Havana. It had been Becker who had handed Reagan the videotape of that action-packed space-opera, whispering in his ear as he did so, *'I think you might want to take a look at this. Our scientists need just a few more years . . .'*

But there was no time to dwell on past successes, no matter how courageous or benign. This latest strutting peacock had his quirks, more than a few if the court cases were to be believed, but they were of little concern now. Becker could cope with this idiot getting his name wrong.

Anyway, everyone was 'Bob' until they were members of this President's inner circle, and that dubious honour was hardly worth the price. In the absence of long weekends spent sailing together in Maine, or even longer weekends spent partying with Washington's high-class whores, Becker was never likely to aspire to such lofty social heights. At least 'Bob' was better than some of the pet names the surveillance tapes showed he had for the more well-upholstered female interns.

Admiring his own stoicism, the Dark Man took a deep breath and began his pitch. 'May I begin, sir?'

The President lit his cigar and puffed on it boldly. 'Hit me, Bob.'

Becker fought back an urge to take the order literally, but overcame it with a smile that could have scared a brick.

'Overnight there have been alarming developments in the former Kingdom of Urgistan. Our friends in British Intel are getting very hot under their starched collars. At this point reports are sketchy, but I can present you with my initial analysis right now.'

The President blew a smoke ring and did his best to look thoughtful. In fact he failed to get past *'used-car salesman picks underwear*'. 'Urgistan eh? Can't have any sort of hoo-haa in our backyard, now can we? Never did trust those Latinos – always swarming across the border looking for work or hand-outs.'

Next to him the Secretary of State coughed nervously. 'Urgistan is in Central Asia, sir. It's a poverty-stricken nation high in the Himalayas. About as far away from us as you can get – without travelling into space.'

The President chewed on his cigar for a moment. 'Central Asia, Central America, wa-hey. So what? Have you ever noticed how all the continents' names end with the same letter they begin with? Spooky ain't it.'

There was a long silence as those gathered took this in. Finally Uncle Sam's favourite cheeky nephew decided to move things on. 'So what's the deal down there, Bob? What's got the Brits' stiff lips all a-tremble?'

Becker's heavy brow furrowed like an earthquake fault line. 'It's the usual story, I'm afraid. Urgistan is home to many distinct racial minorities, and an even larger number of religious cults – makes San Francisco look tame by comparison. Seems the local hard man, General Noroco, who you might remember overthrew the absolute monarchy in last week's military coup –'

The President waved him on, obviously as aware of Urgistani internal politics as he was of the sexual harassment laws.

' – has seen fit to crack down on the diverse nationalist elements. He's riding roughshod over their justifiable claims for autonomy as a way of diverting attention from his country's extreme poverty and lack of cable TV. He's a dangerous lunatic who must be stopped. You know the score by now.'

The Head of the Joint Chiefs tutted and nodded in a commendably understated way.

The President threw him a glance and placed both hands on the chair arms beside him. 'Fascinating, Bob!

Do we have any national interests in not letting him get away with this heinous crime?'

Becker put on his most sincere expression, the one he'd practised for hours during his long-forgotten youth. 'Not directly. We do, however, have evidence Noroco is about to embark on a brutal policy of ethnic cleansing. Satellite recon shows major troop movements in the area – there's been a 100% increase in military telecommunications. After all, it's what men like him nearly always do at times like this.'

Despite the fact that the closest this President had ever come to ethnic cleansing was the photo-opportunity they'd staged for him in Harlem removing graffiti from that school wall with a bucket and mop, he was more than convinced by this damning evidence. Becker saw his chance to strike for the kill, as well as get in some opportunist slander.

'As usual, the situation caught the CIA boys on the hop.' It was so much easier when the Chief wasn't an ex-Agency man himself. Those Langley assholes made convenient scapegoats when you needed someone other than International Communism to blame. He'd been laying the groundwork for his next move for years.

'They might even have kept this data from you on purpose – we all know they're not keen to see you have a second term.'

The President turned to the brown-tongued crony who was destined to be his Campaign Manager in the coming election. He didn't have to embarrass anyone by putting his unspoken thoughts into words.

The smartly dressed advisor almost fell off his chair in his haste to pass on his optimistic assessment. 'It's not going to hurt our chances any, sir. A short, sharp, victorious war never did anyone's popularity any harm at all. If you count what we did to those rebel French Canadians up in Montreal last year, one more victory would make you the winningest Commander-in-Chief since Ray-Gun Ronnie. Two-for-two looks mighty good from where I stand.'

A far away look had come over the President's steel-grey eyes. He could almost picture the statue now – knowing smirk, hands on hips, trouser zip bulging as it showed the first signs of giving way. As decisions went, his next one wasn't difficult to make.

'What are his capabilities, Bob? Any sign of nukes just yet? I bet the Brits sold him one of those superguns, seems about par for the course – though they never look all *that* big to *me*. Know what I mean?'

Becker ignored his master's suggestive wink and school-boy nudge. Shaking his head soberly, he continued. 'They have the usual mix of clapped-out ex-Soviet hardware – 1960s' vintage at best. Not even the French would accept this guy's credit. He's got some of their older stuff, but that's just Argentine and Iraqi cast-offs – probably full of bullet holes already. Our boys should turn it to scrap metal in no time flat.'

The President turned on his best baby-kissing smile, the one that could turn a college cheerleader weak at the knees from twenty paces.

'That'll wrap it up, Bob. Sounds like a just cause to me! I want that place crawling with stealth fighters and news-crews before you can say "collateral damage".' He affected a plumby British accent – what he achieved was closer to Dick Van Dyke.

'*Make it so, Number One.* Geeze, I've always wanted to say that. Bye the way, what's our standing in the polls right now?'

That was as far as the debate went. The War (capitals were now appropriate) was as cut-and-dried as the Com-mander-in-Chief's hair. There just remained the formality of obtaining a quick 'bouffant styling' from the United Nations Security Council, and they'd be ready to start selling tickets any world leader facing re-election would be scrambling to obtain. Anyone less worldly-wise than those present would have been forgiven for choking on their mineral water and Danish pastries, but to these people 'cynicism' was just a word in the dictionary half-way between cyanide and cyst.

As the meeting adjourned Becker allowed himself a moment of quiet satisfaction. The glance he exchanged with the Head of the Joint Chiefs told him that the General felt the same way. The Committee would be well pleased with the work they'd done this day.

But something was tugging at the back of his mind – a dark uneasiness he knew he could share with no one. His orders to set off the chain of events he'd unleashed today had come too suddenly, not at all like the carefully weighed and considered edicts the Committee usually percolated down to him. This, after all, was the same organization which had taken until 1941 to conclude WW2 could be the making of the industrial USA. He'd heard that those Japanese admirals had been a nightmare to bribe, but a way had been found in the end.[1] He was going to need a similar level of cunning if he was going to uncover the real motives behind these subtle ploys, of which he was the mere messenger.

Then, of course, there was always the matter of his continued suspicions regarding Madame Chairman.

Surely Urgistan could not be connected to that other business, the ongoing struggle even Becker at times tried to banish from his mind? Jesus H C, how he wished he had a copy of The File to check his facts. Was it a coincidence that a copy of his most prized database had gone missing? It was surely too much to hope it was.

---

[1] 'Oner-ible Geisha certainly looked female at time.'

'Tough luck, bud. Be there on December 7th, or the world's press get the pictures. Bye the way, I thought Göring was a pervert, but you guys make him look like Eleanor Roosevelt on a quiet night in.'

Like a long-married wife who discovers her husband has started growing a moustache and taken to wearing leather caps, ever so slowly a terrible suspicion began to form in his mind.

19. Exposé

Kate pressed rewind on the battered edit-suite video and cast a weary eye over the page of untidily scribbled notes. It was not easy making sense of her haphazard scrawl at the best of times, a crippled spider on its way home from a heavy session at the pub, as one colleague had put it, but on this occasion the subject matter would not help anyone make sense of her thoughts in the slightest.

Kate was in the midst of frenzied last-minute research for the much-anticipated UFO special. The research was frenzied because the deadline was fast approaching and after the regular end-of-show appeal for contributions her office had been swamped with submissions from what seemed like a solar-system-wide haul of cranks and nutters. It was hard to move without tripping over the details of Clive from Barnsley's telepathic radishes, or some delusional religious freak convinced that only their cat could receive coded communiqués from beyond Orion. 'Quantity' was not going to be a problem, 'quality' on the other hand . . .

The pressure was on to keep coming up with red-hot items. On a competing channel Bezant's World of The Bizarre was eating into their audience share. The ongoing World's Longest/Straightest Banana Competition was a masterpiece of Dalian proportions. If Maxwell's team didn't do something quickly to spark ratings, heads would roll. At the production meeting that morning they'd been told in no uncertain terms that the UFO Special *had* to be a killer.

Maxwell had asked how the guest list was shaping up. It had been Kate's unpleasant duty to tell him that while she had been researching the intriguing story of the sexually-abused West Country farmer, her co-worker tasked with reeling in the Temple of Planet Love had gone on long-term sick-leave, and no progress had been made. An unfortunate lapse, but with their staff turnover what did he expect?

Maxwell had hit the roof. 'These guys are a must for the show,' he'd fumed. 'Get someone reliable down there, Jennings, right away. This cult's gagging for a bit of PR. Besides, orange robes and shaven heads look great on TV. Now this farmer's kinky liaison; will he be willing to re-enact it with a greyed-up porn-star?'

Kate had broken it to him gently that this would not be a good idea.

Once the meeting had adjourned she'd rushed back to her office. A quick telephone conversation with a spaced-out cultist later, and Kate was relieved to discover the Temple of Planet Love was still keen to take part – in fact, half the audience were destined to be members of the organization, having booked the tickets in advance. The cult's founder and spiritual leader could meet her today for an exploratory interview. And yes, if they wanted him he was more than eager to be a guest. Kate had got the impression straight off that he wasn't exactly shy when it came to publicity, though she had no idea yet just how badly he wanted to be on *this* particular show.

So that morning Kate had journeyed down to the cult's luxury Sussex mansion, with a bored cameraman in tow, to gather information which Maxwell could use on the day. It was the recording of this meeting that currently whirred along in the tape-deck before her – she still found it difficult to believe some of the things it contained.

There was something about the interview which bothered her in an indescribable way, and it had little to do with the New Age bollocks sprouting from the charismatic leader's mouth. She almost jumped out of her skin when the rewinding cassette reached the start and stopped with a loud clunk. Numbly, she pushed the button marked play and a shiver ran down her spine.

The guy went by the name of Cornelius Jackson, whether that was a stage-name Kate didn't know, wherever it came from there was no denying he certainly had on-screen presence. Even through the camera lens his enthusiasm hit you like an express train full of salesmen. With a shudder Kate remembered how much stronger it had been in the creeping flesh.

Jackson had little piggy eyes and a smile that barely reached up to them. The small round spectacles he wore made his pupils seem ever more distant. There was madness in those eyes, but also a strange, almost hypnotic deviancy.

He had been dressed simply in black robes, their colour setting him apart from his saffron-clad disciples. On the breast of his tunic was a swirling multi-hued geometric design that made you dizzy when you looked at it. Above it was a Chinese symbol of eye-watering design. His voice had been calm and serene in an infuriatingly unpleasant way.

'Welcome, my child, to our simple home.'

He had reached forward and touched Kate's knee, in a way that told her he'd be prepared to make her *more than* welcome any time she liked. Kate had squirmed beneath his touch, but had pressed on all the same.

'Tell me, Mr Jackson, how you came to found the Temple of Planet Love?'

Then Jackson had started on what was undoubtedly his favourite topic – his own life story and his ambitious master plan for the future of the human race. Kate didn't think she'd met anyone so full of themselves her entire life, and she'd met Jimmy Maxwell. Just what might happen if they got together she didn't like to think. Some critical-mass of ego might be reached, the ensuing explosion taking out half a continent.

'Many years ago I came to this land out of the ancient slumbering East. My origins are not important now, and in truth I find them hard to recall. But when I reached these shores I found a society torn by anger, greed and the unhappiness caused by low libido. I made it my humble duty to spread a message of harmony and tolerant love for all mankind . . .'

Jackson had elaborated at some length. Kate had heard most of it before; from Moonies, Scientologists and various pissed-up sixth-form suitors, she'd just never heard it all in the one place. Cults flourished in these confusing times. It seemed all you needed to set one up was an alluring web address[1] and an accident with your laundry, but few could compete with Jackson's creation for pure oddity value.

When they'd been younger, she and Dave and a group of earnest like-minded friends had flirted briefly with nihilist philosophy, but they had quickly come to the conclusion that it wasn't worth the effort. It seemed Jackson had persevered. It was hard to escape the conclusion that dedication and perseverance weren't always a good thing.

The bits about peace and love were all very appealing, but did humanity really have to devote itself to an almost comatose waking daze to achieve it? Kate didn't think so. Sensing her doubt, Jackson had offered to show her one of the cult's ceremonies in the flesh. Kate had politely declined; she'd heard just how 'in the flesh' these things could get. None-too-subtly she'd changed the subject by questioning him on the organization's aims.

As best she could make out the cult had few objectives – it simply wished to gain as many converts as possible through its doctrine of tolerance, understanding, nasal-chanting and compulsory free-form gang-bangs at every available opportunity. If nothing else this credo was at

[1] www.weirdo.orgy.ok

least popular with the rank-and-file – it beat a stale biscuit and sip of economy Bordeaux any day of the week, including Sundays. As a result Jackson's Temple of Planet Love was growing even faster than its founder's ego and bank balance.

Of course this expansion came with a cost. The Temple had drawn a great deal of publicity in recent months, not all of it good. The parents of certain converts had kicked up an almighty fuss. Some claimed Jackson to be a complete cult. Others claimed that description was just one letter out. Kate knew how she felt on the matter. She didn't trust him any more than she'd trust a used-car salesman. And wasn't that exactly what he was doing? Jackson had cobbled together a clapped-out loony theology by welding into one the scraps of others already written off by the test of time. The resulting spirit-vehicle was no doubt little safer to passengers than its resprayed road-bound counterparts. And when it crashed, as she knew it would, the results were bound to be messy.

As she watched the tape for a second time, Kate came to a painful conclusion. Seeing as Jackson was able to talk (relatively) lucidly on his subject, and had done more than a few TV interviews in his time, it was hard to escape the conclusion that they'd have to have him on. When the alternative was Clive from Barnsley and his mystic root vegetables, Cornelius Jackson didn't seem so bad after all. He was going to be on the show, there was little Kate could do to stop it, but something else was nagging at her mind.

Suddenly Kate hit the pause button. In a blinding flash she knew what she'd been subconsciously looking for all along. Squinting against the harsh glare she put her face close to the monitor, until the flickering image was nothing more than a collection of multi-coloured dots, but she had to be sure. Dear God, it was there all right – there was no mistaking it. Suddenly she felt her armpits dampen and her flesh break out in a nauseating cold sweat. In an instant all her worst fears had been confirmed.

In the centre of Jackson's forehead was the faintest trace of an ugly red welt. Standing orders dictated that details of anyone who bore this taint should be delivered to a very special destination with crash priority.

Kate rose from her chair and checked the corridor outside. At this late hour the studio was virtually empty – a lone cleaner emptied a bin further down the hallway, otherwise the place was deserted. But Kate still did something she'd never done before – she locked the edit-suite door. She didn't want any disturbances for the next few minutes. Best not to take any chances.

Taking a deep breath she opened her bag and pulled out a highly specialized piece of equipment. Shortly she had left the prosaic world of daytime chat-shows far behind and was moonlighting on behalf of her other career.

20. Rolling Along

He was finding it far from easy going but dutifully Dave pressed on with his study of the large blue folder Frank had given him.

The cleverest way to lie is to tell the truth up to a point and then stop, leaving your victim to infer the incoherent nonsense you want them to believe. This technique has the in-built advantage that, if the full truth comes out, your credibility remains intact whilst your victim is shown to be an irrational scare-monger of the most half-baked kind.

In the early days this tactic was behind all our dealings with those well-meaning civilians pathologically obsessed with the so-called UFO phenomena. The fact was that the Committee did not have a clue what was going on. Yes, we had an entire scrapyard full of crashed saucers, but no inkling as to what the motives or technology behind the 'Visitors' actually were. If this information ever leaked out it was potentially far more damaging than the knowledge we were being visited by an apparently 'alien' civilization. We had to make the public believe we were in control, and fast. Desperate times call for desperate measures.

A favourite ruse was to put out a report that at a certain time a communications satellite, or shower of meteors, would be entering Earth's atmosphere. If it were true, then all the better. We'd then stage an elaborate hoax, involving the usual mix of high-powered projectors, black-ops helicopters and stealth aircraft, far in excess of what could be expected from the specified event. If it could be arranged we might include a guest appearance from one of the Visitors' craft, though their unreliability and incompetence was a major drawback. The initial 'cover-story' would perform three functions.

Firstly, it would ensure the event was witnessed by the maximum number of people, UFO freaks being the sort who took an unhealthy interest in astronomy and space science.

Secondly, it would imply that we, the dark powers of authority, knew in advance that an 'event' was going to take place, were behind it, and were attempting to explain it away with a feeble fabrication.

Finally, since it would be obvious to any rational observer that what they saw could not have been the mundane event described in the cover story, they'd assume we were hiding the test-flight of some super-secret alien-acquired craft, or practising for the day when we finally broke cover and established the 'New World Order', converting the planet's population into brain-fried sex-slaves en passant. Preposterous! The common man never fails to overestimate the organizational abilities of his shadowy masters. But we could use that to our advantage. Nothing sets a conspiracy theorist's juices flowing quite like a government denial dissipated in the proper way. Headlines such as *'Authorities Claim Weather Balloon Caused West Coast Panic!'* went further towards cementing our credibility than our true bewilderment ever warranted.

The end result would be that the public would assume that there *was* an 'alien presence', and that the benign paternalistic 'powers that be' had it all wrapped up, filed away and understood. So what if there *was* a conspiracy to keep secrets deemed to be in the national interest? Most voters were happy not to know as long as they had access to cheap caffeine and alcohol, and forty channels of cable TV. Any official silence was to keep crucial data out of the hands of the Russians, who might be boarding their Antinovs as we speak. Our good friends on the other side of the Iron Curtain were more than happy to co-operate in this reciprocal agreement – we fulfilled much the same role as a bogey man for their own cowering, downtrodden plebs.

The important thing was that the great unwashed believe that we, their social betters and superiors everywhere, understood why the Visitors were here and were learning whole new technologies from them. Of course in reality nothing could have been further from the truth.

Dave's reading material was getting too much to take. Wearily he reached for the battered camper van's battered transistor radio and turned it on. He couldn't be sure but he suspected the strange Heath Robinson device beneath it was one of the few remaining eight-track music cassettes. No doubt it had been gathering dust since, much to its flip-flop-wearing owner's dismay, the last of *The Beach Boys' Greatest Hits* in that doomed format had been sunk into some festering New Jersey landfill. With a shudder Dave clicked the volume knob to 'on'.

Unsurprisingly, considering the monumental information junkie in the driving seat next to him, the set was tuned to a news station. A short jingle, which somehow managed to pack a lifetime's worth of melodrama into its three tight bars, was followed by a newscaster's excited voice.

'In a shock development today, Professor JT Barstow of the University of Portland was beaten senseless by masked attackers outside the WZMX building here in sunny Sacramento. Prior to the unprovoked attack the Professor had been taking part in a heated phone-in debate concerning the breakdown of civil society and general good manners in our nation today. Professor Barstow, an acknowledged expert on the symptoms of social collapse, had been explaining his own theories on what causes normally polite people to become psychotic on the very slightest pretext.

'Experts were quick to claim this incident marks the first recorded case of what is already being called "*Rage* Rage", or the irrational hatred of minor academics with half-baked theories for just about everything. These same experts quickly went on to demand immediate police protection and Federal funding to research the phenomenon. The Professor, who is recovering from head wounds at a local hospital, was unavailable for comment.

'And now, national news. In New York City the Civil Rights for All American People movement said it would go to court to protect the American Nazi Party's right to burn down CRAAP's Manhattan head office. The statement came as grass-roots members of the civil liberties organization picketed firefighters trying to put out the blaze at their downtown HQ.

'"Just because the ANP are crypto-fascist disciples of hate doesn't mean we can take away their First Amendment rights," claimed a spokesperson for the organization, as she fled screaming from the building. "I'll die to protect their constitutional right to freedom of expression."'

Yes, you probably will, Dave thought.

Frank reached over and turned the set off. 'Hey! I was listening to that.'

Frank shook his head. 'You shouldn't absorb that shit, man. They make it up to mess with your mind. They don't need no subtle subliminal stuff when they're shovelling you that shit. Trust me, I did three years on PsyOps back in the seventies.'

'Are you seriously suggesting that someone, somewhere makes up bizarre news stories just to loosen our grip on reality?'

Frank's face took on a crazed far-away expression. 'Have you any better reason why the world is getting weirder?

When we're thoroughly numbed we won't bat an eyelid when *they* make their final move.'

Much as Dave found it hard to believe that someone had been beaten up because of his loopy theories (even in America), he found it harder still to accept the notion it might be part of some planned manipulation. He countered with the most rational counter-argument he could come up with.

'Bollocks! If your theory is true how do you know it's not part of what they're trying to achieve? I once had a girlfriend who'd swallow most things, given enough cider and black, but even she'd gag at that one.'

Frank's chiselled features took on a look of exquisite pain. Obviously this was a point he'd pondered long and hard. 'Just because you're paranoid doesn't mean they're not out to get you. Things are getting flaky round the edges. The centre cannot hold. If this goes on we're all going to be dribbling idiots before they're through. Someone has planned it this way to further their own secret agenda. Personally, I don't plan to be taken in.'

Dave gestured towards the large blue file he'd discarded on the seat beside them. 'I suppose you got this particular paranoid classic from this ridiculous manuscript. Though if the bit I was just reading was true, nothing could be further from the truth. How do your account for those sections? Yet more inverse black propaganda?'

Frank gave Dave a long look, the sort that had once been used to break raw recruits. 'As a matter of fact I was aware of these plots long before I obtained our copy of MJ13. I'm afraid it goes even deeper than you seem to think. If the guy who wrote it is right, even the shady types behind our governments are swinging in the wind. It's just that only I have the proof needed to blow it all to kingdom come.'

It's been observed that irony is indeed a funny thing, as fickle as a pissed-off fairy and as cruel as a jackboot to the groin, but over the next half-second Dave and Frank found it hard to be philosophical about such things. For that matter, over the next half-second Dave and Frank found it hard to be anything other than terrified out of their sunburnt skin. At that precise moment a monumental explosion shook the rear of the van, almost throwing it off the road like a child's unwanted toy. In that half-second Dave was convinced Frank had rigged up some sort of pyrotechnic device to give credence to his words, but when he glanced back to see the rear of the bus skidding to a halt a smoking shell fifty yards further up the freeway, he had to admit this was unlikely.

'What the fuck was that?' he screamed, scrambling for a hand-hold as the cab tilted back at a crazy angle, a frenzy of sparks flying up from the blazing asphalt behind him.

Frank was too busy trying to steer the now two-wheeled van to care. 'Get under the dashboard,' he yelled, forcing Dave's head down one handed.

Before Dave could protest they collided with something soft and yielding, then an instant later something much firmer, which judging by the impact could be nothing but a towering brick wall. This second collision slammed Dave into the footwell with staggering force. Frank had used a conveniently placed cactus to take the sting from their speed, then crashed into the sandbank at the edge of the deserted road. The former commando's ribcage took the force of the steering wheel, but before Dave knew it his companion was pulling him out by his hair into the frigid desert moonlight.

'Gotta keep moving,' Frank panted against his pain, 'black choppers overhead.'

Dave was about to ask 'What black choppers?' when a huge dark shape swooped out of the night, barely missing him by inches. The down-draught from the rotors almost knocked him off his feet, but eerily there was no sound. Dave would have crumpled in a heap on the roadway if

Frank hadn't grasped him by the arm and yelled, 'Come on, gotta get our friend out of the trunk!'

Within seconds they were back at the smoking remains of the caravanette's rear end. Dave felt sure that if anything was left of 'their friend' it would be burnt to an unrecognizable crisp – nothing could have survived that explosion intact. Optimistically, Frank sprung the trunk's latch and reached eagerly inside. The creature hadn't exactly smelt pleasant before its latest ordeal, but being flash fried in the boot of a psychedelic passion-wagon had done nothing to improve its unique aroma. Despite its latest tribulations it was still in one piece. It was still a rotting mess, but it was a thick-skinned rotting mess.

Frank sensed the returning danger before either of them saw it. 'Duck!' was all he could manage before a flurry of explosive shells arrived with a bone-trembling roar. A second black chopper was providing covering fire as its accomplice swung round ready to strike.

Dave found himself sprawled on the ground with Frank and the lifeless alien piled on top of him. With the sort of breathtakingly inappropriate clarity of vision that can only come at a moment of life-threatening danger, Dave calmly noticed a gaping hole in one of the alien's grey shoulders, just inches above his reeling head. It seemed Frank had not quite been quick enough getting it out of harm's way. Though he was in no position to appreciate it at the time, Dave would later realize this was the moment he well and truly lost it. It was from here on that the whole terrifying pantomime seemed take on a surreal, other-worldly quality that left him watching events as if from a great distance. It was all he could do to contain the shrill snigger that backed up behind his blistered and bleeding lips.

In an orgy of battered limbs the three did their best to sort out which appendage belonged to which. 'What the hell are they trying to do to us?' Dave yelled, part of him still clinging to the hopeful delusion this was some unfortunate mistake.

'Kill us would be my first guess,' said Frank, peering over a smouldering cactus at their re-forming pursuers. 'It could also be my last. Seems they want Grey Boy real bad.'

Away on the indigo horizon Dave could just make out two dark shapes as they wheeled and turned. They looked for all the world like giant mosquitoes. Dave saw the missile pods light up a split second before the bowel-emptying shriek reached them. Before he was even thinking about reacting Frank was once more dragging his battered hide across the rocky desert floor. All three arrived behind the roadside sandbank just as the hyper-sonic rockets reached the remains of the burning bus.

If he hadn't been so personally involved in the whole sorry incident, Dave would have appreciated the ensuing explosion as an impressive, and no doubt ruinously expensive, piece of movie special effects. Particularly note-worthy was the way the entire section of VW caravanette launched sixty feet straight into the air, not to mention the way it returned to earth just metres from his spinning head.

Dave let out an insane high-pitched giggle that Frank was quick to recognize. The 'Khe Sanh Chuckle', as it had been known in his platoon back in 'Nam, was a sure sign of the imminent onset of a debilitating bout of pre-post-traumatic stress disorder, and wouldn't be tolerated in a unit he commanded. Frank set about slapping Dave across the face with more gusto than was strictly necessary.

'Time to bug out, Lash Larou. Their night-scopes will be maxed-out from the fires. This is our last chance to get away.'

Dave was about to ask where the hell were they going to *get away to*, in this pancake-flat featureless desert, when he saw the outflow pipe for the first time. It jutted from the roadside sandbank twenty feet from where they lay, discharging its festering cargo of sewage into a drainage ditch running parallel to the road. Frank had evidently seen it too because, while still lying on the ground, he set about hauling Dave and the tattered alien in the direction of its welcoming darkness.

The smell was not pleasant, but then neither was the concept of being used as target practice by the dark and sinister forces of the Military-Industrial-Entertainment Complex who were rapidly reorganizing behind them. With this sobering thought in mind, and a badly grazed hand clasped over his over-worked nose and mouth, Dave scrambled after Frank into the dark and beckoning hole.

21. It Came from the Desert

Billy-Bob and Jolene had been 'going steady' for three months. They were both seventeen and attendees of the Richard M. Nixon High School in the town of Meadowfield, California, tucked away in this, one of the more inhospitable parts of the Mojave desert. It possessed neither meadow nor field, just a dusty scorched plain stretching out in all directions as far as the eye could see – or rather, as far as the perimeter fence of the abandoned Strategic Air Command test range, where Uncle Sam had let off some of his fruitiest whoppers back in the days when both superpowers felt no shame in atmospheric release.

Billy-Bob was the school's star quarterback and held the All-State record for crushing beer cans on the side of his head. Jolene came from a slightly more sophisticated background. Her father was the town Chief of Police and he had hammered into her from an early age the importance of not letting boys get past 'first base'. This stringent doctrine had engendered in the young Jolene the two overriding pillars of her ankle-deep personality. Firstly, it had given her an undeniable air of sweet innocence that had seen her through those difficult early teenage years, when so many of her friends had found themselves being slipped a crippler beneath some sweating jock in the back of a rusting pick-up truck. Many said her face would be her fortune. Jolene's dewy-eyed innocence and shoulder-length blonde hair seemed certain to ensure she would be elected prom queen at the end of her final term. Secondly, and less happily for her mental health, it had fixed in her mind a bewildering association between baseball and sex. From an early age she had hung around Meadowfield's parks and sandlots, a faraway look of barely understood longing in her big watery blue eyes – the smell of a well-oiled catcher's mitt could send her weak at the knees. Billy-Bob might have been a star quarterback, but he also played a pretty mean short-stop for the 'Nixon High H-Bombs'.

Tonight, like so many other nights that summer, they were up on 'The Bluff' overlooking town in Billy's pride and joy – his pink '57 Chevy convertible. But tonight was going to be different from all those other nights of frustrated heavy petting and endless recitation of baseball statistics. Tonight Jolene felt certain she was about to give up a game-winning grand-slam home run – always assuming Billy-Bob could sort his bat out. From her point of view initial signs from the top of the mound were good.

'The Bluff', as it was known to the local teenagers socially well adjusted enough to be interested in such things, was not the most scenic of dating spots, but then Meadowfield was not the most scenic of desert towns. Since the end of the Cold War had closed the local Air Force base, much of the life had seeped out of the sleepy town. But this dust bowl had been on a slow downward spiral long before that fateful day. It was a far cry from the heady 1950s, when Meadowfield was renowned across the land as the closest settlement anywhere to an open-air nuclear test facility, a scant ten miles out across the glow-in-the-dark desert. There had been a brief flurry of interest back in the hey-day of Hollywood B-moviedom, when a string of low-budget producers had sought out the place for its quaint rural charm and uniquely shaped cacti. But once the real dangers of shooting in this part of the desert became apparent there had been a lot less enthusiasm for filming in such a realistic location. Authenticity was all very well and good, but at the risk of instant-onset leukaemia was it really worth it?

Meadowfield's foremost make-out spot reflected this sad decline. The derelict sewage plant that nestled into the sandy hillside behind the track where the young people parked might not have smelled as bad as it once had, but it didn't exactly add an air of ambience. At least it was good for scaring the younger kids with tales of deformed mutant space-monsters lurking in its uncharted depths, crawling out of its labyrinthine pipe system at the drop of a clapper-board.

But local history was the last thing on Billy-Bob's mind this star-crossed night. He was very much in lust, and at long last meant to chomp on Jolene's cherry, stone and all. For her part Jolene envisioned things developing in a slightly more romantic fashion, though compared to her date's testosterone-soaked fantasies a Hell's Angels' gang-bang would have looked like one of Barbara Cartland's finer moments. As if to signify this was indeed a special night they had the Bluff all to themselves. No one and nothing was going to interfere with the World Series of love that was about to erupt in their pants. As the warm desert breeze blew over the town and into their faces, they sat hand-in-hand and danced a coy verbal tango.

'Oh Billy-Bob,' sighed Jolene, gazing up at the evening sky. 'This is such a . . . special night. Did you see that shooting star? Just like one of Nolan Ryan's better fastballs.'

Billy-Bob said nothing for a moment, as ever faintly disturbed by Jolene's peculiar obsessions. Eventually he replied as best he was able. 'Mmmrrph grrrp UURRKK!'

Even for someone as famously inarticulate as Billy-Bob, Jolene felt this was just not trying, conversation-wise. If he thought caveman mumblings were going to loosen her rah-rah skirt and double 'A' trainer bra, he had another think coming. But when she turned to tell her over-optimistic suitor as much, she was surprised to see two dirty hands stretched across his mouth. 'Mmmmrrph!' he said, one more time, as one of the grubby hands reached for his car keys.

Instantaneously a nervous and strangely accented voice whispered in Jolene's ear. 'Look, I'm really sorry about this, but do you think you could be quiet for a moment, otherwise the sadistic nutter next to me might have to kill your friend. And that would just be a bit messy now, wouldn't it?'

Jolene was no more prepared for these surprise visitors than she was for this level of politeness from what she assumed to be a potential mugger. Her tinny butterfly brain struggled to make sense of these bewildering developments, then crashed flapping madly to the floor. It was only then that she noticed the smell. It was a peculiar aroma, a mixture of blood, sweat, raw sewage and the stink of something which had been a long time dead. Jolene decided she didn't like it.

Meanwhile Dave was not in any better spirits. His and Frank's plan had been a desperate one, but since it was the only one rattling around the box marked Plans, he'd taken it. They had emerged from the outflow pipe, along with their rotting grey companion, covered from head to foot in matter nearly as decomposed as the alien. Then they spotted the lone car, along with its two preoccupied young passengers. Frank's strategy was to blend a subtle mixture of stealth, surprise and the thinly-veiled threat of extreme violence to perpetrate a car-jacking. So far it was going smoothly. The fact that they had no weapons didn't troubled Dave for a second. He had no doubt that Frank could kill with his bare hands. Soon enough the pair sat in the rear seats of the brightly painted convertible, the alien propped up between them. Frank had the car keys, and their quaking hostages just where he wanted them. What to do next was the only problem on the horizon. Frank now said something which Dave was glad he had never heard before in his short and, as he was fast coming to realize, sheltered life.

'Right, dudes, get out of the car and get naked.'

It didn't take long. The teenagers were sufficiently terri-fied by the two visions (not to mention smells) of hell to co-operate with an almost embarrassing haste. The strange grey mutant their attackers had brought with them did nothing but amplify this feeling of mortal dread. Within minutes Jolene and Billy-Bob were stripped down to their underwear and trussed up back-to-back with tightly bound items of clothing. Dave had found a patchwork blanket in the trunk and kindly lain it on the ground for them to sit on.

Under different circumstances Billy-Bob might have considered this a successful end to the evening, that's if *both* he and his sweetheart hadn't been gagged and restrained, while a gang of deformed radiation-fiends made off wearing their clothes in his automotive pride and joy. Just what Jolene's daddy might say when he came out looking for them was anyone's guess, but Billy-Bob wasn't looking forward to finding out.

As they accelerated off into the darkening night Dave looked down at the ridiculous contraption they sat in, and at the ridiculous clothing he now wore. The young chap's letterman jacket, with its gaudy mushroom-cloud logo exploding across its back, was baggy round the shoulders but rather tight at the waist. But, Dave had to admit, Frank did look nicely at home in his new dress.

'Great,' Dave muttered. 'I always like to make my get-away from a crime scene in as inconspicuous a manner as possible.'

'Needs must,' mumbled Frank from the driving seat next to him, as he adjusted a shoulder strap as if he'd been doing it all his life. 'And our need is as must as most.'

The grey monstrosity in the back said nothing, it just stared up at the starry night sky, a bulging satchel grasped between its rigor-mortis-locked arms, as it dreamed its eternal dreams of home.

22. Treason

Maryland, USA

The dark and murky room was filled with the sort of dark and murky men who gave middle age a bad name. Not that the place was crowded. Just three individuals hovered amidst the dust-shrouded office furniture, their air of self-importance filling the space where their bellies finished. These were 'big' men in girth and big in ego, well used to ploughing their unstoppable furrows through the battlefield of international commerce. And they were each well used to winning, and not at all used to being kept waiting.

Patience did not come easily to any of the three. They circled each other like caged tigers, not meeting each other's eye, nor crossing each other's path, least some hideous fight develop. Boardrooms were only ever capable of holding one such individual – any more and blood would flow, to be splattered across oak-panelled walls like rusks in a nursery. With the patience of an unexploded bomb they awaited their host's arrival.

'Where the hell is he?' the largest cigar-smoking man muttered, taking a shot of his heroically sized bourbon. 'That little shit has finally gone too far. I've got better places to be than this.'

A slimmer man wearing glasses, though still amply well-fed, brushed off a dusty seat. 'He will have a good reason to call us here. We'd do well to listen carefully to what he has to say. He's not the only one who suspects all is not as it should be.'

His companions shot him suspicious glances, as if this was the last thing they'd expected to hear from one of their own. 'Thinking out of the box' was not well regarded in the company they kept. 'The Committee' was conservative with a capital CON, and had been known to kill to protect its reputation.

The third man was Japanese. He had once been a scrawny computer nerd, but in the course of building his billion-yen games conglomerate the business lunches had taken their toll. Uneasily he shifted his sumo-like frame. 'Dangerous talk for such a place and time. If not in exalted company, one would fear for one's honour. But wait, honourable Ronin approaches.'

A quiet 'ping' marked the elevator's arrival across the deserted lobby. Six piggy eyes fixed on its sliding doors. The cold mechanical brains behind each set realized too late that if this was a trap then their days were numbered, down to decimal places in fact. Without a sound the doors slid open, and a dark figure stepped out.

'Gentlemen, so good of you to come.' The new arrival glided over to the drinks cabinet, unwrapping himself from the folds of his big black trenchcoat as he did so. In his hand he held a small package. He moved with a quiet confidence, as if he knew his way around.

Cigar Man broke the uneasy silence. 'Why have you brought us here, Becker? A little melodramatic, wouldn't you say?'

The building had once been the administrative centre of one of the multitude of government intelligence agencies Becker oversaw as part of his legitimate 'day job'. With the winning of the Cold War it had been mothballed, along with its parent agency – a dusty monument to more lavishly funded times. But then Becker had plenty of other pieces on his invisible chessboard. The Dark Man's voice was stable, giving no hint of the turmoil he felt inside. Becker was well aware this might be his last throw of the dice.

'Colleagues, I have called you here this evening because

in my opinion your minds are the most open to what I have to say. As we all know, when the Committee is in session it can be dominated by its more . . . regal members.'

The three exchanged wary glances. Spectacle Man folded his arms defensively. 'I think we're all aware of your opinions on the wisdom of her policies. All of us were privy to the last Pine Gap Executive Session. Some would say you're dangerously close to paranoia, if not outright insubordination. Not the qualities one would wish for in an intelligence chief. Need I remind you that you are a tool of policy, not a full member charged with its forging?'

Becker shook his head and took a long drink. 'I am only an associate member, of that I am well aware. Certain of our hierarchy take great pleasure in reminding me of that fact at every opportunity. But this time the facts speak for themselves.'

'What facts?' It was Cigar Smoker who spoke up now. 'I read your last report. We're rational men – slander and hearsay cut no ice with us. You won't sway our minds with anything but the hardest proof.'

Becker looked him straight in the eye. Cigar Smoker looked away first, though not before a bead of sweat had broken out on his fat round face. 'You'll have your evidence in good time. But first let me ask you a few questions.'

As he rounded the desks to sit opposite the three, Becker's eyes flashed in the dim lamplight. 'What have the Visitors ever done for us? What breakthroughs have we garnered from their technology these past fifty-five years? Haven't you ever wondered at just how pitiful it is?'

Cigar Man sneered in a hideous manner, flashing a jaundiced smile of tombstone-yellowed teeth. 'Our corporate research facility has a thirty-tonne GM bunny in a basement bunker hutch. It's most cost-effective, we do all our cosmetics testing on different parts of its fur; keeps our lab overheads to a minimum. I don't know what it does to our competitors, but it scares the living shit out of me.'

Becker nodded his swimming head. 'Yes, and how much research have we needed to do ourselves to reach this point? An artificially growth-hormone-induced share, I have no doubt. Sure they're handy as a cover story for the cattle mutilations, but the Greys have taught us nothing new – apart perhaps from how to perform an inhuman square-dance. Check with your top lab people on your return.'

Sumo Man was eager to agree. 'Computer industry bear this out. Our researchers learn more from devices we develop to decode alien artefacts than we do from artefacts themselves. Most puzzling. Grey technology, how you say – *utter borrocks*.'

For a split second Becker had to suppress the horrific image of the 'Research Scientist' dancing along to an infuriating disco beat with the rest of his Village People chums, but thankfully it quickly subsided. The artist in question must have been one of the eager hopefuls who didn't make it past the last audition. Maybe the 'Red Indian' and 'Construction Worker' weren't so bad after all.

Spectacle Man was nodding slowly. 'I do believe you could be right, Becker. Even though aerospace technology has advanced in leaps and bounds, very little of this progress has come directly from the Greys. Most of what we've learned has been negative in nature, from our unsuccessful attempts to back-engineer their science. More puzzling still, they seem to have no knowledge of how it works themselves, almost as if . . .'

'As if they were planted on us,' Becker finished for him. 'Yes, we've come a long way, but haven't you ever stopped to wonder just how much further we should have come if we really *did* have access to advanced alien technology?

It's a great deal further than we have come, I can assure you now.'

The Spectacle Wearer removed his glasses, tiredly rubbing the bridge of his long nose. 'Which begs the question, just what are they doing here? Where's this leading?'

Sumo Man also looked concerned. 'You spoke of evidence, honourable Becker san?'

The Dark Man nodded, a wry smile etched across his pencil-thin lips. 'Gentlemen, walk this way.'

He led them through a set of imposing swing doors and down a long musty corridor. It was well that Becker had brought a flashlight, the building was as silent as a tomb. At last he brought them into a small auditorium, a slide projector set up before a broad white wall. Without a sound the Dark Man reached into his suit and produced a small package. Carefully he unwrapped the slides and slid them into the carousel. 'I'd advise you to take a seat,' was all he said as he powered up the projector.

'These shots were taken from a low earth orbiting satellite. The bird was flying over Windsor Castle, England, while the Chairman was busy hosting a garden party in the grounds. Arrangements must have been hasty, because the toilets were of the open-topped canvas-walled variety. The box you can see at the centre is a chemical commode.' Becker pointed out the series of stalls with a laser pen.

'This is fascinating,' the big man mumbled from behind his cigar, 'but if you'll pardon the expression – where's the beef?'

Becker clicked the next slide into place, a far more detailed close-up shot. 'I'm sure you recognize our redoubtable leader in the centre of the frame. I know it's not polite to photograph a lady whilst powdering her nose, but under the circumstances I felt justified in authorizing this appalling breach of etiquette.'

All three of his guests strained forward to get a better

look at the confused image. Deftly Becker twiddled with a small knob to bring the photo into crystal clear focus. A gasp went up in unison from the three men. A large cigar tumbled lazily to the floor. Its former owner was the first who felt able to speak. 'But she's got . . .'

Becker nodded. 'I know, the abdominal tentacles seem to be a feature of all their kind. Though in this case they seem to be far more extensive than any I've seen before, covering the entire lower half of her body. A true case of *anus horribilis*, I think you'll agree.'

The three corporate heads looked on thunderstruck. 'You mean . . . you've seen this sort of thing before?'

Becker nodded. 'The creature we knew as Kennedy was not quite so extensively tentacled, though its appendages more than made up in girth what they lacked in numbers. Strange, the rumours at the time said he was hung like a horse – in retrospect I think an octopus would be nearer the mark. Might be the only external difference between the males and females of their kind.'

Spectacle Wearer was visibly shaken. 'What in God's name does this mean? What sort of hellish perversion of a human being have we been taking orders from all this time?'

Becker's manner held no trace of triumphalism. 'It means, my friend, that what I've suspected for the past decade is all too true. The Committee has been subverted at its highest echelon by a cunning inhuman force. I always had my private doubts that our last Chairman simply fell off his yacht. But that's not all – I fear our policy to spread unreason and paranoia has been orchestrated to meet some agenda other than our own.'

Spectacle Man took a deep breath. 'If I remember correctly, just the point you tried to raise at Pine Gap?'

'That's right, before I was virtually bundled out the door by our worthy Chairman.'

Becker's accomplices exchanged long hard looks. The

Japanese executive finally broke the silence in a hushed tone. 'Can you tell us more, Becker?'

'I fear, gentlemen, that events are coming to a head. Their plan to generate irrationalism amongst the general public is accelerating apace. Cult activity is at an all-time high, so too are UFO sightings. There's something not right about this developing conflict in Asia – the Chairman wants a war in Urgistan for reasons I cannot fathom. Why it should be now I do not know, but a reckoning is fast approaching and we must be ready to play our hand. Everything I've discovered over the past thirty years has been recorded faithfully in one place.'

'And where is this record?' Cigar Man spoke as if in a waking daze, all of his overblown bluster deflated, seemingly becoming physically smaller before their eyes.

For the first time Becker's face was flushed. 'It's been temporarily . . . *mislaid*. But rest assured I'll be reacquiring it all too soon. For now there's more important issues you must know.'

Spectacle Man began taking notes as Becker carried on. 'Our leader has kept things from you, just as we keep things from the unwashed masses. They've lied about the usefulness of the Greys, they've lied about the true motives for their policy to spread apathy and paranoia. Most of all they've lied about this,' Becker gestured to the oversized inhuman image filling the wall before him. 'I have other satellite shots, of an unmapped South Sea atoll, which seems to have a worrying connection to this. But perhaps most disturbing of all I have my suspicions regarding a revolutionary consumer product they seem ready to launch. You will be briefed on my findings in good time.

'In short, gentlemen, the leadership of the Committee are a bunch of two-faced, multi-limbed, cheating sons of bitches. Much as you no doubt saw yourselves, except this time we're the victims. Doesn't feel too good, does it? We've been suckers far too long – it's time to yank up

Madame Chairman's flies and reach for the breath-freshener. We've swallowed her evil load far too long. Are you ready to spit it back in her face?'

There was a stunned silence from his audience, but Becker could tell he had them now – either that or he'd scared them half to death. Under the circumstances that might be no bad thing.

'What can we do to repair this situation?' Cigar Man spoke up for all three.

Becker rose to his feet. 'The Committee is lost to us forever. We have to right these wrongs alone. Gentlemen, the future of the human race rests in our hands. Now we have to put them to work.'

23. Deadly Toys

Marshall Swift sat in his palatial office overlooking the Thames. It was into the small hours and all his staff had gone home – for this fact he was almost insanely grateful.

In his lap lay a package from a very special client, a client he hadn't seen since she'd sat in his office and offered him the opportunity of a lifetime just a few short days ago. It had been delivered by a nervous courier earlier that morning, faceless behind a motorbike helmet much like the one Marshall's patron had herself worn. In fact, to say the parcel merely 'lay' in his lap was to do it a grave injustice. It seemed to throb and quiver under his every touch – as if, such was the potency of its contents, to pick it up, let alone open it, would be to sell his very soul. Marshall suspected it contained a video, either that or a bomb. Going by what little his visitor had told him it was difficult to judge which might be worse.

With shaking podgy fingers he broke open the seal and slipped his hand inside. Mercifully his first guess had been correct. The package contained a VHS cassette, but also an ominous hand-written letter. It was scrawled in a spidery disjointed script, on Buckingham Palace notepaper.

'Dear Mr Swift, I need not tell you this information comes to you in the strictest confidence. Any security breach on your part will be met with immediate death.'

Marshall didn't need to have it spelled out so boldly; he was well aware of the magnitude of what he was getting into. If he'd needed any confirmation of his darkest fears then this was it. The note filled him with foreboding, but also with a corrosive, jealous glee.

'Play the tape and much will be revealed.'

So he watched the video, and that's when things *really* started getting strange. Everything which had gone before seemed reasonable by comparison. The tape held a maddeningly vague presentation on the product his client wanted him to push – vague because precious few details were revealed. The pompous voiceover even stated no samples would be available until the main production run was complete – security considerations were cited. How was Marshall supposed to promote a product he's never even seen? Yet try he must– the stakes were way too high not to give it his best shot. Excitedly he reflected that this project would need the full weight of his organization behind it. He'd reassign his top creative teams in the morning. Even their current high-profile projects paled into insignificance next to these towering briefs.

Marshall's organization was becoming a victim of its own success. His services had been so much in demand of late, something was going to have to give. Was the war in Central Asia linked to what was going on? If what his visitor had told him was even half true then that conflict was small potatoes. Swiftsure PR itself would need all its decks cleared to help further the Committee's clandestine will. NATO could take its Euros and shove them up its multifaceted multinational behinds.

But even that might not be enough. This was a product that required a highly specialized set of skills to promote an industry niche which even Marshall's firm had been morally dubious about stooping into in the past. Loath as he was to admit it, he was going to need outside help. There weren't many independents left, but those few that were would be glad of the trade. Once he'd cautiously sounded them out he'd get permission from his clients to bring them onboard.

Reaching for his telephone, Marshall went about setting up an unprecedented meeting with the few competitors he had left. They'd be at home by now, but that was no bad thing. It was best this was not done through official channels.

24. Documentation

The building Frank pulled up outside wasn't just shabby, it made the other decrepit tenement blocks in this part of south-central LA look like the condominiums of the gods, topped off by RAFUPie[1] populated penthouse suites. Dave wouldn't have been surprised to hear a distant klaxon and for the whole festering pile to come crashing down – but such a mercy killing seemed too much to hope.

In the abandoned lot across the street a car was burning merrily. Although it was the middle of the day not a siren could be heard. The fire department did not come to this part of town without a police escort, and the police only came in armoured trucks. But if half of what Frank said was true, and Dave was beginning to fear that it just might be, at least one resident liked it perfectly well that way.

Everywhere Dave looked there was litter; wherever there was litter there was graffiti. Some of the litter had graffiti on it, some of the graffiti had litter on it. Not a spare inch was left uncovered. In many cases it seemed spray paint was all that was holding many of the walls together. Bleakly, Dave reflected that this was the sort of neighbourhood where even the rats carried mace.

'Wait here,' advised Frank as he exited the convertible and jogged across the pavement to a substantial metal door. Dave didn't need telling twice.

One block away a small group of scruffy youths was gathering on the street corner, eyeing the newcomers with uneasy suspicion. One gang member toting a car-jack was quite openly measuring up the Chevy's chrome wheels –

---

[1] Rich Armed and Fortified Urban Professionals, as distinct from the suburban-dwelling WIGC-BBS (We Inhabit Gated Communities, Bye Bye Scum).

cash-till dollar signs ringing up behind his wraparound shades, for all Dave knew.

Nervously he looked around to see where Frank had got to. The ex-commando was conducting a heated discussion through a small sliding hatch high up on the pock-marked metal door. Presently Frank returned, a sour expression on his weathered face. 'We're in luck, Hooch is in and will see us now.'

'Problems?'

'I had to sweet-talk his lady into letting us see him. Had to tell her we were onto something big. Too many people learning about our grey friend for my liking. There's an entrance round the back. Grab our shit, we're going in.'

Dave reached for the satchel and its priceless load, while Frank hurried around to the boot. A fast search of the vehicle during a pre-dawn road-stop had revealed a large sports holdall containing a muddy gridiron kit. This had been put to one side, ready for the moment they needed to move their dead companion unobserved – now that moment had arrived. Billy-Bob's dirty uniform was tossed to the gutter, making way for the ripening alien corpse. It was not a perfect fit. When Frank had finished, and after much crunching of fragile inhuman bones, two tattered grey feet protruded from the bulging zipper.

'It will have to do,' was all he said in answer to Dave's questioning gaze.

At a steady dog-trot they made their way along the rubbish-strewn sidewalk and turned into an even dirtier rubbish-strewn alley. Haste would get them noticed, but neither wanted to linger in the open for too long. This was no time to tempt a mugging.

Frank was counting doors to mark their progress when Dave stopped dead in his tracks. Frank carried on for a second, nearly bumping into the cause of Dave's change of pace. This proximity would prove significant later on.

The hulking figure that blocked their path had slipped from the shadows without a sound. On either flank two accomplices glided to meet him. Maybe their mothers would have found them pretty, but somehow Dave doubted it. 'Worldly wise' was about the nicest thing you could say about each face. The one at the front had a bad rendition of a spider's web tattooed across his features. In his hand he held the sort of machete which could have startled a mangrove swamp. Dave felt all the moisture in his mouth pack up and leave home.

'Watch it, grandpa,' said the new arrival, holding up a big hand before Frank. 'This is our turf and we want transit tax. Ante up, how much you got?'

Frank stood dumbfounded for a second, the large lumpy sports bag grasped tightly under his left arm. No one said anything about the feet sticking out from his armpit. Under the circumstances Dave considered this to be a small mercy.

Frank eyed the taxman with a strange mix of contempt and pity. 'Oh, we've got way more than you can cope with. Why don't you have some of this.' His free hand moved with blinding speed, forming a clenched fist as it did so.

The young ruffian never knew what hit him. If, much later on, he had been forced to guess, he would have said a heavy-duty pneumatic pile-driver had made contact with his face, though what this was doing at the end of Frank's arm was another matter. Much would be made that evening, in the sleazy bars and crack-houses around town, of how 'Spider' Harry had been jumped from all sides by the hippie freak's henchmen – though just how many would be a bone of contention starting more than one bar-room brawl. As the local hard-man collapsed to the floor, his face a bloody mess, his two friends beat a hasty retreat which would have done an Italian army proud. Dave didn't think he'd seen anything move so fast, with the possible exception of Frank's fist.

Frank stepped over the crumpled figure without so much as a second glance. 'You want to get that nose sorted out, sonny, looks too good for the rest of your face.'

A little further along they came to the door Frank was looking for. Calmly he beckoned Dave into the dingy archway. 'Look, man, are you cool about what we're here to do?'

Dave's head swam for a moment, then went under for the third and final time. This was one roller-coaster ride he had no desire to throw himself from, because at that precise moment he felt certain they were a long way above the ground. 'I'd feel a whole lot better if I knew just who this character is. Are you sure we can trust him?'

Frank lay a reassuring hand upon his shoulder. 'Have no fear, Dave, Hooch is one of us – a committed quartermaster in every revolutionary war on-going. He'll run guns for the Black Panthers as readily as the Klan, and can get his hands on everything and anything. This is your one stop shop for it all, from clean IDs to fertilizer truck-bombs.'

'Sounds like quite a guy. Another one of your psycho friends from Planet Crazy?'

'I've known Hooch quite a while. Think of him as a signalman on the underground railway of the night. His house is a way-station for fellow travellers and the dispossessed. If he were working for the Feds, their secret death camps would be a lot more crowded than they are by now. Let's go in.'

Frank banged heavily on the door's scarred surface. After the sliding of a great many bolts and deadlocks a small crack appeared and darkness seemed to flood out. Shortly Dave found himself standing inside a rotten-smelling corridor, while overhead a bare bulb failed to light the rubbish-piled corners. Their hostess looked them up and down with an unnerving cross-eyed stare. The skinny figure before them was female, it was hard to miss that fact. A dirty string-cupped bra sagged above her filthy day-glo hot-pants, which topped off long bruised legs ending in plastic high-heel shoes. A thick crust of make-up seemed to have skidded across her face, as if applied from a passing bus. Judging by the wanderings of her wall-eye it was impressive that she'd hit the mark at all. She looked as if she needed a bath, and smelled like she needed several in a row.

'Life's been treating you well, I see, Biancha,' said Frank merrily. 'Business must be good.'

'We get by.' Biancha didn't seem predisposed to chat, ushering them through another doorway into a small and smoky room. When the guests were inside she squeezed in behind them, slinking into a shadowy corner.

The big man behind the cluttered desk didn't rise to greet them, but his face lit up in good-natured recognition all the same. Hooch didn't exactly look the part of a professional revolutionary, his large gut barely contained within a faded sweat-stained shirt. His head was bald and sunburnt, like a sickly pink tomato. Between two chubby fingers he held a fat Cuban cigar – no doubt an added extra, tagged onto the last shipment from old friends down Havana way.

Hooch wiped a big greasy hand on his shirt and held it out to shake. 'Franky boy! Heard you had a spot of bother out back. Nothing that ruffled your feathers, I hope.'

Frank shook his hand as he shook his head. 'Just some juvenile high spirits is all. I gave them an unarmed combat lesson the old-fashioned way. Don't know what's become of this town, everyone seems armed to the teeth. Plain lazy if you ask me.'

Hooch nodded philosophically, as if they were chatting about a drop in grammar standards. 'Last word I had you was training those Michigan crazies on how to topple the Federal State. Get too hot for you up there?'

'Nothing I couldn't handle. But I've got some new heat all my own.'

With little sign of haste Hooch got down to business. 'So, what's this package you're so keen to offload? Been brainwashing kidnapped heiresses again? You know how it ended last time.'

Frank measured his co-conspirator beneath a steady gaze. Hooch had been a good man once, but in this game times changed with deadly speed. Frank's delay in answering was as imperceptible as it was slight. 'Final incontrovertible proof that the Government has access to crashed alien technology. The Cosmic Holy Grail that proves they've been lying to us all along.'

Hooch scoffed, small ringlets of smoke escaping from each nostril. 'Yeah, right. And Canadians only fuck reindeer if they can't catch their sisters. Pull the other one, Frank, it's got a belfry strapped to it.'

Frank said nothing, he simply reached for the bulging holdall he'd placed on the floor and hefted it onto the desk. Taking his time he propped it up and made a great show of dusting it down. Hooch watched avidly, an amused smirk smeared across his fat, cynical face. Carefully Frank undid the zipper and began to unfold its contents.

Moments later Hooch was staring spellbound into two bottomless black eyes. Imperceptibly the big man let out a measured breath. His own gaze never left the slumping corpse before him, as his voice held a deathless hush. 'Is this the real thing?'

Frank nodded. 'Pretty, ain't he? Kinda like seeing your first ever AK burst take down a target.'

Hooch nodded slowly, as if he were scared his head might come off if he moved too fast. Nervously he ran a shaky hand over his cue-ball scalp and licked his big bloated lips. After a moment of breathless awe his piggy eyes narrowed and he leant in for a closer look.

'Er . . . Franky baby. Should its arm be hanging off like

that – and aren't those bullet-holes peppering its skin? Not exactly in pristine condition, is it?'

Frank shifted uneasily in his chair. 'It hasn't been a picnic getting it this far, I can tell you. Some folks seem keen to stop us in our tracks, isn't that right, Dave?'

Dave was startled back to life in the shadowy corner where he'd been watching the exchange. 'That's putting it mildly,' he stammered. 'Someone in authority wants this guy back very badly indeed. Bad enough to convince me it's the real thing.'

It was only now that Dave had a chance to study the creature since his first tense meeting with Frank. At this rate there was going to be very little left before Kate got to see it. A few scraps of grey skin and oddly shaped bone was hardly going to convince the most hardened sceptic as to the significance of their find. Hooch seemed to have reached much the same conclusion. Already he was making out a list in a tattered notebook.

'I can see you'll need some help patching it up. A little embalming fluid wouldn't go amiss. But what's the long-term plan? Where are you thinking to hole up? Gonna have to be mighty careful how you splash this to the press. Washington and the UN have got the TV networks sewn up.'

Frank's voice stayed level. 'We're taking it to London. We're gonna break the story over there.'

Hooch looked at Frank dumbfounded, his fat cigar dripping ash across his fatter belly. 'London! Have you lost your senses? What about customs?'

Frank leaned forward. 'Think about it, Hooch. If you can just get us out of the country we'll have it made. The powers of oppression don't bind so tight over there. Davey's got media contacts too.'

Dave nodded as if he was having a fit. On careful consideration he thought he just might be – a long drawn out one, starting the first moment he met Frank.

Hooch seemed to consider this for a minute. Then he tore the page from the notebook and started making a fresh list. 'We just might be able to make this work. Not gonna be easy, but then the battles worth winning are never a stroll in the park. How tall are you, son?' he asked, turning to Dave.

'5'8, 5'9. Depends if I've had any bits blown off that week.'

Hooch made a note. 'Frank, old buddy, this is a major achievement. I'm proud of you.' The big man moved around the desk with surprising grace, crushing Frank in a bone-powdering hug. 'Those bastards in power won't have a pot to piss in by the time this gets out. Come with me, I've got just what you need.'

25. Terminal Termination Blues

Late that afternoon one of Hooch's small fleet of nondescript motor vehicles slipped from his underground garage and made its way through the shattered neighbourhood. This was not an area where you stopped if you could help it. Car-jackings had been known to go through multiple generations – each set of perpetrators becoming the victims themselves until, by some mystic 'wheel-of-life' process, the original owners stood a slim chance of getting their transport back.

Not that this was much of a possibility on this occasion. Potential car-jackers worth their salt would have been quick to realize they were biting off more than they could chew. The vehicle in question was an armour-plated 'people-mover' wearing 'clean' licence-plates fresh on that day. Hooch's hench-girl Biancha was at the wheel; in the rear sat three passengers, one of whom was strapped into an imposing, bulky wheelchair.

When they came out of Hooch's garage Dave wasn't surprised to see the convertible they'd arrived in stripped to its steel shell and mounted on concrete blocks. It looked like a cloud of mechanical locusts had passed it by, stripping off anything of value and leaving just a smoking husk.

But as the local dangers were left behind Dave's troubled thoughts turned to those that lay ahead. Hooch's final words still rang in his ears. 'Just show them these,' he'd said, handing them the freshly forged diplomatic passports. 'You can get any shit through customs if you're one of their international club of parasites. Our boys take shit in and out of their countries, we allow their guys to do the same – no questions asked. *Quid pro quo*, except you wouldn't want your back scratching with some of the con-

see or hear. I'll catch up later. There's something I've gotta take care of first.'

Before Dave could protest Frank was gone, slipping into the milling crowd like a puma into a swaying jungle. Dave cast an apprehensive glance in the direction his companion was heading. A hundred yards through the swarming traffic he could just make out a colourfully painted yellow van. Every few minutes a snatch of infuriatingly off-key jingle would reach his pounding ears. With a sickening nausea Dave realized that nearby an unsuspecting ice-cream vendor was merrily plying his innocent trade – he was well aware of Frank's prejudice in the frozen snack department, but surely this innocuous retailer couldn't be the target of his companion's attentions at a moment like this? But he'd learnt it was best not to analyse too deeply when Frank was involved – it did more damage to your head than to Frank's perverted world-view. Events around him had a habit of taking their own violent course that no sane human had a hope of controlling. Grimly Dave followed his comrade's instructions and marched on head-down. He didn't have to wait long for his composure to be put to the test.

After a distant shout of '*take cover*', the initial explosion reverberated around the buildings, its echoes shaking the glasswork in a teeth-loosening manner. From all corners of the crowded car park the sounds of a thousand car alarms rose up as if in tribute. Dave turned in the direction of the ice-cream van, all too certain of what he might see. A tower of flame was rising up from the vehicle, its erstwhile customers scattering to the four winds. Gradually, a series of secondary explosions ripped through what was left of its gasoline tanks. Dave could do little but look on open mouthed in awe.

Presently Frank loped back from an unexpected angle, his face an unreadable mask and a small smudge of soot bellow one steely eye. Dave shot him a look of stunned disbelief, as he tried to keep his voice under control. 'What the hell was that for?'

Frank gave a dismissive shrug. 'If they were watching they're going to be preoccupied for a while. Lockable petrol caps might be something they want to invest in for the future. Military Intel is an evolutionary process. I've just helped cleanse the gene-pool.'

Dave shook his weary head. 'And what if it wasn't *one of them*? What if that was an innocent ice-cream van you just blew up?'

Frank gripped the back of the wheelchair and started pushing. 'Ain't no such thing as an *innocent ice-cream van* – you should know that by now. Let's move it out, partner.'

There was no real answer to Frank's logic. To the sound of a riot of wailing sirens the pair calmly pushed their companion into the cavernous terminal building, the modern-day cathedral of glass and steel arching above them to a dizzy height. Hooch's information seemed to be as accurate as Dave prayed were his forgery skills. Straight ahead, the Omega Airlines check-in desks were busy with early arrivals. The trio's tickets and reservations were real enough; it was everything else about them that was phoney. Shortly their documents would be put to the test.

When they showed their reservations to the dentally-privileged airline staff, along with their diplomatic papers, they were hurried through to a VIP lounge away from the common herd. 'Vladimir Ivanov' in the chair was given a few curious glances, but nothing that put his disguise to the test. It seemed rank still held its privileges, even if you were only a Lithuanian chargé d'affaires travelling economy class.

'So far, so good,' muttered Dave as they made their way to passport control. Hooch had assured them that normal security checks were a mere formality for diplomatic travellers, but Dave could not really bring himself to believe it would be so easy. Even tightly gripping the wheelchair's moulded handles, Dave's white hands were visibly shaking. What neither of them knew was that shortly after 'Biancha' had make her radio transmission the staff manning the diplomatic-section security checkpoint had been replaced by a completely new shift of workers. The uniforms looked brand new but some of them were ill-fitting, as if being worn for the first time.

Shortly Dave and Frank stood before one of these apprentice officials, not that you would have known to look at him; his sleeve bore the stripes of a sergeant in the Federal Customs Service. Before them in the queue a Middle Eastern gentleman wearing dark glasses and a drooping moustache had been waved through carrying a large bulky package. The immigration officer had not given him a second glance, let alone asked to see what was inside the bag. It could have been ticking for all Dave knew. Metal detectors were nowhere to be seen, just a handful of tired-looking diplomats sipping drinks and reading papers beyond the token barrier that blocked their path.

'Next,' came the tired murmur from the bored official. Dave pushed the wheelchair up to the kiosk and stopped, certain he was about to be deafened by clanging alarms. From the corner of his eye he noticed that one of 'Vladimir's' scrawny arms had fallen into his lap, exposing a battered three-fingered hand.

'Passport?' said the guard, not taking his eyes from the pad of forms in front of him. Dave handed his over, along with 'Vlad's' fictitious documents. Despite the officer's evident disinterest Dave felt the need for an explanation.

'He very sick,' he stuttered, his best Lithuanian accent in no way improved by the rising note of panic in his voice. 'Must get home to see babushka before he . . . you know . . . croaks it.'

The guard didn't look up to see the cutting motion Dave made with a finger across his neck. 'Whatever you say, sir,' he said, already reaching for Frank's papers. Frank gave Dave the very slightest shake of the head as he bundled him out of the way and took his turn at the desk. Dave needn't have worried. Within seconds they were through and wheeling their silent charge along the deserted departure lounge, its wayward arm safely tucked back inside.

Despite their success Frank did not look a happy man. 'What's up? We're through, aren't we?'

Frank's troubled face barely moved as his eyes scanned the spacious room. 'I don't like it. Something's up. This is getting too easy by half.'

Dave found it hard to share his friend's suspicions. 'Maybe Hooch is as good as you said he is. I've seen nothing to suggest anyone's twigged us since we got here. If you ask me, taking out that van was pushing our luck, but then I've come to accept your idiosyncrasies. Hooch expects such things from you. Everyone has their little idiosyncrasies. Maybe Hooch's is that he doesn't screw up.'

'Don't count your chickens, Dave. You talk too much when you're crapping your pants. Sit down and shut up before I shut you up for good.'

Suitably chastised, Dave did as he was told. When their flight was announced they both got up as calmly as they were able, removed 'Vladimir's' handbrake and made their way to the waiting plane.

26. Indigestion

Aero-Dynamics Inc. Research Facility, Mojave Desert, California, USA

Three days after meeting Becker in the deserted office complex, Spectacle Wearing Man was preparing to pilot his executive jet out of the country. He'd done just as the Dark Man had told him – the components the Security Chief had requested had been couriered to the drop-point earlier that day. What Becker wanted with that much plutonium didn't bear thinking about too closely, but Spectacle Man thought he could guess. Now it was time for those implicated to make their getaway, before it was too late.

Even though he was head of one of the richest and most influential corporations in the country, able to bend the ear of Air Force Generals and Presidents alike, the Spectacle Wearer held no illusions as to his organization's ability to protect him when this storm broke. Best to lie low somewhere distant, for the months or years it took to blow over. With this in mind he was performing the final pre-flight inspection of his plane, before taking off into the setting sun. As an experienced pilot he knew better than to cut corners where his own safety was concerned. With even more care than when he scrutinized a balance sheet, he wiggled the flaps and ran his gloved hand along the wing's slender aileron cord.

On the flight-ramp nearby some of Uncle Sam's most secret toys glistened in the desert sun, all black paint and sharp edges. Technicians scurried over them preparing them for their coming baptism of fire. Urgistan would offer an ideal stage for their talents, no doubt leading to AeDyn obtaining an even bigger slice of the ever-dwindling military procurement pie. It was all Spectacle Man could do to suppress a chuckle. Under different circumstances he'd be relishing the coming deluge of TNT and napalm.

With a wistful smile he turned his attention back to his own more humble hardware. Progressing in the familiar ritual around the nose, he checked the pitots for unwanted obstructions. The port side wing was next, where the control surfaces were rigorously inspected. Everything was spick and span, as befitted the CEO's private plane. He stared down at the undercarriage with satisfaction. He'd be well out of this mess soon enough. Just the engines left to go.

It was then that he first noticed the low electrical whirring noise. For no good reason the hairs on the back of his neck stood on end. It was an unfamiliar sound, almost as if a starter-motor was about to engage some larger engine. Spectacle Man had good reason not to recognize the strangely unnerving hum – not once before had he been this close to a spooling-up jet engine at start-up. Strapped into the cockpit was his preferred position at moments like this.

The gaping-mouthed CEO experienced one second of pure ball-tightening terror, during which his greed-filled life really did flash before his eyes, before he was sucked in along with the rushing air, to become intimately acquainted with the barely subsonic turbine blades. He didn't stay there long. One short second later, he was deposited at the back of the spluttering engine. He had made his journey by plane in record time. It just wasn't the one he'd anticipated.

*   *   *

Tinsendo Corporate HQ, Nagoya, Japan

Far across the slumbering Pacific Sumo Man stepped into the express elevator on the top floor of his firm's towering head office complex. It was one of the tallest skyscrapers in Japan, a monument in concrete and steel to Tinsendo's domination of the world computer-games market. Sumo Man had just attended a high-level meeting with his company's top executives, where the main topic of debate had been the level of gratuitous violence to pursue in their follow-up to the classic *Virtua Zombie Street Kick Boxer VI*.

The meeting had gone well. All agreed that as their target audience increased in age, and attention spans shortened to barely measurable levels, the amount of blood and guts in *VII* would have to go through the roof. Mention had been made of a new device pioneered by R&D which could squirt a mixture of blood and sweat at the player from a screen attachment at appropriate moments in the game – all were keen to see this worthy feature included. On this happy note the hungry corporate samurai had decided to adjourn to the excellent sushi bar across the street.

As the sweating overweight executives packed into the sumptuous elevator, their brains fixed on the inviting dishes of tuna-friendly dolphin and 'twice-shredded blowfish stew' they would soon tuck into, few objected to the breathless crush – after all it was virtually a national custom on these overpopulated isles.

It was an express lift, designed to transit the sixty floors between the penthouse boardroom suite and street level in the fastest possible time, but none of the tightly-packed directors expected to reach the ground quite as quickly as they did. Subsequent investigation would reveal a previously undiscovered bug in the building's master computer to be at fault. Under certain conditions the '+' sign in the lift control software seemed to transform itself into a '–', thus accelerating the high-powered device in the wrong direction, i.e. downwards, when gravity alone would have more than sufficed.

* * *

Nomsento Corp. Arable Production Test Centre, Kansas, USA

Meanwhile food was more than just 'on the mind' of Becker's last remaining co-conspirator. The Cigar Smoking Man was the living embodiment of a life insurance salesman's worst nightmare. He was a keen meat-eater and over the years his one-track diet had built up a veritable herd of decaying Texas longhorn in his straining colon. He liked his meat not so much rare as extinct. But it wasn't this cancerous mass that killed him, neither was it another terrifying visit to the thirty tonne vivisection bunny housed deep under the innocuous looking research establishment.

As he stood out near the open-air barbecue on that bright and sunny morning, Cigar Man prepared to sample the latest end-product of his corporation's genetic research programme. With a gusto he normally reserved for profit and loss accounts he set about the bloody T-bone steak as if his life depended on it.

But it wasn't the lab's worth of bovine growth hormone which had been pumped into the cow over its short and painful life which killed him, but rather the 20cc of pure strychnine that somehow had found its way into the juicy steak minutes before consumption. The poison hit his bloodstream like an out-of-control express train, exploding his straining heart as if it were an over-ripe tomato in a vacuum tube. Cigar Man was dead before his flabby carcass hit the dusty ground.

27. Semtex Boogie Woogie

Becker hurried through the deserted underground car park, his dark face a mask of gathering gloom. The rows of silent vehicles stretched out on either side, mute sentries to his thunderous passage. The Dark Man was a tornado waiting to happen.

Events were not exactly proceeding to plan.

Without breaking stride Becker marvelled at his own talent for understatement. If things went any 'less well' he'd end up dead, or worse still a laughing stock, harried from the Committee like some gangling imbecile. His three confidants had been removed from the game, scrubbed as easily as the amateurs that they no doubt were, and that *bothered* him. His enemies were dangerously close to breaking cover; that could only mean one thing. For the time being at least he still judged himself to be safe. Any attempt on his life would signify to the others that his fears were well-founded – his opponent could not risk that until she was a good deal stronger, ready to begin her deadly end game in fact. He feared that day was coming soon. All told, things were careering worryingly out of control.

Granted, he was still able to track the two irresponsible sneak thieves who had stolen his coveted file, but his continued inability to stop them was proving more than a passing annoyance – it was a slight to his professional pride, and Becker was a very proud man indeed. The alien carcass itself was no longer his paramount concern. What he wanted back, with all his heart, was that manuscript. He'd been a fool but MJ13 was the last copy he had left. How it had fallen into the three-fingered hands of the renegade Greys he had no idea – somehow they had stolen it from his personal suite at the Nevada site. The worrying possibility that they had been taking it to their real masters was too fanciful to entertain. What mattered now was that it was retrieved. The idiots who had it no doubt barely recognized its significance. It was enough to make him fume.

The Dark Man's anger was sharply cut across by another barely recognized emotion. It was an infuriating experience, like trying to place a song from a single line of lyric. Becker halted in his tracks as he savoured this strange new sensation. It was almost enough to bring a thin smile to his bloodless lips. Could it be ... *fear* that he was experiencing, for the first and only?

Of course he was well used to the over-arching mortal dread of his seemingly hopeless struggle – it was the daily catalyst that drove him on. But that was a slumbering, long-term 'strategic' fear. It was a small-scale 'tactical' fear which now pulled him up short, the sort that he'd never known before.

Slowly, as if entirely of their own accord, the short hairs on the back of his neck stood on end. Warily Becker's eyes scanned the rows of empty vehicles, all senses straining to catch the faintest clue. Barely a hundred paces ahead his own armour-plated Mercedes awaited; any ambush would be targeted there. Nothing moved.

Then it hit him. Someone was watching him from behind.

Becker became so convinced of this fact that it was all he could do not to spin round to confront his hidden pursuer. A cold certainty told him that was not a good idea.

With the sort of low cunning that had been known to cause foxes to lead packs of hounds along busy railway tracks, Becker made a great show of checking all of his jacket pockets for some mislaid personal item. Dejectedly he turned on his heel, as if resigned at having to retrace his steps – the retrieval of this trivial belonging the only thing on his mind. It was lucky for him that he did so when he did.

As his calm eyes scanned the dark basement to his rear quarter the 20 lb of high explosive strapped beneath his car detonated like a subterranean sun. The garage was filled with a fiery inferno of flame and twisted metal, as the vehicles next to his own were transformed into deadly burning shrapnel. The expanding blast-wave reached out a huge hot hand and pushed Becker off his feet. When he hit the concrete he lay pancake flat, his instincts taking over.

When the fire had subsided Becker gazed out from beneath his sheltering trenchcoat, his eyes wide with shock and horror. Hazily the smell of burning hair reached round from the back of his scalp. It wasn't how close he'd come to death that had him worried, it was what this open assault on his authority signified. With a grim deter- mination he ground together his mighty jaws. This whole affair was getting personal.

28. Airborne

The languid bulk of the big 747 climbed to its cruising altitude and set a course directly into the rising sun. Inside the pressurized cabin Dave stared across at Frank and barely fought down the blitzkrieg panic attack he felt sweeping his system. All of his gung-ho machismo had evaporated amidst the rarefied atmosphere, to be replaced by the sort of sick dread which threatened to make him physically ill. The younger man's bewilderment was poorly hidden on his lined and tired face, as dejectedly he gulped at his third drink. Just what was he letting himself in for by throwing in his lot with this madman? They'd been more than lucky thus far; sooner or later that luck was bound to run out.

The pair had already committed enough crimes to get them put away for a very long time indeed. Theft of government property, falsifying documents, transporting a dangerous biological hazard across international frontiers, and to cap it all a pathological attack on an ice-cream van because they can't be trusted. Which made Dave an accessory to murder. He was well aware that the United States took a very dim view of foreign nationals committing acts of sabotage on its soil, even if it did only extend to the destruction of dairy-based snack vendors. 'Green cards' were hard enough to come by when you pursued a legitimate career, let alone when your passport read 'International Terrorist'. It was ironic really – Dave had always looked down his nose at the raving conspiracy freak fraternity and scoffed at their paranoid ramblings. But now, with mounting shame and disbelief, he realized he was helping to swell their burgeoning ranks.

All it took was a quick glance at the thing strapped to

the wheelchair beside him to remind Dave it was not all part of some horrible cheese-induced dream. He knew he couldn't be imagining the bizarrely disguised creature, not unless his nostrils were capable of hallucinating just as severely as were his bulging eyeballs.

Somewhere along the way since leaving Hooch's establishment the industrial-strength deodorants sprayed on the creature seemed to have worn off. Clearly the stewardesses had noticed this too. They'd made a great fuss of tending to 'the poor man' and strapped his chair down in the specially allocated spot. Dave had found it necessary to tell them their charge was 'very tired' and just wanted to sleep on the return journey to his homeland, in order to make them ease back the unwanted attention.

On Dave's other shoulder Frank was engrossed in the journal that they'd come to refer to simply as 'the file'. Frank seemed to spend every spare moment poring over the great tome in the hope of discovering some fundamental inner truth.

For a second Dave watched his companion's eyes race over the pages of tightly packed script. Every so often Frank would let out a softly incredulous snort, as he obtained final confirmation of some long-held theory or belief. It made Dave decidedly nervous, even though his facility to experience that emotion had been seriously numbed over those past few terrible days. By the time they reached Heathrow there were going to be few secrets left unknown to Frank. How this would affect his already unstable behaviour Dave shuddered to think.

Next to him Frank let out an excited whimper. 'Dave, old buddy, you've gotta read this section.' With that he shuffled the armour-plated folder into his companion's lap. 'Take it from the top, home-boy. I reckon this should make a few things clear.'

At first it was almost embarrassingly easy. The more outlandish the hoaxes we orchestrated, the more they were lapped up. Partly this was due to the fact that the Visitors' *real* behaviour was undeniably bizarre. The populace had got used to accepting the prevailing myths – all we needed to do was make our deceptions fit the existing pattern to have them widely believed.

By stifling serious scientific debate, while encouraging and financing the lunatic fringe, we were able to discredit any serious attempts to understand the phenomena. To the public-at-large the saucers quickly became the preserve of the crazies. This gave us the time and space to regroup, while our high-profile agents muddied the waters with occult mysticism and new-age twaddle. Our friends in Hollywood were particularly helpful in this respect.

But that was before I began to suspect the full implications of what we were being ordered to do. When I began to understand the inherent danger in the policy to encourage 'conspiracy theories' I quickly showed the evidence to my masters on the Committee.

There are none so deaf as those that do not wish to hear. If what I was saying was true we had been unwittingly playing into the hands of our opponents – for some, this was too much to bear.

It was my conclusion that the Greys were not in fact an advanced master race, reconnoitring our planet as part of some mass contact scenario, but the pawns of a darker force operating to a far subtler inhuman agenda. You only have to study their behaviour for this hypothesis to become apparent.

What 'cosmic master race' worth its dilythium-crystals would travel millions of light-years to Earth, only to manifest itself to a group of hippies, form a crop circle, scare the ass off some inbred hill-farmers, then crash in an out-of-the-way spot? It didn't make sense, and doesn't to this day. All the evidence from the Greys we've managed to capture backs this conclusion. They show no sign of understanding the engineering behind their 'ships' and are more interested in studying their Earth-bound counterparts than in teaching our scientists anything new. All the subjects I've met showed about as much sign of being the vanguard of a super-intelligent alien race as most of our 'democratic leaders' show of actually running their countries.

But my unmistakable conclusions fell on deaf ears. In replicating and exaggerating their behaviour, for what we thought of as our own advancement, we were doing nothing but furthering their own mysterious ends.

It's a common mistake of the small-minded cranks who pursue us, to assume that the Black Government holds to one coherent view on all matters. This assumption runs against human nature, especially the human nature of the sort of power-rich headstrong people who make up the 300. Trying to get them to agree on policy is no easy task, and one that gave my predecessors an endless headache. I have it on good authority that WW2 started as an intramural squabble between special interest groups.

It was the hereditary leader of one of the 'great families' who was forever giving me the most trouble. If she hadn't have been so wealthy, and her covert power so all embracing, I would have gladly had the frosty bitch taken out.

'One finds it hard to believe,' she'd say with the infuriating arrogance that only comes with long-running family power, *'that One's financial contributions cannot be better spent than to arrive at such a hair-brained conclusion. Claiming that "their behaviour is designed to lead us down the path of irrationalism" is not acceptable, Becker. One is not amused.'* Much later, when she

was able to 'whack' the one high-profile agent I was able to infiltrate into her family, I knew she'd meant business all along.

This realization was in part what prompted me to write this memoir. As you read this, no doubt an insignificant prole cast adrift amidst the great unwashed mass of humanity, you must be told that the future of our race rests in your own trembling, slippery hands. If I can go some small way to convince you of the danger, then my treachery might not be in vain.

'Jesus,' said Dave. 'If this guy was any more full of himself he'd be committing a criminal offence.'

'Yeah,' agreed Frank, 'but what if he's on the money? He seems to know what he's talking about. His theory fits all the facts.'

Dave snorted. 'Oh come off it! His theory fits all the facts he chooses to include. The bookshelves are full of nutters claiming to be insiders in the black world of government conspiracy. My magazine gets letters every month from "former operatives" and "ex-high ranking civil servants". Most of them are sad attention-seekers. If the military-industrial complex leaked like they said it did we'd have all drowned long ago.'

Frank looked unfazed. 'Perhaps, but how many of those guys' manuscripts got discovered clasped to the chest of that thing sitting next to you?'

Dave had to concede his friend might have a point.

29. A Line in the Snow

Urgistan, Western Himalayas

Once the decision had been made to punish the wayward rogue state the international community was quickly mobilized. The White House had been first to parrot its scripted lines, but then the Committee ran it almost as a legitimate front for its more shady dealings behind the scenes – just as it had done since the first day Thomas Jefferson rolled up a trouser leg and chanted 'All hail the All Seeing Eye. Which way's east?' Becker's absence was noted but not considered in any way out of the ordinary. Such was the scope of his official brief, he was often gone for weeks at a time.

There were, however, other players on the world stage who had to be levered into action, or inaction, as the case may be. Cooperation from India and China was a priority. Fortunately political ideology might sound good from a little red book, but few let it get in the way of business concerns. Like a well-oiled machine the Black Government slid into gear, and did what it did best – manipulate.

Each element of the gathering coalition followed their own narrow self-interests, but in doing so furthered the Committee's clandestine ends. The skill of the unseen puppeteers was to make the myopic national leaders see where these self-interests lay. More often than not the prancing fools obliged, their empty-headed duplicity tattooed across their grinning faces for all who knew to see. Greed and ambition were constants amongst the political classes. The Committee's techniques for playing on them spanned cultures and centuries.

The story of the evil General Noroco's ruthless ascent

to power was soon known from Baltimore to Bangalore. Twenty-four-hour cable news took some beating for hammering a point home. 'Napalm Noroco' was clearly a man of savage ambition, prepared to stop at nothing in his quest for regional power. He had no qualms venting his hatred on his beleaguered people. It was said on occasion he even locked them up if they broke the law. In the same breath the name of 'Colonel Yajik' was whispered in hushed tones. This much-feared hard man was identified as Noroco's chief lieutenant, a hated enforcer amongst the downtrodden mountain clans and commander of the crack 5th Mobile Division – a unit so skilled at camouflage that no trace of it could yet be found. Adorning a thousand news specials, snappy animated graphics illustrated the pair's merciless, bloody rise.

In time-honoured fashion the inevitable evidence was uncovered of a plot to acquire nuclear secrets, Noroco no doubt intending to hold the world to ransom. It was clear to all right-thinking people that these dangerous maniacs had to be stopped, and stop them the UN would.

The coalition had right on its side. Coalitions always did. No less an august body than the United Nations said so. Resolution after resolution was passed condemning Noroco's brutal regime. Soon enough the killer mandate was ratified, demanding Noroco disband his mighty army and halt the persecution of Urgistan's racial minorities – or face the consequences. The thirty-six-hour deadline would give him little chance to comply. But the big players didn't have it all their own way. Some of those smaller tin-pot voting members were getting harder to cajole – some demanded even bigger favours. It was fortunate the international banks were on side – they might not give a damn, but dams were another matter entirely.

From a range of twelve thousand miles, in bunkers far beneath Washington and Colorado Springs, brave Air Force Generals planned the campaign in meticulous detail.

Their aim was as simple as the aim of their bomb crews was accurate – to reinstate the rule of law, as well as deplete munitions stocks, which had shown an unfortunate tendency to creep up of late. Nothing runs down a smart-bomb mountain quite like a short sharp air war. Across the arms-dealing world fresh catalogues were printed off to accommodate the new winter collections, as zebra-grey camouflage fabrics made sudden appearances on the catwalks of Paris and Milan.

Urgistan had been branded a Banana Republic. It had no oil, it commanded no trade routes and it had no hope of facing down the world's might. It was a country the term 'backwater' could have been coined for. But all the same, in newsrooms across the globe, atlases were dusted down and computer graphics firms commissioned. Urgistan's fifteen minutes of fame were destined to arrive with a 'bang', and some blinding phosphorous flashes.

30. Communications

Becker was back at his mountain retreat high in the West Virginian hills. He wouldn't normally have returned to such an insecure locale, but there were things he simply *had* to do. For one he needed his tool-box to assemble the very special components the Spectacle Wearing Man had shipped to him at such great cost. He was relying on the fact that his assassins would assume he was dead, and wouldn't have the cabin watched. This was born more from hope than realism.

The Dark Man wasted no time in re-establishing the encrypted data-link to all his field operatives on the other side of the Atlantic. Some of the messages left in his mail box showed a disquieting long-term trend. But there were more important immediate problems with which to contend – Freemantle and his reformed snatch-squad were proving more difficult to raise than the dead. That frock-wearing faggot in Rome no doubt had a clearer line to the Big Guy upstairs.

'Come again, Cadmium Vole, I'm not reading you clearly.' Becker fought to overcome his frustration as he spoke into the slender microphone attached to his laptop computer. The Zyclon 6000 might have been the very latest in covert military communications systems, but it had looked a lot more impressive in the salesman's brochure – shinier too.

As so often with things electronic, when you brought it home and took it out of the box, discarding the blizzard of polystyrene nuggets, the real thing was a bit of a let down. The bikini-clad girl the manufacturers had used to model it in the arms catalogue must have been a midget, thought Becker, as he fiddled with a plastic frequency dial.

If this was 'state of the art' then it was more of a mouldy cow sawn in half than the enigmatic smile on the 'Mona Lisa'.

Three-thousand miles away, in the spartan back bedroom of a well-disguised safe-house not far from Heathrow Airport, Captain Cyrus Freemantle (aka Cadmium Vole for the duration of this mission) was coming to much the same conclusion. He couldn't help but wonder if they would have been better off with two plastic cups and a very long piece of string.

'It's the ionospheric radio interference again, sir,' he said slowly into his own dangerously snappable microphone. 'It's making communication rather difficult.'

Back in the Appalachian wilderness Becker watched forlornly as a meaningless series of *s and #s were printed out across the top of his screen. The Zyclon 6000 was reportedly able to translate voice input into text in real time, but at the moment it just looked like it was writing the script to a dirty movie. It seemed that the highly advanced encryption system, designed to make an intercepted signal indecipherable to anyone without the correct code, was in this case turning the already garbled message into complete gibberish. Behind the scenes the machine's MovieOS™ operating system was not helping matters either, adding its own random stream of characters for dramatic effect.

Even across the appalling satellite link Becker's anger was clear to discern. 'I know WWWOOOHHH causing it you FFFFRRRTTTTY. Try using the other PPPPRRRMMM.'

Freemantle fiddled at a few knobs for appearance's sake, but knew deep down the task was beyond him. The Black Operations unit he headed had lost its best communications technician back in the blood-soaked Nevada desert.

Becker spoke very slowly and clearly into his pickup.

'Listen carefully, this is very important. I won't repeat it again. You must make the snatch as cleanly as possible. It is imperative that you DON'T draw attention to yourselves. The kidnappers should be arriving on the three o'clock shuttle. Call me back if you don't understand any of this message. Signing off now.'

Over at his end the only phrases intelligible to Freemantle were *'imperative'*, *'recover'* and *'draw attention to yourselves'*. After the details of the flight the message trailed off into an ear-splitting series of click and whistles. The 'End of Message' sign-off came as a blessed relief. Based on what he knew about the 'merchandise' they were charged to recover, Freemantle's imagination found it all too easy to fill in the blanks.

Once he'd shut down the system and marched through to the shabby lounge which served as his men's ready-room, Freemantle's voice held no hint of any lingering doubt. 'Saddle up, troops, looks like the bad guys are rolling into town.'

31. Satan's Little Helpers

London, UK

They say there exists honour among thieves. Who 'they' are is a matter for debate – most obvious candidates being the thieves themselves. No matter how little respect you have for yourself or your peers, every community needs a lower rung to step on – some lower order of scum to tell itself it's superior to. This rule applies even to those cursed misfits employed in the advertising business.

Among admen there is a moral hierarchy of sorts. Just as armed robbers self-righteously beat up paedophiles in jail, so Marshall Swift looked down on the sad collection of reprobates he'd gathered before him, in this dingy smoke-filled chamber, with a disgust bordering on contempt. It was midnight in the world above, though you wouldn't have known that inside the strategy war-room deep beneath the open-plan splendour of Swiftsure Towers. Marshall's audience were lost in shadow – in more ways than one.

The man himself stood at the head of a large oval table, weighed down with croissants and Pierre bottles. By his side was a bulky projection carousel – a remote control balanced casually in each hand. His guests were fanned out around him, all eyes curious yet guarded in a uniquely vigilant way. He'd obtained special permission to talk to them; his clients were the sort of people who liked to be kept in touch.

You wouldn't have thought his visitors were human filth to look at them. They were immaculately groomed and well dressed to a man. And that's exactly what they all were – there was enough testosterone in this room to spark a small-scale war, and to keep it going long enough for the French to sell arms to every side. That wasn't to say Marshall's guests were at all Neanderthal – all present had high IQs, and had been educated in the best universities tuition fees could buy. Yet there was a terrible darkness in every soul, due in part to the pact each had made with his own personal devil. They were the lowest of the low, the sickest of the sick, the writhing tapeworm feeding off mankind's juicy innards. These were admen who made commercials aimed at children.

Marshall cleared his throat. His guests needn't know of the Committee's entire plan, he just wanted their help to make one part of the scheme click. And with these evil geniuses on side that shouldn't be a problem.

'Gentlemen. I've called you here this evening, to this unprecedented meeting, because last week an unprecedented client came to me with an unprecedented product. Vast though Swiftsure PR has become,' there were a few begrudging snorts of derision at this point, 'the fact remains this brief lies outside our normal scope of operations. That's why I invited you here – to offer you, the elite specialists in your field, the chance to climb on board and help me row this baby home. We're not talking about the new Coca-Flakes account, you understand. This deal involves enchiladas of the biggest and juiciest kind.'

Now at least he had their curiosity sparked if nothing else. Marshall gestured with the projector's remote to the whiteboard behind him. 'Allow me, if you will, to cut you an oven-fresh slice of future pie.' The machine whirred into life, and the first slide clacked into place.

At this point, in this obsessively informal industry, it was traditional to include a shot of the speaker propping up his skis while smiling for the camera, and to make some quip about 'last year's holiday snaps getting mixed up' – then the audience would titter feebly and the presentation would begin. The absence of this harmless if annoying custom served only to underline this meeting's gravitas. The first slide held nothing but a giant question-mark.

'Colleagues, let me ask you a question. Time and time again which demographic group proves most susceptible to our skills? Which segment of society shows itself most easily swayed by our fast talking and slick presentation?'

'If you don't know the answer to that, then we're wasting our time.' It was one of Marshall's most bitter rivals who spoke up now. Over long years of competition Boardman had seen his own agency ground into the dust by Swiftsure PR. 'Otherwise why would you have called *us* here?'

Marshall demurred in mock respect. 'Of course you're right, you know the answer better than most. The perfect audience for what we do – I speak of course about the naïve young. But let's not get hooked up on mere chronological age; huge swathes of society remain immature for much longer these days, living at home with parents in an indefinite adolescence.'

Marshall snapped up a fresh slide which showed revenue from toys sales spiralling up and up. As sophistication and complexity increased, so did price. And despite the vagaries of demographic bumps the market wasn't getting any smaller. As many adults bought toys for themselves these days as for the kids. They were the ideal consumer item, hoovering up the mushrooming levels of disposable income in a bulging fungus-friendly bag – a truly booming sector, without a natural upper limit.

'Leisure products represent our perfect market – any decent adman's recurring wet dream. You guys sat around this table represent the perfect creative unit, one that I will forge behind a perfectly crafted campaign. We can build a monument to advertising's highest ideals – one that couldn't have been bettered if Elvis had recently had time to endorse a whole warehouse worth of merchandise.

There's only one ingredient that we're missing – so trivial to the purity of what we do, yet so crucial to our holy cause. My client has it – the perfect pre-teen product.'

An expectant silence of terrific weight came clanging down. Marshall clicked the next slide into place.

The image filling the wall was hazy and indistinct, interference lines betraying the fact it had been captured from a VCR. It seemed to show a multi-coloured fluffy creature, all bulging puppy-dog eyes and wayward limbs. It looked for all the world like something a Canadian fur trader might merrily club to death – just with more than the usual number of legs. This vision of cloying loveliness was the most horrific thing many in the room had ever seen, yet it somehow managed to be amongst the most compellingly attractive. Already many present were hypnotized by those bottomless, disquietingly alien, bush-baby eyes – though they seemed black pits opening into an eternity amidst the frigid uncaring stars.

'Gentlemen, meet Poke-It-On – the cute collectable cuddly-toy with a difference. The distinction being, it thinks for itself. Never before have such wonders of microelectronics, artificial intelligence and bio-engineering come together in an aspirational young person's product. Come next Christmas the kiddies and fan-boys will be going bonkers over these little fellas.'

A handful of blank and cynical faces remained around the room. It was left to Boardman to voice this minority's misgivings. 'It not exactly . . . the most original concept I've ever seen. This sort of beast has been flogged to death for years.'

Marshall's zeal kicked in like a turbine. 'Not one like this, there hasn't. It's the collectable semi-intelligent companion that's also a fashion statement – every one unique. You can splay its legs and push it on your forehead like a hat! Hence the name – you "poke it on". When everyone is wearing one we'll all stand out from the crowd. It's gonna be a winner! These babies will all but leap off the shelves to snare potential customers.'

Boardman's eyes were as dead as his smile. 'I don't see why. We've seen it all before.'

Their host ground his teeth in frustration. 'Look, Poke-It-Ons are virtually self-aware. They've got more brains than your average cat or dog, and don't take months to house-train. I can show you footage of them in action that will blow your mind.'

'How's it done? They don't even look synthetic to me.'

Marshall took a deep breath. 'Look, I'm not a man of science . . . It's done through some sort of genetically manipulated gubbins inside the thing. It's a cyborg, in fact – part animal, part machine. You'd almost believe they were alive to see them move.'

'I'll believe that when I see it.' Boardman folded his arms.

'OK, perhaps you will.'

Nodding smugly, as if he'd planned it all along, Marshall lifted the second remote control and pointed it at the projector. Whirring mechanically, a video machine sprang to life, to play its pre-cued tape. The recording Marshall had watched two nights before was projected onto the screen. He didn't watch it again; he'd studied it countless times in the days in between. Instead Marshall watched his visitors' eyes as they grew and grew like saucers. When all had seen the first batch of Poke-It-Ons in action, jaws were retrieved from the carpet and eyeballs were popped back into heads.

Marshall knew that he had them. 'I'm told these critters are already huge in Japan,' he triumphantly declared.

There remained just one obstinate dissenter. Boardman wasn't so easily convinced. 'Can we see some sales figures – market demographics and the like? I was over there last week and I didn't see anything of the kind.'

Marshall looked ready to resort to violence, as a fervent

passion burst across his face. 'Details, details! If you knew how significant these things are going to be to the entire human race, you wouldn't let mere details get in the way. We've just got to concentrate on selling them here and now. What's that factor you chaps are always prattling on about?'

Boardman seemed to have developed a sudden interest in his nails. 'The "nag factor" we call it. If you can spark that then you've got it made. No matter how poor, most parents will give in to their brat's pestering in the end. After all, there's always high-interest credit.'

Marshall was pulled up short in his tracks. Even for a hard-bitten pirate-captain of industry such as him – complete with the obligatory eye-patch, peg-leg and stuffed parrot to boot – this was a shocking admission to have so starkly delivered. He had children himself – he never saw them, admittedly, but he knew they existed, the same way most people suspected God was there. The thought that their young minds were manipulated by sick perverts like Boardman each time they turned on the TV in their rooms made him want to run home to protect them. Boardman's entire professional life was dedicated to making the lives of other parents, other human beings, harder than they needed to be – often the poorest and least able to pay for the vapid dreams he pushed. In these days of saturation marketing almost everyone was exposed to the same multimedia campaigns. Aspirational advertising knew no bounds of nationality or credit-rating. And of these facts Boardman seemed inordinately proud.

The visitor seemed to read Marshall's thoughts, and rose to meet the challenge. 'Don't look at me like that. We help motivate the proles to earn a living and bring home the dough. Where would we be if people weren't constantly driven to want the best? We'd be living in a social dark age, that's where.'

Marshall sighed and rubbed his eyes. It was hard to

escape the conclusion that the world would have been a better place if Boardman had been strangled at birth.

'As a theory of what drives human endeavour you've got to admit that's pretty flimsy.' Marshall never thought he'd hear such words from his own mouth, but his guest's bare-faced admission had him riled. It was with difficulty that he struggled to regain control. 'Perhaps we shouldn't get immersed in ethical theory – let's focus on the job at hand.'

Now there was something on which they could all agree. Everyone in that crypt-like room had been making a speciality of that particular manoeuvre their entire working lives. All except one, that is. Boardman's spotty assistant Kevin had only been with him for six months. In that time he was yet to develop the crusty armour-plated exoskeleton necessary to get ahead in advertising, or even to survive. Currently he had a query he felt duty-bound to raise.

'Those kids in that recording, the ones with the product wedged on their heads, they looked . . . well they looked vacant. Didn't seem *right* somehow to me.'

Marshall looked at him as if noticing a nasty stain for the first time. 'That was the light of blissful rapture shining in their young eyes. Are you so cynical you've forgotten what it looks like?'

There circulated a round of approving titters, as Kevin lowered his head in shame. Boardman glared at his quivering underling, but he himself had one more point he wanted to raise.

'Can you get us some samples? We have to know what we're going to sell.'

Marshall coughed uncomfortably, but had worked out this answer in advance. 'That's all part of the uniqueness of this brief. This merchandise is surrounded by the tightest security. Until the first shipment arrives on these shores there'll be no leaks to dilute growing demand. The first anyone sees of them, they'll be jumping off the shelves.'

'No prototypes or pre-production models?'

Their host shook his head sternly. 'Absolutely none at all.'

Boardman looked surprised, but nodded. 'I like that – be mean to keep 'em keen. It's worked in the past.'

'That's right,' urged Marshall. 'That way when they do hit the stores the public will strip them bare. You don't maximize sales by flooding the market too soon.'

'So when do we get to see the product?'

Marshall's grin spread from ear to ear. 'My contact informs me that all those involved in the campaign will be invited to a VIP unveiling at the top-secret production facility in the Far East just days before the launch. It should be quite a show. As long as we lay the groundwork for the Poke-It-On's success we all stand to profit greatly from this deal. The retainer alone reads like a small country's GDP. We all get a slice of the pie – there's plenty of business to go around.'

When a satisfied confirmatory titter welled up from his guests their buoyant host knew he had then hooked. Marshall rolled his sleeves up and got down to work.

'Right! Let's get some cappuccino and sun-dried tomato focaccia bread delivered. No one leaves this room till we've nailed this baby down. And I *do* mean to the floor.'

*   *   *

In the small hours of the next morning, in the front seat of Boardman's Jag, Kevin was still strangely troubled by what he'd seen.

'There's something not *right* about this, boss, something not *right* at all.'

'Cut the moaning, you whining brat. In this game you never look a gift commission in the mouth – especially one with its lily-white thighs spread wide and a come-roger-me-senseless smile splashed across its face. I doubt if even Marshall knows what he's onto. It's almost our duty to rip him off.'

Ahead of them at a deserted intersection the traffic lights inexplicably went straight from green to red. Boardman swore bitterly and slammed on the brakes. There was no one here to notice, but you could never be too sure; his licence already had more endorsements than a washed-up actor's voice-over career.

As they skidded to a halt Kevin saw the street was not completely empty. On the kerb two lanes away sat a lone and shivering figure. Trade looked less than roaring for this squeegee windshield-cleaner. It must have been very cold and lonely at this ungodly hour – he was wearing a full-face balaclava. No sooner had the car screeched to a halt than he jumped the metal railings and began jogging purposefully over, a heavy bucket swinging in his hand.

Before he had arrived Boardman wound down his window with a snarl. 'It's fine as it is, chum, thank you very much. Now fuck off before I call the pigs.'

Rude perhaps, but Kevin had heard far worse from his arrogant boss. Nevertheless he couldn't help but feel the stranger's reaction to be somewhat excessive. The newcomer reached inside his swaying bucket and, instead of a dripping sponge, produced something very different indeed. Boardman didn't see the long barrel of the silencer until it was far too late.

Two shots rang out on the deserted West London street. Soon the interior of Boardman's Jag was spottier even than Kevin's face. The echoes had barely subsided before the squeegee merchant was gone.

32. Reception Committee

Heathrow, UK

Dave and Frank stood before the final hurdle separating them from their freedom: the passport check-in desk and on to the baggage carousels beyond. This would be yet another test of Dave's frayed nerves, but as Frank was so fond of saying, they'd demolish that swaying rope-bridge when they came to it. Now it stood before them, and it was a long drop down to the raging torrent beneath.

Dave's rational half could see there were no more gun-toting British Transport police on duty than on any other day, it just seemed that way to him. How 'Vlad' felt about it, propped up in his electrified wheelchair and reeking of air-freshener and Omega Airlines travel wipes, was anyone's guess, but if the inhuman expression on his glazed black eyes was anything to go by he was way past caring. In several places the bandages had begun to fray, giving tantalizing glimpses of the grey-green flesh beneath.

Like almost everyone else, no matter from which tin-pot banana republic, Dave held his own nation's security forces in far higher regard than any evidence warranted. Johnny Foreigner might be easily deceived, but the good old British Customs and Excise were bound to see through their flimsy lies. It was almost with a perverse pride that Dave looked forward to capture.

'So you're the guys smuggling the decomposing alien into the country? Step this way for a thoroughly unpleasant internal examination.'

Beside him Frank was a picture of professionalism. He had no good reason to believe they were destined to get away with this stunt, but then there had been no good reason to believe they'd get anything like this far. Worrying about it now was going to do precisely zero good. As they took another step towards the mundane passport counter, Frank's head tilted towards his perspiring companion.

'Easy there, ol' fella. No reason to figure they've rumbled us yet.'

Dave could barely bring himself to speak, such was his terror. The sane and sensible part of his mind was telling him, in a loud persistent voice, that the best he could hope for was to spend a very long time at Her Majesty's pleasure, hopefully not simultaneously at the pleasure of a fat, bald, heavy-metal-loving cellmate with a fungal nail infection. At worst he would be propping up a motorway flyover before you could say 'Enemy of the State'. Whichever way it turned out, his social life was heading for an all-time low.

Despite the way panic-filled minutes seemed to stretch into agonizing hours, all too suddenly it was their turn at the counter. Dave had a vague sense of Frank stepping up first and proffering his fake passport, sure that any second they were to be cut down in a hail of gunfire. But once the bored official took a cursory glance at his phoney diplomatic papers, Dave's companion was ushered through without a fuss.

Now it was his own turn. With ice-cold hands he pushed 'Vlad' into position and applied the handbrake. Nothing he'd ever been through had prepared him for a moment like this – not even the time he'd plucked up the courage to ask Kate for a dance at the third-form disco. His feet were two blocks of lead, his tongue a beached and bloated whale. With the sort of gulp that an anaconda could have used to swallow a small deer, Dave stepped forward.

'Passport, sir?' The official's voice held no emotion at all.

'Nnnnmmm . . . Noooo aliens to declare today, thank you,' came Dave's more than garbled reply, as he threw the officer his documents.

The passport official looked at him steadily for a heart-stopping second. 'What was that you said, sir?'

With an effort of will Dave got his haywire tongue back under control. 'What I mean to say was . . . we have no Eileens to declare.' He pointed at his companion, 'He Vlad, me Constantine. He very sick . . . er, Comrade.' *Nice subtle recovery*, the calm part of Dave told the rest of him, as he winced inwardly.

The tired bureaucrat had met enough nutters in his time to spot one several miles off. This idiot was evidently several children's TV presenters short of a drugs bust.[1] Lithuanian 'care in the community' obviously extended to employment in their diplomatic service. Still, his English was very good considering he was little more than Broadmoor fodder – no doubt a Slavic serial killer waiting to happen. The officer's shift was over in ten minutes; he had no intention of getting to know this bumbling fool any better than he needed to. Besides, those rubber gloves didn't half make his fingers smell. With a twitch of his eye he handed Dave's papers back.

'Green channel on the right, sir. I just check passports here.'

And that was all it took. Twenty yards further on Dave and 'Vlad' joined Frank at the baggage carousel, as the other passengers began the ritual scramble for their luggage. For these three weary travellers there were no such worries – they carried all their baggage with them, much of it piled on 'Vlad's' bruised and battered lap.

'Nice move, 007,' was all Frank could bring himself to say. 'I can see I've taught you well. Walk this way and try not to open your fat fucking mouth.'

---

[1] This is a customs official's idea of a joke.

Within minutes they were through the exit, proceeding along the roped-off walkway that led to the crowded terminal. Dave was not the most worldly-wise of travellers, there were Venezuelan Hermit Shrews with more air miles than him, but even he sensed all was not well as soon as they entered the frenetic chamber. The concourse was no doubt as busy as it ever was, but even that did not explain the strange air of unreality that hung over the teeming crowds. Dave cast a questioning glance at Frank, and fought back rising panic when he saw his accomplice had sensed it too.

'Keep walking and play it cool,' the former commando mumbled, as he led them along with the stream of trolley-pushing travellers just landed from their own flights.

Above the general background murmur and subdued flight announcements, Dave could make out a strangely discordant troop of pipes and bells. For some reason their formless nonsense tune set his teeth on edge in a way impossible to describe. Banishing the sound from his head, he forced himself to think happy thoughts.

Dave hadn't asked Kate to meet them at the airport, he had wanted to reveal his career-blossoming find under more considered circumstances. But as he gazed at the ranks of strangers on the other side of the barrier, half-heartedly holding up name cards and licence plates, he would have done anything to have seen a friendly face. As it was, all he had was Frank and his focused stare to keep him warm.

Just as they were nearing the end of the barriered section, within easy credit card range of the ubiquitous airport shops,[1] Dave began to hope against hope that he could

---

[1] Despite what airport designers might like to think, this is not a common train of thought: *'I've just stepped off a plane. I know what I need – an overpriced pair of socks, and a pair of earrings you could more economically buy wrapped up in a Christmas cracker. Now where can I purchase such things?'*

finally relax. 'Holy shit, I think we've made it,' he muttered to Frank, an adolescent quaver in his voice.

For no obvious reason Frank's face became as black as thunder, as if attempting to remember some slippery yet crucial fact.

It was then that their attackers made the hit.

Dave floundered for three seconds as he tried to work out what was going on, then floundered for several more when he realized the task was beyond him. The morning catch, when cast upon the concrete floor at Billingsgate fish market, often took events more in its stride. Under the circumstances Dave had good reason to look confused.

The small party was jumped simultaneously from two sides by two quite different sets of assailants. From the right came a group of smartly dressed young men, their dark glasses and black leather gloves the only items of clothing at odds with their otherwise immaculate appearance. It looked for all the world as if, tired at last of pointing off into the middle distance and chuckling soullessly to themselves, members of the military wing of the Male Catalogue Model's Liberation Army had decided to spring from the page and finally kick some butt.

A big gloved hand landed heavily on Dave's shoulder. Its owner had an American accent. 'This is where we repossess our property, sir.'

In desperation Dave looked round for guidance from Frank, but the ex-soldier was nowhere to be seen. Then he saw the second group of attackers – and things really went off the deep end. His new American friend seemed more than a trifle alarmed by this development too.

Dave had heard of the Temple of Planet Love. Who hadn't? But this knowledge in no way prepared him for the sight of a platoon of the freaks in full flood. Casting aside collection tins and brightly painted tambourines, they streamed over the barrier like an orange tide, barging travellers from their path as if they were leaves in a storm.

Too late Dave realized he and Vlad were their intended targets. Desperation coursing through his veins, he crumbled in a heap to the floor and did his level best to protect them both. 'Don't hit me! Spare my face!'

Meanwhile, his hand still clamped on Dave's shoulder, Captain Cyrus Freemantle was quicker to react. He saw that his carefully timed ambush was itself under attack and adjusted his meticulously laid plans accordingly.

'Kick shit out of the hippie freaks!' he screamed to his men, as he began leading by example. The first pair of saffron-clad cultists went down beneath his scything forearm like corn before a reaper.

Forgotten for the moment at the feet of the escalating mêlée, Dave crawled for cover up against Vlad's electric wheelchair. Above him the fight was getting dirty. The orange-clad cultists danced around their more conventionally trained foes, lashing out with bewildering flurries of jump-kicks and karate chops. Completely unnecessarily, no doubt born of pure frustration at their inability to pin down their opponents, one of Freemantle's men landed a thundering left hook on Vlad's delicate skull. Dave could just make out the sound of disintegrating alien bones above the clamour of battle, and the approach of distant sirens.

At this point he knew that if there was going to be anything left of Vlad by the end of the trip he was going to have to extricate him from this madhouse as fast as possible. But where had Frank got to? With a level of bravery he in no way felt, Dave got to his feet – after first ducking a cultist's wayward head-kick. It was then that he spotted his companion.

He had prised off a long section of steel-tubed barrier, and with a blood-curdling battle-cry was now charging into the fight with it jammed under his arm like a battering ram. Four of the combatants went down beneath his relentless onslaught, sweeping up others in their wake like some belligerent human snowball. Frank paused only when he reached Dave's position.

'Get him out of here!' he yelled, pushing Dave back into the still-occupied wheelchair. Heroically and with obvious relish, Frank set about covering his partner's escape.

Ever since Hooch had provided them with the electrically powered contraption, Dave and Frank had been taking turns pushing Vlad around – based largely on the correct assumption that he was in no fit state to operate it himself. What their resourceful underworld contact had failed to point out was that unless they manually disengaged the complex gearing system, when pushing against the motor they were in fact charging its already powerful batteries. And this machine was more than adequately provided for in this department – it was a Cheetah 2000, a sleekly designed sports model intended to give wheelchair-basketball players all the zip they would ever need.

When Dave pushed forward on the stubby control column all this pent-up energy was released in the twinkling of a punch-blackened eye. At a velocity Evel Knievel would have been proud of the shuddering chair set off apace, rearing up in a fearsome wheelie before it had gone ten yards. With a terrified scream Dave was pinned back on Vlad's battered carcass by the raw force of acceleration! The crowd of onlookers parted like the Red Sea and Dave ploughed through them uncontrollably.

For a second all the protagonists stared in amazement along the path cut through the teeming crowd. For a heartbeat all was still. Then the head cultist got back to business by landing a shuddering uppercut on Freemantle's gaping jaw. That was the moment any carefully laid military plans sailed out the window. Freemantle's men and the cultists set about each other with reckless abandon, all thought of missions and objectives cast aside. When the airport police finally arrived, complete with tear-gas and baying hounds, they found it near impossible to prise the warring factions apart.

While the fight continued Dave and Vlad were experiencing the ride of their lives. Possibly Vlad had been on journeys that raised more hairs from his bald head, but then less than a week ago he had crewed an ion-drive UFO as it crashed into a remote desert hillside. Experiences like that tended to take quite a lot of living up to. Nevertheless at the moment Dave would have taken his chances with a plummeting flying saucer, compared to this.

The fickle machine seemed to take on a life all its own. Dave jerked the useless joystick this way and that, but on the highly polished floor the steering had little effect. On his left a Bureau de Change flashed by at frightening pace. To their right a mobile fudge-seller barely got his hand-cart out of the way in time.

Then Dave saw it, burning panic welling up in his throat and threatening to overcome him. Approaching at literally breakneck speed, a towering advertising hoarding blocked their path. 'Omega Airlines – the last airline you'll ever need' read the caption in bright letters that would stay with Dave forever. There was room to pass beneath, but could he get his head down before decapitation?

Still perched on top Vlad and the chair, he somehow managed to limbo beneath the wooden barrier. Inches behind his head Vlad was not so lucky. In a shower of splintering chipboard he left an alien skull-sized hole in the bottom of the shuddering board.

But the drama was not over yet. Still accelerating, they hit a partially loaded baggage car, its tailgate lowered to aid cargo stacking. The obstacle served as a makeshift ramp, launching them over the rows of cowering tourists taking cover beneath their seats. The wheelchair sailed through the air majestically for a strangely peaceful second, before crashing back to earth with a bone-shuddering impact.

Still their charge continued. Excitedly a group of Japanese tourists recorded their passing for posterity with a battery of flashing cameras. Somewhere nearby a small child cheered.

Dave did his best to steer for the spacious sliding doorway that fronted the terminal's glass-fronted façade, swaying the chair from side to side like a demented gondolier. But try as he might their course took them inexorably towards the imposing curtain-wall, sixty feet to one side of the rapidly evacuating doorway. It wouldn't be pretty, but it would at least bring their nightmare ride to a conclusion, one way or another.

Yards short of the life-threatening barrier Dave's white-knuckled hands finally found the handbrake. Closing his eyes he tugged it with all his might.

The wheelchair stopped instantly. Dave and Vlad didn't.

They were catapulted forward like a couple of mannequins. Dave opened his eyes, only to close them again very quickly indeed. Moments later he trampolined off the bulging safety-glass, rebounding backwards to near enough where he'd parted company with the chair.

Vlad's ballistic properties were subtly different. During the course of his long hot journey his pallid papery skin had split in several different places. Here and there major internal organs bulged just beneath his tacky bandages, threatening to become major external organs at a moment's notice. His advanced stage of decomposition, coupled with an atmosphere he was never meant to know, had not done his personal hygiene any favours. With a sickeningly loud '*splat*' he impacted on the perfectly smooth glass and stuck there, limpet-like – his four twisted limbs flayed outwards by the sheer force of the collision.

From the spot where Dave's battered body skidded to a halt, he gazed up through two barely focused eyes. From the corner of his mouth his swollen tongue lolled, dribbling a puddle of blood-specked spittle onto the hard floor. The last image he saw before losing consciousness was the wet squelch of amniotic fluid that Vlad had left as, his weight finally overcoming suction, he slid slowly down the cold glass wall.

Seconds later Frank was by his side. 'Wake up, Dave, we don't have time to fool around.' The ex-commando had retrieved the chair and now hoisted Dave into it. Working quickly he grabbed Vlad by the scruff of the neck and deposited him in Dave's lap. Without so much as a glance over his shoulder Frank legged it through the nearby automatic doors, and into the teeming traffic beyond.

33. Reunions

Kate sensed something was wrong as soon as she put her key in the front door. It was no one specific thing, just the sure knowledge that her home and place of refuge had been compromised.

A more retiring soul would have backed off there and then, retracing their steps to the underground to run for their life, or taken a trip to the nearest police station to see if one of their good apples could make her an appointment that week. But neither of these options were available to her, for reasons she was not keen to share. Steeling her nerves she opened the front door and stepped into the dark room.

She didn't have to search long to find evidence of her visitors. One of them was slouched casually in an armchair opposite the door, clipping his toenails with her kitchen scissors and drinking a diet coke. Kate was about to ask who the hell he thought he was when she caught sight of Dave. Her oldest friend was lying on her couch, a damp flannel draped across his forehead and a low moan rising from his lips.

'What the fuck is going on?' she asked, for once feeling her choice of language to be entirely justified.

The man lounging on her armchair rose with casual grace. 'Hi babe, you must be Kate? Heard a lot about you from wavy Davey over there.'

Several choice replies sprung to mind, none exactly suitable ways her mum would have considered to greet a guest. Kate studied this overly-familiar house-breaker. He was of no discernible age, the lines on his weather-worn face at odds with the sharp freshness in his glinting eyes. An unruly mass of frizzy grey hair was held back by a sweat-stained bandanna. He wore what might once have been a white cotton vest, above a pair of ludicrously creased and stained suit trousers. Every inch of his parchment-brown skin was covered by tattoos or old scars, in some places both. He was perhaps the most wizened individual she had ever seen, but animated by the sort of youthful vigour that wore you out to look at him.

'Sorry to have to drop in unannounced, but in one of his rare lucid moments Davey told me you were expecting us.'

Kate's grip on reality wavered for a second. 'Yes, he emailed that he was coming back. And that he would have . . . company.'

Frank's eyes narrowed infinitesimally. Hurriedly Kate broke away from their unnerving spell. 'What the hell have you done to him?' She glided over to Dave's side, where he seemed to be reliving a particularly unpleasant dream.

With a small yelp he woke. Forlornly he tried to sit up. 'Kate, it's in the bedroom, you gotta see it.'

She lay a comforting hand on a bruised shoulder. 'Easy there, old fella. Looks like you've been in the wars. See what happens when I'm not around to take care of you?'

Frank joined her at Dave's side. 'Your pal's a real hero. I couldn't have got it through without him. If they ever get round to handing out medals for this op, Davey will be first in line.'

Kate glared up at Frank. 'How did you manage to get in?'

Frank cast a wry glance over his shoulder to the still open window. 'Let's just say home security isn't all it should be these days. You could do with some professional advice.'

'Thanks for the tip.' To her annoyance Kate found herself studying the corded muscles of his forearm. 'Now, is someone going to tell me what's going on?'

Dave pulled himself upright with a wince. 'It's easier if we let you see for yourself. We put Vlad in your bedroom to get him out of the way.'

Before Kate could ask who Vlad was, she found herself standing at her bedroom door flanked by her two companions. The curtains were drawn, it was dark inside, but that didn't stop the waves of pungent aroma radiating out like the after-shocks of an earthquake. For a second she thought she might collapse. Frank grasped the top of her arm to steady her. Kate tried not to notice the warmth of his iron grip. As her eyes grew accustomed to the dark she made out the inhuman form slumped in the dented wheelchair. Two huge lifeless eyes stared back at her from the gloom. For a while her mouth moved but no sound came out, until finally her straining larynx stuttered into gear.

'My God,' she muttered, 'it's one hell of a mess. What did you do for the poor thing to end up looking like that?'

Dave sounded hurt. 'OK, so he sustained a little "transit damage". We weren't exactly travelling first class. Not a warm lemon towel in sight the entire trip.'

The 'transit damage' Dave referred to was quite extensive. Most of the bandages that had constituted Hooch's disguise were long gone. In their absence the creature's tattered skin was all too visible. It would take more than a lab full of Parisian beauty-technicians to restore its youthful complexion. In several places sharp fragments of bone jutted from the bruised flesh. If he hadn't been long dead Vlad would never have walked again, such was the damage to one knobbly knee.

'Look, Kate, I know this is hard to believe, but when Frank recovered it from the downed UFO he found something else too – something that could turn out to be even more important.'

Kate held very still, displaying no outward signs of emotion as Dave went on. 'The creature seemed to have stolen a document, a handbook for the running of the "Black Government" that controls our elected officials. The true power behind just about every throne.'

Kate put on her best incredulous expression. 'And you have this file too, I presume?'

Frank pointed to the queerly designed satchel resting on Kate's bed. 'There's your baby.'

Kate slumped against the doorframe and slowly rubbed her weary head. 'Perhaps we should . . . take him to meet my producer in the morning.'

Despite his injuries Dave let out a whooping cheer. He would have kissed her but he could see she'd been through enough for one day. His spirits soaring, he stumbled back to the couch to try and sleep.

Frank wheeled Vlad from Kate's bedroom, pausing to retrieve the satchel as he did so. As he left, his eyes met hers. 'I'll keep this guy with me, if you don't mind. Don't want him disturbing your beauty sleep. Got a feeling it's gonna be a long day tomorrow.'

Kate met his stare and matched it. 'Could be longer than any of us imagine.' With that he turned and closed the door.

When she was alone Kate produced a small hand-held computer from a cluttered bedside draw. After extending a telescopic aerial she typed into it six short words and pressed a large button marked SEND.

Merchandise reacquired. Ditto MJ13. Please advise.

34. Operation 'Golden Yak'

All around the borders of the rebel state of Urgistan the forces of truth and justice prepared to rain down their retribution. Their target was one man, and the fearsome military machine he had built around him. He was clearly a dangerous lunatic, prepared to flout the authority of the entire civilized world.

This picture of a Himalayan Hitler painted by the world's media was missing only the billowing black cloak, rakish top-hat and taloned hands. A distant peel of thunder wouldn't have seemed entirely amiss when he appeared on TV screens. Eager to obtain a jump in the ongoing ratings war, more than one keen junior news editor actually suggested adding the sound-effects, before being talked down by older, wiser heads, who knew subtler ways to sway the public mood.

Inexplicably and almost overnight Noroco T-shirts appeared in gift-shops across the American Mid-West. Any loud noise nearby caused his red-LED eyes to glow madly. 'WE BOMBED THE A-BOMBABLE SNOWMAN' bumper stickers put in a timely appearance.

This was a just war, as were all wars in this television age. All necessary criteria had been met. Somewhere, someone was doing wrong, and it was up to the global policeman wrapped in the Stars and Stripes to see to it that he got his just deserts. Most importantly of all, there was no way this perp could 'whack' back. International justice had a habit of turning a blind eye when nuclear-equipped apprentice superpowers were at fault. Tibet and Kashmir weren't far away, but they might as well have been on the dark side of the moon.

As usual there would be no civilian deaths, just 'col-

lateral damage'. The gallant Coalition pilots wouldn't be entering a war-zone, but a *'permissive environment'* (that's if the Urgis were able to shoot back after the first few seconds of the fearsome onslaught). The Western soldiers weren't going to slaughter their Urgistani counterparts, but *'degrade their offensive capability'*. Dead women and children might make for bad PR, but bug-eyed teenage conscripts were fair game. On air bases scattered across half the globe, safety pins were pulled from Cold War bombs older than some of their intended victims.

As tradition demanded, North Korea pledged support to the beleaguered state. Its leader was a consummate professional, trained at the best clandestine drama schools the Committee had to offer. He knew his role well; he had played his part many times before.[1] This last act of smiling betrayal was the final nail in Urgistan's soon to be crowded coffin. Nations which had previously reserved their doubts fell into dead-eyed line behind more hawkish neighbours.

The Coalition itself was an international affair – the PR managers would not settle for anything less. A last-minute round of shuttle diplomacy, incorporating everyone apart from the Urgistanis, had served chiefly to crank up 'air miles', but had done little in the cause of peace.

As usual the British Foreign Office completely failed to predict the outbreak of hostilities, even though this time it had been intimately involved in orchestrating them – an irony not lost on the hordes of Oxbridge-educated ex-KGB men who filled its shuffling ranks.

The French also provided valued assistance. No one had kept the invoices, but it was suspected that Urgi equipment comprised mainly of ancient Franco-Russian kit. At length weary French officers briefed their Coalition part-

---

[1] On the international stage, it's not 'pride' that comes before a fall, but 'North Korean support'.

ners on their systems' known weaknesses. The prospects for battle were looking up.

The Germans were also present in force, even though the last time the Luftwaffe had been this far east the blackened soil around Stalingrad had been all they'd seen. This time they hoped for a gentler ride. The Dutch had offered to send a hospital ship, until it had been pointed out Urgistan was as far from the sea as you could get, and ten thousand feet higher. With a smile the Dutch planners went back to their 'special cakes', so popular around the conference tables.

And so the stage was set. The audience had its popcorn, the world's press had its show. TV Telethons for the refugees were already being planned. At 0500 hours on the day the ultimatum expired, the bombs were loaded for one last time. In a scene repeated all across Southern Asia, in the ready-room of the 666th Stealth Bomber Wing the unit's CO gave his men their final detailed orders.

'Right boys, let's bomb the living crap out of them.'

35. On the Run

Washington, USA

Becker slipped past the newsstands, past the blaring head-lines of imminent war and into the departure lounge toilets as if in urgent need of bladder relief. The only good thing about the coming conflict was that at least it pushed Elvis's brief comeback tour off the front pages, but Becker had little time to worry about his opponents' mischief right now.

As he entered the rest room there was nothing about his manner which suggested he was anything other than a man with an immediate desire for ceramic assistance. He even managed to hobble with slightly crossed legs. But it was no long-awaited call of nature that prompted this visit to the bathroom. Once safely enclosed in a spacious cubicle he jammed his heavy-armoured briefcase against the inside of the door – all that lead shielding came with its price but also had its uses, as the X-ray operators would soon fail to discover. Moving quickly, he placed his travel bag on his knees and got down to work.

Amongst other things it held a wide rectangular mirror. Arrayed beneath it was the sort of make-up kit that could have made a Hollywood starlet flush with envy. Next to these items he propped his newly acquired passport, the ink barely dry and the photo darkroom fresh. It had been an age since Becker had needed to operate undercover in the field, but it was with a palpable excitement that he rediscovered lost talents. His hair was slicked back and darkened with an oily gel. Once it had been spirit-gummed into place the moustache needed only minimal trimming.

When his reflection matched the photo down to the closest detail, Becker gave himself an assured nod.

Next to go was the dark business suit. This was stuffed into the removable cover which housed the toilet cistern. From the bag Becker produced the sort of travel clothes only a tourist would wear. The Hawaiian shirt would provide ideal camouflage if he happened to find himself in a Turkish brothel circa 1967 the open-toed sandals lacked even this partially redeeming feature. If his enemies caught him now, cyanide dentures would not be needed – the Dark Man felt certain he would first die of shame.

But his appearance was only half the picture. As he slid back amongst the travelling throng Becker moved differently. All his mannerisms had changed. He seemed shorter and somehow twenty pounds lighter. Even without the disguise his own mother would have been hard pressed to pick him out.

He passed through the checkpoints and onto the waiting plane without further delay. The red-eye flight would at least give him time to think, a commodity which had been in short supply these last few hectic weeks. Contact had been lost with both his key London resources; this was definitely *not a good thing*. Freemantle was a liability, he should have known better than to trust that useless grunt with a mission as delicate as this, but the way Becker and the assault team had been prised apart like a well-cooked clam was still a slight to his professional pride. The captain should have been pensioned off to the funny farm like some other tools Becker had discarded over the years; but wait, he thought with a wry smile, wasn't that half the reason he was in this mess right now?

The Dark Man's isolation from his other operative was even more disconcerting. It was all too possible they were receiving contradictory orders from his superiors. All told, he concluded, it was high time he arrive on the scene and take personal command. Besides, he'd outstayed his welcome in Washington. At least he had the tracking device, its comfortable mass weighing reassuringly against his hip. And there was always that surprisingly heavy briefcase, stowed in the luggage rack above his head – Madame Chairman might soon be getting an unpleasant surprise.

When, eight hours and six time-zones later, Becker passed through the same Heathrow terminal which Frank and Dave had used he hardly paused for breath. He didn't linger at the police checkpoint, vainly appealing for witnesses to yesterday's chaotic riot, nor did he stop to gawk at the small army of cleaners still attempting to remove the oddly corrosive stains from the plate-glass windows near to the door. As Becker strode down the terminal's steps to hail a waiting cab there was a grim determination burning in his heavily made-up eyes. Fate might have initially dealt him a losing hand, but this was one game that was far from over yet.

36. Grey Dawn

The reply which lit up the screen of Kate's hand-held terminal, in the midst of those sleepless pre-dawn hours, filled her with dismay and alarm. So much so in fact that, regardless of standard operating procedures, she immediately sought confirmation of her instructions – which she received back immediately. Still, hers was not to reason why, she thought to herself as she slipped beneath the covers to snatch a few precious hours of rest.

Before either of her guests had risen Kate was up and about making the relevant calls to her TV boss's home numbers. Busily, she set about orchestrating what looked to be the breaking story of the century. Her claims were met with derision at first, but her calm insistence coupled with her reputation for reliability won through the further she was passed up the chain of command. By the time the pot of fresh coffee had finished percolating, the BAFTAs were as good as in the bag.

The fact that today's show had been scheduled long ago to focus on the recent wave of UFO sightings seemed too good to be true, to such an extent that Kate paused for a moment to ponder the bizarre synchronicity of the affair. It seemed that today she was destined to have more on her plate than simply the jittery needs of a demented Somerset farmer, who in light of recent developments didn't seem half so demented after all. Several worrying possibilities danced through Kate's restless mind – but no, that was pure paranoia, wasn't it?

On the sofa and armchair in the living room Dave and Frank slept the sleep of the dead. In the war-torn wheelchair next to them Vlad slept the sleep of the dead too, but with more commitment. The bullet holes and broken limbs did nothing but add to the overall effect. Judging by the state of them the tale of a hair-raising journey from Nevada was all too easy to believe. If a fraction of it were true it was a miracle they were here at all. But there was something about all this which bothered Kate on a deeply primordial level, something which slithered away under a mental rock if she so much as looked at it from the corner of her eye.

With a troubled yelp Dave suddenly came to. When he saw his oldest friend standing above him he gave a weak smile. 'Bad dreams. I've been having a few lately.'

Kate handed him a coffee. 'You look like you could do with this.'

Kate shuddered to think just what he must have gone through to get this far. Frank was some leader of men. Despite herself she felt a tremendous surge of pity. Dave was clearly way out of his depth, in what Kate knew to be a very deep and shark-filled pool.

His groggy eyes strayed to the grey monstrosity slumped next to him. When he saw it Kate watched him flinch as if struck by a physical blow. 'I wasn't cut out for this, was I?' he said when he saw her studying him closely.

'I don't think any of us were,' she said, crouching next to the sofa.

Dave shook his head. 'I spend all my working life searching for proof – when I finally find it it nearly gets me killed. Don't know where I'd be without friends like you. I'll be forever sorry I dragged you into this.'

'Some of us didn't have far to fall.' Kate gazed at him for a long while. 'Look, Dave, there are things you should know – things about me that I've kept from you.'

Dave pulled himself upright by her side, his eyes shining with hopeless optimism. 'There's only one thing I need to know. And that is, have you realized yet we were meant to be? Wouldn't we make a great team? I always said I'd prove myself to you one day – well, that day has come. By the end of the week we're going to be recognized across the world – doesn't that excite you?'

Now it was Kate's turn to shake her head. Dave was nothing if not consistent in his determination to win her over. 'No, Dave, you're missing the point. This has got nothing to do with "us" – I'm helping you because ... well, because you're a friend. But I've got a past you know nothing about. I'm involved in things I can barely explain myself.'

Dave looked at her, bemused. 'But I know you better than anyone, have done since we left school.'

'Those three years I spent in the States, you didn't know me then.'

'That was a college exchange programme. How much trouble could you have got into over there?' But Dave's eyes held a horrible uncertainty. Kate decided she liked them better the other way.

Before she could answer, Frank sprung suddenly awake. 'Charlie in the forest, all around – TRIGGER THE CLAYMORES, SARGE!'

'Don't worry,' said Dave, 'he's always like this first thing.'

When Frank had convinced himself he wasn't in the midst of a Vietcong-filled jungle thirty years ago, Kate went to fetch them breakfast. Just as he always did when he had a moment of spare time, Dave reached for *MJ13* and started reading.

There was a grave danger at this time that the public would learn just how little we knew. This was in the days when I was still firmly behind 'Unified Conspiracy Theory' as an instrument of policy. The faked sightings were progressing well, but were never going to influence a mass audience that way. Most of our elaborate productions were always going to be seen by the

'Anorak and Sandal' crowd – 'Von Danikens', as we called them in the trade.

We concluded that what we needed at the time was a widespread injection of paranoia into the mass consciousness. Our remedial efforts to hijack credit for the JFK killing had gone better than we hoped, but we needed still more kudos as cunning all-powerful puppeteers. My growing concerns prompted me to put our top psychological warfare section onto the problem. What they came up with succeeded beyond our wildest dreams.

We'd known for a long time that TV fiction presented the most effective way of hitting the biggest audience deep and hard enough to make a difference. When our elite creative writers came up with the concept of a show revolving around a Shadow Government plot to suppress contact with ET, many were sceptical about this apparently suicidal move.

'It's too close to the truth,' they said. 'It will be too obvious we're trying to appear cleverer than we actually are. The more sophisticated members of the public will see through it for the inept manipulation that it is.' How wrong those blubbering Committee members proved to be.

Of course there was the usual bickering between the FBI and CIA as to which organization should provide the dim-witted heroes. As it turned out I had the casting vote. Seeing as we'd recently got a former Chief Spook into the White House, to experience the fleeting high of a quick twiddle with the levers of illusionary power, I felt it only fair that the FBI get their way this time.

We judged the content of the show to be so direct as to not require any of the usual subliminal messages. Soon enough the whole manipulation was swallowed without a hitch – ironically enough becoming a rallying point for the paranoid and dispossessed. There was only one downside – I didn't think much of the chain-smoking fool they got to play my part. Statistical Command soon informed us that a significant percentage of the public believed we knew more than we were letting on about aliens; an even higher percentage believed there was some sort of 'government plot' behind most everything that went on – oh, if it were only true. All that remained was to slowly turn the show into a comedy parody of itself, thus further muddying the already clouded waters.

As far as most of the Committee was concerned this was a situation beyond price – the population would never know the horrible truth of how little we understood what was going on. Of course, I was slowly coming to understand this was far from a good thing. Somewhere far away our opponents unseen were merrily wringing their pallid hands in glee.

Dave thumped the big file shut. Something about these underhand shenanigans was nagging at the back of his mind. If the author of this work was right, there existed a high-level conspiracy to encourage belief in conspiracy theories. He seemed to think this policy furthered some deeper, darker motive barely understood.

What had Dave bothered was the ease with which they'd got Vlad this far. Frank was good, but he also seemed imbued with monumental good fortune. Could it be they were being used to propagate this outer conspiracy? Sure, someone had been trying to stop them – those black choppers had not been sent to speed them along – but, as MJ13 showed, the monolithic Black Government was far from the monolith it seemed to be – it was rife with internal bickering. Unless, of course, MJ13 was part of the conspiracy itself.

Wearily, Dave sank his head into his hands. This was too much for him to take this early in the day, and what a day it promised to be.

37. Studio

Once they'd done their best to eat breakfast the three accomplices set out for the TV studio with Vlad in tow. None of them felt much like eating, but Frank had insisted, 'This is not a good day for a low blood sugar level,' as Dave rushed to the bathroom to lose his bowl of iron-rich Wheato-Flakes. For his part Frank did not seem the best exponent of his own advice. His morning meal consisted of six cups of strong black coffee, followed by ten minutes of chanting meditation. When the percolator pot was empty he'd started chewing on the grounds. Kate had to tell him to bring them with him if he wanted to miss the worst of the morning traffic.

For Dave the journey was not a pleasant experience. He found himself jammed into the back of Kate's small hatchback, Vlad's wheelchair poking into his neck from the boot, and its former occupant sprawled across him in a most disconcerting manner. As Kate weaved her usual snaking course through the rush-hour traffic the limp alien was thrown about as if suffering a particularly nasty fit. On one occasion another startled commuter found himself peering into Vlad's bottomless eyes, before Dave unpeeled the smashed grey face from the quarter-light window.

Only one other aspect of their journey had seemed in any way out of the ordinary. Kate had asked for a description of yesterday's airport attackers. Frank replied that they had been uniformly nondescript, ordinary travellers to a man. Dave was about to remind him of the orange tie-dyed sheets, tambourines and ankle-bells of at least half their foes, when he suddenly thought better of it and shut his mouth instead. When they pulled into the dim underground car park, Dave was more than glad to untangle himself from his fruity-smelling companion.

Kate's arrival had evidently been expected. Their party were met at a service elevator by a small group of research staff, but their manner was anything but reverent – in fact it was shockingly mundane. 'Yeah, nice alien. Now who's going to fetch this barking-mad farmer from the station?' was about the most emotive reaction they got.

As they rode up to studio level Kate looked edgy and alert, as if she thought more was going on than met the eye. Frank just looked alert, as he always did when travelling through unfamiliar territory. Dave had to try hard not to become more and more disheartened. He had expected to be greeted like a hero, but instead seemed destined to be just another fifteen-minutes-of-fame freak, hauled before some dull-witted audience desensitized by endless cookery game shows and *Dallas* repeats.

'Jesus H!' wailed the harried Floor Manager when he caught sight of their alien charge. 'Get that thing to make-up *this instant*! We can't have it going on the show like that, we have a reputation to consider. Now where's those darling scientists got to? Sebastian, get me my running order now!'

Dave had to fight back a moment of panic as Vlad was wheeled away. It was the first time they'd been separated in the days since meeting Frank – though it seemed more like a lifetime. Frank too was ready to snap at this development. It took Kate's soothing hands to reassure him all would be well. Nevertheless he snatched the satchel as it passed and hung it around his neck. With a menacing scowl he allowed himself to be dragged off into a studio corner, to be pumped for his side of the tale.

With a horrible certainty Dave saw the way Kate looked after their moody leader. 'I can't believe you fancy that lunatic. He's nearly old enough to be your dad. Did your judgement pack up and leave home while I was away?'

Kate blushed and turned her back. 'I don't know what

you're talking about. Why do men always reduce every-thing to sex?'

'Who said anything about sex?' Dave's head was spinning with a sickening mixture of bafflement and jealousy. 'Look, Frank's a mate and everything, but that doesn't stop me from realizing that he's . . .'

'Completely stark raving bonkers,' Kate finished for him. 'Yes, I know, but that doesn't make him a bad person.'

Dave could barely believe what was going on. Finding a crashed dead alien and successfully smuggling it back through customs paled into insignificance compared to the unbelievable developments that were happening in his friend's heart and mind. With a hopeless bafflement he realized that he would never understand women. He didn't even try to keep the bitterness from his voice.

'I wouldn't waste your time on him, darling. Had most of his wedding-tackle blown off by a land-mine in 'Nam – has to piss through a tube to this day. They could have sewn it back on, but he says he prefers it that way, keeps him focused on the job at hand – or not at hand, as the case may be.'

Kate said nothing, she simply stared off onto the stage, where Frank was explaining to one of her wide-eyed assistants how to take down a Shadow Government ice-cream van with nothing but two house-bricks, a length of twine and a safety match.

Further conversation was cut short by the arrival of Jimmy Maxwell himself on set. Before every show the great man liked to greet each member of the crew in person, a technique he'd learned writing self-help books prior to his days in TV. Eventually, after many 'high-fives' and much over-enthusiastic whooping, he made his way to the two simmering friends. Kate was obviously well used to his antics because she made good her escape. Dave was left to fend for himself as Maxwell pummelled his hand.

'Hey, that's a nice model they've got in make-up. I love

the way you've roughed it up a bit. Was that chicken offal I could see poking out? Gives it that air of macabre authenticity.'

Dave fought hard to keep his voice level. 'It's not a model. It's a real dead alien. Frank pulled it from the wreck of a UFO in the Nevada desert seconds after it was shot down trying to escape. You wouldn't believe the lengths they've gone to getting it back here.'

Maxwell looked at him blankly for a moment. 'Whatever,' he said finally, then honoured Dave with his famous flashing smile. Dave buried his head in his hands and did his best not to cry.

'There, there,' soothed Maxwell with all the sincerity of a praying mantis. 'The first TV appearance is always hard. Just remember to stay in your seat, don't swear too much – all that bleeping gets us in trouble with the suits upstairs – but above all, enjoy yourself. That's what it's all about. We're in the entertainment industry after all.'

Dave looked up through his tears of impotent rage. 'You just don't get it at all, do you?' But Maxwell was already gone.

The three were given precious little time to themselves. The show was to be taped at 10 AM, ready for transmission later that afternoon. Dave himself was hurried through make-up, where he was patronized to within an inch of his life by a barely pubescent female midget, then questioned by one of Kate's researchers – who seemed more interested in whether he'd had any sexual contact with 'the Visitors' than in speculation as to their motives or culture. He was handed a guest-list on which, Dave was relieved to see, were the names of some of the nation's foremost UFO researchers – well-respected peers to a man. Nodding approvingly he saw that Professor Ralf Harding was amongst them. It seemed that despite its trashy reputation *The Maxwell Show* did not do things by half. Before he knew it, Dave was being briefed on the running order by the sweating Floor-Manager.

'Right, ducky, here's the plan. You and your chums are our star attraction – that means we wheel you out last for the big finale. Until then you wait in the green room.'

Dave could barely keep up with the bewildering series of responses necessary to communicate with the energetic little man. Seconds later he found himself ushered through to 'hospitality' as his manic host rambled on.

'Help yourself to the fruit bowl. Shirley Bassey, we had her last week – god I *love* that woman – she recommends the papaya-flavoured mineral water. Which reminds me: your friend with the muscles – where *did* he get that bandanna? You've got to ask him for me, would you? There's a love.'

Dave was glad to see the back of him, if nothing else just to give his throbbing eardrums a rest.

Near a long heavily-laden table Frank was glumly munching a kiwi-fruit, furry skin and all. He was gazing intently at a TV monitor hung in the corner of the room, showing the last-minute preparations for the show. Even as Dave watched, his friend's mood seemed to darken.

'What's up? We're about to splash this story once and for all – that's if anyone actually cares to watch this junk.'

Frank simply nodded towards the flickering image. 'Looks like some old friends have taken the trouble to turn up in person.'

The monitor showed a wide shot of the back of the studio. As technicians and cameramen made final adjustments, members of the audience were beginning to take their seats. Maxwell's show attracted a diverse crowd. There were obsessional fans who followed him all over the world, some who queued up weeks before a filming – even when not strictly necessary. But this crowd looked stranger than most.

Dave's eyes were first drawn to a large dark haired-man

in the front row, with sunglasses and the sort of Hawaiian shirt you could have used to power a small town. Behind him a row of seats was rapidly filling with the distinctively clad initiates of the Temple of Planet Love.

'Oh my God,' was all he was able to say, before he started shaking uncontrollably. Frank took him by the shoulders.

'Keep it together, Dave. We're not gonna get out of this if you start panicking now.'

'But what are we going to do? They've got us cornered this time.'

Frank's lined face took on a quizzical expression as he spat out the remains of the kiwi, hitting the bin from all of twelve feet. 'No need to write us off just yet. I figure there's more to this than meets the eye. Think back to when we arrived at the airport. Were those pyjama-wearing freaks trying to stop us or help us through?'

Dave's shaking subsided for the moment. Now that he came to think about it there had been two distinct groups involved in that swirling fight. The first group of clean-cut young men had most definitely been intent on halting their progress. Just as they attained the upper hand the cultists had struck.

'It was almost as if they ambushed our ambushers,' muttered Dave, the first droplets of comprehension percolating through his troubled mind.

'Right,' said Frank, picking the last of the seeds from between his teeth. 'Those boys wanted us to get this far, and they were willing to risk all to do so.'

Terrible hope flashed in Dave's eyes. 'That's great – isn't it?'

Frank looked pained, as if badly let down by a star pupil. 'I can say without any shadow of doubt that you have never been so spectacularly wrong your entire life. We don't know why they want us on TV. What are their motives in helping us? I'd rather trust the military lizards who jumped us in the first place than this lot. At least you know where you stand with them – under twenty feet of water with concrete insoles perhaps, but at least you know where you stand. Grab your shit, Dave, we're blowing this joint.' Frank was at the door in a heartbeat.

'What about Vlad and Kate? We can't leave without them.'

'We'll collect *him* on the way out. They've put Vlad in the wings ready to go on stage. As for your girlfriend – we'll discuss her later. Shake it, Dave, let's move like we mean business.'

It was all Dave could do not to move like he had malaria, but he followed Frank all the same.

*　　*　　*

As Kate watched the final preparations going on around her she experienced none of the excitement she normally felt at times like this. Instead she was filled with an ominous foreboding. Orders were orders, but there was something not right about what was going on today. Initially she had been certain she could fulfil her responsibilities without any harm coming to her old friend. Now she was not so sure. This whole situation stank of a set-up to her.

When she'd seen the members of the Temple of Planet Love troop into the gallery en masse she'd felt a moment of panic. But there was nothing strange about them being here. Frank and Dave had been unable, or unwilling, to put a name to yesterday's assailants; she had no reason to suspect they'd been involved. Worrying though it was, their leader was a guest on today's show. Considering its subject matter, his disciples had every reason to be here.

Which brought her back to Dave and Frank's remarkable find. From where she stood, Kate could clearly see Vlad on the other side of the stage. Still seated in the less than appropriate wheelchair, his black eyes seemed to mock her from the smothering darkness. The make-up department had done a remarkable job patching him back together – most of the stitches didn't even show. Despite this Kate couldn't help but feel that the *Jimmy Maxwell Show* T-shirt was a mistake they'd all come to regret.

As the last of the warm-up men shuffled off the stage Kate could almost smell the tension in the charged studio air. Whatever went on, this would be a day none present would forget. When the familiar signature tune blared from the speakers, she had to lick her bone-dry lips. Maxwell would not be far behind. Suddenly the APPLAUSE lights went on and the audience obediently responded. That was when she saw the man in the Hawaiian shirt in the front row, and the blood froze in her veins.

*   *   *

If Kate could have seen what was currently happening outside the studio complex's plush foyer, she would have been even more alarmed. Without warning two dark unmarked vans screeched to a halt and disgorged their cargo of black-clad young men. If she could have seen behind the balaclavas and gas-masks each wore, she would have noticed many sported black eyes and fresh bruises. Not all were armed, but those that were made up for it through sheer weight of fire-power. As they sprinted up the concrete steps a fairy grotto of laser-target spots danced around their jack-booted feet.

Captain Cyrus Freemantle's elite platoon might have allowed themselves to be surprised at the airport, but this time they were taking no chances, and if the look of grim determination burning in every eye was anything to go by, no prisoners either. Pausing briefly, he consulted the floor-plans he carried stuffed down his bulky bulletproof vest. 'Go Go Go!' he yelled, for no discernible reason.

With military precision they stormed through the plate-glass doors, their leader pistol-whipping the lone security guard who stood in their way. Freemantle had no need to consult the large wall map at reception he knew exactly where he and his men were going.

*   *   *

Frank and Dave retraced their steps to the hushed corner of the sound stage. Underneath a bright 'ON AIR' sign Vlad was being chaperoned by the Floor Manager and two of his well-built assistants, the sort of burly men needed on a show like this to keep order amongst warring guests.

Frank had always favoured the direct approach. Single-mindedly he waded in, dragging Dave behind him. 'We're here to collect our friend, we're not taking part in the show.'

Desperately the panic stricken Floor Manager spread-eagled himself across Vlad's recumbent form. 'Stop right there, I won't stand for this sort of behaviour on my set!'

Frank was in no mood for theatrics. 'Step aside, queeny, before I do it for you.'

Horrified, the Floor Manager beckoned his brawny assistants, who moved up to chastise the unruly guest. They were large and well muscled, but their sunbed tans and tight T-shirts told Frank more than he needed to know about their trips to the gym. He hit the first one hard in the solar plexus with three stiff fingers, the other he saw off with a standing kick to the head. Both went down like they had no intention of getting up again.

'Murderer!' screamed the Floor Manager. 'What have you done to my boys?'

'Exactly what they were about to do to me,' said Frank, calmly releasing Vlad's handbrake. 'Come on, Dave, we're leaving.'

As the pair turned to go the first of Freemantle's men rounded the corner at the end of the corridor, guns and truncheons at the ready. Simultaneously, the first tendrils of tear-gas reached their flaring nostrils. 'I think a slight change of plan might be needed,' said Dave, his voice rising several octaves.

'Quick, on the stage,' ordered Frank, performing a 180 degree turn that flung Vlad's scrawny neck around with a sickening crunch.

'But that's the only way out!' Dave flapped in the general direction of the fast-approaching troopers.

Frank grabbed him by the hand. 'Forget it, Dave, publicity's our only hope now.'

38. The Emperor's Real Clothes

Events off stage were barely noticed by those taking part in the recording. A certain West Country farmer, seated in a specially darkened area and referred to only as 'Mr Smith', had just told his harrowing tale of alien visitation coupled with bovine sexual abuse. He had been countered by Jackson, leader of the Temple of Planet Love, who had pointed out what a great honour it was to be selected by the 'Elder Ones' to provide a donation of his seed, whatever their methods of seduction. Smith had claimed that, honour or not, it was only polite to ask first.

After that things had got more bizarre, and rather heated. Jackson's followers in the audience had started chanting, and several of the distinguished panel of UFO experts had become outraged at this blatant trivialization of their beloved subject.

Things were warming up rather nicely, thought Jimmy Maxwell to himself smugly. Later he would barely get a chance to reflect on the bitter irony of this notion. For the time being the first signs of trouble went unheeded. None noticed the two dull thuds followed by a strangled scream that came from the wings, just as none noticed the shouts of alarm or loud crashes as Freemantle's soldiers continued to storm the building. All in the studio were too rapt in their own petty precious concerns. Professor Harding was busy taking just about every one present to task.

'And as for you, Maxwell, your show's a travesty of journalism! My colleagues were promised reasoned debate and a chance to air our views. Instead we get this nutter,' he yelled, gesturing towards Jackson, 'and his brain-washed hordes. It's fantasy!'

As if on cue Dave and Frank stumbled on stage, pushing their wheelchair-bound companion with them. Maxwell knew full well they weren't scheduled on yet, but like the true pro that he was he took their arrival in his bounding stride.

'Well, that's where you're wrong, Professor. Never let it be said that we don't break new ground on this show, because we've got our very own world exclusive right here, folks, right now. Give it up for Dave and Frank, ladies and gentlemen, and their entirely genuine crashed alien carcass!'

Not really sure what they were seeing yet, the studio audience nevertheless went wild with glee. They'd been promised a big finale, and no doubt this was it; all present knew a show-stopper when they saw one, even if it did look like Frankenstein's glandularly deficient midget brother. As one they jumped to their feet and started whooping and cheering as if welcoming a returning hero, rather than a couple of shifty strangers pushing what looked like a misshapen, fire-damaged tailor's dummy.

Dave and Frank flinched under the sudden lights and oppressive wall of sound. A mob was not a pretty sight at the best of times, and this crowd was even less attractive than most.

Frank grabbed a clip-on microphone from one startled academic. 'I just want yo'all to know that the Shadow Government that runs our lives has tried to get this thing back since we hauled if from a saucer in Nevada. The jack-boots of their UN Gestapo troops are kicking down our dressing-room door at this very moment. The revolution starts here. You can have liberty, or you can have peace, but you can't have both for long – grab a gun and man the barricades. Live free or die!'

The audience went into paroxysms of delight – but then

they always did when something controversial was said. The truth of the statement wasn't the issue, just that it was given voice at all over the magical medium of TV generated its own reality.

The panel of experts, meanwhile, were peering intently at the thing slumped in Dave's wheelchair. Leaning over the microphone nervously, Frank's companion felt the need to add to his friend's heartfelt manifesto.

'I think what Frank was *trying* to say is that we have here final incontrovertible proof that we are not alone in the universe. We also have proof that our political leaders have been keeping this knowledge from us for the past half-century.' Dave patted the large satchel hung tightly around Frank's neck. 'I'm sure they won't want to appear on camera, but we are currently being followed by some very disagreeable individuals.'

The audience set up another round of boisterous cheering, which under the circumstances seemed a rather odd reaction, but the pattern was too firmly set. Dave noticed that a man on the panel, wearing a complex arrangement of black and orange bed-sheets, was looking at him in a most peculiar way. He didn't get the chance to peer back for long.

From his darkened booth Farmer Smith cried, 'That's one of them grey elves!' and instinctively reached to protect his genitals.

Professor Harding was studying Vlad ever more closely. Suddenly he seemed to reach a monumentus conclusion. 'The thing's a fake!' he screamed hysterically. 'You can clearly see the stitches where it's sown together! They could at least have spent more time on their home-made special effects. Do they think us idiots to be fooled by such simple trickery?'

Dave was no stranger to bowel-knotting frustration. He had his love-life to thank for that, but events today were threatening to tip him over the edge into madness.

'IT'S NOT A FAKE!' he howled. 'There's a logical explanation why it looks that way. Can't you just listen to our story?'

But proceedings had already moved on apace. This was not the Oxford Union Debating Society, not even the Mother's Union Macramé Society if truth be known. Intellectual rigour was about as welcome as a leper in a whorehouse.

One of Harding's esteemed colleagues had risen to inspect the alien at close range. After wiggling one scrawny arm with considerable vigour it came off in his hand, in a shower of sooty skin and powdered bone. 'FRAUD! It was stapled on!' he yelled, holding it up above his head like a trophy. Instantly the mood of the crowd turned ugly. There were boos and someone at the back set up a chant of 'Off, off!'

At last Maxwell felt the need to intervene. It was all very well allowing the guests to vent their feelings, but when the props started getting damaged you had to step in.

'Why don't we allow Frank and Dave to tell us their tale?' he said in his best conciliatory manner.

But the new arrivals would never get their chance. At that moment Freemantle and his band of freelance commandos dispelled any myths as to their camera-shyness and crashed the party in a way as brutal as it was direct. Half a dozen stun-grenades bounced on stage to be followed by twice that many black-kitted men. Frank at least had the sense to cover his ears and eyes; the rest of those present were not so quick. Seconds later most were falling around, blinded, deafened and half-choked by the eye-watering fumes.

Freemantle made straight for the wheelchair-bound alien. 'No prisoners, men – apart from the one we came for!'

Dave saw the red laser spot on his chest just in time.

'What the . . . ?' he yelled, as Frank pulled him to the floor. Behind him, an instant later, Maxwell was all but cut in half by the ferocious burst of explosive 9mm shells.

Ralph Harding jumped to his feet and shouted, 'If you think we're going to be impressed by these childish gimmicks you can –' until he was mowed down in a similar fashion.

From out of the smoke Frank saw a long arm, clad in the sleeve of a garish Hawaiian shirt, grasping for the clasp of his heavy satchel. Instinctively he kicked out, pinning it to the floor and snapping it at the wrist with a loud crack. Its owner's cry of pain was lost amidst the general commotion.

Freemantle put his hand on the back of Vlad's chair. 'Time to go, Sparky.'

It was at that moment that Jackson recovered from his initial shock and remembered his task, though his cult's intervention hardly seemed necessary now. Jumping on his chair he yelled to his followers. 'To me, disciples of Love. You know what you have to do – be not afraid to crack heads!'

As one his entourage surged forward, using the audience's front ranks as stepping-stones along the way. With commendable, if not misplaced, professionalism one burly stage-hand attempted to stem the flood. He was carried backwards by the orange rush, to crash painfully into an upright scaffold stanchion. At first few appreciated the importance of this seemingly trivial event, but as soon as the high-powered lighting suspended above began to crash down, braining troopers and cultists alike, none were left in any doubt. Soon the stage was swept by a flood of arcing electric sparks.

Though you wouldn't have known it to smell him, Vlad was still filled with most of the embalming fluid Hooch had so thoughtfully provided. The thick noxious liquid had been seeping through his skin's larger holes for the

248

past 6,000 miles, but most of it was still inside the tattered corpse. In addition, in a vain attempt to disguise the stench, Dave had been spraying him liberally with aerosol deodorant, coating his skin with a tacky patina of incendiary man-made slime. Simply put, the dead alien was a mummified petrol bomb waiting for a light. When the 12,000 volts from the lighting-rig passed through this volatile cocktail of flammable chemicals, there was only ever going to be one outcome. Vlad went up like an inhuman torch, the heavy wheelchair beneath him bucking like a psychotic rodeo mount.

One hand still gripping the chair, Freemantle began to dance a terrifying electron-fuelled fandango, blue lightning streaming around him.

'Noooooo!' screamed Dave, scrambling for the fast-cooking fruits of his life's labour, sparks from the inferno flooding across the stage and burning cinders of flesh raining down around him.

'Give it up,' Frank yelled in his ear, pulling him back to the relative safety of the floor. 'It's not important any more. We've got to get out!'

But the chances of that happening took on depressingly lengthening odds as Freemantle was flung clear, landing amidst a tangle of fleeing guests. With smouldering hatred the young officer locked bulging eyes with Frank, his balaclava pushed from his head by his new Afro haircut. A spark of recognition flashed between them – nothing compared to the current that had just raced through Freemantle's shuddering body, but powerful enough all the same. Madly he staggered to his feet, with murder burning in his eyes. The objective of his mission gone up in smoke, Freemantle charged his recurrent tormentor, pistol in hand.

'Die, you fuckers!' he screamed, cocking the weapon on the run.

But before he'd gone three steps a hulking studio camera

slammed into his side, bludgeoning him under its squealing castors. Calmly Kate stepped out from behind the weighty device. 'Use the back exit!'

Frank dragged Dave to his feet and followed her, as behind them the remains of Freemantle's men set about emptying their ammo clips into Jackson's dancing followers – belated revenge for the ambush at Heathrow. As the old antagonists resumed their violent acquaintance, Frank, Dave and Kate slipped away through the gunsmoke.

There followed a panic-inspired flight, which later Dave could do little to remember. Kate knew the backstage maze of corridors and offices like the back of her hand. Once down an echoing stairwell the three spilled into the basement car park. It was only at their vehicle that a heavily wheezing Dave looked back, distraught.

'But we lost Vlad! We let the bastards take him from us.'

Frank wiped a smear of blood and soot from his face. 'I wouldn't worry about it, Davey. It wasn't him they were after. This is more important now.'

His grizzled hand came to rest on the strange alien satchel tied about his waist, and its bulging, sinister contents.

39. Evasions

Through a blinding wall of pain Becker became dimly aware of the wail of distant sirens and the rumble of stampeding feet. For a terrible moment he feared he must have wet himself, but then saw that the overhead fire-sprinklers were showering him with a gentle rain. It had been a long shot, following his manuscript to these studios in the hope of obtaining the opening he needed, but then he was fast running out of more carefully considered options.

As he struggled back to consciousness the professional part of his brain reflected that mission success rates were seldom improved by the uncoordinated arrival of wayward subordinates – who hadn't so much grasped the wrong end of the stick as hammered it through an eye-socket and into their delicate frontal lobes. Becker might have been hurt and frustrated, but he was not nearly distracted enough to forget the instigator of his most recent woes. He intended to get a firm grip of the right end of the stick and to use it to beat Freemantle until his nose bled.

With an ugly snarl the Dark Man hauled himself upright with his one good arm and stumbled over to where the young officer lay unconscious on the bloodstained floor. He paused only once, to smash a big fist into the prying lens of an abandoned TV camera that had come to rest nearby.

Becker was in no mood for excuses, just as he was in no mood for small-talk. 'What the fuck do you think you're playing at, Freemantle? I was closing in on them when your goons arrived. If we live through this fiasco I'll make sure you're court-martialled like no one's ever been court-martialled before.'

Freemantle looked up from his concussed daze, one eye

not even trying to point in the right direction. 'But we accomplished our goal. The target was taken out – burnt to a crisp in fact – whatever you wanna call it, boss.'

Next to him the electron-fried remains in the steaming wheelchair bore mute testimony to his words. If the charred mess of cartilage and bone had ever been a living creature, it would have taken the world's greatest veterinary pathologist to even attempt to guess which one it was – Rolf Harris would have had no chance.

Becker shook the soldier like he was a large black-and-blue milkshake. 'That wasn't the mission! We were meant to be keeping this situation under wraps. When the film of your exploits gets beamed around the world there won't be a Stone Age tribesman in the Amazonian jungle who doesn't get to see it! That was about as discreet as a fist up the rectum. You're a disgrace to your uniform.'

Freemantle looked up wearily. 'But you told us to . . .'

Becker sensed time was running short. He knew the Armed Response Units couldn't be far away. 'I don't care what you think you were told. Listen to me, Freemantle. Our leadership has been compromised. They're playing for the other team now. I'm the only one of the Committee not taken in by their two-faced double-dealings. If you've got an ounce of patriotism left you'd best take what's left of your men and head for the hills. Do you understand me?'

Freemantle's eyes refocused for a moment, then rolled far back in his head as his body slumped, a limp dead weight.

Becker swore again, but he didn't have time for sophisticated schemes. Already a fast-response paramedic crew was treating a bullet-riddled cultist nearby. Dropping Freemantle's flaccid form he made off through the clearing smoke. He still had the tracker, and that meant he still had hope.

Behind him he could already hear the strident challenges of the first of the police officers as they picked their way carefully through the zone of destruction.

*   *   *

Becker wasn't the only one to slip away from the war-torn studio before the forces of law and justice arrived.

Most of his attendant followers seemed destined to stay behind, due in no small part to the debilitating effects of 9mm dum-dum bullets, but Jackson saw no reason why he should hang around to face the music. Police station interview rooms seldom played the grooviest of tunes. Awkward questions and unpleasantly suspicious minds tended to be the order of the day, and both were bad for his yin-yang balance.

He had no doubt that he would eventually be tracked down to the cult's rural hideaway. It was well documented that he had been a guest on that day's show – even a cursory glance at the transmission tape would reveal his full part in the massacre. But by then the trail would be cold, and his allies would be able to haul him from the flames of justice. It had happened many times before, it would happen many times again. It was truly liberating to know you had friends in very high places, especially when you'd just done exactly as you were told.

What he needed now was to get back to the mansion to destroy any incriminating evidence. Some of the things that lurked in its deepest vaults were embarrassing, to say the least.

*   *   *

The mood in Kate's car as it mounted the motorway slip-road was of stunned disbelief. All three passengers were cocooned in a semi-daze of despondency.

Huddled on the rear seat Dave seemed lost in a permanent state of shock, his red-rimmed eyes replaying the same scenes of death and destruction over and over again.

Up front Frank was wrapped in his own concerns, a worried scowl clamped across his forehead. One scared hand sought the clasp of the big satchel, toying with it as if it were a lucky charm. Only Kate in the driver's seat seemed capable of coherent speech.

'Do you know who those guys were? The ones with the SAS fixation, I mean. I think I can place the pyjama-clad fanatics.'

Frank studied her carefully. 'I recognized a few. That unit tends to suffer rather high attrition rates, though it was less so when I supervised their training. Standards seem to be slipping.'

Dave looked at him, gob-smacked. 'You *knew* those maniacs? I thought you were making up all those tales about the Black Berets.'

Frank didn't honour him with a response, as a faraway look came over his eyes. 'I always did tell Watson to keep his weapon down. Looks like it proved his undoing – those New Age freaks sure can fight barehanded. Give me a battalion of them and we'd take the world.'

Kate seemed unimpressed by Frank's battlefield reminiscences. 'That's as maybe, but how did they all know we were going to be there? Not only the cultists, but the boys in black as well?'

Dave's shock turned to confusion. There was something about this that didn't quite add up. 'Jackson and his gang of born-again hippies – they seem to turn up whenever we've got our backs to the wall. Am I alone in having noticed that?'

Frank shook his head. 'You're not alone. It's almost as if they're following us around. Gonna have to find out why, some day soon – only polite to ask.'

Dave paused. 'Which brings me to another point. Just where are we going exactly?'

Frank watched the girl closely as she changed lanes to overtake a large white van. 'I know a place where we can lie low for a few days. I assume that's what you want to do. My uncle's got a cottage in the Lake District – he said I can use it while he's away on business.'

Dave nodded just a bit too eagerly. 'Sounds reasonable to me – I think I need a break. What about you, Frank?'

Frank hugged the big file case close to his chest and peered at Kate. 'Why not? Figure we ain't got any place else to go.'

40. 'Golden Yak' Goes In

At his less than space-age HQ, General Noroco was hard
pressed to fathom the world's reaction to his pleas for help.
He hadn't expected to be hailed as a hero for announcing
his nation's troubling find, but to receive from half the
planet what amounted to a declaration of war struck him
as tantamount to overkill – either that or there'd been
one hell of a party and the rest of humanity had the
mother of all hangovers. The frantic president didn't want
to think about such a concept as his tiny army prepared to
do battle with the gathered military might of the assembled
Western World.

Maybe he was just a simple soldier, naïve to the machinations of international power politics; nevertheless he
found it hard to believe that his claims had been given a
fair hearing. Admittedly, as a clarion call for assistance
they weren't exactly *that* easy to believe, but that did
nothing to lessen the ancient threat that had been
unearthed. He was even ready to admit the way he'd seized
power from that traitorous king might look bad on paper,
but there had been no time for the niceties of democracy.
Drastic times called for drastic measures. The Urgi people
at least remembered enough of the old ways to lend him
their wholehearted support. If only the rest of the world
would open their myopic eyes.

One minute the foreign diplomats had been demanding
Urgistan stop its pitiful attempts to contain the 'alleged'
resurgent menace, the next they were calmly informing
him the strike missions were on the way. It was hard to
see how such a sudden transition could have taken place,
hard enough in fact to make him wonder if some deeper
motive was at play. Noroco was a practical man and dis-

missed this paranoid delusion. He was a combat-scarred veteran, not subject to jump at shadows like a raw recruit. But still his doubts lingered.

Had Urgistan's name come up in some covert lottery held deep beneath the Pentagon's fortified vaults? Was his homeland destined to be that decade's 'enemy of record', as Libya, Iraq and countless others had been before? Surely, riddled as it was with communists and paid informers, not even the American State Department operated by such unfair means. There must be some other force at work. It was a tribute to his faith in his fellow man that Noroco ascribed no darker motives to his foes.

But the recently installed president would get no further chance to develop his theories. Sick with exhaustion, a trembling messenger fell through the bead-curtain door and handed him a tattered note. It informed him that the first planes had already crossed the border. It was no ruinously expensive radar installation, maintained by drunken Russian 'advisors', which had generated this valued intelligence – Urgistani technology did not stretch so far. From high on his sunny vantage-spot a fearful goat-herd had watched the first stealth planes snake down the twisting valley. Noroco turned to his recently demonized right-hand man.

'Looks like the game's up, Yajik. Your last-ditch efforts have failed.'

From his spot across the cluttered desks, Yajik looked up from what he was doing. 'Then I can stop licking these stamps now?' he said with his bone-dry tongue half-hanging out, and a look of terrible despondency on his haggard face.

Besides him a towering mound of unfinished correspondence threatened to make him the first casualty of war. When the normal diplomatic channels had let them down, with puppy-like enthusiasm Yajik had set about resorting to the more personal touch. Armed with a three-year-old copy of *Hi!* magazine (and the innocence of the very young or very stupid) he had written letters to as many of the world's celebrities as he could manage, explaining at length the terrible wrong that seemed destined to be committed.

From the other side of town a rattling series of explosions, which Noroco suspected to be the Central Post Office launching into orbit, signalled that perhaps this mail would not now be delivered in time.

'Never mind that,' said the general with a weary sigh. 'Why not share a last drink with me, old friend?'

Noroco had little fear of death, but like the rest of his tiny army he'd deserted the ramshackle barracks long ago. His men had been sent home to their families, with orders to lie low. There was no reason why more should die than had to. Noroco had no doubt that his time would come. He trusted the accuracy of Western bombing no more than he trusted the motives of their diplomats and politicians, but he saw no reason why his spirit should be called by the sky-gods any time soon. With the calm fatalism of his forefathers he poured himself a bowl of green tea, and took a long refreshing sip.

Yajik meanwhile found it hard to be so philosophical. 'I beg you, master, take cover!' he wailed, as he cowered beneath an overburdened table. Already the air was thick with an acrid ancient dust, shaken loose by the force of the nearby concussions.

But Noroco would have none of it. 'Get out from under there, you snivelling cull. This building is in a residential civilian district. Not even our sunglass-wearing friends are stupid enough to target this part of town.'

Yajik considered pointing out that there was no reason why they should target any part of the country, let alone this half-horse town, but thought better of it, as a rolling series of blasts shook the street's foundations.

'Better safe than sorry, Master. Your death now would serve no purpose!'

Noroco was about to administer another ear bashing to his wailing accomplice, when a dawning realization broke across his face. He was not a handsome man at the best of times, but now his leathery features seemed illuminated by a serene inner light.

Grabbing the Urgistani military's last remaining portable radio, he ran from the shaking building, out to his waiting Trabant staff car. Maybe his death could serve a purpose after all.

41. Invitation

Death was the furthest thing from Marshall Swift's mind. The way he was feeling right now he was certain he could live forever. It would be the least prize the Ferrari-driving, champagne-guzzling gods of PR could bestow on a marketing genius such as him. It was all he could do to stop rubbing his hands together with glee, like some horribly perverted version of Lady Macbeth. His over-polished face seemed cast in a permanent rictus smile; several members of his staff, upon seeing it, had run screaming from the room – but not for any of the usual reasons.

All Marshall's distilled exuberance was down to one simple fact. The advertising campaign he'd created for his strange and mysterious clients had exploded across the continent into a resounding success. Billboards and TV screens all over Europe were festooned with Poke-It-On's cloying image. There were features on the Six O'Clock News; questions were being asked in Parliament (most often, 'Where can my children get one?')

The badges showing you'd placed an advance order were appearing on celebrities across every land. On the catwalks of Paris and Milan they were often all that protected the model's modesty. In playgrounds and housing estates from Barnsley to Baku, those poor unfortunate kiddies not hip enough to have one were singled out and tormented remorselessly in ways which only young children and mail-order book clubs know how. At high-brow dinner parties the hot topic of conversation was what colour your pre-booked furry companion was going to be – at least it made a change from that unpleasantness in Urgistan.

Marshall hadn't needed to go far in promoting the product's virtues. He'd simply suggested through clever spin that everyone else was going bonkers for the little creatures, and before long it became true. He liked to think he'd supplied the electric cattle-prod, then stood back and let mankind's herd instinct take control. The 'Pokey' craze crossed international frontiers quicker than a fully laden NATO jet, and showed less signs of flagging than a Swedish porn star's peroxide-blond handlebar moustache.

The fact that the critters weren't available in the shops yet just added to their appeal. Marshall knew the mystique of well-fuelled expectations was even more malleable than injection-moulded plastic and fire-retardant nylon fur. When the merchandise was finally unleashed on an eager public, back orders alone promised to shift them as fast as they could be shovelled from container ships' bulging holds.

High in his penthouse office suite, Marshall threw his head back and laughed with all his might. Word had it that parallel campaigns had been just as successful in the US and Far East, but the adman didn't let this rumour deflate his Zeppelin ego for one minute. As famous victories went, this triumph promised to be Marshall's Agincourt and Trafalgar all rolled into one. He had no doubt there'd be a juicy bonus awaiting him at closure, but for the moment at least he was content to revel in his own breathtaking ability.

Sure, Boardman's untimely death had been a disappointment. Loath as Marshall was to admit it, his experience would have come in handy, but as it was, his own skills had been more than enough to carry the day. So what if violent car-jackings were on the increase – who had time to worry about random crime and society's moral fibre when you held the nation's credit card details clutched in your hands? Not Marshall, that was for sure. All he needed now was for one minor detail to be taken care of and his magnum opus would be complete. He simply required the secretive manufacturers, somewhere far off in their hidden production complexes, to literally 'deliver the goods' and they would be laughing all the way to the merchant bank.

Happily, he turned on his office TV just in time to see the seventh rerun that day of their top commercial. Kids across the land would be sitting down to their alphabeti-spaghetti, but devouring Poke-It-On in their dreams.

To a beyond-annoying upbeat tune a troop of laughing children danced across a sunlit meadow, cartoon Poke-It-Ons resplendent in their eye-watering colours frolicking along behind – just like friendly puppies, but with a double-digit IQ and a surplus of legs and antennae.

But what the kiddies started doing next you couldn't do to your average pup, not without Rolf Harris rushing round from Battersea Dogs' Home to redecorate your walls with a hideous mural in protest.[1] When the soul-destroying jingle changed to an oddly discordant hum, each child reached for the nearest computer-generated Poke-It-On and rammed it onto their foreheads like a squirming, living cap.

The creatures seemed to wriggle into place with a multi-legged shuffle, then sigh with an almost human moan of pleasure and contentment. A second later each child sank into a state of blissful rapture – dewy eyes rolling back in small heads like marbles in a jar.

Marshall couldn't put his finger on it, but for a moment something struck him as unspeakably depraved about this symbiosis. But his moment of doubt was quickly squashed. He was well practised at keeping his scruples under wraps. Anyway, the catchy music, which had now kicked back in with full force left little room for conscious thought.

> . . . Poke on, Poke on,
> Poke on a Pokey today . . .

---

[1] Remember, a dog is for Christmas, not just tobacco-company research.

Even sat in his office Marshall experienced an annoying urge to rush out and buy one. It was almost as if there was something subliminal in that song. Of course the rules didn't allow for that sort of thing these days – government busybodies everywhere – but there was just something behind that nauseating melody . . .

Poke on . . . a Poke-It-On . . . todaaaay. Go on kids, poke on a Poke-It-On today!

Finally, the image of near-comatose children was replaced by a close-up of a particularly cute and cuddlesome Poke-It-On (ONLY £39.95, PLACE YOUR ORDERS TODAY! Deliveries coming soon.)

The commercial was truly a marvel of modern technology, much like the product itself – which, as far as Marshall knew, no one outside the mysterious factory had yet seen. The Pokeys in the advert were, without exception, creations of the very latest computer imaging technology – so cutting-edge that rumour had it the animators had to wear chain-mail gloves. Before he could become unnaturally aroused by the thought of all the techno-wizardry at his disposal, the adverts were interrupted by a news flash.

It seemed that earlier that day some sort of grizzly publicity stunt on a daytime confessional chat show had gone horribly wrong and many people had been hurt. A police firearms team had responded and the fools in SAS-style fancy dress, messing around with a fake alien, had been blown away. Swathes of the studio audience had been mown down too. Marshall was appalled – they had been valuable consumers to a man.

It was truly sickening the way everyone seemed to be jumping on the alien bandwagon these days. Little Grey Men were cropping up everywhere, to help promote the most diverse of goods and services. It was nearly as bad as the way the Millennium had been hijacked a few years before – the whole event descending into an undignified scramble to cash in. Some unprincipled people just made him want to retch.

Marshall's contempt was interrupted by the sound of a small explosion emanating from the intercom unit on his desk. The device wasn't malfunctioning, this was just how MovieOS™ informed you a message had arrived.

'Package for you, Mr Marshall, sir.' His PA sounded as fed up with these new personality-driven computers as was the rest of the staff. 'There's a black-clad motorbike dispatch-rider waiting in reception. Says he won't leave until you read what he's brought and delivered a reply.'

Moments later Marshall was alone in his office once again, this time with the package on his desk. You didn't have to be Einstein to guess who it was from. He was quickly learning the means by which his royal benefactor operated. Eagerly he tore the parcel apart.

What he found inside was a hand-written letter, this time on unheaded notepaper, but he recognized the spidery script all the same.

Dear Mr Swift,
Congratulations. You have done better than any of us could have imagined. Even Oneself – and One has *very* high expectations for this undertaking indeed. You could almost say it has been One's 'Pet Project' for more years than One cares to mention – even more so than the Corgis.

It is now time to consider the matter of your remuneration. After careful consultation with One's colleagues, we are prepared to offer you a very special opportunity, a chance that befalls few men in each generation.

The ultimate reward for your loyalty is not destined to be financially based . . .

If this was where she offered him a knighthood he'd ram it right back up her pampered Teutonic behind. And if she was going to suggest front-row seats for her eldest son's latest marriage she could keep them too. Marshall had no desire to watch that jug-eared buffoon getting permanently hitched to his favoured mount – in his humble opinion you'd need more than a stiff upper lip to want to ride that nightmare beast round the paddock, blinkers, bridle and four hundred years of inbreeding or no.

. . . though you will of course be paid lavishly in hard cash.

Phew, close one.

The special opportunity One is honoured to extend is an invitation to join a highly exclusive club – a club whose members are helping to shape Tomorrow's World.

This was more like it. Here was a club tie that would surely open doors – splinter them to matchwood, in fact.

If you wish to take up our cordial offer please place two samples of blood in the specimen jars provided, and send them back with the courier your PA is currently unsuccessfully trying to 'chat up'.

The initiation ceremony, should you care to join us, for both yourself and the elite few others selected, will coincide with our product's VIP unveiling at our Corporate HQ. Details of journey arrangements to follow.

One looks forward to you permanently joining our organization, for all eternity and beyond.

Yours, in ermine,

Liz 2

Marshall didn't need to waste time thinking about it, this wasn't the sort of proposal you turned down in a hurry – the financial equivalent of a supermodel asking you in for coffee and a shag. OK, so some of her requests were a little peculiar – not to mention the nagging suspicion as to why the world's richest woman would want any more cash – but when you had a chance like this you didn't let trifling details make you reach for the brakes.

Without a second, or even first thought, Marshall pulled a penknife from his pocket and pricked his thumb – which was the other way round to how he usually did it, but it gave him more than the normal thrill. Wincing slightly, he squeezed a small quantity of his (reassuringly still red) life-fluid into one of the thin plastic tubes and snapped it shut.

Little did he know it but this wasn't an offer he could have turned down if he'd wanted to – not unless he'd craved a second visit from some less savoury callers. Folk who crossed the Committee had a habit of falling off yachts, or slamming into underpass stanchions after first being run off the road by mystery cars.

But then there were plenty of things Marshall was yet to discover about his regal client, though not all of them would remain hidden for long.

42. Your Days Are Numbered

The Watchers are obsessed with Numerology and the Occult, just as their Nazi cohorts were – those loyal servants who currently slumber deep under the Antarctic ice ready to be awakened. Prime amongst the ancient runes and symbols the Old Ones worship is the number 42 – the true Number of the Genetically-Engineered Beast.

42 is the number of nut-chips you get on one of their ice-cream cones.

42 is the number of their secret deep-sea bases.

42 is the number of verses in the full version of 'American Pie', the ones which make clear its original demonic message. The ones the CIA made Don MacLean cut out.

On an island in the South Pacific, close to the 42nd parallel the Watchers have 42 very special 'guests', which they use to help spread paranoia and confusion. They are being used up by the day.

Never trust anyone who declares this sum significant. They are without doubt a high-ranking Watcher agent unleashed upon Earth to spread fear and delusions wherever they go.

Page 42, Becker, *MJ13*

43. Communion

Kate was as good as her word. They found her uncle's holiday cottage after a long drive, nestled in the folds of two barren hills, slumbering beneath a bleak expanse of moorland. Dusk was settling on the landscape as they pulled onto the gravel driveway, the first cold stars twinkling from a stark sky. Dave at least was eager for the prospect of a warm bed. Beside him Frank's snores hinted that he was not in such a hurry. Like all military men he was capable of sleeping anywhere.

Kate was first out of the car. 'I'll go and check he's left the key in the usual place.'

Oddly Dave noticed she took her bag with her. Rubbing his face he got out to stretch. 'So what do we do now? I know he didn't get us very far in the end, but I almost miss that scruffy grey beggar.'

Frank had sprung awake in an instant. Moodily he was peering at the darkening horizon. 'Don't worry about him, partner. He's gone to a better place. As for our next move, we'll discover what that should be soon enough.'

Dave considered asking him what he meant, but saw the look in Frank's eyes and thought better of it. He didn't think he'd like what he'd hear. He was relieved when Kate returned with the key, and they entered the farmhouse to prepare a simple supper. The electricity was off but they soon found a ready supply of candles. The choice of food wasn't great, but Dave tucked into his corned beef and beans with gusto. It was enlightening what not eating all day as you fled for your life could do to your appetite.

When they were finished, and the first splashes of rain were beginning to pepper the windowpanes, Kate rose to clear the things away. As she reached for Frank's plate their eyes met and she graced him with a tired smile. With frightening speed his hand shot out to grab her slender wrist.

'I wouldn't be in such a hurry to leave us, if I were you.'

Kate squirmed under his tightening grip. 'Stop it, Frank, you're hurting me.'

Dave was on his feet in an instant. 'What the hell are you thinking of, you stupid brain-fried grunt. Let her go!'

But Frank was having none of it. 'Sit down and shut up, Dave. You've really got no idea, have you? Go and look up "gullible" in the dictionary, it'll say "*cf. Dave*".'

Kate's eyes locked with Frank's. 'Do as he says, Dave. There's more to this than either of you know.'

Frank grinned and nodded. 'Ain't that the truth, sister? And you're about to give us our first lesson.' With his free hand he reached into his ever-present satchel and produced an unfeasibly large gun.

Dave stared wide-eyed at its boxy metallic shape, the polished chrome glinting in the dim candlelight. His sense of reality was quaking beneath him once more, as Frank cocked the hammer and pointed it at Kate's head.

'Picked this up from one of my former colleagues back at your studio. Don't reckon he'll be needing it anytime soon.'

The ex-commando continued to train the gun on the girl as he let her go. Backing off, his lip curled in an ugly sneer. 'Now babe, are you going to come clean about your part in this mess, or am I gonna have to replaster that wall with your pretty brains? How did our black-clad friends know where to find us?'

Kate held very still, a look of sick acceptance on her face. 'If you'll just let me explain, you'll see that our interests coincide.'

Dave could barely believe what he was hearing. 'Tell me this isn't happening, Kate.'

Frank answered for her. 'Take a look in her purse. I'd

be interested to see if it contains anything . . . out of the ordinary.'

Dumbly Dave complied. He found much that he'd expect amidst any young woman's things. Lipstick, credit cards, a small bottle of mineral water, more paper hankies than seemed strictly necessary. Only one item struck him as odd. It looked at first sight like a small palm-top computer, the sort that was briefly fashionable before people realized a notebook and pen didn't need batteries. When he snapped it open he got the shock of his life. It didn't exactly have a rotating satellite dish built in, but the array of antennae and sensors that popped out told him this was no normal personal organizer.

Frank saw his astonishment. 'In case you're wondering, Dave, you can't buy that shit on the high street.'

'This can't be happening,' Dave mumbled to no one in particular.

Kate looked sad, but in no other way alarmed. 'Oh, it's happening all right. It's because people have stuck their heads in the sand too long that they've got this far. My boss is working to ensure they don't get any further.'

Dave nearly dropped the hi-tech communicator in shock. 'Your boss! You mean to say you're working for the scum mixed up in this? But I've known you since we were in school. You're a TV researcher, on a daytime confession show, not some female Harry Palmer dodging poisoned umbrellas and talking in code!'

It told Frank all he needed to know about his friend, that he was perfectly capable of believing in flying saucers and little grey men, but couldn't accept that the girl he loved led a double life. Not for the first time he pondered that humans were funny creatures.

Kate's eyes didn't leave Frank's. 'Those years I spent at college in the States, well, I've got news for you, Dave; I wasn't just at USC, I was a little bit further east – out in the desert in fact. That was where I received my training.'

Dave sounded aghast. 'But you sent me letters and post-cards. I even got a photo of you and some buck-toothed football-playing idiot.'

Kate gazed at her friend pityingly. 'You really don't get how big this is, do you?'

Dave looked dumbfounded. 'And your job in TV, the one I think we can assume you no longer have – well, not since your employer got blown away by Frank's trigger-happy chums?'

Kate paused for a moment. 'That was set up for me as part of my mission. I was monitoring certain . . . changes our society has undergone.'

Dave shook his head in disbelief. 'I'm sorry, but I find that hard to believe. If this is your idea of a joke, it's in very poor taste.'

'It's no joke, Dave. If the fools running the Committee get their way there won't be anyone left laughing.'

Throughout the exchange Frank had been looking at Kate in an odd way. His eyes still held mistrust, but also the beginnings of dawning comprehension. 'This is very touching an' all, listening to you two get reacquainted, but we don't have all night for Davey-boy here to whip his world view into shape. I think, Kate, that perhaps you'd better take this story from the top. Just who exactly are you working for?'

The moment was broken by the squeal of tyres from the gravel forecourt outside. Seconds later two powerful headlights cast the drifting shadows of the three com-panions across the cottage's plaster wall. For a moment all seemed frozen, dismay smeared across every face. As their silhouettes dissolved into the blackness, so appar-ently did their chances of survival.

'Oh my God,' blubbed Dave. 'This is it. They've come to get us! And this time there's no escape.'

Kate held up both hands pleadingly as Frank nervously glanced from the girl to the door then back again. There was a back exit, but he'd have to leave Dave behind. Could he chance it that they didn't have that way covered? The odds weren't looking good.

For the first time Kate's voice held the slightest tremor. 'I know this looks bad, but there's no reason to panic. I didn't mean for you to meet this way, but you left me little choice. That's not who you think it is outside.'

Frank formed a triangle between himself, the girl and the door. 'It better not be, because if it is then you die with us.'

By then they could all clearly hear the sound of heavy boots crunching gravel underfoot. The pace was measured, and it came from only one pair of shoes. Dizzily Dave remembered that he'd left the door on the latch. As the handle of the door turned, the young reporter thought he might faint with fright. Nearby Frank licked his lips, as Kate tried to will a peaceful resolution. When the farmhouse door swung inwards their guest stepped up and filled the frame, a hulking shadow against the encroaching indigo night.

Frank panned the gun to aim right between the stranger's eyes. It wasn't the sort of high percentage shot he'd been trained to take, but if this was the end of the line then he wanted to go out in style. To be caught in some elaborate trap was no fitting way for a hero to end his days. If this was how it ended then this arrogant son of a bitch was going to be buying duty-free next to him on the last ferry-boat to Hell.

The figure took one silent step forward, and soft candle-light bathed half his craggy face in its baleful orange glow. Ever so slowly Frank's jaw dropped. So did the gun.

Dave saw the new arrival was a man of indeterminate age. Old certainly, but infused with a terrible vitality that threatened to burst forth from his crumpled clothes. Dave looked from the newcomer to Frank and back again. Their physiques were very different, but they were unmistakably hewed from the same resilient stone. They shared that same permanent middle-distance stare, as if afraid of what they might see if they looked closer to home. The stranger's voice was as deep and resonant as a drum.

'Relax, soldier. I'm on my own.'

Frank's face was a writhing sea of emotion, as a strange mixture of suspicion and half-remembered recognition fought it out for supremacy. His distrust seemed finally to win out. 'But I thought you were . . .'

'Dead?' Becker finished for him. 'There are plenty of folks who'd prefer to see me that way. As of yet they haven't got their wish.'

Frank's brow furrowed with concentration. 'You were the one at the studio? Dark hair, front row. Hawaiian shirt you should need a licence for. Sorry about the arm.'

Becker shrugged. 'That's OK. I didn't take it personally. Good to see you haven't lost any of your old speed.'

Frank's intensity didn't waver. 'That's not where I remember you from, though. Not where I remember you "buying the farm"?'

The Dark Man shook his head. 'We go back much further than that. Though I don't blame you if your recollection falters. It's no doubt for the better that you've forgotten more than you know. Though I see Kate must be trying to help you remember.'

She still had her hands raised as a result of Frank's high-calibre quiz. She now lowered them and moved to close the rain-lashed door. 'You took your time. I was beginning to think you'd got lost.'

Dave got the impression he was getting left behind. 'What the hell . . . you told him where this place was? Have you completely lost your senses?'

Kate glanced at her old friend. 'You know nothing about this. Perhaps this is our chance to set the record straight.'

Turning to Becker she helped him out of his heavy overcoat. 'Are you sure you weren't followed? Let me have a look at that wrist.'

Becker gave her a withering look. 'At this point I could say something about grandmothers and the sucking of eggs, but seeing as yours was such an acerbic old bat I'll let it lie. The last thing we need are the ghosts of the dead adding to our problems. The arm's fine – nothing a few aspirin can't take care of.'

Dave glanced from Becker to Kate. 'I'm starting to feel like the odd man out. Do you three know each other from somewhere? I'm developing a major complex here.'

Frank scoffed. 'As if you didn't have one already.'

Kate ignored him. 'I didn't need to direct him here. The old place belongs to him, after all.'

Now it was Frank's turn to sound incredulous. With a rare lapse of professional standards he gestured towards Becker with the gun. '*He's* your uncle?'

Kate looked genuinely guilty. 'Actually no, he's not my uncle, he's my dad.'

Dave would have slithered to the floor if he'd had the energy. 'Jesus wept,' he sobbed. 'This is getting too much. Will someone *please* explain what's going on?'

Frank too seemed deeply troubled. 'Yeah – I want some answers fast, and I'm not afraid to expend ammunition to get them. I've seen this dude before, but where and when and for which side does he fight?'

Kate sighed wearily. 'Sit down, boys, shut up and listen.'

The Dark Man beckoned for the girl to do the same. 'You too, Kate. I've kept it from you for long enough – this horrible truth that I carry with me like a cross. You've served me blindly until now, like so many of my unwitting tools. You of all people deserve to know the facts, as best I can tell them. Loyalty has its price.'

Kate lay a gentle hand on his broken arm. It was the first sign of outward affection Frank and Dave had seen. Wearily, Becker began to tell his tale.

44. The Awful Truth

As the storm took hold, blowing eerie discordant tunes through the open flue and sending candleflames dancing, Becker's story unfolded like a vast and hazy route-map to a place no one wanted to visit.[1]

He told of the secret society that underpinned the affairs of man, the Committee of 300 he called it, and not without a shudder. Its members formed a semi-hereditary ruling elite, membership passing through inbred generations like some haunted antique clock. Democracy was a sham, elected officials pawns and playthings, nothing more than strutting peacocks who took the fickle praise of history, and the fall when things went wrong. The Committee's goals were more enduring and more primordial – the retention of its covert grip on power, at a cost paid in the lives of the faceless horde.

Every ruling caste needs its servants, and this one more so than most. Becker himself had been such an accomplice, a trusted retainer of this bickering oligarchy, charged with wielding the far-reaching powers it could not entrust to one of its own kind. This assignment had given him a perspective that few men would crave, the vision to stand back and watch his master's decadent decline and imminent fall. Secret it might have been, but the Committee's toppling would send shock waves around the world. The final earthquake to lay low a tottering civilization.

How such a disaster could take place, in spite of his own best efforts, clearly filled Becker with rage and shame. The Committee had always been obsessed with tradition, its shady roots stretching back to a dimly remembered

---

[1] i.e. Hull.

Masonic past. It was Becker's hypothesis that these latent occult leanings, coupled with a love of intrigue for its own sake, had been turned against the organization by an external force – 'the Silent Watchers', he called them, contempt permeating his voice.

Somehow the upper echelons of mankind's shadow leadership had been subverted through trickery and infiltration. The Greys were nothing more than a red herring, a distraction intended to lead humanity down a bizarre path of Luddite irrationalism. Knowledge of their existence was widespread, Becker had been unable to prevent that dissemination, but their true nature had been kept from an increasingly credulous and superstitious public. The awful truth had been hidden, wrapped up in a veil of lies and carefully staged hoaxes. Better mankind believe in a fictitious hi-tech alien presence incarcerated by a uncaring government than that it know the full facts. If the truth ever seeped out the effects on human consciousness and optimism for the future would be incalculable. But this goal was just what the Watchers seemed intent to achieve. Their motives could only be guessed at, but that they were benign seemed too much to hope.

The Committee's policy of controlling mankind through paranoia and fear was soon concocted to complement this subversive agenda. This new idea found fertile ground in the gullible and distracted minds of certain members, tapping an unpleasant undercurrent that had flowed by all along. Some were not content that their political puppets merely take the falls, some wanted them loathed and mistrusted as well. This was how the arch manipulators had themselves become the manipulated, a point Becker had struggled long and hard to bring to light.

For the past forty years a covert Black War had been fought between Becker's own dark agency and the inhuman schemes of the Watchers. With the recent attempt on his life, that war was covert no more. The Black War had taken on a terrible white heat.

When he'd finished the three sat in silence for what seemed like a lifetime. At last Dave felt able to speak.

'No, I can't accept it. You're making it up. My magazine gets letters from freaks like you all the time. I'll bet you've got a budgie, wear an anorak and live at home with your mum.'

Becker locked Dave in a vice-like stare. 'I've got ulcers older than you. Take it from me, son – I know what I'm about.'

Frank seamed more prepared to believe, though no more trusting. 'Why have you come to us? Wouldn't your friends in high places make better allies?'

Becker sat back and spread his arms. 'My enemies have broken cover. Their need for stealth is gone. If they can risk an open attempt on my life then their grip on the Committee is complete. My former contacts are lost forever. I wouldn't be surprised if their car bomb was planted by my own staff, in response to some trumped-up charge. In fact I'm a little embarrassed by their performance. I trained my people better than that.'

'I know the feeling,' Frank muttered. 'But why should we take you in? What do we have to gain?'

Becker pointed to the alien satchel Frank had placed on the kitchen table. 'You have MJ13, but that's just a record of the facts. Do you expect any more success getting it published than its author?'

Dave gazed at the battered sack that had come with them through so much, and at the bulky blue folder he could see poking out. 'What the hell is that thing?'

Becker sighed. 'MJ13 filled many functions over the years. It started as the primary briefing document for those inducted into power – the operational bible for the carefully selected few allowed to join our clan. I was responsible for its update, dissemination and security. Only I had the clearance to see it written down in one place. The whole sordid affair.'

'Must have looked bad when it went missing. You say it started out that way. What did it become?'

Becker's spirit seemed to sink before Dave's eyes. 'I allowed my own beliefs to percolate through its pages. By the time the master copy was stolen it had become a personal rant against the policies of the Committee. The Watchers knew I was onto them, yet they still sought to leak the document, along with some corroborating biological material. They obviously thought my ramblings would not be believed, doing my cause more harm than good. I'm afraid I have been fatally naïve.'

Dave's face had suddenly gone dreadfully pale. 'That email you sent me, Frank, the one that triggered our meeting . . .'

His words trailed off. Frank was slowly shaking his head. 'Gotta admit, I always wondered how you showed up in Las Vegas. Seemed too neat to be true. Our telepathic link's never been the same since.'

Dave was looking sicker by the second, his voice almost pleading for a sane reply. 'Then who told me to be at that diner – what was it they hoped to achieve?'

All he got in answer were harried looks from the others. Slowly Frank shook his head. 'Shit, man, these dudes are smart.'

Becker seemed more certain of his facts. 'It fits their modus operandi. MJ13 was taken from my office by a not-so-stupid Grey. Perhaps they're not the harmless smokescreen I first thought. Their masters seem to hold some sway over them even in captivity. The one who took it fled with a crew of his zombified friends.'

'Until their saucer purposefully crashed in the Nevada desert,' said Frank, a hieroglyph-carved penny dropping with an ominous clang.

'That's right,' said Becker. 'But you weren't to know. If it's any consolation you have my eternal admiration. You successfully smuggled the thing out of the country despite my best efforts to stop you.'

'Thanks,' said Frank sardonically. 'We noticed. But it wasn't entirely one-way traffic.' He looked at Dave. 'We got the feeling we had some help along the way.'

'This is all pure bullshit,' his companion muttered.

Becker's brow darkened. 'Then you felt the dark hand of the Old Ones at work, or whatever other appendage they use in its place. By the time you'd got it to the TV studio, the attempt on my life had been made. I pray that they believe it to be successful. By that stage control of my last few remaining assets had been thoroughly usurped by the real powers behind the throne.'

'That's why I was told to get the boys onto the box,' Kate said.

Becker nodded. 'And when Freemantle and his men crashed the party it did nothing but draw attention to the Watchers' subtle scheme – their true intention all along.'

Kate's face held a look of sick concern. 'And the Temple of Planet Love, how do they fit into this?'

Becker shrugged. 'That's a bigger question than you can know. Though I suspect they were at your studio merely to add fuel to the fire. And to ensure events proceeded with a bang.'

A distant look descended over Frank's flinty eyes. 'Oh, they went with a bang all right. 'But what do they hope to achieve, these "Watchers"? Why play these games? I don't give a shit about these stuck-up aristocrats you used to work for, but why bend them out of shape?'

Becker paused for a long while. At first Dave thought he wouldn't answer. When he did it seemed to cause him great pain. 'I . . . don't . . . fully understand. But something's coming, some major play for the destiny of this fragile rock, and when it comes we don't want the dice to fall their way.'

His statement was met with another silence. Becker leaned forward in his chair.

'You asked what you have to gain from me. I can offer more than just an explanation for that overblown doorstop you've been lugging across half the globe. I know how we can strike back at the Watchers, perhaps wipe them out for good. You are right, Frank, this is not the first time that we've met.'

45. Machu Picchu Revisited

Becker looked carefully in turn at each of the three conspirators seated around the table, as if weighing up the measure of their souls. His own daughter, her best friend in denial and a burnt-out grunt who looked likely to crack at any moment. As far as armies went he had served with better, in fact he had seen better units dissolve in terror, but then this threesome made up his last remaining hope. When Becker spoke it was with a calm air of authority he no longer felt.

'We are up against an opponent of frightening subtlety and inhuman intellect. It's only in the past weeks that I've come to realize just how clever they are. They make the short-sighted conclusions in that manuscript look like fairy tales.' Becker gestured to the large blue ring-binder at the end of the table. Dave noticed his hand displayed a slight tremor. Frank saw it too.

'Up until now, hoaxes and half-truths have been their weapons of choice. Have no doubt, however, that your recent TV appearance will be used to further their plans. Their power grows stronger, the stakes are raised by the day. When we strike back it must be with irresistible force.'

Frank's 'thousand yard stare' seemed to double in distance. 'How can we do that? Where do we aim?'

'Patience. First you must know your enemy, as you know yourself.'

'Sun Tzu,' nodded Frank approvingly. 'The first rule of war.'

'Funny,' muttered Dave. 'I always thought "military intelligence" was an oxymoron.' He was roundly ignored. Becker went on.

'This is not the first time I've faced this foe directly. For the past twenty years I've been probing for a potential weakness, gathering information where I can. Once before I felt strong enough to strike.'

'Let me guess,' said Kate. 'South America, '92? Don't remember hearing much from you that year.'

Becker nodded. 'I was otherwise engaged. After my agency's success in setting up the Gulf War I was in a position of relative strength within the Committee. Oil money has deep pockets, as well as deep gratitude for its favoured sons. I held political capital that I haven't before or since. I was able to use it to test a theory, to set up a reconnaissance mission in force. Of course, most of the Committee thought I had taken leave of my senses, but they couldn't deny the war hero who'd so recently helped them play out their petty games. If only I'd looked harder into their acquiescence. My target was in the Andes – a place I'd long suspected to be a seat of enemy power.'

'Machu Picchu,' muttered Frank, a haunted, distant look in his eye.

'The ancient Inca capital,' nodded Becker. 'Say what you like about them, but at least the Old Ones possess a flair for the dramatic. When we were ready to launch the assault I needed my best man at the cutting edge. Sergeant Frank MacIntyre commanded the first chopper to hit the ground.'

Dave's voice was on the verge of breaking up. 'What went wrong?'

Becker let out a weary sigh. For the first time he looked his true age. 'We were betrayed higher up the chain of command. That was how I learned the true extent of their penetration of our leadership. But we paid a terrible price to obtain that information.'

Frank's mind was yanked back unbidden, to a time before the militias and the confused political meetings, where pipe-bombs were packed with fertilizer as tightly as back rooms were packed with eager faces. Before his life in the shadows, when he'd drifted through the vast American subculture of paranoid gun-nuts and redneck survivalist freaks, to ride with them along the chaotic railways of the night.

He was taken back to that fateful day when he and his elite band of troopers rode their black helicopters across the boundless jungle, their booted feet dangling scant inches above the lush tree canopy. He could hear the heavy '*whop-whop*' of the rotor-blades right now. For the first time Frank's memories cleared, as Becker's words tumbled on.

They hit the landing zone in tight formation, the Black-hawks setting down on a high plateau amidst a natural amphitheatre of bizarrely shaped hills. As ever their planning was impeccable. Satellite photos had shown where the deserted Inca palaces were located, thermal scans which cyclopean structures led down into the slumbering chambers and galleries lacing the hill. But Frank's Black Berets never got that far.

Their enemies had been waiting for them around the clearing. Hidden between ancient temples and vine-clad step-pyramids, they'd unleashed a withering crossfire with a horrific array of deadly weapons, both familiar and unknown. The ambush had developed with terrible force. Frank saw his comrades scythed down around him, the elite of the covert military establishment reduced to so much flayed flesh and shattered bone. Next to him his radio operator went down, both legs cut clean off at the knee by a laser beam's searing heat.

The landed choppers started popping like Fourth of July firecrackers, their screaming crews spilling out like blazing human torches. Those still circling made off around the dome-shaped hills, swaying corpses swinging from the abseil-lines. Back in the killing zone Sergeant MacIntyre valiantly attempted to rally his men, but to no avail. With a slow-motion clatter he was cut down by a vintage WW1 machine-gun.

For what seemed like a lifetime all was still. Then, once they were sure of no further resistance from the dead and dying scattered on the plateau, the ambushers cautiously crept from their jungle-infested dens. Frank's body was picked over by a multitude of three-fingered grey hands. When the creatures finished pilfering his kit, he was dragged down into their dark and dismal lair, through the vats and laboratories where they conducted unspeakable experiments. And that was when his true nightmare began.

Drifting in and out of consciousness, Frank was carried to a large and vaulting chamber cut from living rock. At its far end stood a potent symbol of Watcher power, taking up the entire rear wall – a crudely built brick pyramid overlain with the all-seeing eye. Around it skulked and scurried the fruits of past harvests. An army of lobotomized local Indians peered on from the gloom, their minds as vacant as their bruise-ringed dead eyes. Positioned at the room's centre was a genetically engineered organism of monstrous design – a pulsating telepathic mind-hub that linked this den of slaves to their distant, faceless masters. From its vein-laced purple dome sprouted a multitude of specially-adapted tentacles, each tipped by a beckoning skull-sized cap. Like the handful of other survivors, Frank was to be indoctrinated into the ways of the Watchers, to become yet another willing slave. And when this was done, when each knew the full details of the inhuman plot, their brains would be harvested for one crucial emotion – the single critical enzyme the Watchers needed to survive.

One by one the men were attached to the thing, their minds to be scrubbed clean, ready to receive fresh instructions.

Becker had been on board the command chopper, watching helpless as the first wave of his men were slaughtered where they stood. Hurriedly he drew in the tattered remnants of those who'd survived, the second wave of back-up staff fortunately still in the air. Medics and signal technicians were quickly press-ganged into combat troops, radios and stretchers swapped for carbines and grenades. Confident of their victory, the Watchers' grey sentries had lowered their guard. When Becker's men went back in, it was with the force of avenging angels.

Casualties were horrific, but the soldiers had vengeance as well as military discipline on their side. Steadily they fought their way down through that infested honeycombed hill, wasting Greys at a rate far outstripping their own losses. At last Becker and a handful of suicidal volunteers made it to the central chamber. The Greys and human drones fought fanatically to protect their living link to HQ, but they were like a sand wall placed before a surging tide.

Becker realized the significance of the throbbing communication terminal as soon as he saw it, and what it must mean for the unfortunate troopers held in its thrall. A hastily tossed grenade put an end to the monstrous download of information. But for those men strapped in, their salvation came too late. All died instantly as a result of the disconnection, expressions of blessed mercy stretched across every face. All died, that is, except for one sergeant – his brain clearly more resilient than most. Frank was dragged kicking and screaming back to the surface by Becker, as the rest of his men covered their retreat. None of that valiant rearguard made it out alive.

'We had one chopper still operational, along with a small group we'd left top-side to cover any escape. We didn't really expect to be coming out alive. I needn't tell you, we got out of there in a hurry. I knew I should have busted Freemantle after he didn't volunteer to go with us into that hill, but after that débâcle we needed all the warm bodies we could get.'

Frank looked at him with horrified fascination. 'What happened to me after that?'

'When we got back Stateside you received the best medical treatment known to man. Your body healed, but your mind seemed lost to us forever. You spent months with our top psychiatrists. They invented whole new batteries of tests to probe your twisted psyche. We suspected even then that it held clues to our enemy's true intent. I'd be surprised if you can even look at an ink-blot without flipping your lid. I have to tell you that you drove more than one of your doctors clinically insane. In the end we had to call it a day, there were only so many willing to volunteer for service on your case. We struck a special medal for those that tried. Those still in one piece finally admitted they could extract nothing from you – nothing that you'd witnessed strapped to that infernal living device – no knowledge of what it was trying to harvest from your soul.'

'Suppressed,' said Kate. 'The brain edits out ordeals it can't begin to comprehend.'

'Or finds too shocking,' added Becker. 'Your memories are buried deep. Once I knew we'd got all we could from you, we suppressed what recollections you did have and turned you loose. Just another brain-fried grunt wandering the streets, balls in hand.'

'Gee,' said Frank. 'I'm touched by your concern. Wasn't I in line for a pension? I would have expected at least a bullet in the back of the head.'

'It was the least I could do to set you free,' said Becker modestly, 'after your years of faithful service to the cause.'

Frank looked at him oddly. 'There's one thing I don't understand. When Freemantle told you it was me who had the Grey, how did you track me down? I wasn't in the habit of using my real name.'

'With this,' said Becker. He unbuckled from his belt what looked like a tiny mobile. Thumbing a switch he pointed its stubby aerial at a spot just behind Frank's left ear. A scarlet bulb on the plastic case began flashing at a blistering pace. 'RANGE 0 METRES' read the device's compact display.

'Great,' muttered Frank. 'People always said I had a chip on my shoulder. Now I find it's in my head!'

Kate was evidently learning much for the first time too. 'So the Machu Picchu site, it wasn't the Watchers' main base.'

Becker shook his head. 'I had underestimated them once again. It was nothing more than a regional centre – a jumping-off point for them to draw in new recruits. We encountered their usual screen of Greys and enslaved humans, but nothing that even looked like a live Watcher. We shut down one branch office – a pyrrhic tactical victory, because they're opening up new franchises all the time.'

'That's a fascinating story,' said Dave, with only a trace of sarcasm. 'It goes a long way to explain Frank's deplorable mental state. But what bearing has it got on our current predicament?'

Kate shifted uneasily in her chair. 'I think I can tell you that.' She and Becker exchanged a knowing look. He prompted her to go on.

'My first mission on leaving the academy was to monitor social changes in the UK. For this sort of delicate work we only use field agents familiar with local culture. I grew up here after all.' She glanced at Dave, who pretended not to notice. 'The last two years I've been specially tasked with investigating the rebirth of superstition and irrationalism: UFOs, crop circles, mystic cults and the like.'

Dave's eyes narrowed. 'Or shaven-headed orange chums, so keen on helping us get on TV?'

Becker nodded. 'They're the legitimate human face of another Watcher branch office. The one specifically tasked with subverting the UK.'

'Christ,' muttered Frank. 'If they're the legitimate face I wouldn't like to see the illegitimate one.'

Becker's steady gaze fell on him like a lead weight. 'You might be gazing on that countenance soon enough. You see, Frank, your mind, and the cultists' own brain-hub, are the only keys we have to unlocking the Old Ones' plans.'

46. Please Aim Here

Noroco fought back a massive yawn. He'd been driving through the night and was currently paying the price for his unflagging persistence. Beside him in the battered Trabant his army's only operational portable radio bounced along with every pothole in the road. The twisting mountain track was rocky in a way that only up-country Urgistan and celebrity marriages could be. If any of the three of them reached the Kara-Kuri region in one piece it would be a miracle, but not half the miracle it would take to end this war, and to bring the true threat to the world's fickle attention.

But as Noroco had reflected more than once on that long slow journey, if you had no hope you had nothing at all. It was just seconds after such a moment of giddy optimism that his spirits suffered a near fatal blow.

The roadway he had followed snaked up along a steep escarpment, the wall of stark grey stone to his right broken only by a series of widening gullies. These minor obstacles had been getting larger for the past hour, but until now had been spannable by simple culverts in the road. Not so the large gorge that currently blocked his path. Until recently it had been crossed by a rickety trellis bridge. He could still see its fire-blackened remains blocking the tiny stream four hundred feet below – no doubt an early target for the Allied bombs.

Noroco got out of the car and shielded his narrow eyes against the high-altitude glare. Ten miles up the desolate valley he could just make out the start of a shattered region of blasted soil and twisted rock, the first indication that he was nearing his destination. And did his straining eyes deceive him or was that a threatening hillside of corrupted ice and discoloured snow nestling between the peaks? His first tantalizing glimpse of the haunted Kara-Kuri glacier. Reinvigorated by his discovery, the general pulled the radio from his useless vehicle and considered his next move. To his left the land fell away sharply, but it should be passable with care.

An hour later he was having second thoughts about this assessment. He had scrambled down the wide scree and reached the valley's barren floor with considerable difficulty. Dusting himself down he'd set off up the canyon at a purposeful striding pace, but he hadn't gone twenty paces when the brooding silence was shattered by the low rumble of speeding jets away to the south, the booming echoes of their sonic shock waves reverberating off the canyon walls like distant thunder.

'This way, you fools!' Noroco yelled, jumping on the spot and waving a hand in the direction of the far-off glacier. 'That's what you should be bombing, not our peaceful towns and villages. Come on up and take a look!'

Miraculously, as if following his bidding to the letter, two of the tiny dots above the horizon peeled away from the formation and began to head straight towards him. For a moment Noroco experienced a flash of blinding elation, then a bout of stomach-emptying terror – against all the laws of chance his plan seemed to be working.

*   *   *

Onboard the lead F-13 fighter Lieutenant Duggan, USAF, peered at his magnified infrared display and frowned. The target was still a long way off but the range was closing rapidly. A lone figure seemed to be running up the rocky valley, clutching something to his chest and pointing hysterically ahead of him. Several times the man fell, but on each occasion got quickly to his feet and continued his headlong flight. The reason for his stumbling progress was that he was not looking where he was going; Duggan could have sworn he kept glancing over his shoulder, right back at him. The young officer was getting something garbled across his radio too.

'*Bomb me when I get there! It's our only hope . . .*' it seemed to scream, over and over again. Duggan snorted in disgust – some distant commercial station no doubt. This altitude played havoc with UHF transmissions. Scowling, he retuned to his squadron's control channel. His readjustment came just in time.

'Cloud Nine to Angel Leader. Explain course change!'

'Have spotted a target of opportunity entering Sector 7. Am investigating ASAP.'

There was a long pause before the radar controller came back on-line. 'Angel Leader, be advised Sector 7 is off limits. We have it from the very highest authority that it's a Restricted Zone. Am vectoring you out of there.'

Before Duggan could reply a new voice crackled in his headset, its tone brooking no room for debate. 'Angel Leader, this is Heaven's Gate. Turn back *right now*. This is your last warning before we use deadly force to help you comply.'

Duggan's eyes darkened beneath his mirrored shades – this new call-sign had been in no briefings. 'Identify yourself, Heaven's Gate. How do we know you're on our side?'

The new voice didn't hesitate for a second. 'Never mind who *we* are, just know that if you don't turn back right now you won't live long enough to be court-martialled. These orders come from the highest authority there is. Ever heard of the pale building in DC?'

Quietly, the AWACS controller returned to Duggan's frequency. He sounded sickened and more than a little shaken by this challenge to his authority. 'Do as they say, Angel Leader. Their security clearance checks out. Didn't know top brass watched our moves so closely.'

Duggan knew when he was beaten. These days you

didn't buck the system if you wanted your career to progress – the Air Force still flew mail planes to the Antarctic
after all.

As it turned out, the point was moot in any case; the
lone figure had suddenly disappeared from view.

*   *   *

Noroco raced onwards like a man possessed. He held little
hope that he could reach the glacier before the planes
wiped him out, but he was desperate enough to clutch at
any straw, no matter how bent. Perhaps his imminent
death, so close to the seat of ancient evil, would be enough
in itself to bring the place to the warmongers' attention.

Half turning he yelled back over his shoulder, 'Follow
me, you fuckwits. And bring your short-sighted generals
with you!'

But no sooner had he parted his chapped lips than the
planes once more showed an uncanny knack for
responding to his every word; but this time they far from
followed his orders. Noroco stumbled to a halt as both
aircraft banked hard and set a new course back the way
they'd come. It was almost as if they'd encountered an
invisible barrier and were now fleeing for their worthless
lives.

Noroco's breathless dismay gave way to a terrible fury.
'Cowards!' he screamed, shaking his gnarled fist impotently after the departing jets. 'Don't run away. Don't you
know who I am?'

In a manic frenzy the general tried to reach them on
the radio, but all he got for his troubles was an earful of
frightful static. Just as Noroco began to conclude things
couldn't get any worse, they did – suddenly he was tackled
from an entirely unexpected direction by a pair of burly
Urgi soldiers. Still cursing the Western pilots, he was
bundled to the ground like a fighting yak at a Himalayan
rodeo.

Noroco quickly redirected his ire. 'Get off me, you oafs! I'm your Commanding Officer!'

But before he knew it he was being dragged behind a large boulder by the two straining troopers. He could hardly fail to notice that they were none too careful in their handling of a Head of State. But it was only when he skidded to a painful halt that Noroco's day really began to start looking grim.

Yajik's ugly face beamed down at him, a mask of unbridled happiness and relief. 'Ah, Master. We feared the Outlanders were about to get you. Don't you know it's not safe to parade round in the open like that these days?'

Noroco looked at his sidekick with contemptuous disbelief. 'By all the gods, how did you get up here so fast? I've been driving throughout the night.'

Yajik tapped a stubby finger to his stub nose in a hideously suggestive manner. 'I know these hills like the back of my grandma's hand – and considering how much she used to box my ear, that's quite a bit. If you don't mind me saying so, sir, these parts can be treacherous for those that don't know them. Especially if out strolling without a care in the world.'

'I *wasn't* going on a hiking holiday,' Noroco fumed. 'I was trying to lead our enemies to the source of the contamination – successfully too, I might add – until . . .' His words trailed off as Yajik slowly shook his head with a vacant grin.

'It would have done no good, sir. Our troops report the Outlanders have nothing to do with the high Kara-Kuri – almost as if they are scared of the place. Either that or their leaders know what's up here. Many of our boys have found refuge in these hills.'

All hope drained from Noroco's face, his features turning the colour of a wrung-out teabag. 'Then the Demon awakening and this war are no coincidence. We are beset by enemies from every side.'

Yajik displayed his fine collection of rotting teeth. 'Have no fear, Master. Fate smiles on us like a cut-price whore the day the goat-herds get paid. You have met up with *me* once again – our nation can yet be saved!'

Noroco sunk his head into his hands and wept openly.

47. East Grinstead A-Go-Go

The next morning Dave, Kate, Frank and Becker set out on the long drive south. They had sat up long into that stormy night, pooling every scrap of available information they had on Jackson's Temple of Planet Love. Some of it was disquieting in a most slippery way. It ranged from the inevitable salacious tabloid gossip to the detailed report Kate had faxed to Becker, while Dave and Frank had their fateful meeting in the States.

All of them had heard something of this cult. It was hard not to in these days of incessant turbocharged PR – a phenomenom Jackson was a wilier exponent of than most. There was only one thing they knew for sure. Like so many of the happy-clappy 'religions' of the New Age it had set up home in a small, affluent town tucked away in the leafy East Sussex countryside – a parasitic fungus sprouting from England's green, unpleasant land.

It seemed birds of a feather did indeed flock together, especially when those feathers smelled of incense, were saffron-dyed and hung with tiny tinkling bells. If this cult really believed what it professed, then it made its competitors look like Spockish bastions of coldly rational science. But the four were beginning to conclude Jackson's ideology was nothing but a carefully crafted masquerade.

Soon Kate's car was packed to overflowing. Becker had been able to pull some impressive kit from the cottage's darkest corners, not to mention the large bulky briefcase he hauled from his own hire vehicle with such care. For a time, playing with these new toys, Frank seemed a happy man. Dave concluded that 'holiday home' was looking an increasingly implausible description. 'Safe house' sounded nearer the mark. As they'd slipped down the long driveway the sanctuary it had offered seemed more and more appealing. Becker and Frank dozed on the crowded back seat, as Dave and Kate sat up front.

'You didn't expect to get caught up in any of this, did you?' Kate said.

Dave removed his glasses and rubbed his weary eyes. 'I don't know anymore ... about ... anything. Nothing makes any sense.'

Kate looked at her old friend warmly. 'You know you're not alone. If I ever find the guy who can explain it all to me, I mean to beat it out of him with a very big stick.'

Dave sighed. 'I was so sure of what I knew. There always seemed to be a simple pattern. So many certainties. But then ...'

'Frank comes along and pulls the rug from under your feet,' she finished for him.

'Something like that. The worst of it is I always felt I had a role to play – me and that magazine. All I had to do was gather the evidence, present it in an intelligent manner, and the world would welcome me as a hero. Some of it more passionately than most.' He looked at her pointedly.

Kate kept her eyes on the road. 'People only ever believe what they want to believe, Dave. In discovering the truth you learned it's not so easy to accept. I'm afraid you'll have to be more patient with your fellow man.'

'My patience is wearing pretty thin. From what I've seen I don't know if they're worth saving. And I definitely don't see how I'm the right man for the job.'

'True heroes never do.' That was all else she had to say on the matter.

*　　*　　*

They stopped for lunch at an unappealing service station. None of them felt much like eating; each was too preoccupied with the trials they knew would be ahead – Frank most of all. With each passing mile he seemed to retreat further into a defensive haze of brooding silence.

Finding himself alone for a moment with their shadowy new member, there was one question Dave felt he must ask. He'd scoured MJ13 for an answer, but perhaps surprisingly his searching had been in vain.

Becker seemed amused by Dave's inquiry. 'Kennedy was killed by the grassy knoll.'

'I know where he died, I asked who did it.'

Becker's chuckle was not a pretty sight. 'No, I meant it literally. Kennedy was killed *by* the grassy knoll. A radio transceiver buried inside it triggered the explosive dentures we'd had fitted. When I discovered he was a Watcher agent I had no option but to take him down. What a mistake that turned out to be.'

Dave's confusion only deepened until his vertigo threatened to suck him in. Becker saw that, perhaps understandably, he needed to elaborate.

'It was masterful the way our enemies turned his death to their advantage – subtly leaking that it *had* been a conspiracy all along, to help in their campaign to heighten public paranoia. The liberal martyr laid low by the callous State; what a pack of lies! Of course they couldn't go so far as to disclose the method used – The "Lone Dentist Theory" would have pushed the story's credibility to the limit.'

At least that was one point on which Dave could agree. His head was beginning to hurt with the ramifications of what he was learning. Soon enough, thankfully as far as Dave was concerned, they were on the road again.

By late afternoon they'd covered the three hundred miles to their destination. As they crested a low hill, beneath them in a shallow valley the small town slumbered in the gentle sun. If not the highly polished buckle on London's stockbroker belt, then at least a finely wrought stud.

'We lie up until dark near the target. That's when we go in.' Dave needed little convincing that Becker had done this sort of thing before.

Frank nodded in acknowledgement; a salute would have been inappropriate. Kate was glad to note even this mute reaction.

Out of the four of them only she had visited the area before, visited the very Temple of Planet Love itself, in fact. Showing an unnerving knowledge of the local back streets, she took them to a quiet country lane running behind the sprawling mansion, the track hidden from view by the dense encroaching woodland. Silently she parked the car and got out to stretch her legs. Soon she was joined by the others. They would have to wait many hours for the blanketing cover of night.

'What's the plan?' she asked to no one in particular, as they stood beneath the trees.

Becker peered through the roadside foliage. 'Doesn't appear to be much activity. At least Freemantle's men thinned their ranks.'

'You can say that again,' Dave said quietly. 'I'd be surprised if there were any cultists left.'

Becker seemed sure of his facts. 'You can bet there's at least one present.'

Across an impressive expanse of immaculate lawn the imposing whitewashed walls seemed to sprout from the very soil. There didn't appear to be anyone about. The only sign of human occupation was a hastily parked black Ferrari, skidded to a halt across the gravel drive. For no good reason one wheel seemed embedded in a flower bed.

Becker gave voice to their silent thoughts. 'Somewhere in there is a communications link back to the Watchers' main base.'

'Perhaps you're right,' said Dave. 'But how do we use it to extract the information we need?'

Becker looked at him as if he were very stupid indeed.

'We've got the only subject who's been connected to one of those things and lived to tell the tale. It's not much, but he's got more experience than anyone else could hope for.'

The three of them turned to look at Frank, who had gone deathly pale.

*   *   *

As darkness fell, they set about preparing for the coming mission. Frank proved more than adept at sorting out their impressive array of combat gear. Sternly he stood before Dave, helping him put on a set of ponderous night-vision goggles. Unsurprisingly, his younger companion seemed to be having second thoughts.

'Look, I'm sure this all makes perfect sense to you – heading in there to hook you up to some living database to hack their files – but might they not have just bought a fax machine in the meantime? Technology has moved on.'

Frank was busy smearing a fingerload of green gunge across Dave's face. 'Becker says all Watcher technology is biologically based. Something about it being the only science they really understand. Believe me, these guys usually do things "by the book". Improvisation isn't one of their strong points.'

'You seem well up on the subject. When did he tell you that?'

'Ten years ago, or more. The memories have started coming back. Linking up with . . . what's in there could unlock the rest – make me finally slip my clutch.'

Dave nodded. 'You're suffering a mental log-jam. You just need to wiggle the right bit and the rest will come flooding free.'

Frank's face was grim. 'Or the wrong bit, as the case may be. Secure that webbing, soldier, we're going in.'

48. High and Dry and Dead

Oblivious to the preparations going on outside, Jackson had his hands full with problems of his own. Since hurrying back from the bloodbath at the television studios, where he'd seen the cream of his followers cut down before his bulging eyes, he had spent a fruitless twenty-four hours attempting to raise his masters back at their distant HQ.

They had known how things would turn out, he didn't doubt that for an instant. The Watchers were too skilful at the art of manipulation for any other explanation to make sense. With a mood of dull fatalism Jackson allowed the numbing tendrils of the cult's central brain-hub to wrap around his skull one final time. He feared what he might hear, but not as much as he feared being left out in the cold. It was fresh instructions he sought, not explanations. But even more so than usual, the going had not been easy.

After many energy-sapping hours his consciousness at last cut through the teeming traffic that seemed to flood the Old Ones' telepathic ether – the familiar channels seemed to be building to a devilish crescendo. What Jackson heard back filled him with trepidation and woe, despite the narcotic effects of this unnatural communication. He felt like an abandoned general, cast adrift without hope of reinforcement or rescue. His orders were simple. Remove all trace of the cult from his current location; all evidence was to go up in smoke. Any surviving cultists were to be sent on a one-way trip to meet 'the great fornicator in the sky'. Fat chance of that: they had all been sacrificed for a fleeting moment of fame – getting that one worthless dead Grey publicized on TV.

Its purpose fulfilled, its cover blown, all record of the

Temple of Planet Love was to be wiped from the face of the earth. It was a contingency carefully planned for – all Watcher outposts had ready means of self-destruction close to hand. This would not be the first time their followers had been expected to cut and run.

Jackson was no fool. He knew full well he was nothing but a foot soldier in the coming struggle. His was not to reason why, his was but to get shot at, blown up and commit suicide at his masters' slightest whim. All that mattered was the furtherance of *the cause*. But the word 'expendable' had a bitter ring to it. There was an outside chance he could do his duty and still get out alive. Jackson might have been heartbroken to see years of work turned to ashes but he was not foolhardy enough to consider bucking the will of his handlers – there were some things worse than mere death.

A thought which brought him back to the plight of the cult's consignment of half-mad Greys. They were housed in another place – not far away, but far enough so that their existence was known only to the TOPL's very highest initiates. Along with their allocated transport they were to be sent on one final suicide mission – the orders had been most clear. Stonehenge would soon have yet another tourist attraction – a sixty-foot, apparently 'alien' craft embedded bull's-eye in its centre. That should send the jittery masses into a paranoid frenzy, not to mention set yet another bewildering puzzle for their hapless leaders. Jackson was almost disappointed he wouldn't be around to see the results for himself.

His curiosity was sparked by this grandiose expenditure of resources. The Watchers were seldom willing to commit so openly. Something big indeed must be on the cards, perhaps even the long-awaited ultimate unmasking. But Jackson had little time for idle speculation. Before he could see to the Greys, and his own survival, he had urgent work to complete.

Stoically he spent that evening making preparations for the coming inferno. The cleansing flames must leave no corner of the mansion untouched. Systematically he made the rounds, a can of petrol in one hand and a satchel of demolition charges in the other. One by one he set the fuses, pushing detonators into the yielding explosives as he strung them along from room to room in a snaking line. His tasks completed, there was just one part of his crumbling empire he knew he could not leave behind.

With a heavy heart, but a lighter load of TNT, Jackson made his way down to the basement to rescue Barney, the cult's genetically modified pet guard-gorilla.

Actually Barney's duties extended rather beyond those of mere over-evolved watchdog. He was part mascot, part gigolo-stud – a final test of loyalty standing proud between willing initiates and the final mysteries of this perverse cult. The grey-white, shambling creature regularly took part in cult ceremonies which would have brought tears to the eyes of Catherine the Great's pony. More than one female cultist had been welcomed into the organization's highest echelons by Barney's hairy embrace and brown-toothed smile.

Barney had tentacles sprouting from places where most gorillas didn't even have places, but Jackson had always thought there was a certain baleful tranquillity about the mutant ape – at least there was if he wasn't ripping your head off and dancing on your entrails, a task he had performed on more than one occasion.

Jackson felt that he and Barney shared a special affinity, and one not just down to their prodigious carnal appetites. They were both hewn from the same block after all, noble hunters a cut above the common herd, duty bound to spread their superior seed – filter-pump purifiers of the planetary gene-pool, if you like. Bullshit perhaps, but at least a high-brow moral justification for shagging anything that took your fancy.

Jackson groped for the light-switch at the head of the damp cellar. When he found it the alien howl of longing which rose up from beneath told him his pet had indeed missed him. Treading carefully on the half-rotten boards Jackson descended the stairs, one at a time, to Barney's steel-caged lair.

Barney might have been more beast than man, despite the unnatural duties he'd been forced to perform on penta-gram-scrawled floors, but he knew something was afoot. He'd been left down here in the cold for the past two weeks, unattended save for water and food. None of the hairless-monkey she-things had required his attention in those hectic final days of the cult's existence. Now he was horny and more than a little pissed off. Currently the roving antennae protruding from his bare albino scalp could sense danger on the petroleum-thick air.

Soon Jackson stood before his cage. 'I bet you've missed me, my boy? Never fear – it's to be a new life for us. Let's get you out of there.'

Barney gripped the thick bars with monstrous strength and screamed his best blood-curdling scream; it was very good. If Jackson hadn't been a 42nd Level Initiate of the Great Elder Darkness, he would have wet his loincloth, but fortunately he was hardened to it. Barney wanted something to screw even more badly than he wanted some-thing to kill, but he wouldn't stop to be picky.

With a cheerful naivety that belied his experience, Jack-son put a small key in the lock and turned it with a loud click. Smiling his mirthless smile he opened the cage. Barney burst through like a shot, barging his dismayed master aside like a lose-jointed rag-doll.

'Come back, you little shit! I was gonna take you with me.'

But the sound of Barney's knuckles pounding up the wooden stairs was all the answer he received.

Gathering the folds of his robe about him, revealing

an unappealing lime-green thong and cursing in a most unphilosophic manner, Jackson raced after Barney as if his life depended on it. He knew full well the Watchers' tolerance for leaks. He wasn't Dutch but such was his desperation he currently would have gladly stuck his finger into any sort of bulging dyke who came his way.

49. Gatecrashers from Hell

While their distracted host was preparing an explosive house-warming they might never forget, the four companions performed a textbook infiltration of the ghostly-quiet mansion. Frank led the way, closely followed by Kate, who used what little she remembered of the temple's layout to direct them through its eccentrically curved and silent halls.

Dave had to fight back a sense of growing unease. He gripped the assault rifle Becker had given him until his hands went numb, but he doubted he'd be able to use it if the time came.

This building just wasn't *right*. He couldn't put his finger on it, yet he was sure the architect must have been stark raving bonkers – there wasn't a right-angle anywhere. The snaking corridors canted inwards in a most oppressive manner, bas-reliefs of disturbing design hewn across their surface. Some of the writhing forms looked mostly human; some looked, at least in part, like animals Dave thought he should recognize. What they were doing to each other he didn't like to speculate, but Dave felt certain the RSPCA would have taken a very dim view.

Even the door frames brought him out in a cold sweat. It sounded stupid but he got the impression they'd been designed without humanity in mind. They were low and squat, bulging in the middle in oddly disturbing ways. Dave had to banish from his mind the image of certain 'female' Bulgarian shotputters he'd once watched too closely on TV. But it wasn't just the architecture which was wrong about this place. Dave had the overwhelming impression he was penetrating, if not the lair, then at least a temporary hideout of a slumbering, unspeakable evil.

What seemed like hours later, and after more than one switchback along all-too-familiar spiralling corridors, they came to an elaborately decorated central chamber, the upper reaches of its vaulting ceiling lost to the flickering torchlight. Swirling geometric tapestries hung from the walls, threatening to permanently defocus the eyes of anyone foolhardy enough to look for long. As Becker had predicted, a mosaic of an ornate eye-topped pyramid took up most of the bizarrely frescoed floor.

But their attention was not focused on this pervasive Watcher symbol for long. Off in one corner, looking somehow as if it had been recently abandoned in a fit of rage, throbbed and pulsated a bulbous mass of writhing protoplasm. Dave didn't have to be told this was the communication node they'd come to find; the dreadful knowledge welled up in him of its own accord like a dodgy plate of prawns.

The living transmitter did not make for a pretty sight. Its ribbed trunk was grey in a septic-green sort of way, the sickly leaves growing from its base rat-tail pink. Around its semi-transparent sides a bewildering storm of bulges and lumps wriggled. From its summit sprouted a forest of tumorous alien growths. These pallid tentacles reached for the newcomers in sickening profusion, impatient suckers sensing their racing brain-waves.

Dumbly Frank took an unsteady step towards the abomination. Instantly Becker was by his side. 'Remember what I told you. Keep your mind focused on the task at hand. When you think you've seen what we need to know, break off contact. We don't want to lose the best chance we have.'

'I'm touched by your concern,' muttered Frank.

'No, Frank, you're just touched,' said Becker. 'But you'll have to do.'

Frank stepped forward, into the range of the eager tentacles. Two of them slithered around his waist, as another sought out his forehead with appalling haste. With a wet crunch Dave feared might live with him forever, the biological device attached itself to Frank's brain. After a low moan and a feverish shudder the poor man's eyes rolled back in his head and were gone.

It was difficult to tell which part of the aberrant symbiosis was the tool and which the master, both seemed to feed off each other in a most alarming way. Shortly it was all too apparent that communication was taking place. Seconds after the connection had been established the terminal went into a frenzy of activity. Tendrils whirled through the air and the bulbous frame pulsated, as parts of it cycled through entire spectrums of inhuman colour. From somewhere deep inside rose a ghastly wailing.

'What's it doing? Get it off him!' screamed Kate above the din.

Becker held her back. 'This is normal. Let him be.'

By this point Dave felt he could watch no longer. While Kate and Becker stared at Frank in awe, he took the chance to investigate the echoing hallway. After scant minutes of exploration he was, if anything, even more disturbed.

The murals that decorated the crazily slanted walls were everywhere. His eyes were drawn to them again and again. But these scenes of orgiastic excess weren't all that had him worried. Several choice and highly pertinent questions sprung to mind, which strangely hadn't bothered him up until now.

Top of the list was: 'Why does this building smell of petrol?' Closely followed by: 'What are these small suspicious packages scattered all around the room, and why are they linked by bright red electrical flex?'

Absent-mindedly Dave wandered over to one and picked it up. It comprised three cylinders of a plastic-wrapped pliable material, daisy-chained to others of its kind throughout the maze of tunnels.

'What does *Nitroglikorichen – producen oft DDR* mean?' called Dave, more loudly than he'd really intended to.

Becker was at his side without seeming to cover the intervening space. 'It means,' he said with heroic forced calmness, 'as if we didn't know it already, that we have to get out of this place as quickly as possible. How's he doing, Kate?' As Becker removed the explosive sticks from Dave's blood-drained hands the girl looked over her shoulder.

'It's hard to tell. He's still got that distant spaced-out look. How do we know when he's found out what we're looking for?'

'We'll know all right. You can expect him to come down from this trip with more than a fuzzy tongue and a desire to eat the contents of the nearest fridge. Keep your eye on him, we've got other problems.' But Becker hardly had time to comprehend the significance of his words, because at that precise moment Barney put in his shuffling appearance.

Twenty yards away across the cold stone floor the deformed ape shambled to a halt statue-still in an oval doorway – his albino fur and fiery-pink eyes in stark contrast with the blackness beyond. For a heart-stopping instant all locked eyes in open-mouthed disbelief. Dave barely held back a scream as Barney's spittle rapidly formed a frothing puddle at his clawed feet. For once even Becker seemed lost for words, but their mutual horror was not destined to go uninterrupted for long.

The hall was served by many entrances, as if it were a central meeting point to which all routes led. Yawning portals were positioned regularly around the walls. At one near the gorilla, another new arrival skidded to a halt out of gloom. His mind racing out of control, madly Dave reflected that at this rate the chamber would be full in no time flat. Perhaps a waiter would be around with a plate of hors-d'oeuvre and a tray of drinks. Wasn't this cosy?

For the time being at least, Jackson seemed only to notice his wayward pet. 'Barney, there you are. Bad boy! What have I told you about running off like that? It'll be no vestal virgins for you!'

But then the preoccupied cult leader followed the ape's hungry gaze and in one rage-filled glance he took them all in. Frank and Kate immersed in hijacking his master's most closely guarded secrets, and in front of them Becker and Dave dismantling his carefully laid explosives. Jackson didn't know what they were doing here but he knew where he'd last seen them – back at the TV studios, seconds prior to his followers being mowed down like a field of over-ripe wheat. With a mounting volcanic rage his piggy eyes fixed on Dave.

'You again!' he spat, hot rage flushing his face. Jackson might have been a willing slave to a higher power but that wouldn't prevent him exacting bitter revenge on these meddlers *en passant*. Turning to his watch-gorilla he mustered his sole remaining reservoirs of command. 'Fetch, Barney! Bring those swine to me.' The giant ape sprang eagerly into action.

Bravely Dave screamed at the top of his lungs and dropped his rifle in his urge to get it cocked. It was soon evident that he'd at least remembered to remove the safety catch, because a clip-load of booming shells emptied themselves into the distant ceiling. Under a shower of peppering masonry Becker coolly drew his own handgun and clicked the hammer – but he didn't need to use it.

Barney was having none of Jackson's bullish manner. He might have been a loyal beast once upon a time, but that was before he'd sensed his crazed master's urge to destroy the only place he'd ever called home. With startling speed he covered the distance between them in one leaping bound. Too fast to see, Barney's vice-like paws shot out and grasped Jackson by his scrawny ankles.

'No, don't fetch me, you fool!' cried Jackson, pointing

at Becker and Dave. 'They're the cause of all our woes.'

But it was much too late for reason. Barney might have had the strength of a herd of oxen, and been hung like a horse to boot, but due to a frightful mix-up with his DNA he had the compassion of a trainee PE teacher. With cheerful ferocity he proceeded to swing Jackson over his hairy head like a human fly-swat.

'Eeeeeerrrrggg!' yelled the cult leader, his jet-black cassock hitching up around his waist and his wire-rimmed glasses sailing off forever. But his pleas were to no avail. Jackson's shaven scalp shattered like an egg-shell on first contact with the concrete floor. Yelping with glee, Barney swung him back the other way, increasing the pace and tempo with each fearsome swipe.

From out of this surreal altercation a small black device was flung from Jackson's now-limp body, skidding across the polished marble floor. Deftly, Becker stopped it beneath his foot. Bending to retrieve it he instantly recognized it as a timing mechanism. Dave peered at it from over his shoulder, wide-eyed with fright. In big red flashing numerals the timer read: one minute fifty seconds. It seemed to be counting down at an unfair rate.

'Can't you stop that thing?' wailed Dave.

Becker fumbled with the mechanism. 'The switch is shattered. Must have been damaged by the impact. I think it's time we left.'

He was going to get no argument there. 'Let's get the fuck out of here!' screamed Dave, scuttling back towards Kate and Frank on all fours. For once the girl could only agree with him. Grabbing each of Frank's shoulders with her slender hands, she pulled with all her might. Frank's head came unstuck from a dancing tendril with a sick squelch, the sentient growth retracting into the terminal's trunk.

'Uuuuurrrggh,' moaned Frank, as if roused from a deep and troubled sleep. With a strength belying his advanced years, Becker hoisted the comatose trooper over his shoulder and led the way from the stinking chamber.

As they raced for the doorway Dave peered back, and instantly wished he hadn't. Barney was performing a depraved act that still carried a penalty of ritual stoning to-death in certain of England's more rural shires upon Jackson's bucking corpse. Beneath the pumping ape the cult leader was probably thankful to be dead, though you wouldn't have known to look at his smashed and bruised face. Before he could become hypnotized by the horrific scene Dave was dragged onwards by the scruff of the neck. Becker yelled in his ringing ear, 'No time for sightseeing, time to bug out, soldier.'

With some perverse instinct for survival Kate guided them through the building's labyrinthine halls with what seemed like careless haste. They had very little margin for error. Just one wrong turning and they'd go up with the building. Yet sooner than Dave would have thought possible he found himself gulping in cold night air. They'd barely stumbled fifty paces across the inky lawn when the first detonation rocked the building behind them. Dave fell to his knees as a hot blast of air lifted him off his feet. Kate paused to drag him upright. 'Come on! Gotta make it to the trees before the big one blows!'

Later he would have no recollection of how they reached cover. The bushes and roadway seemed hopeless pain-filled miles away. As they flopped down behind the ditch the first big detonation struck, the mansion's roof launching straight up into the cold uncaring sky. It seemed to hang in space for far too long – strangely still in one piece – before raining back to earth in a shower of charred beams and blackened tiles. Becker hazily reflected that such a conflagration could not have been caused by mere dynamite alone. Just what hell-spawned monstrosities must have cooked off deep inside the furthest catacombs didn't bear thinking about, and fortunately they were in no position to try. For the first time in what seemed like an age they became aware of Frank's presence. The unconscious ex-commando was propped up next to Dave with Kate straddling his hips in a most unladylike fashion.

'I don't like it one bit,' she said to Becker. 'His pupils are dilated and I'm not getting any response!'

Becker reached for the small rucksack Dave wore on his back. He produced a large syringe and carefully flicked the needle. 'Inject him with this, it should do the trick.'

Cursing her clumsiness, Kate found a vein and pushed the plunger home. Instantly Frank's eyes snapped open, and the words began tumbling forth.

50. Hangar 912

Becker and Kate carried Frank to the waiting car, the sweat-soaked veteran still babbling in an incoherent fashion. They had no reason to believe the mansion held further dangers, but when the fire brigade arrived they would inevitably start asking awkward questions, such as, What are you doing with all this ammunition and explosives so close to a scale model of Beirut?

The flames from the fire continued to tower into the night sky with an urgent intensity, their tips flecked with unnatural blues and greens, as god-knew-what hellish chemicals burned off in the ruin's vaults. The inferno must have been visible for miles around. Dave was already dimly aware of the first sirens approaching from the distance. Kate lay Frank's head carefully on the car's back seat.

'Get in next to him, Dave. I need you to keep him upright. He doesn't seem to have full control.'

'I'll do my best, but that injection nearly killed him. Should his eyes be rolling back in his head that way? He's got a load of spit pouring from his mouth.'

But these weren't the extent of Frank's injuries. In the middle of his sun-tanned forehead stood three fresh, ugly red welts. Inside this ring of abrasions was perhaps the most disquieting thing Dave had seen in all that long and terrible night. It was a disc of sore red flesh, perhaps an inch in diameter, surrounded by a charred black line. Closer inspection revealed the grain of Frank's skin to be oddly angled in this zone, one of his prominent frown-lines clearly twisted at a distressing angle. Without needing to be told, Dave knew this wound had been cut by the sickening tentacle that had attached itself to Frank's head. This plug of flesh and bone had been unscrewed in a burrowing quest for his delicate frontal lobes. When the download was over the segment had been replaced and cauterized, though in a hasty and careless fashion. Dave shuddered uncontrollably in the darkness, despite all his best efforts at self-control.

Meanwhile Frank was yelling something about an airfield, and how they must get there before *they* destroyed that too. Hastily Becker administered a second syringe of what he would only call 'a powerful sedative', and strapped Frank in with a rear seat-belt.

'Just drive, Kate. There's nothing a conventional hospital could do for Frank now. We're his only hope.'

'Where do we go?'

'We'll worry about that when we get there. Just go.'

With a screeching wheel-spin they made off into the comforting darkness. It seemed fortunate that Frank had an even higher tolerance to man-made drugs than he did to the worst ravages of Watcher biotechnology. Frank's years as a gutter junkie finally began to pay off. His body had obtained more than just an immunity to just about every infectious disease known to man, plus a few that weren't; it had learned how to survive. Under a dosage which would have killed stone-dead a normal person, not to mention a tougher-than-average African bull-elephant, his battered system established some sort of equilibrium. The gale of fresher air, blowing headlong into his face, did its part too. After thirty minutes of Kate's high-speed driving Frank seemed to be making a tentative recovery.

'South road out of town,' he repeated for the umpteenth time. 'Big field. That's where *they* keep it parked. It's our only way of reaching the glacier.'

'What the hell does he mean by that?' demanded Kate. 'He's been jabbering like a loon for the past twenty miles.'

Becker turned to check Frank's pulse. 'How the hell should I know? Must be something from when he was hooked up.' He threw his daughter a questioning look. 'Well, do you know of this place he's on about?'

Kate sighed. 'No, but I can take us in the general direction. I suppose we've got nowhere better to go.' At the next deserted junction she performed a sweeping U-turn and took them back in the direction they had come.

Shortly Frank had recovered sufficiently to give more precise directions. He took them down pitch-black country lanes and through sleeping villages. Despite his certainty of their route they must have covered many more miles than even the most wayward crow would have flown, so tortuous did their twisting path become.

As the first light of dawn warmed the eastern sky they came to a halt at the gateway to a large flat stretch of meadow. It looked as if the cows hadn't been put out to pasture in a good few years, so high was the grass in places. Early morning dew weighed down the most impressive strands, jewelling thick cobwebs and dandelion-clocks with glistening droplets. But the travellers didn't get a chance to appreciate this rural idyll for long. Tucked away in one corner, brooding in a strangely ominous manner, was what looked like a big dilapidated barn. Becker turned to his one-time subordinate.

'OK, Frank, you've brought us this far. Time to tell us what you saw!'

Frank rubbed the side of his head distractedly. 'I've got the world's worst headache. I'm still trying to make sense of it myself. Can't I show you what's inside first?'

Dave was relieved to see his friend's improvement, but also strangely uneasy. 'Then you learned where the main Watcher base is located? Discovered something of their plans?'

Frank's confusion only deepened. 'Something like that, yes. It'll be easier when we're inside.' He pointed a shaky finger to the rickety wooden structure.

Silently Kate put the car into low gear and drove them

down a muddy, furrowed path. Despite the general sense of neglect, Dave noticed the surface held recent tyre-tracks. All too soon the shabby road ended at a patch of broken ground in front of two large wooden doors. As the bright orange sun rose behind the imposing building the four companions helped each other from the car and stretched their aching muscles. Across the weather-worn shutters was daubed a sign in dripping red paint: *Property of TEMPLE OF PLANET LOVE – Trespassers will be punished in a subsequent life*. Beneath it the artist had drawn a poor representation of a stick-man partly obscured by a red circle with a line through it. Exchanging wary glances, the four companions gingerly approached.

Kate was the first to speak. She'd noticed something odd that she *could* put her finger on. 'Can't remember the last time I saw a deserted cowshed with a lock like that.' She pointed to a slab-sided grey box hung at a convenient height beside one of the doors. Its face held a numeric keypad as well as a small electronic display.

Casually Frank strode over and typed in a six-figure code. If Dave was expecting a fanfare of trumpets and the eruption of fireworks he was disappointed. All that heralded Frank's manoeuvre was a low pneumatic hiss, as if nearby a lorry were resetting its brakes.

'Far out,' muttered Dave. 'Techno-cows from Planet Orgasm.'

Frank looked at each of them in turn, his face that of a man who knew too much and desperately needed to forget. 'This is part of their plan. One of the elements they've been using to trick us for way too many years. Time's about right for the tables to be turned.' Straining against its weight he slid open one vast door and staggered aside. The structure rolled on some silent mechanism, completely at odds with the building's air of decay.

The three others looked on aghast. It was dark inside, yet something large, angular and darker still filled the space. As if he had done so a thousand times before, Frank reached inside and flipped on a light switch. A wide bank of neon tubes snapped on overhead, flooding the hangar in a stark metallic blue.

It was some sort of craft, that much was clear, but this was no comfortably familiar vehicle. Dave thought he might have seen its like before, half-hidden behind clouds and badly out of focus in a hundred grainy photos, sent to his office by the armies of the bemused and the slightly mad. However, this was the first time he'd seen one up close and the first time he'd seen one in the flesh.

The vessel was so triangular it hurt his eyes to look at, so black it threatened to suck him in. It went beyond the Wright Brothers' wildest fantasies, way beyond *in-flight movies* and a *duty-free trolley service* in fact. Structurally, it was an elongated pyramid, tilted on one side, and its apex formed an eye-watering sharp point. The craft's wingspan was far wider than its height, which Dave estimated to be barely two metres at its rear. The whole contraption rested on three sturdy metal skids, the gearing disappearing into the underside through barely visible doors. No other distinguishing features sullied its sterile surface. But above all it was the colour which grabbed your mind and refused to let it go.

Dave was reminded of a poster he'd had on his bedroom wall when a boy, a relic of his first ever trip to a planetarium. It had been an artist's impression of a black hole. But that semi-mythical object had not been propped up in an English country barn, it had brooded far out in the depths of space – which was precisely where this thing looked like it belonged. The ship reminded Dave of the very latest in US stealth technology, though developed to the nth degree. Truth to tell, this device made California's best efforts look like some Stone Age tribe had tried to build a monorail based on one picture of Ivor the Engine.

Becker seemed less phased than most. He wandered

around the craft eyeing it knowingly, as if he were an Arab prince sizing up a racehorse. 'Nice,' he said, nodding approvingly. 'One of the newer models. The Air Force has only been scraping these babies off the Arizona hardpan for the past couple of years. Back in the good ole days it was all saucers, saucers everywhere, with not a moment to think. Time was when the sight of a stray hub-cap could break them out into a cold sweat. These puppies are just so much more . . . *sleek*.'

Kate's eyes were wide with wonder. 'Our friend Jackson must have been highly regarded to be given one of these.'

Frank nodded. 'His was a crack unit. Troops like his always get the best kit.'

Dave's face was an odd mixture of confusion and awe. 'This was his personal sky-buggy? He didn't strike me as the amateur pilot type.'

Becker slowly shook his head. 'This boat wasn't for Jackson's private use. I doubt very much if he even knew how to fly it. It was for use as part of the Watcher deception he helped run – another piece of the elaborate striptease jigsaw they were drip-feeding mankind.' Frank confirmed this theory with a weary nod.

Dave still wasn't convinced. 'But if his loopy cultists didn't pilot it, who the hell did?'

Frank and Becker fell silent and exchanged a knowing look. Suddenly the Dark Man cocked his head to one side, as if straining to hear some sound at the bare limits of perception. The others froze and followed suit. When he picked it out Dave was amazed he hadn't heard it before. It was like a magic picture hidden in a page of dots – once you were aware of it you couldn't ignore it if you tried, and oh, how hard he would try.

From somewhere far away (though not nearly far enough) drifted the dreadful haunting melodies of a folk-music concert in full swing. Dave could picture the scene right now: somewhere nearby a roomful of grown adults, proudly clad in organic Arran sweaters and baggy brown corduroys, sat smoking herbal pipes and drinking gelatinous real ale. With a horrid intensity they would be clustered around a simple stage. Beards and sideburns would be much in evidence, and that was only on the ruddy faces of the womenfolk. Just what archaic forms of facial hair the males might sport didn't bear thinking about. What was certain, however, was that an evangelical light of holy fanaticism would burn in each and every bulging eye as, spellbound, they watched their melancholic heroes gavotte and twitch on-stage.

A terrible and inevitable certainty welled up in Dave. Despite the horrors he'd seen that day – a sex-crazed cult leader posthumously buggered by a mutant gorilla sprang to mind – he felt certain the worst was yet to come. Even if your entire family *had* been wiped out by the 'Great East Anglia Turnip Blight' of 1840 that was no reason to set the tale to music and inflict it on later generations. Times might well have been hard in the 'olden days', but unfortunately they were not nearly hard enough to rid the human gene-pool of the pernicious 'folk-singer chromosome'. Calmly Dave repressed a momentous shudder and tried to think nice thoughts. Within seconds he had failed.

But there was to be no respite for him or the others. Nervously Frank pointed to what looked like a small workman's hut tucked away in a dark recess, the sort used the world over for brewing gut-rotting tea and general unspecific skiving.

'*They* are in there,' was all the cryptic explanation he would give.

Purposefully, Becker strode over to the bolted door. It was in no other way locked, as if intended to keep something in rather than intruders out. Resolutely, he drew his gun from his shoulder-holster with his one good hand and cocked it menacingly.

Frank's tone was far from reassuring. 'You won't be needing the artillery, boss. At least not for now.'

Dubiously his one-time superior put the automatic away. When Frank gave a curt nod, Becker slid back the bolt and put his hand on the shabby brass handle. The door creaked opened with a screech which set their teeth on edge and expelled a pungent draft of foetid stale air. Slowly their eyes became accustomed to the gloom. Down into the dark bowels of the earth twisted a rickety wooden staircase, its boards worn smooth with age. One by one they edged their way onto the planks and descended into the depths. When they reached the lower landing they could barely comprehend what they saw.

Beneath the length of the hangar ran a gallery with a bare earthen floor. Along one wall stood a series of glass-fronted enclosures. But Dave suspected this to be no normal glass. It had air-holes at precise and regular intervals and looked to be made of the same tough, bullet-proof perspex that protected security-conscious bank clerks and nervous PMs. But it wasn't the architectural fittings which caught the eye, it was the cavern's contents which did that, and more besides.

Behind each panel was a small room, linked by a simple passageway. The first few spartan cells Dave studied were devoid of any life – dirty pallets and a few grubby possessions were all that marked any form of habitation. However, this dark warren was far from deserted – it was home to a brood of crazily familiar creatures. Clustered in a dingy central chamber, twenty or thirty Greys had gathered for a morning of impromptu musical entertainment. It was a scene eerily reminiscent of Dave's daydream, even down to the herb pipes and roll-neck sweaters. The throng was gathered around a low stage, where some of their number were about to perform with a plethora of home-made musical devices. It was their tuning-up session which had first caught the intruder's ear.

All told this sight was far, far worse than even Dave could have imagined – at least his band of jolly nature-loving freaks had been human, in the loosest possible sense. Dave's vision had not included the troupe of Morris dancers limbering up to one side, bladder-sticks gripped eagerly in three-fingered grey hands; nor the double rank of a dinner-jacketed male voice choir just starting to hum in Welsh. All that was missing was a kilted piper slowly garrotting a cat for the full ethnic tableau to be complete – oh no, there he was, how could he have missed him? Slowly but surely, like the precious sand in some spiritual egg-timer, Dave felt his sanity begin to trickle away.

But this wasn't the end of the matter by a long shot. When they noticed the newcomers' presence a multitude of innocent grey faces turned to gaze their way. A sea of huge back eyes glittered in the dim flickering light, obscenely bulging craniums bobbing for a better view. Yet after a moment of mildly curious study they got back to their own devices, soon striking up where they left off.

Becker had seen its like many times before. The United States government had a similar, if not slightly higher-tech, set-up at its Groom Lake facility half a mile beneath Nevada. At least the Greys there had the benefit of a well-lit, spacious prison – and only the minor irritation of regular medical experimentation.

Becker shook his head. 'Obsessed with country music, the lot of them. The CIA infiltrated more teams into Nashville than they did into all of Eastern Europe during the Cold War. Not even Elvis could help them work it out.'

Frank's eyes stayed glued to the scene before them. 'It's 'cause the Greys are made from redneck DNA. Ever wonder why it's always farmers and hillbillies making sightings and getting abducted? The Greys are instinctively attracted to their own kind – that's the sort of sample they're always bringing back.'

Becker's brow furrowed, as he seemed to reach some troubling new plateau of understanding. 'Jesus holy shit,' he mumbled.

Meanwhile Dave's jaw was hovering somewhere down around his ankles. 'But if Jackson's cult had their own stock of Greys, why go to all the trouble of helping us get ours into the country?'

Frank looked at him with pity. 'Don't you get it yet? The public rightly considered the cultists to be several high priests short of a temple. They were on a mission to make society steadily less rational. When they engineered a leak it had to come from a more plausible source. It was credibility we provided.'

Becker's voice held no mirth. 'Though to look at the two of you, perhaps they're not so clever after all.'

Frank ignored him. 'Face it, Dave, they used us to further their ends.'

'Then that mystery email that brought us together, that was their doing too?'

'Undoubtedly.'

Dave sank to his knees. 'What have I done?' he moaned pitifully. 'I've helped these bastards in their plans. All my life I've been helping them and not known it.'

Kate helped him to his feet. 'And you weren't to know. You're not the first they've used. At least you didn't help them willingly, like some traitors I could mention.'

Becker snapped out of his troubling thoughts and turned to Frank. 'OK, mister, we've seen enough. This whole diabolical plot goes deeper than even I imagined. Why did you need to bring us here?'

Frank looked at him levelly. 'Because until you knew how far this went, you wouldn't believe what I have to tell you.'

51. Frank Spills the Beans

Silently, they padded their way back up the rotten stair-case. Dave gingerly closed the door behind them, as if they were naughty children covering their tracks after finding hidden Christmas toys. Once they were assembled Frank dusted down a clearing on the bare earth floor and squatted on his haunches, the others gathering around him. With the sort of distant stare which could have got him committed, not to mention fitted with the very latest in back-tied sleeveless suits, he told them what he had learned while attached to the cultists' pulsating brain-node.

Victims linked to those devices were in most cases drugged and damaged beyond repair, unable to exercise free will as they underwent what amounted to mental rape. Frank had been different. His formidable will had burned through the simple vegetative program – crashing the Watchers' communication system like a careering express train. He'd then embarked on a smash-and-grab raid for covert data. Coupled with the suppressed memories of what he'd seen at Machu Picchu, he was able to piece together the wider picture. It didn't make for happy view-ing – and it hadn't come without a price. The Watchers knew he'd probed them, and now they knew he was coming too. Speed was going to be of the essence.

Their enemies were older than the hills (he told them), and more patient than anyone could know. They had come to Earth aeons before the first men stumbled from the Stone Age, club in hand and wife by hair; before the present continents drifted into place. They were a proud and haughty race, banished from their own world for their intolerable religious beliefs by more enlightened kin. A band of cosmic Pilgrim Fathers, wandering the stars in search of weak and feeble heathens to convert – the willing guardians of some imagined grey-man's burden which they were only too keen to lay down from on high. Mankind was destined to play the Red Indian role. None of the listeners needed telling how such a relationship invariably turned out.

But things had not gone according to plan for those first Watchers. They hadn't so much 'landed' on their prehistoric Plymouth Rock as crashed headlong into it – setting a worrying pattern their grey slaves would follow with single-minded determination to this day. Being fundamentalists of the most stubborn kind they had a loathing for technology matched only by their contempt for astral navigation. Genetic manipulation was the only science they could bear. The Watchers' ship was a semi-living being, hatched in some giant jamjar around an alien sun. Other engineering was beyond them, as was anything so mundane as actually learning to pilot this temperamental, hurtling craft. Their strange gods would see them through, and in a way they had. Cushioned in their intergalactic cocoon, many had survived the crash, though at a terrible price.

As the handful of straggling survivors crawled from the wreckage, strewn across a windswept desert plateau, they'd vowed powerful blood oaths to one day rescue their fellow creatures still trapped inside, slumbering through an eternal dreamless sleep of deathless suspended animation.

Millennia passed, ice ages had come and gone. The Watchers bided their time on this strange foreign world. One final bout of earthquakes shook the globe, continents rising and sinking beneath the waves of shallow seas. The forces of plate tectonics indulged in one last petulant fit of hurtling crockery. When it was over the crash site was thrust up to great altitude, to once again be encased in stagnant ancient ice. But now it was the turn of another force of nature to have its say. Fitfully the first human civilizations took root in the fertile crescent, soon to spread like weeds in a sunlit garden.

Always few in number, the Watchers had relied on subterfuge and subtlety to establish a grip on power. The first Mesopotamian kings had worshipped at their outlandish feet, their inhuman reign of terror as brittle as it was incomplete. Reluctantly, inevitably, the Watchers slunk from view, to play their games of manipulation and deception from behind the scenes. Cults and secret societies made up of human converts were the guardians of their power's flickering flame, Masons, Templers and various folk music societies their carefully forged tools.

But it was another institution, at conception completely unconnected to the dormant alien threat, which was to become their greatest and most potent weapon. In the last days of the Renaissance, when the growing complexity of human affairs led to the formation of the Committee of 300, the Watchers knew the perfect vehicle for their sweeping plans had arrived. Here was an all-powerful body of the great but not so good, cutting across national boundaries and the vagaries of culture. For the first time a single institution had the power of mastery over the entire species – and the Old Ones had to have it. Here at last was the means to honour their ancient promise to their sleeping kin. The body forged by the Hapsburgs to cement their boundless wealth would be corrupted to an even darker end. The Watchers' final objective was simple – nothing less than the reawakening of all their kind, and the establishment of overt domination over the witless population of planet Earth.

Becker's voice held an uncustomary tremble. 'Do you know how they mean to trigger this rebirth – how far their plans have progressed?'

Frank looked sickened as he spoke. 'There was only so much I could learn. All I know is it involves something they must take from each and every one of us. As you know better than most, the Committee was corrupted to serve their purpose. With you gone Madame Chairman has complete control. They'll use her and her cronies to harvest what they need. With every passing day they grow stronger.'

Becker's eyes were far away, as if for the first time seeing some hidden truth. 'The war they've started in Urgistan, that's to protect the crash site, isn't it?'

Frank nodded. 'The ship is embedded inside a giant glacier. The locals know of the Watchers through dimly-remembered myths. When the reawakening began the Urgis tried to wipe them out. The Watchers' human servants couldn't allow that to happen – they know their masters will be vulnerable while the process goes on. Using their proxies they set about subduing Urgistan.'

Kate gestured to the triangular vessel. 'Well, if they can build stuff like this then we're done for. It leaves our best efforts far behind.'

Frank shook his head. 'They only have a limited supply of these babies. The black triangles are what's left of the scout-pods from their ship. It's all the Watcher cults can do to keep a handful in the air. Hard technology isn't what they're best at. If they're going to win they have to use more underhand methods.'

Becker took up where Frank left off. 'I've long suspected part of what they plan to do – they mean to sap our will to fight by making us paranoid, cynical zombies, unmoved by whatever our leaders say or do. To this end they've orchestrated a campaign to engender mass psychosis over the past fifty years. But what will be their ultimate *coup de grâce*?'

Dave looked bleak. 'Judging by what I've seen of modern culture, I think we're in very deep shit indeed.'

Kate slowly nodded. 'We have to be stop them here and now – before they're fully awake – before they can make use of all the Committee's hard work. Strike back at their base in Urgistan.'

Dave was in no mood for heroics. 'It's a war zone half-way round the globe. How do we even get there? I don't think the RAF are taking sightseeing bookings.'

Becker glanced up at the brooding black craft above them.

Dave followed his gaze. 'No fucking way are you getting me up in *that* thing! We'd hit the first hill we came to. If the Greys can't stop crashing, what hope have we?'

Becker's patience showed signs of wearing thin. 'My agency recovered several such craft over the years – triangles, saucers and every shape in between. At the time we thought they were recon ships from an advanced alien race – we now know the fallacy of that assumption. Nevertheless, after we scraped off their pilots we put every resource we had into back-engineering their secrets.'

'And what did you learn?' Kate asked without much hope.

Becker's reply was a long time coming. 'That we couldn't find volunteer test pilots fast enough. The attrition rate was very high.'

'Great!' wailed Dave. 'We're chartering a flight with Black Triangle Airlines. *Your pilot today is Ming the Merciless. Please assume your crash positions now.* I want a drink!'

Becker raised a calming hand. 'We stand a better chance than those brave Air Force volunteers. They were learning by trial and error – we have an inkling as to how the technology works – not to mention the only living human adept at jockeying one of their neural links.'

They each turned to look at Frank, the old warrior's ugly forehead scar seeming to throb before their eyes.

'Do I have much choice in what's coming next?'

Becker's face was grim. 'Not if you want mankind to have any chance of freedom.'

They didn't have to wait for Frank's answer. Sadly he gazed up at the hideously beautiful vessel.

Dave tried valiantly to reinstate an air of reason to the proceedings. 'OK . . . OK. Supposing for the moment that we *could* actually get out there, penetrating *en route* one of the tightest air defence cordons in the history of warfare, just what are we supposed to do to these Watchers when we arrive? Politely ask them to leave – use harsh language? I can see a flaw in your plan, and I'm afraid it's a biggy.'

Becker rose slowly to his feet, his old bones popping loudly, causing Dave to jump. 'There is one weapon we do have at our disposal. It's time I showed you my last hold-out, my last-ditch option to stop the Committee in its tracks. It'll more than fit the bill for this change of target. Let me show you what I can bring to the party.'

Eyeing him warily the others stumbled outside. Soon they were gathered around the boot of Kate's car, silently staring at its contents. Becker's armoured briefcase, the one he had arrived with handcuffed to his good wrist, lay open atop the other baggage. Frank nodded knowingly, as Kate whistled between her perfect teeth.

'Only a small one, then,' she said, as calmly as she could muster.

Dave looked bewildered. It seemed to be nothing but a tangle of brightly coloured wires, leading from a circuit board to a grapefruit-sized chrome ball. All this was held in the sort of egg-tray foam packaging precision instruments often came in. Along one of the case's long diagonals ran a steel tube, terminating in the metal orb and connected to more bewildering electronics. Dave thought he recognized a large battery and some sort of timing mechanism.

'I don't get it. What is it?'

Becker smiled his best patronizing smile. 'This beauty was provided by a former colleague – the CEO of our biggest defence contractor. He paid for his bravery with his life. It's up to us to ensure he didn't die in vain.'

'Yes, yes,' Dave was losing patience, 'but what *is* it?'

Becker looked him straight in the eye. 'Nothing major, you understand – just your common-or-garden, everyday, compact nuclear warhead.'

Dave felt his mouth turn dry. 'And we're going to . . .'

'Take it inside the Watcher ship and set it off,' Becker finished for him. 'Destroy their filthy infestation once and for all.'

Dave began to tremble. 'Can't we just, you know, detonate it nearby?'

Frank shook his head, his gaze still far away. 'That'd do little good – wouldn't even scratch their paintwork. That ship hit the atmosphere like an out-of-control meteor and it didn't break up; then in ploughed itself half a mile into a granite mountainside and still stayed in more or less one piece. Only a blast close to the main hub of its central nervous system could take it out. We'll have to find its central cortex.'

Dave glanced from one friend to the other, searching vainly for some vestige of common sense between them. If there was one there he failed to find it. 'Those things are semi-immortal alien gods. They've got secrets and powers we can't even dream of. How do you think we're going to beat them?'

'We'll find a way.' Kate's voice held a glint of steel. 'We'll find a way because we have to.'

Dave didn't seem so convinced. 'We'll *find a way* to get ourselves killed, that's what we'll do. How do we know where the crash site is? How do we get inside? How do we set that device off without taking us with it?'

Becker looked at him sharply. 'Details, details! The future of mankind is at stake. First, as you so correctly pointed out, we have to get there.'

One by one they turned to look at the starkly angular craft lurking in the hangar above them.

52. Fly Me to the Moon

The first hurdle was getting inside the thing. There were no handles or key-holes in sight, not even a hairline crack to jimmy open. Even if there had been, Dave felt certain it would have done no good – this was clearly not a craft that responded to brute force. Its clean lines seemed to stretch on unbroken into infinity, skirting dimensions best left undisturbed and riding the coat-tails of mathematics forever beyond the mind of man. Frank was on the point of giving up when Becker hit the right spot.

The Dark Man simply placed a gnarled hand on a spot on the craft's faceted underbelly and looked at it as if reading a far off road sign, his icy grey eyes squinting into the remote distance. Later Becker would describe the feeling as akin to being attached to the suction hose of a spiritual vacuum cleaner, his whole body sucked dry of spiritual force.

Whatever the workings of this silent mechanism it had the desired effect. As slow as a crematorium conveyor-belt, a thin black gangway descended from the ship, no pistons or levers to drive its remorseless progress. Warily, Frank in the lead, they edged their way up the slope, unsure of what they might find.

If the exterior was all hard edges, then the interior couldn't have been more different if it had tried to – a possibility none of them liked to dwell on. The first image that sprang to mind was the sort of children's play-rooms found in department stores and shopping centres across the land, where stressed parents left wailing brats to embark on their credit-fuelled odysseys undisturbed. Admittedly, the chamber lacked the knee-deep layer of brightly coloured plastic balls, though the overall effect was much the same – everything was padded.

The four found themselves in a small, dim compartment barely lit by a pervasive pink light. There was not a straight line in sight; bulkheads and consoles were sculpted from some pliant, cloudily translucent substance that bulged and shifted beneath their every touch. Everywhere strange curves and eye-watering spirals were given form, alien colours dancing across them like a slow-tempo fairy disco. Condensed moisture dripped from the ceiling inches above their heads, to be reabsorbed into the spongy porous deck underfoot. Four squat armchairs were arranged in a rough diamond, only discernible from some giant's discarded bubble-gum by the matching head-rests sprouting from the back of each. From everywhere and nowhere came a faint mechanical hum, as if they were inside some living transformer. Becker seemed to have seen it all before, succinctly summing up their present circumstances, as well as that of the entire human race.

'Best get a move on. We don't know how long we've got left.'

Hurriedly they began the task of transferring their gear from Kate's car. Frank was at pains to point out it was best they did not tarry too long, and all too soon for Dave's liking they were done. Becker was the last to enter, his ominous briefcase once more handcuffed to his unbroken arm.

'Right, team, time to get down to business.'

One bulbous seat was for the pilot, that much was clear. It squatted at the front of the cabin before a semi-circular arch of multi-coloured blancmange, no instruments evident on its smooth, damp surface. Above it hung a ten-foot-wide featureless lozenge of a cloudy pearl material. Wordlessly, Frank made his way forward to this station, his scarred jaw firmly set.

'Buckle in,' said Becker, flopping down into the folds of the couch to the right and rear of the pilot's.

Before Dave could ask 'What buckle?' his question was

answered for him – the sides of the seat swelled up around him, restricting all motion. For a horrible moment he thought he might go on sinking in forever, to suffocate amidst the bowels of this half-living nightmare vessel. Just as his panic reached a crescendo he came to rest, half encased in the seat's sickening, cloying warmth. Carefully Kate and Frank took their places, alarm clouding each worried face as they went through the same ordeal.

'Just what are we trying to achieve?' asked the girl nervously.

'We'll try a simple hover first,' Becker answered. 'Just six-feet should do. If Frank can master that he's got it cracked.'

None wished to enquire why such a simple manoeuvre would prove so conclusive. Silently their unwilling pilot placed his hands on the console and the entire ship came alive.

Suddenly the dancing lights became much brighter, the faint hum rising to a discordant fanfare. To Dave it sounded not unlike some of the more chemically-inspired 70s progressive rock – in an instant Rick Wakeman's entire musical career seemed to flash through his head. But it wasn't this brain-unhinging tumult which grabbed his attention. The large oval shield in front of Frank cleared, revealing an image of two half-open barn doors, and beyond a stretch of empty meadow. Dave realized it must be the view from the front of the craft – he could clearly see the grass in the swaying breeze outside. The edges of the scene were fuzzy, as if the eye's peripheral vision would only stretch so far.

To the extent the restraining head-rests would allow Frank turned back to the others. 'Am I doing this right?' he yelled to Becker, a rising note of panic in his voice.

Becker wasn't able to nod his head. 'You're doing fine. Just relax and let your instincts take over. The most we could ever establish was your subconscious feeds it instructions.'

'What do I do now?' Frank seemed unsure.

Becker paused for a moment as if considering his answer. Their pilot was not impressed. 'Well, mister know-it-all? This is no time to go shy on me.'

Even above the din Dave clearly heard Becker's sigh. 'Your guess is as good as mine. This is as far as any test pilot ever got.'

Frank looked at him bleakly for a while, as Dave felt all his limbs go numb – at least he'd feel no pain when they were ripped from his body, he mused. Grimly Frank got back to the task at hand.

For a long time nothing happened. Frank sat with a look of exquisite concentration etched across his eroded face, his palms firmly pressed to the terminal as if to keep it down. Beads of sweat formed on his temples and trickled around to his heavily stubbled chin. Still the view from the strange portal stubbornly remained the same – they hadn't budged an inch.

'It's no good,' stuttered Frank from between clenched teeth. 'I can't get us off the ground.'

Calmly Becker licked his parched lips. 'Remember your link to the communication node. This works just the same way, but in reverse. Loosen up, let your emotions take control.'

Frank's brow cleared and he seemed to relax. In an instant the barn doors were gone, replaced for a split second by a blur of confusing colour then by a clear stretch of indigo sky. Forlornly a few faint stars twinkled in their distant orbits, the ancient chasms between them never seeming so cold. There had been little sense of motion, only the faintest surge Dave could detect.

'Where the hell are we?' screamed Kate, the view lacking a reassuring reference point, nothing so mundane as a grimy horizon line in fact.

334

'I think we're successfully in the hover,' said Becker very slowly, as if conscious of accusations of understatement. 'Any chance of learning just how high?'

Their pilot's eyes had gone very wide. 'Their units don't mean much to me. How do I point us down to take a look?'

The forward roll they executed wasn't as instantaneous as their ascent, but it was fast enough all the same. Despite the unnerving lack of inertia Dave felt his stomach rise through his chest and perform somersaults on his lolling tongue – any East German judges present would have given it 5.9 for artistic impression. In a second the frontal view had swung through ninety heart-stopping degrees and they were looking straight back down along the path which they'd so recently come.

The answer to Becker's question was *very high indeed*.

The decrepit barn they'd blasted off from, no doubt currently sporting a nifty open-air roof, was an invisible speck somewhere far below. Way beneath them the highest clouds crowded round the gaping, swirling hole torn through their midst by a sudden slicing vortex, seemingly as stunned and confused as the ship's gawking passengers. Dave couldn't be sure but at the edge of the portal's unfocused vision he thought he saw a glint of ocean, and beyond it a coastline which could only be northern France.

Becker's voice was measured and precise. 'Perhaps a little less altitude would be a good idea, Frank – at least for now, that is.' Before he'd finished the sentence they were falling like a rock on the end of a not-quite-long-enough length of elastic. Their speed was such that the thin air condensed into a raging torrent across the artificial porthole. Kate gave out a horrifying scream. Dave wanted to but didn't have the composure to get one out, his strangled gurglings already lost miles above their heads.

But somehow their pilot rose above it, as their roaring mount showed signs of doing anything but. Much too casually for comfort their 'headlong plummet' slowed to a meagre 'uncontrolled plunge', then with bladder-emptying relief to a mere 'graceful fall'. When it had become relatively negligible (though perhaps still doing a Stuka dive-bomber proud) Dave could clearly make out the feeble mark of man on the landscape beneath. Amongst the patchwork of fields he could just make out one – directly beneath – covered in splintered matchwood, in one corner a freshly air-conditioned barn. He estimated they must have fallen ninety thousand feet in just under a minute. Despite what traffic policemen say, it isn't speed that kills, but sudden slowing down.

Regardless of Frank's success at stemming their vertical death-ride Dave couldn't help but feel what Becker said next amounted to running before they could walk – or worse still, crashing before they could fly.

'Right, Frank, now you've mastered the basics, why don't we get on our way. Urgistan, here we come.'

53. So Much Done to So Many, by Some Who Flew

10,000 ft above Kara-Kuri Province, Urgistan

Dave remembered very little of that hair-raising journey and later couldn't help but feel his amnesia was a blessed relief. His last nerve-ending had burnt out somewhere over (but not far enough over) the Austrian Alps, as the sleek black craft tore down yet another chalet-peppered valley, the sound of scattering cow-bells ringing too closely in their ears.

Frank was learning on the job – you had to make allowances for that – but at the speed they travelled the slightest mistake could prove fatal. Beads of cold sweat stood out on his forehead, as he concentrated to maintain control of the hurtling craft. More than once the passengers found themselves swaying helplessly from side to side as they raised their howling mental voices to will Frank over some looming obstacle. Each time they made it – by the skin of their chattering teeth. It was more than any completely sane individual could bear. Fortunately completely sane individuals were in short supply, and getting rarer all the time.

Dave wasn't certain of anything anymore, apart from the fact that there was now an air traffic controller in Athens suffering from a very nasty nervous breakdown – not to mention the flight-crew of that too-close-for-comfort jumbo jet. But there had been no time for the counting of blessings. The Middle East had shot past, nothing more than a confused and maddening, sandy beige blur.

Frank was just beginning to get the hang of piloting the unfamiliar vehicle as the terrain began to rise up and wrinkle beneath them once again. As they overflew the first snowfields he performed a high-spirited barrel-roll, causing much consternation amongst his gagging crew. It had been a very steep learning curve – almost as steep as the towering mass of ice and Himalayan granite which currently filled their vision-portal like a frosted snow-capped cyst.

'Look out!' Dave yelled, his knuckles white with terror.

Frank flung them into an impossible curve that should by rights have jellified their bones, his voice calmly cutting above their wails, 'That's all I need – backseat drivers.' He shifted their course to a less hair-raising ballistic trajectory, which flung them into the endlessly-frigid blue sky. Each occupant leant back in their seats as the force of the staggering manoeuvre kicked in.

Frank sounded on the edge of permanent dementia. 'If any of you think you could do better, why not step up and take a turn. I'm feeling a little jet-lagged as it is.'

'You're doing fine,' rasped Becker, his ancient chest fighting for every breath against its unnatural load. 'This looks like Urgistan to me. I think we've arrived.'

Dave was less impressed. 'So, we're here. What do we do now? Fly round in circles until the Watchers talk us down? I doubt they're at home to guests so soon after rising. Perhaps they need a coffee first.'

Kate turned to her old man. 'He's got a point. It doesn't look such a small country to me. How do we find the right glacier?'

Before Becker could answer Frank sombrely interrupted, his face as cold and frosty as the clear mountain air. 'Give me time – I'll know it when I see it. This is almost like coming home.'

*   *   *

Major Chuck McMurdoch (USAF) was a combat veteran of the Gulf War (all four big ones), Balkan police actions (almost lost count) and just about everywhere else in between – including the recent aerial pounding delivered to Montreal, to whip the rebel Canuck city into line (when *would* those pussies give up the French road signs?).

He was the undisputed master of his chosen mount[1], the Air Force's number one weapons system jock – a pilot of god-like skill, bottomless experience and cast-iron guts. He was famed throughout the 69th Tactical Fighter Wing ('The Amorous Assassins – *licking Uncle Sam's enemies since 1917*') for his ever-present mirrored shades and trademark Stetson hat. His ability to perform a reverse-inverted Imleman, while loosing off a brace of Sidewinders, was legendary – as was his talent for giving the short soundbite-laden interviews that reporters loved. This wasn't a man who took failure lying down, not even bent at the knee in fact; not amongst his pilots or ground crew, nor the machinery of brain-haemorrhage-inducing complexity they struggled to keep in the air. That's why the anomalous radar returns had him bothered.

The blip kept coming and going, fading in and winking out. It covered the mountainous miles at a dazzling pace – almost as if quartering the region whilst performing some impossible high-speed search. But that was ridiculous, nothing on earth moved so fast. It must be some weird radar echo from these bleak hills. Give him the wide-open prairie of his home state any day.

---

[1] The F-13 Wombat Stealth Fighter™. The very latest sleek-black, tungsten-carbide killing-machine to slip from the Californian aerospace industry's underground bunkers. $120 million a piece, as temperamental as a moody ballerina, and as cost-effective as a nuclear fly-swat. Its design the minimum specification required (or so the Air Force maintained) to be able to knock prop-driven biplanes from the sky above America's Third World enemies well into the next financial period.

Twenty miles further north the rest of his squadron eagerly prowled Urgi air-space, longing for something to destroy. Impatiently, McMurdoch punched his radio to the frequency of Lieutenant Duggan, the northern element's young commander.

'Howdy there, Bravo Niner Four. I have an unidentified radar contact near your position. You able to make visual ID, Duggan? Let it be something to burn – the guys are getting bored down here.'

McMurdoch's subordinate took a while to reply, as ever slightly in awe of the great man. 'Aaaah, that's a big negative Alpha Niner. We see the radar return too, but no visual as of yet. Will keep you posted.'

McMurdoch cursed his luck, no chance to increase his victory record today. Since destroying the Urgistani Air Force on the ground in the first minutes of Eagle Day +1 he had had very little to do. Maybe, he pondered moodily, if they hadn't used quite so many cluster bombs, perhaps they could have made that kite factory last longer.

But suddenly the prospect of further carnage was looking up. Excitedly Duggan radioed back. 'We have visual contact – we have a VISUAL! Holy shit, look at that baby go!'

Before there was time to think McMurdoch had banked his F-13 to the north, the five other planes with him quickly following suit. In his mind at least he was already painting the kill symbols over the black paintwork outside his crowded cockpit – many more and they'd have to give him a longer plane.

'Who've ya got for me today, Duggan?' he demanded. It was too much to dream that the Chinese had got involved, or even (hope against hope) the Russians. He'd been waiting to kick Ivan's sorry beetroot-riddled butt for more years than he cared to remember.

'Can't tell, sir,' came the crackling reply. 'It won't stay still long enough for us to shoot at!'

'Pull your head from up your ass, Duggan, and make your report. Otherwise I WILL come up there, rip your head off and personally crap down your neck!'

But Duggan had worries of a more pressing nature. 'Sweet Jesus! What's it doing? Help us, sir – we're under fire!'

Fuming at this appalling breach of aeronautical etiquette, McMurdoch lit his afterburners and charged towards the fray. The other F-13s followed him blindly, without so much as a questioning thought. Which was just as well; if they'd known what they were up against even these all-American fly-boys would have been filling their g-suits.

*   *   *

Frank sensed the patrolling stealth fighters long before he saw them. Under the circumstances perhaps an understandable oversight – all of his conscious attention had been focused on scanning the endless miles of ice and snow slipping past beneath them for a landmark that would ignite a spark of recognition. But then this craft imbued its pilot with several unique advantages.

For the ex-commando it was a most disquieting sensation. His psyche was hooked up to the craft's alien sensors – input fed directly up his fingers and into his overloaded brain, bypassing the more traditional routes of eyes and ears. A spiritual coupling not unlike really base sex.

Frank knew the interceptors were nearby the same way he'd know some unseen obstacle blocked his path in a pitch black room – he simply felt they were there. Before he knew it he was reacting, dropping out of their zigzag course and assuming a defensive posture to meet the attack. Impatient for a fight, the four American planes turned into a dive and accelerated down to meet them.

Ignoring Dave's screams of 'WHAT'S UP NOW?' Frank

341

searched the ship's jumbled memories for some suitably violent response. When he found one it filled his scarred warrior's soul with lusty anticipation. Gathering his reserves of mental strength, Frank willed the black triangle to protect itself.

What happened next took the triangle's occupants by complete surprise.

*   *   *

But not nearly as much as it surprised the hopelessly eager Lieutenant Duggan.

The leader of McMurdoch's northern element was deliriously happy at having something to do; at long last a chance to kick-start his combat career.

His adolescent daydreams were not long in being cruelly dashed. When he saw what he was up against it dented even his monumental self-confidence. He'd heard rumours that the Soviets had developed super-secret stealth planes from acquired alien technology before the downfall of the evil empire, but he'd never really believed them up until now. After all, Uncle Sam's own Intel spooks spread much the same stories – when the enemy thought he was already beat any battle was almost a forgone conclusion.

Yet reverse-engineered UFOs were the only explanation for what he was seeing charging towards him. The triangular craft danced around the sky in an impossible manner, jumping from one place to another, seemingly not crossing the intervening space. But these bone-breaking manoeuvres were nothing compared to what it did next. With horrible suddenness a small hatch snapped open on its glistening black underside and out shot a ball of sparking cobalt radiance.

Duggan's first thought was that it was some sort of flare, released to confuse any heat-seekers his men might fire. This hopelessly naïve conclusion did not stand up to further scrutiny. The electric-blue sphere hadn't dropped twenty feet before it perked up and changed direction briskly. The thing wobbled for a confused half-second, as if gaining its bearings, then zoomed at the first of Duggan's planes as if it were a wasp with an attitude problem. The closing speed was terrific – if anything the orb moved even faster than its blisteringly quick mother-ship, its jinks and cuts even more precise. Before its target had time to take evasive action the whirling sphere hit it head on, passing through the plane, along its buckling spine, to emerge out of a spluttering jet nozzle unscathed, none the worse for the shuddering collision. The same could not be said for the F-13.

The plane evaporated into an expanding cloud of molten steel and vaporized kerosene, an exploding fog of micro-fine particles blown out of every orifice – at least for as long as there were orifices left for things to be blown out of. In the blink of a popping eyeball all structural integrity was gone, disintegrated into a shower of flaming wreckage, the pilot with no chance of escape.

As the first F-13 ceased to exist Duggan desperately radioed his distant CO, but didn't get a chance to chat – their enemy had no intention of playing hit-and-run. It was with perverse fascination that Duggan watched as a similar fate befell the rest of his command; the same burning blue ball dashing between each like an epileptic butterfly of death, leaving smoking havoc and burning mayhem in its wake.

In less time than it would have taken to issue a warning his was the only aircraft left intact – performing a macabre tango with the black triangle through the cold clear air. This unhappy equilibrium was not destined to remain balanced for long. Still travelling near enough flat out, and screaming at the top of his exploding lungs, Duggan's first thought was that his plane had disappeared. Then he did too.

*   *   *

When McMurdoch and the rest of his men got within visual range they could barely believe their eyes. Even at twice the speed of sound the details were gruesomely apparent. The sky was filled with burning wreckage, shredded wings and twisted metal descending in lazy spirals. There was no sign of Duggan's four-ship flight, just the lingering aroma of flaming death and a few embarrassed clouds of black embittered smoke.

But the sky was not entirely empty. Amidst this scene of plunging carnage hung a suspicious dark shape, all jutting points and hard edges. Around it orbited an electrified orb of sizzling blue lightning. The vessel hovered in one spot, doing its level best to look innocent and not quite pulling it off. It seemed for all the world to be saying: 'Yeah, what of it?'

The craft might have wanted him to believe butter wouldn't melt on its fuselage but McMurdoch knew better – he knew the stuff would bubble and blacken in no time flat. He didn't know *how* it had happened but someone was going to pay, and pay dearly, for this obscene waste of government resources. In the absence of a more likely culprit, such as the entire Chinese Air Force, or a bored Himalayan god with a blazing hatred for American pilots, this sinister black triangle would do.

'Tally-ho!' McMurdoch yelled, loosing off a stream of explosive cannon shells as he closed on the vessel at supersonic pace.

But the target proved more elusive than McMurdoch would have believed possible, blinking out of existence as the tracers rattled by. Impossibly it winked back into reality half a mile behind the rearmost of his planes, matching the formation for speed every step of the way.

And so it began; battle was joined, a dance of death with both partners unafraid to stamp on a few toes. It wasn't a pretty fight but it was over very, very quickly – mercifully quickly for McMurdoch and his men.

For this skirmish the cobalt sphere stayed close to its angular mother-ship, weaving around it in tight frenetic arcs. As the black triangle zoomed alongside each F-13 in turn it lashed out in a single fierce sortie, returning as if attached by some powerful unseen leash. Without exception the unfortunate planes exploded one by one, a shower of sapphire sparks and incoherent radio chatter all that marked their passing. Not one pilot had time to eject.

It wasn't so much a 'dogfight', more like a rabid wolf being unleashed on a kennel of unsuspecting poodles; this was pure slaughter from start to finish. Never before, in the field of human conflict, had such an almighty kicking been dealt to the USAF. If it had been a boxing match any humane referee would have called it off after the first punch, but there was no referee present. All too soon the battle hurtled towards its inevitable conclusion. Three, four, five planes went down under this relentless charge, until just one foe remained.

Only McMurdoch had escaped the frenzied path of destruction. Performing a never-before-seen manoeuvre, which he'd had in the back of his mind for quite a while but hadn't had the guts to try, McMurdoch twisted out of the path of the electro-flail and got on the tail of the jinxing craft. Fighting back the blackout he felt encroaching from the awesome g-force, McMurdoch vowed to make his advantage count – this would be his one chance of a kill.

Visions of Congressional Medals of Honour (posthumous of course) racing through his head, McMurdoch knew just what he must do. Pointing the nose of his plane down at the vulnerable vessel, he set about attaining ramming speed. It didn't take him long to get there.

* * *

Inside the black triangle all its occupants saw McMurdoch coming but only Dave had the presence of mind to react.

'YAAAAAAAAAAAAH! HE'S GONNA HIT US!'

Before even Frank could respond there was a thundering impact as the F-13 tore a gaping hole through the triangle's broad flat roof. For a second there was a deafening ripping noise, akin to tearing flesh and popping cartilage, then nothing but the shriek of the jet-stream filled the void.

When the initial shock had passed it was horrifically obvious what had happened. The nose and cockpit of McMurdoch's plane skewered the triangle's cabin like a badly harpooned whale. Both craft formed an insane hybrid which was never meant to fly – and seemed unnaturally determined not to. The bizarrely mating planes set off on a single-minded brand-new course, straight downwards towards Urgistan's craggy peaks.

For a terrible moment Dave gawped wide-eyed at their pilot lolling semi-conscious against the straps of his ejector seat. Around him whistled the racing air, above him spun a swathe of clear blue sky that by rights shouldn't have been there. Above the wind Kate yelled at the top of her lungs, somehow managing both monumental volume and understatement in one breath.

'Do something, Frank.'

For his part McMurdoch had no intention of sticking around to find out what anyone else might do. Concluding for once that discretion *was* the better part of valour, at least where gatecrashing UFOs was concerned, he reached between his legs and yanked with all of what was left of his might. At last his groping fingers found the ejection handle and he pulled like a man possessed. Seconds later he was accelerating upwards into the crystal morning sky, the triangle's occupants left far behind.

Back inside the UFO the cabin was now filed with clouds of noxious thick white smoke – the legacy of McMurdoch's rocket-assisted departure.

'Level us off, Frank!' howled Kate.

But their pilot could barely hear her. The pain of the traumatic damage had been channelled through his screaming cortex – momentarily Frank had blacked out with shock. When he came to the cabin was filled with cloying fumes, his view through the elliptical viewing portal non-existent. Frantically he waved a bloodied hand before his face, and almost wished he hadn't – a vast snow-wrapped hillside hurtled towards them more quickly than seemed polite. Summoning every ounce of his stubborn will Frank focused on his shattered craft and willed it upward – but his efforts were to be in vain.

At a speed that would have worried an over-keen artillery shell the black craft ploughed headlong into a towering snow bank, and bounced like a crystal vase.

54. Unhappy Landings

Frank wasn't the triangle's only passenger to be affected by the craft's pervasive personality. Dave knew only pain, that and the fact he must get out of the wreckage as soon as possible to go and find some hill-farmers to hassle.

Either group would do – on points of detail the Watchers weren't fussy. The mission was to firstly spread the word to those elements of society most susceptible to irrationalism: the woolly-minded and the mystically inclined. The specific flavour of 'nutter' didn't matter – web-authoring techno-druids served just as well as sports presenters[1] with messiah complexes – their spiritual kin all over the world simply more credulous than most. Just as it had once been the priests and the prophets at the vanguard of the Watchers' subversive campaign, now it was the swollen armies of numerologist accountants[2] and Feng Shui civil engineers.[3]

So it had been in the beginning, so it would be for evermore – or at least until the Old Ones were ready to play their final winning hand. This had always been the way of things at smoking crash sites from time immemorial – preordained in the stars, written by the cold alien intelligence that lurked amongst them.

How he knew these things Dave had no idea. The

---

[1] Right first time! Turn to back page for details of your prize.

[2] 'Oooooh. £13.1313 million – not a good amount to keep in an account. Best give some of it to me.'

[3] 'Statistics prove that bridges built East–West are slightly less likely to fall down than those built North–South. Those completed on a Tuesday also seem to better stand the test of time. Additionally, no bridge constructed along a ley-line has ever collapsed. Risk Analysis Theory therefore proves that bridges built East–West, along a ley-line, on a Tuesday, can never fall down. The bill is in the post.'

images seemed to well up from out of the very couch on which he lay, almost as if the ship itself were trying to get in a last session of indoctrination before its link with him was cut forever. Dave allowed himself to be lulled by its peculiarly compelling voice, all individuality subservient to its greater, darker cause. By the time he staggered from the wreckage he would be programmed to act as bizarrely as inhumanly possible – just like one of the hordes of grey plague carriers which had done so many times before.

But someone was not playing along with the script. Suddenly Dave was being pulled from the protective confines of his acceleration couch by strangely familiar hands, and comforted by a recognizable soothing voice. As if surfacing through a bath of cloying mental treacle he slipped out of his trance.

'Come on, Davey boy, don't go all floppy on me – I bet you never thought you'd hear those words from me!'

Kate struggled to pull him upright, bracing herself against the slanting deck. With a low grunt she yanked Dave to his feet.

'Wha . . . what happened?' he mumbled, saliva trickling down his chin.

'We crashed, in case you didn't notice. It's kind of hard to fly with a stealth fighter embedded in your wing.' She nodded to the smoking wreck strewn around them.

The black triangle in which they'd journeyed so far, so fast, was decaying before their eyes. Large chunks of it were falling off and steaming in the fierce high-altitude glare. The stench was terrible: it smelled like Vlad.

Nearby, Becker was helping Frank out of his own chair. Their pilot looked terrible, pain and shock hung across his dazed features like a gruesome Halloween mask.

'I did my best, just couldn't control her . . .'

'You did just fine, soldier. Take a sip of this.' Becker handed him a badly dented flask. The briefcase was still

349

handcuffed to his wrist. With one arm broken and the other weighed down by a warhead, getting the flask to Frank's lips was a bit of an ordeal. Then together they staggered over to the other two survivors.

Dave shook the last traces of the Watcher spell from his throbbing head. 'I don't get it,' he muttered. 'Why aren't we dead? I don't think Frank exactly performed a textbook landing.'

Becker was no student of physics but he'd seen it all before. 'The same reason the g-forces didn't splatter us when Charles Lindbergh here flung us around the sky. Their craft generate some sort of inertialess field. Enough to give a sense of motion, but not to squash passengers flat as pancakes. It dampened down the shock of our final deceleration.'

Kate nervously eyed their surroundings. 'The snow might have helped too.'

The craft was half buried in a wide snowfield at the top of a broad crevasse. Further down the hillside this slashing scar narrowed into a deep tree-lined gully, snow runoff forming a bubbling mountain stream. Above them the peaks stretched in an endless line of ice and snow – grim guardians of ancient secrets best left forgotten. It should have been colder at this altitude, but the heat from the crash, along with their own adrenaline-filled blood, kept the shivers at bay, at least for the time being.

It was only at this point that the full magnitude of their predicament came crashing home. They were stuck half-way up a mountain in the middle of a major war zone with nothing but an atom bomb to keep them warm. It was going to be a long cold night unless they found some food and shelter quickly.

Becker seemed to have reached the same conclusion. 'Probably better if we don't stick around. Our Air Force friends will soon be on their way to search for survivors.'

'And at worst?' Kate's eyes held their first real doubt.

It sickened Dave to see it. Whatever his own doubts she had always been the rock to which his spirit clung.

Becker said nothing, he simply trudged off through the virgin-white snow. Dumbly, one by one, the others followed.

The going was slow. Carefully they picked their way down the rocky mountain towards the sheltering camouflage of the overgrown ravine. When they reached the jagged tree line Frank looped forward to take up point, all his field skills needed to find a path through the thickening bush. But behind him all was far from sweetness and light. This time Dave was not going to let their strategy go undebated. He stumbled alongside Becker as they made their way through a fragrant rhododendron stand.

'Do you mind telling me, just what *is* the point of any of this? We're stranded in this wilderness without a hope of achieving what we came for. Why don't we just hand ourselves in to the authorities right now?'

Becker hardly slackened his remorseless pace. 'Oh look, there's the UN headquarters.'

'Listen, mate, I watch the news. This place is about to become the sort of battlefield Robocop would be proud of. Just about every civilized nation on Earth is holding back ready for the ground invasion – you know how these things work. In the meantime, don't you think they know when so much as a gnat farts up here? We're probably on Candid Camera as we speak – hello GNN!' Dave waved at the clear blue sky.

Becker swotted back a low branch that nearly knocked Dave off his feet. 'If we were, they'd have taken us in by now. These "authorities" you're so keen on – if they caught us we'd be dead within the day. You know that as well as I.'

If Dave had ever known it then he seemed to have forgotten in a hurry. 'Maybe – but that sounds like better odds than we've got right now. If we just *explained* to someone in authority what we know, then they'd *have* to listen.' Becker didn't even grace Dave with a withering look as he rambled on. 'We don't know where the Watcher ship is, or how we're going to get in *if* we get there. I don't mind a bit of risk but I never volunteered for a suicide mission.'

All of a sudden they had caught up with Frank, the former commando staring at the three of them in speechless exasperation. 'This is not easy, guys; searching for a glacier filled with late-sleeping space aliens. Our odds are in no way improved by the SHOWER OF SHIT BEHIND ME YAPPING AWAY LIKE DELEGATES AT A SPEED-FREAKS' CONVENTION! Can it, why don't you?'

Becker turned to stare Dave straight in the eye. The young man tried his best to match him, but his attempt failed as miserably as had his plea for reason.

'I can't argue with the facts, but apathy gets us zilch. This is our only hope now.' Becker held up the heavy steel case.

Dave couldn't bring himself to look at the thing as he stepped up into Becker's face. 'We're lost, we're hungry, and on the run from an all-powerful alien conspiracy and the world's assembled military. I think I've got every reason to feel *despondent*. Fate couldn't get more unkind if she tried!'

'Can it, soldier!'

'Oh yeah, WHO'S GONNA MAKE ME?'

At that moment a series of loud clicks from the foliage around them broke the tension. As one the fugitives turned. Dave almost collapsed to his knees when he saw them; only Kate's arms stopped him from sprawling to the floor.

From behind an impressive battery of vintage bolt-action rifles a small army of anxious Urgistani faces stared on in wide-eyed surprise. Despite Dave's assurances to the contrary, it seemed fate was winding up her long right leg, ready to kick them in the balls once again.

55. With Friends Like These

'Let me get this straight,' tittered General Roderick Noroco, his broad Asiatic features a picture of bemused concentration. 'You planned to creep into our poor besieged country, locate the slumbering evil which has haunted us for aeons, and then wipe it out before it can awaken to enslave all mankind?'

Becker looked at him with all the dignity he could muster, which under the circumstances wasn't very much. 'In essence, if not detail, that is correct.'

Behind Noroco the rabble of scruffy soldiers and scabby henchmen broke into gales of uproarious laughter, as if on some unspoken command. Noroco himself smiled warmly, as he placed both gnarled hands on the age-blackened table before him. He sat in a high-backed wooden chair, its ancient carved surface ingrained with brain-scrambling grime-filled detail. Above his moth-eaten military cap arched the low sloping ceiling of one of the crude tent-habitats of the hill dwellers – a hole cut in the roof extracted the acrid blue fumes from a smoky peat fire that smouldered feebly off to one side. The structure had once served as the village meeting-hall, its former occupants long since fled to the relative safety of the lowlands – laser-guided bombs currently the least of their worries in this remote part of Urgistan. Before Noroco, the four tethered captives shivered in the scant heat given off by the flames.

In light of their host's merriment Becker felt the need for further explanation. 'We've learned of a dark conspiracy to victimize your nation – the real motives behind this war on your proud and resilient people.'

Noroco raised a questioning eyebrow. Becker knew this

could be his one chance to save their lives. He didn't let his nerves show.

'It's so that the high-ranking Watcher agents who've taken control of the Committee can protect their masters' lair. The unwitting fools at the head of the world's governments are nothing but puppets.'

The packed room exploded into fits of laughter, more than one of the harried troopers staggering to the floor under the weight of his comrades' back-slaps. Bemused as ever, Dave wondered just how many could understand Becker's words at all, let alone make sense of them. Glumly he concluded that it mattered little – with this crowd's mood of terrified, manic gaiety they would wet their pants at the slightest provocation. Bernard Manning would have killed for an audience like this.

Beside the general, Yajik – his ever loyal lieutenant – elbowed the great man's ribs in a manner not quite in keeping with his presidential dignity. 'And we say the inhabitants of the Kara-Kuri are barking mad. Those folks are nothing compared to these Outlanders.'

Noroco laughed for a moment longer, in a rather forced manner, before very suddenly stopping with the finality of a lethal injection. Behind him the rest of his men did the same – many of the more worldly-wise (those with transistor radios, or who could read the carefully worded pamphlets dropped over the past two days) had been exposed to Allied propaganda painting their leader as the very archetype of the evil goose-stepping dictator. Whether they'd known him for years or not, they thought it wise not to take any chances.

Exasperated, Noroco half-turned to glare at his men. 'You know, you don't *have* to do that. I'm not about to shoot you for chuckling out of turn. Apart from anything else I hardly think we can spare the manpower. Now, where were we?'

Annoyed, Noroco turned back to his unwilling guests

and leapt suddenly to his feet – he was quicker in getting there than most. All five foot of his stocky frame thrust out his barrel chest. When he spoke it was with extravagant dramaticism.

'Stupid Outlander perhaps – or maybe, exceedingly brave new comrades! It pains me to say so but I had reached much the same conclusion myself. Not even the US State Department could be so unfair.'

Urgistan's vilified leader held out a scarred hand, which Becker took with considerable trepidation. But this was no wily ruse. Noroco pumped his arm like he was a non-swimming sailor bailing out a sinking ship.

'Either exceedingly brave or exceedingly stupid. We should discover which.' Nearby, Dave let out a contemptuous snort which hinted at his true feelings on the matter.

Noroco continued unperturbed. 'Ever since those two-faced North Koreans ran screaming from our corner we've been completely friendless. The Iraqis and Libyans don't want to know us – even the Serbians have been sending our mail back unopened. You're the first people who've come to our aid, and for that we are grateful.'

The troops behind Noroco broke into a spontaneous cheer. Their general shot them a glance out of the corner of one beady eye, as if to say *'Don't push your luck,'* but he let their merriment run its course. They'd had precious little to cheer about these last few troubled weeks and might have little in the days to come. Since the Allied bombing had started this small band had constantly been on the move from one valley to the next.

Noroco fixed Becker with a suspicious gaze. 'So what do the leaders of this "Committee" want with our homeland? And how do we know you're not part of one of their fiendish tricks?'

The Dark Man took a deep breath. 'The Committee currently serves the agenda of the Watchers. Now that reaping time is here its leaders mean to reactivate the crashed ship and awaken their frozen race.'

Noroco nodded sagely. 'I had guessed this flimsily excused war must have something to do with the Hill-Demons. You know that some of them are already on the move? Abominations not seen for a hundred generations walk these mountains once again.'

Becker looked at their captor with what might have been a burgeoning respect. 'Then you must be aware of the urgency of what we have to do. I beg you, let us be about our way.'

Noroco's brow darkened. 'Not so quickly, my friend. My entire nation has been bent on nothing else but their destruction since we rediscovered this dormant threat. What makes you think you can do better than the military might of Urgistan – home to the finest warrior-people the gods ever cast upon the earth?'

Despite the scattered cheers Frank wasn't about to let his crack unit be disparaged in this way. Diplomacy was all very well and good but the morale of his team came higher up his list of considerations.

'You haven't seen us in action yet, grandpa. We're gonna hit them harder than they've ever been hit before – we'll pass through'em like a dose of napalm-salts.'

Noroco eyed the four disdainfully, Dave and Kate shivering in obvious discomfort. 'Yes, I can see, though in my humble opinion perhaps more SOS than SAS. And if the reports from my sentries are anything to go by, your arrival should wake even those Watchers still deep in slumber – for just four people you make one hell of a din.'

Frank jutted out his jaw. 'We'll take our chances.'

Noroco's gaze returned to him, studying the faded war-horse carefully – one old warrior sizing up another. 'The servants of the Watchers will already outnumber you by several hundred to one. If the legends are true there may be thousands more on the way – and I hear they can be quite – what's your word for it –*irascible*, yes, they can be irascible in the morning.'

Becker butted in. 'We know what we're up against.'

Noroco didn't break stride. 'And they have access to black-magic spells, countless horrors best left unimagined. The old tales tell of their complete mastery of nature. They can conjure up hellish monstrosities beyond your wildest dreams. You would confront these creatures bare-handed?'

Dave thought about voicing his reservations, but was beaten to it. Becker clapped his former sergeant on one sinewy shoulder. 'Oh, they don't outnumber us. You see, we have a secret weapon – we have Frank.'

Kate had been silent for most of the exchange, watching her father perform as she always had, with a confused mixture of fear and awe. Now she knew she had to speak.

'Frank is not the only secret weapon we possess.' She returned her father's frosty gaze. 'It will prove to them we're on their side. They have a right to know, it's their country after all.'

Silently Becker looked back at Noroco, and seemed to reach a difficult decision. Without a word he hefted his heavy briefcase onto the smoke-aged table and pulled a small silver key from a chain around his neck. Within a second it was open.

Hurriedly the assembled throng crowded round to take a look. Few, if any, knew what an atom bomb should look like, but most guessed this bewildering tangle of stainless steel and circuitry more than fitted the bill. Becker simply nodded in response to Noroco's unspoken question.

Their host seemed in a happy daze. 'Ironic, really. We spent the best part of last month scouring the world's arms fairs for one of these beauties, all to no avail – even the Israelis wouldn't return our calls. Now one falls right into our laps. That's karma for you, don't you think.'

Becker's face was sour. 'I wouldn't know about that. But

if you can get us inside their ship, and we can set this thing off, we've got a fighting chance of ending their threat once and for all.'

56. Initiation

The helicopter ride had been as long and dull as it was uneventful. Marshall Swift was glad when their faceless pilot informed them it would soon be over. He'd given up trying to guess where they were heading hours ago, though he knew it was before they'd left the dusty lowlands and headed up out into this endless wilderness of towering rock and freezing snow.

They'd taken off from the remote Bangladeshi airfield, the isolated jungle-shrouded strip temporary home to perhaps the densest concentration of private jets the world had ever seen. Just as each of the assembled dignitaries had been told, the big twin-rotored black chopper had been awaiting their arrival; ready to take them to the Poke-It-On production facility for the grand unveiling.

When the forty VIP passengers were assembled in the helicopter's palatial hold the magical mystery tour began. Marshall was no student of geography – he quickly became disorientated while in the air – but it was hard to escape the conclusion that the craft's complex series of spiralling manoeuvres had been designed to confuse any amateur navigators amongst them. Marshall was unable to calculate the course they'd set, and since then had spotted few landmarks to aid him along the way.

The same could not be said regarding his fellow passengers. The excited adman knew enough about international finance to recognize a significant proportion of his fellow guests. Several were, at least indirectly, corporate clients of his. He'd taken enough Yoke-Cola dollars over the years to almost rot the teeth from his head; while GNN's European account more than kept him in coke. The heads of both multinationals currently sat side by side, not ten feet from Marshall, engrossed in mounds of their own paperwork.

It was Marshall's conservative estimate that two-thirds of the planet's private wealth lounged aboard this craft, sipping Bloody Marys or reading the *Wall Street Journal* – and that was just the ones he recognized. There were plenty of other shady characters Marshall had never seen before but who more than fitted the bill as candidates for ownership of the other third. The whole cabin reeked of excessive consumption, worse even than a pasty-faced nineteenth-century poet.

Near the forward bulkhead the founder of Nanosoft Computers tapped away at a portable keyboard, no doubt plotting new ways to slow down his software to help sustain wavering sales of newer, faster hardware. A row behind him the three Arab sheikhs with their chubby fingers on the stop-cock of Middle Eastern oil shared a private joke, perhaps comparing notes on the latest slur campaign to discredit the electric car.[1] The thought of the life insurance policies which would pay out if this plane crashed brought Marshall out in a cold sweat.

If he'd known how low they were flying he'd have sweated all the more. If he'd known of the trigger-happy

---

[1] Mix-n-Match Sluromatic™ smear campaign. Twice yearly, until the end of time, pick any three from the following and 'leak' to the press.

- Batteries take a week to charge and only drive you 4.2 miles.
- The cars lack zip, preventing you from avoiding accidents.
- They make you glow in the dark.
- Pedestrians hit by electric vehicles risk electrocution.
- Milk delivered by float gives you cancer.
- Auto industry workers will have to be put to death if conventional cars don't sell.
- Electric motors make a nasty 'whirring' noise.
- Jesus/Allah/Buddha/L. Ron Hubbard wants you to buy petrol.
- Unless we suck it from the ground, oil might re-form into dinosaurs, who would probably eat us.
- Best one of the lot. Great big electro-generating power stations (incorporating economies of scale and pollution monitoring suits) are less efficient than a tiny internal combustion engine you lug around with you.

NATO warplanes policing the 'No-Fly Zone' they were currently penetrating, he would have done well to avoid a nervous fit. He wasn't to know but this last danger was the least of their worries – unwittingly the planes were being vectored away from the chopper, their mission more to keep prying eyes at bay than to keep the luminaries of the Committee from hurtling towards their final fate.

But all this was unknown to the happily pampered crowd on the silent stealth helicopter. Marshall swallowed dryly and took another gulp of his own scotch. For some reason this exalted company was making him nervous, while at the same time giving him a perverse thrill. To be admitted to such an august body meant he'd truly arrived as a player on the world stage – either that or they needed someone to serve the tea. Was this really the star-studded launch of a ground-breaking children's toy, or was there more here than met the eye? With a shaking hand he downed what was left of his drink and reassured himself he would soon be getting everything he deserved. He'd sold tougher dreams in his time.

Suddenly they seemed to be circling an unseen landing-pad. Marshall strained to look out of a small round portal, badly annoying the head of Japan's biggest investment bank as he did so, but his efforts were to be in vain. Outside the weather had closed in, swathing their destination in mist and swirling fog. Through some prodigious feet of piloting skill (which Marshall felt sure best went unobserved) all too soon they had landed, and the huge rear doors were lowering with a low mechanical hum. Shielding their eyes against the hazy glare, one by one this select crew of pirate-captains of industry made their way into daylight.

It was like nothing Marshall had been expecting – no remote Chinese sweatshop, no River-Kwai-style jungle hellhole. He'd been ready for a hi-tech robotic production facility, manned by inscrutable white-coated technicians all humming the company song and doing very slow karate first thing before work, but he hadn't been ready for this. Range upon range of towering mountains marched off along a frigid skyline as far as the eye could see. From off the wind-swept landing-pad an icy walkway led to a dingy tunnel. The isolation of their surroundings caught Marshall's breath – it must have taken super-human skill to land the helicopter here. Further speculation was cut short by the familiar tones of a clipped upper-crust nasal accent.

'One is so glad you could come.'

Each and every guest turned to look at the Committee's Chairman with apprehension and something bordering on awe. She wore a simple white robe, the thin material seemingly scant protection against the bone-numbing cold. Nevertheless the grey-haired matriarch stood statue-still without so much as a shiver, her frail body unfazed by the incessant blasts that whipped down from the brutal peaks above. The crowd's self-selecting spokesman was a robust businessman who, judging by his informality, must have met their hostess many times before. He needed to shout to be heard above the strengthening gale.

'It's time for answers, Madame Chairman. Why have you brought us here? We thought we were finally to see this factory of yours.'

Their hostess honoured him with her best Mona Lisa smile. 'All in good time. This is indeed where those oh-so-profitable creatures shall hail from. Appearances can be deceptive – as you, in particular, should know.'

Without further ceremony she turned and led them off the pad, gliding through a crumbling archway of intricately crafted stone. As the group stumbled along after her Marshall's gaze fell upon the carvings obscenely cut into the frosted rock – and at the disquietingly familiar symbol set into the capstone. One by one the party passed mutely beneath the seal of the pyramid and its single unblinking, all-seeing eye.

Once inside they were ushered into groups of four or five and prompted to wait at a series of iris valves set along the tunnel wall. Their attendants were short and swathed in white robes from head to toe. Marshall tried not to notice the disjointed way they walked, or the three-fingered hands that beckoned the guests to their places. If this was the pinnacle of global corporate hospitality he'd run the gauntlet of Pimms-soaked brain-dead toffs at Henley any day. Suddenly, all those hat-wearing neighing horses at Ascot didn't seem so bad after all.

No sooner had the guests been sorted than the low doorways before them dilated with a quiet hiss. A whiff of pungent gas escaped as the assembled dignitaries crowded into these strange lifts. When Marshall looked back from the small chamber he saw a peculiar row of half-open pipes set against the opposite wall. What this strange place might be he had no idea. Next to him Nanosoft's bespectacled CEO gripped his ever-present laptop to his shallow chest.

'Gee, neat mansion. Our hostess must be quite a *Star Trek* fan.'

Before Swift had time to respond their brief journey came to an abrupt halt. The stomach-churning deceleration was cushioned by the chamber's padded sides, but it was considerable all the same. Soon, all forty visitors were brushing themselves down in a new and bewildering open space. Darkness shrouded the distant walls, large hooks hung close to their heads from the dim ceiling. Somehow their hostess had got there ahead of them. She stood serenely on a low pedestal – a blue-rinsed vision in white, stark against the encroaching gloom. Her face was a mask of barely suppressed gaiety, a horrible eagerness burning behind her cold eyes.

'Gentlemen. The moment of your final initiation is at hand.'

Despite his misgivings Marshall let out a loud whoop of delight, his shredded nerves raising his voice to a childish shriek. 'And about time too. Do we have to roll up a trouser leg and bare a nipple? Shouldn't there be weird markings on the floor?'

Against his better judgement he peered down at the deck between his jittering feet. It held no arcane symbols but was ridged and grooved in a disturbingly zoomorphic way. Dark stains clung to it, somehow managing to coyly give the impression of once having been blood. Other, less wholesome discolorations left the mind boggled and the stomach wrapped up in knots. Whoever negotiated the cleaning contract for this facility needed to be hauled up for an immediate performance review. Subconsciously, the adman began to salivate at the prospect.

Meanwhile, their hostess stared back at Marshall with tolerant disbelief, an expression she was very good at after long years of practice. 'Oh, nothing so formal, my dear boy – One wouldn't want you falling at this final hurdle. You just lie back and relax. Think of England if it helps. I usually do.'

Nearby one fat corporate chairman was far from happy. 'What about the merchandise – when do we get to see it? I've no time for these stupid games. Got to be in Dusseldorf in five hours for my 11:30.'

Her Majesty fixed him with a frosty stare, another manoeuvre she had perfected. 'There is the small matter of *one* trifling ceremony we *do* have to perform – an ancient rite all who seek the hidden knowledge must endure. The wisdom of the Old Ones does come at a price.'

'Great!' sighed Marshall. 'I can't wait to join the club. Where's my blindfold? Don't tie the noose too tight.'

Their hostess held up her hand and smiled her best enigmatic smile. Despite his turbulent emotions Marshall was reminded of her picture on the back of Britain's fast-disappearing bank-notes.

'Patience, my eager children. There are simply a few questions One is duty-bound to ask.' She turned back to the others in the restless crowd.

Dusseldorf 11:30 man looked sour as he glanced around him. 'We know better than to blurt out the Committee's business. None of us are keen on the idea of falling off a yacht. Our pilots back at the rendezvous point don't even know we're here.'

Nodding serenely Madame Chairman's compelling stare fell with full force on Marshall's sweating brow. 'Is the campaign to sell the Poke-It-Ons at its height? Do we have customers breaking down toy-store doors to buy them, as we speak?'

For a terrible moment Marshall felt unable to respond, such was his relief and glee. 'Yes, your Loveliness. The consumer frenzy has begun. There'll be widespread rioting if the units don't ship soon. Your own Prime Minister has had to recall troops from Urgistan to be ready to contain the mob. Is it time for your loyal servants to receive their reward?'

Nodding contentedly their hostess seemed satisfied with this news, but she was in a minority of one. Nanosoft's boyish chairman wanted more meaningful answers. 'But how can we cash in if we don't satisfy consumer demand? I know profit might be for wimps these days, but this is going too far. When do we see the product? I've begun to doubt it exists at all.'

Several of the others added their bawling voices to the growing clamour of discontent. Someone shouted: 'For once "Geek-Boy" is right. It's time to fish or cut bait. Show us the money, or we're on our way home.'

Their hostess bowed in mock respect, not without diffi-culty due to an oddly bulging waistline. Her penetrating nasal tones never held more contempt. 'You'll never know how much pleasure it gives me to introduce you. Gentle-men, meet Poke-It-On. Poke-It-On, do your stuff!'

What she did next took them all by complete surprise. Suddenly she turned on her royal heels and beat a hasty retreat as if her life depended on it. No sooner had her stunned guests realized what was happening than their scampering hostess was gone – disappearing through a waiting lift door that closed behind her with a rapid hiss.

'Well, this is very improper, I must say.' It was a sober-suited minion who spoke up now. 'I've never been treated so rudely in all my life.'

Marshall concluded the corpulent business man should get out more. But his thoughts, just like those of all the others, were soon overtaken by a sickening gastric rumble emanating from above. Over their heads, and creaking like a ghost ship, a wide cylindrical chute heaved into view, its hinged cover overlain with the mark of a bleary eye. Along with the rest of the Inner Circle of the Committee of 300 Marshall Swift gazed upwards towards the frightful spout. With a heavy clang the hatchway swung open, and a multitude of frenzied Poke-It-Ons poured out – falling onto waiting foreheads like acid rain upon a field of corn.

There were many more of the creatures than were needed to go around. Viscously the strongest amongst them fought it out for the honour to ride a thrashing host. The screaming Committee men tried in vain to pull them from their succulent scalps, but chubby fingers more used to picking over corporate lunches, or counting out bank-notes to high-class whores, were no match for this hatchling brood.

Within minutes it was done. The Committee was once and for all under the complete control of the Watchers, any need for subterfuge long and truly gone. There were a few lingering screams but they didn't last for long. The last thing Marshall heard before the lights of his free will went out one final time was the hollow inhuman laughter of their hostess hidden somewhere far away. But that wasn't the end of the matter at all, hardly the beginning of an indeterminate nightmare coma with no promise of an end. Marshall's own personal Poke-It-On seemed to tap in to a well-developed aspect of his psyche, almost to feed off it in fact. But this gorging wasn't entirely for its own benefit. What it harvested it transmitted to some other place – some battery of coalesced psychic power gradually filling with an evil intent.

But Marshall only had this flash of insight for a moment. Within seconds he had been assimilated into an impersonal mindless gestalt, his body nothing more than a hollow and drained husk. The Great Harvest had begun.

57. Four Play

A howling Himalayan wind tore down from the high peaks chilling the bones of the small party of cautious travellers to the very core. Far off into the distance marched the towering silhouettes of range upon range of silent icy sentinels, the jagged backbone of the planet stark against the crystal-clear sky. Dave would have been breathless at the sight of such exquisite beauty, if he hadn't already been breathless from the climb. The fur coats provided by the nervous Urgistanis didn't help either. Dave was certain strange things nested in his – the weight slowed him down to a stumbling crawl.

The others were in better shape, Frank and Kate benefiting from their military training and the constant state of readiness their particular careers entailed. Becker seemed as sprightly as a mountain-goat – despite his advanced years more than keeping up with the foremost of the Urgi guides. The heavy load he carried did not hinder him. As he stopped for yet another breather, Dave pondered that it must be the proximity of his final nemesis which spurred the Dark Man on. It took the equally breathless Yajik to pull Dave to his feet.

'Come on, Outlander. Better we do not tarry.' Steadily they caught up with the platoon of wary Urgi soldiers.

The route Noroco took them led ever upwards in a series of bewildering switch-backs, through a sequence of increasingly bleak valleys, the scouring mountain air growing thinner at every turn. The Glacier of the Hill Witches was a place well known to generations of Urgistanis, a locale referred to time and again in the most blood-thirsty of their arcane myths. But that wasn't to say this route had been well trodden over the years. Their destination was guarded by the most deep-rooted taboos, as well it now seemed by the combined might of NATO's air forces. Twice on that difficult trek they'd needed to take cover from Allied planes, the roar of the jets and distant sonic booms the only sounds breaking the vast foreboding silence. Each time the party had untangled itself from the sparse undergrowth Becker had confidently informed them they had not been seen. If they had been spotted the response would have been as fast as it would have been brutal.

By mid-afternoon on that first day's climb the group began to pass mounds of heaped stone, tattered remnants of brightly coloured streamers flapping atop the pyres on the gusting breeze. Tersely their guides informed the four foreigners these were powerful wards, placed by earlier generations to contain the slumbering perversions which awaited them above – more than one of the frightened tribesmen making signs to dispel the evil eye as they did so. Dave couldn't help but feel that if a hail of .303 bullets couldn't do the trick then a few ribbons weren't going to help.

As the fiery red sun set behind the escarpments to the west the subdued travellers made a simple camp. Two miles to the north, up a narrowing rocky vale, a craggy ridge-line separated them from their ultimate destination – the alien-infested Kara-Kuri Glacier. Noroco calmly assured them that this close to night it was best not to camp too near the haunted spot. They would have to cover the last few miles at dawn. His almost casual words pumped a fresh dose of fear into Dave's already bulging veins. Under a thick musty blanket, strung up to keep the worst of the snow-flecked gale at bay, Kate and the terrified young man struggled to stay warm.

'Fancy meeting you here.' Dave's teeth chattered as he wondered if he could get away with putting his arm round her.

Kate made the decision for him. She well remembered her Arctic survival training. 'You can get closer than that. I'm not going to bite – though there might be things out there that would jump at the chance.'

As he nestled closer Dave looked at her long and hard in the gathering gloom. 'I hope this is all going to be worth it. I don't like the thought of our sacrifice just so your dad can go out in a blaze of glory.'

Kate sighed deeply. 'Sometimes you just have to *have a go*, no matter how futile the attempt. It beats sitting by and watching things crumble around your feet.'

Dave looked disconsolate. 'I don't know about that. I'd trade our present circumstances in for a bit of blissful ignorance any day. Kate, I'm scared.'

As if on cue a lurching shadow fell across their billowing hide. Then Frank's face peered down at them. Dave seethed inwardly as this potentially tender moment was interrupted. The grizzled ex-commando was handing out ammunition as he made his inspection rounds, checking on the preparedness of their sentries and pickets.

'Everything OK with you guys?'

Kate made room for him on the ledge. 'Dave's scared. I think we all are.'

The young man looked embarrassed as Frank hunkered down. 'All right, Kate! No need to spread it around.'

'I wasn't spreading it around, I was just telling Frank. He's one of us – you should know that best of all.'

The man himself looked at Dave oddly for a while. 'Nothing wrong with a bit of fear, partner. Thins the blood, keeps you on the move. Pure unadulterated terror once got me from Da Nang to Hanoi, and back again. You'll do fine when tomorrow comes.'

Dave's blush deepened. 'It's not so much that I'm jumping at every shadow. It's just I feel . . . a little inadequate surrounded by a bunch of emotionless hard cases like you.

Even the Urgis seem forged from solid steel. Becker doesn't seem to have a nerve-ending in his body.'

Frank shook his bandanna-swathed head. 'Oh, they're scared all right, they just don't show it. You gotta admire those tough-arse little guys. They know only too well what we're up against, but don't bat an eyelid as they march to almost certain death. I don't know if they're brave or clinically insane. Your assessment of Becker is closer to the mark.'

'Jesus,' muttered Dave, 'that's reassuring to know.'

Kate gazed up at the gaunt American. 'How about you, Frank, any nerves tonight?'

Frank stared off into the blindingly indigo sky, seemed to count the stars for a while, then looked right back at her. 'I had those circuits burnt out long ago. Sometimes that's not entirely a good thing.' With that he pulled away, loping off towards where Becker and Noroco sat deep in grim-faced council. Kate's eyes followed him wistfully.

Not for the first time Dave studied her serene face, and felt an ugly knot inside him tighten another turn. 'Heaven help us if we're relying on that psycho to pull us through. I don't know why we don't just give up right now.'

Kate glared back at him sharply. 'We don't *just give up* because people like Frank keep us going. Do you think we'd have got this far without him? He's not a quitter, Dave. Unlike you.' With that she pulled the covers around herself and turned her back on him.

There was not a lot he could say to that. Bleakly, Dave got his head down as best he could, to drift off into a troubled nightmare-haunted sleep. More than once he woke up to find his worst dreams were coming true. Tomorrow threatened to be a long and painful day.

* * *

That next morning dawned bright and clear, as if the very elements were attempting to lull the party into a false sense of security. But to the north a bank of sombre clouds had gathered during the night, forming a monumental wall of brooding grey terror. Silent flashes amidst the bubbling maelstrom hinted at conditions yet to come.

Yajik seemed to take great pleasure in telling the four huddled Westerners how fierce storms, brutal enough to make grown men long for death, could sweep down in minutes from the vast Tibetan plateau sprawled beyond the impassable Kara-Kuri range. As ever, Frank insisted on looking on an increasingly slender bright side – a convenient blizzard would cover any escape they might have to make. Dave doubted their planning needed to extend that far.

Not that their strategy, as it stood, was likely to win any prizes. If the French Foreign Legion ever started awarding Palme d'Ors, in the category of 'Best Foreign-Language Military Operation', then General Custer and the Seventh Cavalry were more likely to be getting a phone call and an all-expenses-paid trip to the Riviera. *Get inside the Watcher ship, penetrate the central hub complex, plant the bomb and get out again, as fast as possible*, was about as far as this masterpiece went. If anyone survived then that was a bonus. As Becker said himself, it wasn't going to be easy, but it would be as direct and brutal as a broken bottle in the face.

The time had arrived to decide who would make up the final assault team. Those not selected would stay behind to fortify the current forward base camp. After a hurried consultation with both Becker and Frank, General Noroco clambered onto a large flat stone to survey his anxious troops.

'I need volunteers to accompany us on the last leg of our heroic mission. If you're up for it, take one step forward. I have to warn you, though, it's not likely to be . . .'

Thirty threadbare Urgis literally fell over themselves in their haste to rush to the front. Yajik, who had been hovering by his President's side, was swept backwards by the surge of fur-clad bodies, as he himself leapt forward with his arm raised in the air.

It didn't make for a pretty sight: a confused scrum of flailing limbs and cursing bodies quickly developed. Several untimely fights broke out as every tribesman struggled to get more 'forward' than those around him. It seemed Noroco's followers were more scared of their all too tangible leader than they were of any dusty legend.

Noroco cast tired eyes towards the heavens. 'Gods, give me strength,' he muttered. 'Look, I'm not going to execute *anyone* who fails to volunteer – surely you must know me better than that by now. When did I last order a firing-squad to shoot anything other than fireworks?'

His words did nothing to dispel his men's selfish sacrificial frenzy. At the forefront of the fast-escalating ruck Yajik put his head down and drove determinedly for the rear, sweeping several of the more scrawny Urgis along with him as he went. 'Look, I'm volunteering, sire!' he cried, one scrawny arm held defiantly aloft.

Noroco had seen enough. Reasoning that if his troops insisted on being afraid of him then the least he could expect was some good old-fashioned military discipline, he put-on his best parade-ground Sergeant Major's voice.

'Atteeen-SHUN!' he screamed at the top of his lungs.

The fighting abruptly ended, several rollicking punches hanging ponderously in mid-air. One by one Noroco's men began to look at each other warily, then back at their exasperated commander – who had planted his hands on his hips and turned a most unattractive shade of puce.

'How many times do I have to tell you, I am NOT an evil dictator. You don't have to believe *everything* those lying Outland scum – no disrespect to our guests,' he shrugged apologetically towards Becker and Frank – 'what those lying Outland scum claim on their CIA-scripted news bulletins.'

After a brief pause, in which the general regained some

of his presidential composure, Noroco singled out one toothless, decrepit Urgistani soldier, suspended by the lapels by a more burly comrade.

'You there, Talmuk. I know for a fact you've got more wives and children than you know what to do with. How do you think they'd manage if you didn't come back? What in the name of all the sky-gods are you doing volunteering for a mission like this? Get back in line this instant, and that *is* an order.'

Meekly Talmuk did as he was told, muttering under his breath that if there was a better incentive for going on a suicide mission than having 'more wives and children than you knew what to do with', then he was yet to hear it. But Noroco was clearly in no mood for insubordination. His ominously quiet voice belied a volcano of barely suppressed menace.

'Now, I want all you men who've got wives and families to take one step backwards – and to stay there. This is likely to be a one-way trip.'

Reluctantly a majority of the Urgistanis took a shuffling step to the rear, downcast eyes monitoring their peers all the while. Noroco hadn't finished yet.

'And out of you lads who are left – if you'd really rather not come along I don't want you volunteering. It's perfectly acceptable to want to stay behind. I'm not exactly keen on it myself. We'll not stoop to the level of our enemies, no matter how badly they make us try. Come on now, don't make me get angry . . .'

Out of the corner of his eye Noroco spotted furtive movement. 'That doesn't include you, Yajik. You're coming with me. We'll need your occult expertise.' Slowly the defiant front ranks thinned, a growing knot of the middle-aged and the un-heroically sane forming to the rear. At last just seven young Urgistanis stubbornly remained rooted to the spot, each set of eyes suspiciously darting from one to the other.

'Right,' said Noroco, happy at last, 'that looks more like it. I want you boys to know I'll tolerate no heroics from any of you. If I see any grandstanding you'll have me to answer to. Now collect your kit and get ready to move out in five minutes.'

In the flurry of activity which followed, Dave found himself confronted by Kate. 'You know, you don't have to come,' she said to him as kindly as she was able, the sensation of kicking a loyal puppy still foremost in her mind. 'Perhaps it would be better if you waited here with the supplies.'

Dave might have been terrified out of his wits but there was no way he was letting the woman of his dreams disappear into some honeycombed hillside, infested with genetically engineered alien slime, never to be seen again. If she was going in, he was going in with her – if only to fire the bullets that would ensure neither was captured.

'Count me in. I've got as much to contribute as the next man – especially when the next man's Yajik. When I'm through with those green suckers they'll curse the day they ever crossed my path' . . . was what he meant to say, but what actually came out was a strangled wheezing, accompanied by some quite impressive dribbling.

Anyone who didn't know him better would have thought Dave was having some sort of fit. But Kate had seen it all before. She could tell by the way he frantically clutched the vintage bolt-action rifle the Urgis had given him that Dave wasn't going to be put off. Decidedly unconvinced, she wandered off to make her own preparations.

Frank quickly replaced her by his side. 'Easy there, partner, no need to develop combat fever just yet. Here, I want you to carry this.' He held out the battered satchel Dave had first seen slung round the neck of their long-since-departed Grey friend. Inside it bulged the ominous armoured edges of Becker's MJ13 manuscript.

Dave looked at it in disbelief. 'I can't believe you're

still hulking that thing around. Don't you think it's served its purpose? We don't want it slowing us down when we run screaming for our lives – not that I think that tactic will do much good.'

Frank looked at him oddly for a while. 'Just trust me on this one, Dave. I want you to have it.'

Dave regarded him bleakly. 'Just like you asked me to trust you when I met you in that diner?'

Frank refused to rise to the bait. 'Here you go. Slip the loop round your neck and I'll pull it good and tight. I've got a feeling it could come in handy.'

Reasoning fatalistically that it would do little harm to humour his friend, Dave did as he was told. The weight around his neck was no heavier than the weight already around his heart.

The four original conspirators were joined by General Noroco, Yajik and the seven Urgi volunteers – forming an inauspicious number, but seeing what they were already up against it hardly seemed to matter. Apart from Becker's nuclear-tipped briefcase, which he wore slung across his chest papoose fashion, their weaponry was far from awesome: Noroco and Frank carried their only automatic fire-arms. But then, as Becker so joylessly pointed out, if this assignment came down to fire-power alone then it would already be too late to matter. Stealth was to be their only hope of success.

As the hazy yellow sun was obscured by the first strands of cloud, heralding the approach of the shadowy darkness rolling in from the north, the final thirteen travellers set out silently to cover the last few desolate miles to the brooding glacier, and whatever awaited them within.

58. Penetration

Frank dived for cover behind the craggy granite outcrop which served as the group's temporary windswept home. His one-man recon sortie had been inconclusive, but in a positive way. He was out of breath, but only due to the dizzy altitude. Huddled behind the meagre obstacle a line of sombre faces stared back at him expectantly.

'Nada. There's nothing up there to see.'

'I can't believe we've got this far unopposed.' Becker peered from cover, towards the forbidding tunnel's gaping maw. Crouched beside him and shivering against the cold, the others did the same.

Up the gently rising slope, covered by a thickening layer of dirty yellow snow, led the twisting path they had picked their way along that fearful morning. But Dave knew that wasn't quite right; the path no more led up to the stygian chasm than it led up to a waiting wizard at the head of some decayed yellow brick road. Somehow the winding track seemed only to lead *down from* the ill-omened hole, worn away by centuries of scurrying inhuman toes – a one-way valve drip-feeding trouble and strife to the oblivious human race. By proceeding onwards they would be swimming against an incessant tide. Nothing new in that.

'Perhaps it's a trap.' Noroco couldn't bring himself to hope they would gain entry in such a simple fashion.

The hurried conference turned to regard Yajik's shivering form. 'Don't look at me,' shrugged the reluctant Urgistani. 'Just because my Gran told me a few ghost tales doesn't mean I know their tactics. Your guess is as good as mine . . . better, I'd be prepared to wager.'

'There are *no* traps,' insisted Frank, a little perturbed at their failure to take him at his word. 'At least not out in the open. I didn't get a good look inside but the place looks completely deserted from what I saw.'

Not for the first time Dave had his doubts. He was trying not to notice that Frank had scrawled '*Born to Kill*' on his filthy sweat-stained bandanna, in what he could only hope was an oddly-crusted red dye. 'I thought we were looking for a crashed alien ship? All I see is a dirty great mountain undercut by that foul-smelling cave.'

'It's in there all right.' Frank gestured above them, into the mass of dark grey swirling cloud.

Dave peered up though a veil of steadily falling snow. What he'd at first mistaken for a towering mountain rising up from the rocky valley floor at a near right-angle was in fact not stone at all, but a dirty age-old wall of solid ice. Millennia of ceaseless pressure had compacted the soil and rock the glacier carried into thickening strata of hardened moraine. It was through this dark, dense matter that some unseen hand had carved an entrance tunnel at the base. Dave strained his eyes studying the twisted hieroglyphs that danced around the portal. For its capstone the burrow bore a disquietingly familiar symbol – the triangular form of a brick-built pyramid, overset with a patiently watching all-seeing eye.

Frank pointed to the oddly regular cavern mouth. 'That leads up into the glacier – and into their ship buried within.'

The thirteen companions were silent for a moment, some of the Urgistanis waving a bewildering array of magic charms, as the howling wind whipped about their flapping, tattered uniforms.

At long last Kate broke the morbid silence. 'If we stay here much longer we won't need to worry what's inside. This storm won't take prisoners.'

It was plain to them all that she was right. Just as Yajik had predicted, the blizzard was sweeping in with dreadful suddenness. If they delayed any longer they wouldn't be able to see a hand in front of their frost-bitten faces, let alone navigate the last hundred yards to the cavern's jaw – scarring the glacier's face like a screaming mouth.

Becker glanced across at Frank. 'OK, soldier, lead the way.'

A manic glint entered Frank's pale blue eyes as he cocked his sub-machinegun with more force than was strictly necessary. 'Right people, move it out. Let's go kick some alien ass.'

59. Attackus Interruptus

As soon as they were inside the pungent crypt, away from the intensity of the worsening blizzard, the sound of the gale dropped to nothing more than a moaning whisper. As far as Dave was concerned the black silence which embraced them was infinitely worse. Urgistani soldiers lit their meagre store of oil lanterns as the young man hunkered down to ponder their predicament – and did not much like the conclusions he came to. Better a good clean frozen death outside than the breathless suffocating fate which no doubt awaited them inside this hellish warren.

From out of the darkness Kate glided to his side. 'How you doing, sunshine?'

'Not so good, to tell the truth. I just want to get this over and done with, one way or the other.'

'That's what we came here for,' she replied, checking the magazine of her rifle. 'Have some faith, Dave, we'll pull through. It's thanks to you and Frank we've got this one chance. Remember?'

Dave's heart lifted. Kate was right. It was at least partly thanks to him. It wasn't much, but it was better than no hope at all. He was just beginning to rekindle a flickering spark of hope when the relentless urgency of their quest tugged them on once more.

With a cheery smile that hid her true thoughts, Kate helped Dave clamber to his feet. 'Look lively, Frank's moving us out.'

The cavernous entrance narrowed to a snaking tunnel but didn't branch off into any other corridors. If it had done so navigation would have quickly become a problem – the icy walls that slipped past were as bleak and featureless as the snow-covered Urgi landscape outside. At times they were subjected to strong blasts of foul-smelling air which whistled down the tunnel from out of the shadowy depths. Weakly, Dave pulled a rough Urgi scarf up around his nose and mouth, as much to hold back the vomit as to exclude the reeking bouquet.

As they moved further into the haunted glacier Dave discovered the silence was far from complete. Every so often the frozen river of ice and powdered rock through which they travelled would give off a series of bone-juddering creaks and groans – as if it were some ancient iron bridge which had slipped its moorings and was on the point of collapse. But even these dreadful sounds were not the end of the matter.

From the uttermost depths of the mountain welled up the distant reverberation of age-old machinery pounding out an incessant rhythm. It seemed to reach out and twang a discordant harmonic buried somewhere deep inside Dave's over-burdened heart, and try to tear it still beating from his heaving chest. But there was something not quite right about the heavy drum-like beat, some subtle flaw in its teeth-loosening rumble. For some reason Dave got the impression all was not well with the engines driving the remorseless sound. Somehow they had been running down for thousands of years, and would soon grind to a halt completely if not tended to by a mechanic with a bit of WD40. How Dave knew this he had no idea. All he knew for certain was that if the hellish samba went on much longer it would shatter the fillings in his teeth. It was no surprise to discover he'd suffered a mild nosebleed.

Next to Dave and Kate, Becker kept a constant record of their progress, every hundred metres tying a fresh knot in a length of nylon string he kept suspended from his webbing. Noroco followed close behind, machine-gun cradled across one brawny arm. Frank was just a dim shadow out in front. Yajik and the other Urgi soldiers brought up the rear.

They journeyed in this fashion for several hours, the gently sloping gradient leading ever upward. Dave's only measure of time was his needlessly complex digital watch, which he'd turned to face inward on his wrist in a sad attempt to appear more professional. There was no other measure of progress through the subterranean world, just the soft pounding of their footfalls and the distant rumble of running-down gears. Twice they had to pause to refill the oil lamps from their fast-dwindling supply of fuel. At long last they came to a sudden halt. Each and every traveller sensed they had entered a large empty space.

Becker held up his flickering lantern to pierce the encroaching gloom. Above their swimming heads the curved walls of a vaulting hemispherical chamber stretched up to a shadowy unseen roof. Around the perimeter of the vast room stood a multitude of empty doors, their squat inhuman design mimicking the corridor down which they'd journeyed. Above this line of exits ran a narrow ledge carved from the frozen walls; atop this shelf another row of pitch-black portals stared back like mute unblinking eyes.

Grimly Becker turned to the speechless Noroco. 'You'd better get your men to mark each passage as best they can. They all look the same to me, even the one we came through.'

The general nodded in agreement. 'Otherwise we might never find our way out of this maze. How do we know which one to choose?'

All eyes turned to Frank, who stood thirty yards further into the cavern, sniffing the acrid breeze like a hound on the scent of something big and mean. None could hear the words he muttered over and over to himself – 'The Hall of Whispers . . . the Hall of Whispers.' He had seen more than he ever wanted to of this ancient meeting-place, and of the blasphemous rites that went on within.

Meanwhile Noroco had trotted back to pass on Becker's

instructions to his men, but before he could do so he got his first nasty shock of what would turn out to be a surprise-filled day. At the tail of the party Yajik was accompanied by just two white-faced Urgi soldiers. Noroco valiantly attempted to keep a rising note of panic from his voice.

'Er – Yajik, where are the others?'

Noroco's chief lieutenant looked on aghast, each of his limbs seemingly developing a quivering life of its own. With a barely audible squelch his remaining self-control dribbled from him and made a dash for the exit. 'We . . . we don't know, Great and Noble Leader. Perhaps they . . . wandered off?'

'WANDERED OFF!' Noroco's voice reverberated round the empty chamber, generating a fearsome echo. 'Have they gone to look for butterflies? Why, pray, did you not think to tell me this . . .' Noroco gave a massive mock shrug of his broad shoulders '. . . sooner?'

Yajik looked like he might burst into tears at any moment. 'Because . . . we were frightened of what you might say.'

Dave, Kate and Becker hurried back to discover the cause of the commotion. When he saw the general's expression, Becker's own face drained of colour. 'Er – where are the others?'

'Don't you start too,' fumed Noroco.

Kate found herself involuntarily raising her gun, and peering at the dizzy carousel of entrances spaced around them. Dave's testicles quickly packed their bags and caught the first express train north, into his quivering body, his fingers shakily groping for the safety-catch on his own rifle. At least Becker hadn't lost his usual gift for understatement.

'We can safely say that this is *not* a positive development.'

Was Dave imagining it or was the oppressive drum-beat

getting louder, the rhythm increasing in tempo? It had haunted their subconscious for so long it was hard to tell. 'I don't like this at all,' he sobbed quietly to no one in particular.

'Me neither,' breathed Kate next to him, as they both turned back to back and tried unsuccessfully to cover each and every opening.

Noroco looked at his deputy, dumbfounded. 'Let me get this clear,' he said with infinitely forced patience. 'You decided, to keep from me, the fact that our men have been picked off one by one, in case it PISSED ME OFF?'

It was all Yajik could do to nod his head.

Noroco's face seemed to illuminate the festering air around him with its own incandescent scarlet glow. 'And this restraint on your part, it's meant to have cushioned the blow, I take it?'

Yajik could say nothing in reply. Trembling furiously he simply reversed his rattling rifle and rammed its muzzle into his gaping mouth, badly chipping his few remaining teeth in the process. Both short scrawny arms unsuccessfully stretched for the trigger as he tried to balance the gun between his wobbling knees.

Noroco leapt towards his subordinate and knocked the weapon from his grasp, sending Yajik skidding across the rough-hewn floor like a rag doll. 'Get up, you maggot! We don't have the manpower to spare for such luxuries as suicide. You're a disgrace to our proud warrior race.'

At a dead run Frank rejoined the party. 'What the hell is going on back here? What's all the noise? Where are the others?'

Before Noroco could give a suitably cutting reply a mighty blast of stale air passed through the cavern, extinguishing all the flickering lanterns.

'Shit,' said Becker, from out of the pitch blackness.

Dave was about to scream, but never got the chance. Seconds later the lurking ambushers struck.

60. Multiple Organisms

Grendel Mk XVII was the very latest living prototype to spring from the Watchers' age-old production line of genetically engineered monstrosities.

Technically speaking he was what was known as a 'Lurker', but then that was a catch-all classification covering a wide range of shambling horrors with too many teeth and the personal habits of a first-year medical student. Barney, the Temple of Planet Love's pet watch-gorilla, bore a passing resemblance to G17 (as he was known to the handful of cultist technicians who'd lovingly nursed him from the hatching-vat) the same way John Noak's sheepdog Shep bore a passing resemblance to a twenty-tonne killer giant squid with an aggression complex.

Grendel had two arms and two legs, but that was where the similarities ended. Instead of a head he had nothing but a broad tooth-filled mouth, sprouting from a raised bump where his neck should have been. Despite the detrimental effect this had on his cranial capacity, not to mention eyesight, this arrangement had the undeniable benefit of at least getting his razor-rimmed mouth closer to his bottomless stomach. Grendel was a first-rate sentry, but also a prowling, growling garbage disposal unit well suited to recycling any trespassers unlucky enough to stray nearby.

He came from a distinguished line. His more conventionally headed, if less well-tentacled, relatives had been terrorizing Urgistanis (and the few hardy mountaineers foolish enough to venture into these hills) for more years than mankind cared to remember. Way back in the depths of history a revered ancestor had given a gang of Danish Vikings a torrid time – so torrid in fact that their entire race had struck out to do some freelance raping and pillaging in a search for a more peaceful existence.

But that wasn't to say G17 was a perfect specimen, in fact far from it. Watcher technology was not what it had been – things had been getting flaky around the edges for quite some time. Skills once mastered were being perverted by each dwindling generation of mindless Grey servants, distorted by fawning human cultists. As a result Grendel's DNA was a hotchpotch of conflicting information, a potpourri of battling chromosomes and cells. He was the final mutated bastard child of a decaying and desperate race.

You could tell all this just to look at him. He possessed no internal organs at all; inexplicably they were all hung from the outside of his twelve feet of corded muscle. Grendel didn't exactly 'wear his heart on his sleeve', it was just a bit further up his arm. As if this wasn't enough (and for most people who saw him, it was) Grendel had one more bizarre congenital abnormality suspended about his person: one all the more embarrassing seeing as he was at least nominally male. Between his bowed legs swung a ponderous set of pallid cows udders – the terrible legacy of his hijacked DNA.

One feature he did share with Barney was the almost *de rigueur* abdominal tentacles. The Watchers' servants were very 'big' on abdominal tentacles – you could almost have said it was their trade-mark. As it was, if some uppity mortal scientist got a bit too close for comfort with his genetic research, the preferred Watcher method of intimidation was to get their patsies on the Committee to have him denounced as a 'modern-day Frankenstein', dabbling in fields man was never meant to know. Mob mentality could be left to do the rest. There was very little pure R&D that went on anywhere in the world that didn't fall under the all-seeing eye of the Black Government. Alternatively, the Watchers could always send round a troop of Lurkers and their kind, with instructions to maim first and ask questions later – but only then if they so desired.

Once upon a time a radical young Grey designer, serving his apprenticeship amidst the very deepest hatching-pens, had drawn up concept sketches for an entire range of artificial creatures totally lacking in the 'A-T' department. This had caused much consternation and mirthless laughter around the Kara-Kuri HQ, even after said designer had been melted down and his genetic material used to pioneer a new range of sentient kettles. The Watcher minions might have been few in number but there was no way such free-thinking heresy could be tolerated. That way lay madness – not to mention the twin evil blights of logic and reason.

But there was no such risk of original thought pervading this fun-filled day. The orders that Grendel and his squad of 'Lesser Aberrations' had been given were both simple and direct, which was just as well as subtlety was not one of Grendel's strong points.

There was just one corridor down which the intruders could come (so the Mistress had told him): the humans would surely be traversing the single ground-floor entrance into the Watchers' glacial home. All Grendel and his chums had to do was pick off their hired help one by one, so thinning out the ranks to allow the principal ambush force to capture the main players alive. This they had done with consummate professionalism and glee, long gaunt arms yanking feckless Urgi soldiers into darkened alcoves to meet their silent and grizzly fate.

The final trap was set as the unsuspecting fools entered the deserted Hall of Whispers. It was only at this stage that they even noticed their team had been sliced off salami fashion from the rear. What cretins these man-things must be.

As he brooded in the shadows Grendel had needed to

fight back the enormous belch which welled up from the pit of his recently filled stomach. He'd consumed the Urgistanis he'd abducted with frenzied relish, though at the time he'd thought that a touch of tabasco sauce wouldn't have gone amiss. Now he was glad none had been to hand – indigestion could play havoc with a carefully laid trap. As it was he needn't have worried. The frightened jabberings of the man-creatures spared his blushes. As predicted, when the ambush struck they collapsed into a confused panic.

Grendel's mistress had been quite clear in her instructions: the intruders' leaders were to be taken alive at all costs, the eldest one especially so – no sacrifice of Lurkers or Greys was too high a price to pay towards this end. Grendel wasn't bothered by this stricture, the word *expendable* contained way too many syllables for his tiny brain to comprehend, but the concept was burnt into each and every cell of his vast and bloated body. Even if he had been capable of such an emotion Grendel had no cause to worry. Once the darkness came crashing down the invaders were subdued in the briefest and most one-sided of struggles. When their burning lamps were extinguished they were plunged into total darkness, the Lurkers and Greys well capable of operating under such conditions. As terrified shrieks rang out and the blazing muzzle flashes from useless fire-sticks strobe-lit the chaotic scene, the humies went down one by one, waves of small Grey bodies overpowering and pinning them to the floor.

Quickly tied and trussed the pitiful man-things had cried with all their might, their grating piggish voices calling to uncaring gods and pleading for desperate mercy until the bitter end – but their cries were destined to fall on deaf ears. In powerful unseen arms they were hauled away to meet their doom, not to mention to get rogered senseless by it.

Yelling in triumph and rushing down narrow corridors,

Dave's screaming form held high above his spittle-flecked mouth, Grendel failed to notice that his command had come up one captive short.

61. Blow Your Mind

Frank lay motionless in the side-tunnel until he knew the ambushers had departed. It took all of his discipline to remain still as the captives were carried off howling like terrified animals, but he knew his intervention at this stage would do his comrades little good. At least as long as he remained free they had a slender chance of survival. He put off calculating just how slender this chance might be.

When he sensed the last of the shambling monstrosities had run off screaming into the bowels of the hill, he inched his way forward on all fours, moving by touch rather than sight through the claustrophobic blackness. Bleakly he mused it was fortunate his sense of direction was better than his sense for danger had become – when he returned to the spot where his friends had made their futile stand his searching fingers found just what they were looking for. Tobacco-stained teeth flashing a mirthless smile he hefted the comforting weight of the second sub-machinegun into the crook of his arm. Noroco's ammunition pouch was not far away. Quickly he loaded fresh clips into both this weapon and his own, and slung the heavy sack around his shoulders. Frank guessed this was no time to be running short of rounds.

Quietly he set off through the tunnel the attackers had taken, delving ever deeper into the diabolical maze that made up the Watchers' warren. For the time being at least it wasn't hard to track their progress – he followed the receding screeches of the Lurkers' madcap flight as closely as he dared.

*   *   *

Dave was filled with horror, which for the moment at least was better than the belly of the nightmare beast he was precariously suspended above being filled by him. The mutated creature ran screaming down the pitch-black corridors, seemingly following a blind route map all its own. It was quite a ride, and Dave had been on a few dandies lately. He sensed more than saw the blur of hidden dangers whizzing past his head. His upturned face grazed scant inches below the racing ceiling, the frequent stalactites threatening to rip him in two.

When Dave's voice could hold out no more his screams subsided. What lay beyond the next checkpoint he could only guess at, but Dave suspected they were unlikely to accept Luncheon Vouchers or supply complimentary lemon-scented towels.

The young man's croaking silence brought little relief. Now he was able to hear the shrieks of the others, the superstitious pleadings of the Urgistanis intermixed with the cries of other more familiar voices. From out of the clamour rose Kate's frightened tones. Despite his own panic the plight of his companions filled Dave with a rising tide of rage. A burning desire for revenge welled up inside him like a volcano waiting to explode.

All too suddenly their headlong flight came to a juddering conclusion. Without thought for broken bones or cracked skulls their jabbering captors cast them down in the centre of a dimly lit hall, Dave's teeth clattering together like a cue ball striking a tight pack of reds. Within seconds his mouth had filled with the bitter taste of blood as, coughing like a beagle, he spat out what he hoped was only the tip of his tongue.

It was only then that the foetid stench hit him, almost making him add to the mangled scrap of bloody flesh lying pathetically on the floor. The age-old stagnant air was thick will a cocktail of repellent odours: rotting vegetables mixed with embalming fluid well past its bury-by date.

Slowly the panicking captives untangled themselves from the mêlée of bleeding limbs and took stock of their insane surroundings.

'Holy gods above,' whispered Yajik. 'This is where we die.'

Noroco was less fatalistic, though his voice held an equal measure of despair. 'Silence in the ranks. Where's your dignity? May the gods have mercy on our mortal souls,' he muttered as he staggered unsteadily to his feet.

Dreading what he might see, Dave clambered to his badly skinned knees and followed the general's fearful gaze.

They were in the midst of a broad oval cavern, the floor lit by a pervasive green phosphorescent light. The ceiling was lost far above, the distant walls in oddly writhing shadow. What Dave had first taken to be solid rock was nothing of the sort – though cold and hard to the touch it was a substance which had once been far more fluid. Try as he might he couldn't help but notice one unappealing feature: every curvaceous inch was smeared with a residue of thick, viscous slime.

Everywhere, swirling formations welled up from the rolling deck, their peculiarly shamanistic contours suggestive of fused and welded bone. Sprouting from many of these features, dotted around the room in bewildering profusion, a multitude of Watcher brain-hubs flourished, each a carbon copy of the one beneath the deserted HQ of Jackson's loony cult. The dancing fronds growing from the top of these telepathic beacons seemed to beckon to them like inhumanly erotic dancers, each one promising an eternity of blissful oblivion. It looked for all the world as if the bowels of some vast and twisted creature had become fossilized in crystalline metallic stone, and were now slowly thawing out as a colony of budding parasites pushed through its ruptured flesh. This unwelcome image yanked Dave back to the ghastly hybrids which had dragged them to this lair. Grendel and his pack of mutant cronies huddled off to one side in eager anticipation of further orders from some unseen master.

Dave realized that somewhere along the miles of silent corridor they must have left the honeycombed Urgi hill-side and entered the remains of the ghostly Watcher ship. But there was yet more to this awful place than first met his bloodshot eye. It was only now that he noticed what had hijacked the Urgistani's attention. The source of the sickly verdant light was glaringly obvious, almost hypnotic in fact.

One of the cave's vast arching walls was quite different from the rest. It was square and regular, cut from green translucent glass. And it held a slumbering nightmare vision within its boundless fertile depths.

Out of the frying pan, and into God's very own nuclear-powered wok, Dave thought. Before he could further study this obscene wonder a strangely familiar clipped female voice pierced the threatening gloom.

'Ah, Becker. One sees that we meet again. And you seem to have made some new friends. How comforting that must be for you in your old age.'

The speaker sat atop a high-backed throne on a raised and studded dais, the structure seemingly oozing from the gooey adhesive floor. Though at first glance human, there was an unnerving stiffness about her nature that Dave thought he had seen before. And then there were the billowing white robes gathered in her lap which appeared to writhe in an obscenely suggestive manner. Behind her, a giant Watcher brain-hub, much larger than the rest, throbbed and wriggled to an insane rhythm all its own.

Dave saw Kate's head snap up in instant recognition, her eyes glaze with sickened disbelief. He himself was too dazed to be surprised by anything anymore. With a frown he struggled to remember where he'd last heard that overly precise accent. Dimly the sherry-soaked memories of a myriad festive Speeches to the Commonwealth welled up inside him like a putrid Christmas pudding. His newfound knowledge explained a lot.

Becker clearly had less wholesome recollections of their hostess. He rasped his reply between strangled gasps. 'Not as comforting as the thought of seeing your abhorrent life ended, you arrogant bitch.'

Dave couldn't help but feel a simple show of good manners would have got them further – not far perhaps, but maybe their imminent deaths would be rendered all the quicker. Politeness was the general rule when addressing your hostess, especially one who welcomed callers as this one did. It was then Dave noticed another interesting factlet. The Dark Man's face was bruised and beaten but his heavy briefcase was still lashed securely to his torso. At this stage a clean death would come as blessed relief.

Becker's former mistress seemed amused by his hopeless defiance. 'You always were a feisty one, always flouting the authority of your superiors and social betters. And as so often in the past, on this occasion so terribly close to discovering the truth. It will be well worth the years of nagging One endured to see a man as conceited as you reduced to a lobotomized husk.' She threw her old grey head back and laughed uproariously. When she continued it was with a measure of satanic glee.

'But first, One wishes you to know the full magnitude of your defeat. Not just for the pleasure it will give, but to maximize the yield you yourself shall provide to further sustain the Masters' waking.'

Becker looked back at her defiantly. 'I think I can guess the details. You were a double agent corrupting those fools on the Committee to do your bidding, while simultaneously reigning queen of this foul hive.'

She looked at him with inhuman contempt and the first traces of a mad smile. 'Oh, that One should aspire to such lofty heights! I am a mere servant, Becker, just like your worthless self. Though I, at least, knew the leaders I truly served. I am nothing but the midwife, the patient nursemaid masterminding the conditions for the Old Ones to be born again. One can modestly say One has done a fine job. If only you could say the same.'

As she spoke Dave's eyes were drawn back towards the translucent wall behind her. It seemed to be filled with an army of writhing shapes, indistinct at present but dividing and taking individual forms before his bulging eyes. Becker sounded on the point of collapse, his voice carrying none of his usual conviction or sense of purpose.

'You'll never get away with your scheme. When the governments discover what you plan they'll blast this infernal hill to oblivion.'

The pale old woman smiled her joyless smile. 'One begs to differ, my troublesome child. Your feeble warnings have been to no avail. We have your squabbling leaders just where we want them – their shrivelled gonads cupped in our taloned hands. Now that the meddlesome Urgistanis have been subdued nothing can halt the long-awaited reaping.'

She looked down haughtily at Noroco, whom Yajik had to restrain to prevent him charging to an untimely, futile death. 'It is only proper that we have such exalted guests,' her frail hand waved in a well-practised gesture. 'As we speak the first batch of Masters are ready to arise. The fruits of our first harvest will stir the greatest amongst the Patriarchs. Soon your own contributions will be added to our hoard. And when every home on the planet contains a brain-hub ready to latch on, then the great psychic download can begin. The first shipments of transmitters depart tonight. Soon we will have enough of our crop for all the Watchers to awake!'

It was only now that Dave realized the full horror of what he was seeing. The green glass wall was filled with thousands of floating beasts; large, pallid bipedal forms that stirred restlessly from an eternal slumber. But it was a far from featureless enclosure. Fifty feet up its sheer face a row of eerily familiar orifices were linked to the floor by narrow lubricated strips. At the foot of each ramp a gaggle of Grey slaves rinsed thick amniotic fluid off Ancient Masters who had slithered forth from the giant holding-tank one by one. As Dave watched spellbound another popped from a contracting vulva and slid to the ground with a wet thunk, there to be caught by a team of eager three-fingered hands. When the Watcher had been washed down, the scurrying Greys attached a frond from the Great Brain-Hub to its pasty forehead and stepped back as of one. An expectant second passed. Slowly, the creature began to shake and tremble, then its cold dead eyes snapped open and it came wide awake.

Dave's breath caught in his throat; he felt certain he would choke with terror. There were plenty of Watchers still left to come, maybe tens of thousands by Dave's best estimate, but already two dozen or more were being walked round in a single ragged line – their ancient circulation stimulated back to life by the busily attendant Greys.

Becker could see what was happening too, the big man barely containing his surging emotion. Venomously he turned back to their grinning hostess. 'You make me sick. Isn't it enough they'll come to dominate mankind? Why did they need you to drive us to the brink of insanity first?'

Madame Chairman regarded him with weary, cynical eyes. 'You overestimate their cruelty. They are a pragmatic race, just like you or I. In fact, more like you than you could ever imagine. They do nothing without good reason.'

'Then why the campaign to spread conspiracy theories and paranoia? Do they hope to sap our will to fight? They might be in for a nasty shock, idiot politicians notwith-standing. There are plenty of free spirits who'll resist them.' Becker struggled to prevent his thoughts turning to Frank;

Madame Chairman was no doubt capable of plucking the very thoughts from his mind as he spoke.

The evil handmaid shook her grey head. 'Nothing so subtle, though your society's apathy doesn't hurt our cause one bit. There was a far more concrete reason for what we have done.

'Paranoid fear is the most potent human emotion, a powerful mental stimulant, turbo-charged caffeine for the soul. When the Watchers' ship crashed all those in suspended animation suffered massive neural trauma. The craft itself was a genetically engineered organism; the pain it suffered was channelled through its life-support circuits and into its unconscious cargo. Those few left unscathed put their damaged kindred into a deeper trance to slowly heal their terrible wounds. In order to revive them we now need the most powerful drug of all, the one that can only be obtained from every man and woman who currently walks this earth.'

Becker's gaze had become clouded and distant, his voice barely above a whisper. 'The abductions and the hoaxes. The Greys' bizarre behaviour . . .'

Their hostess nodded. 'For the past ten thousand years we, the humble servants of the Watchers, have lovingly ripened the crop. Only when we judged mankind to be sufficiently paranoid could we show our hand. Now you are ready, reaping day has come. Already the first of the Masters stir . . . Behold!'

The captives turned towards the moving shadows. As a swathe of cowering Greys slowly parted a handful of taller pallid figures dizzily shuffled forward.

Dave's throat was thick with awe. 'But they look just like . . . us.'

To look upon the Watchers, it seemed an overstretched Hollywood special effects department had decided to make savings on the budget. They were pale, they were emaciated to the point of anorexia, and they were groggy from their aeons-old sleep, but they were unmistakably human.

Their hostess gave a mirthless chuckle. 'How else do you think the body chemistry would be compatible? We aren't in the movies now. Your filthy race is nothing but the feral offspring of their mutated runts. The descendants of semi-civilized retarded exiles who "went native". When we handful of *true keepers of the flame* saw what had occurred we also saw our chance to one day wake the Great Architects themselves. Humanity is nothing but a pampered veal-calf, fattened for the butcher's knife. Well, your time at the block approaches, and you shouldn't feel a thing. Your true masters are coming home, and it's time to pay your dues.'

Dave sank to his suddenly jelly-filled knees. 'This cannot be happening!'

Their hostess rose to her bloodless feet. 'One is proud to say it has already begun. As we speak the final preparations for the draining of your entire race are well under way. We've had some false starts in the past – Hitler and Stalin both badly let us down – but this time there'll be no mistakes. What's more, just like so many unknowing humans, you *all* will help the cause. The more anxiety we can harvest the quicker the Masters' rightful sovereignty can be resumed. Anyone feeling sufficiently nervous yet?'

She threw a wrinkled finger in Dave's quivering direction. 'YOU look like a more than suitable candidate. Attach him to the brain-hub now!' Her hollow laughter rang like a diabolical bell.

A squad of fervent Greys sprang forward and Dave was dragged screaming to meet his fate. Cosmic kissing-cousins mankind might have been with the Watchers, but Dave had no desire to feel their snaking tongues wriggle between his lips, or to have their clammy hands grope across his firm young bosom. Seconds later he was held before the vein-riddled bulbous mass that made up the Central Brain-

Hub, its tentacles frenzied with delight. Dave struggled impotently against the unnatural strength of his diminutive captives, but his thrashings only served to tighten their grip. The Greys flung him down to the icy deck, one satanically grinning elf pinning each trembling limb.

This cold floor will give me piles, thought Dave for no good reason, as a sensuous creeper untangled itself from the mass of fronds sprouting from the organism's blushing pudenda. As it danced towards his waiting forehead Dave realized it would take more than Preparation H to save him now.

'Be strong, Dave,' cried Kate forlornly from twenty yards away, where she was pinned by yet more brainless Greys.

As the gyrating tentacle suckered onto Dave's forehead with a sickening squelch, all thoughts of haemorrhoids disappeared from his mind.

*   *   *

Frank peered from the dark passageway where he hid, carefully weighing up each player's every move. The cavern was filled with Greys interspersed with larger shambling figures. Off to one side the nightmare creatures which had ambushed them sat on their bony haunches, snapping at each other impatiently. Despite their fearsome slavering teeth and ripping claws, for the moment at least Frank didn't give them a second thought. There was nothing he could do to take down either group right now. Frank was focused on the captives. He didn't know precisely what he was looking for but he'd know it when he saw it, and when he saw it he'd have to be ready to move fast.

When he spotted Dave being dragged forward his heart sank. Frank knew better than most what one of the Watchers' transmitters could do to the fragile balance of the human mind. But his sadness was touched with a desperate hope.

If anyone was downright pig-headed enough to resist

such an infernal device it would undoubtedly be Dave. Frank's cast-iron complex of unshakeable beliefs still held dents from the handful of debates he'd had with the obstinately rational young man on their journey across the States. Few people were able to rationalize away many of Frank's theories. In the face of overwhelming evidence to the contrary Dave had been one of the few who'd tried. The fact that Frank's paranoia had been more than justified was not the point. The time for right and wrong had long since passed. If anyone could fight back against the pervasive forces of fear and dread it was the pale young man currently in the thrall of the Watchers' living master computer. The only question was, did he know it?

It wasn't much but it was all Frank had to work with. This might be his one and only chance. As silently as he was able he removed the safeties from each gun and hoisted them to his shoulders. Frank needn't have worried about detection. All eyes were turned to the bitch on the stage, who seemed to be reading something from an oddly familiar book. When the strands of the brain-hub stopped their swaying and acrid smoke started pouring from its seams, Frank was the least surprised of anyone – what's more, he was ready.

With a crystal clarity of vision he saw the time for action was at hand. Yelling an inhuman war-cry he began his thundering charge – a hail of 9mm shells heralding his arrival. It was time to crash the party, and Frank had brought a rag-topped bottle filled with hate.

*　　*　　*

The mind the Watchers' Master Brain-Hub tapped into was a battleground of conflicting emotion. Dave's psyche was adrift in an unprecedented sea of mental flux, the lurking icebergs on the horizon shards of jagged decaying kryptonite.

He refused blindly to believe what their hag-like tormentor had hold them, it was too insanely outlandish to be true. Even at this final hour Dave clung to the belief there *had* to be a rational explanation for everything that he'd seen – it was almost a matter of faith. He knew deep down all aliens *must* be virtuous higher beings acting out a *Star Trek* scenario in reverse, noble adherents to some virtuous exploring cause. That the Greys were on a five-million-year mission to crash into deserts and abduct hill-farmers to foster paranoia didn't bear thinking about, and Dave wasn't about to try. Maybe this was an experiment in mass psychosis – some sociology student's idea of a bad joke. Dave clung to this forlorn hope like the blindly faithful dogma that it was, the Himalayan stockpile of evidence to the contrary rejected with every sinew.

Such was his concentration that he hardly noticed as the hieroglyph-covered satchel was ripped from him, hardly batted an eyelid as the document he'd fought so long and hard to protect was handed to his cold-eyed nemesis. Like a frail old nanny settling down for story time, Madame Chairman hefted its prodigious weight into her bulging lap. Turning to a random page she read out loud Becker's most guarded thoughts, rendering an uncannily perfect imitation of his voice.

'There exists the very real possibility that the so-called alien presence is not at all what it seems. It is my disquieting belief that we have been the victims of a subtle and cunning manipulation.'

She seemed to find these words amusing, no doubt the hopelessly naïve meanderings of a juvenile intellect. Laughing at the top of her genetically modified lungs, and with more strength than she could have humanly mustered, she flung the weighty tome in a spiralling arc through the fume-thick air.

As the book he'd carried so far skidded across the slimy floor Dave was filled with a mad and passionate rage.

But he was also filled with memories. Memories of Kate's frightened shrieks, memories of the long fruitless hours he'd spent trying to make sense of this whole bewildering situation, also memories of his own burning desire for revenge. Most of all he remembered something he'd once read between MJ13's battered bullet-riddled covers, a half-deduced central truth Becker must have intuited in a moment of divine madness.

Their ability to manipulate mankind is dependent on our willingness to accept the existence of their powers.

Dave now saw the essential truth of what Becker had only guessed at. The Watchers could only win by preying on man's dormant fears, amplifying and twisting them to serve their selfish needs. Without human paranoia they were less than nothing.

Summoning up all his personal store of rationalism and reason, Dave saw a way to strike back.

* * *

Frank knew none of this. In fact he currently knew very little apart from his berserk battle-rage. It enveloped him in a swirling red mist which pervaded every reflex and reaction. He was a creature, not of thought, but purely of action, a killing machine bent to just one purpose.

A stumbling crowd of Greys and Watchers had gathered round the brain-hub, dull dead eyes transfixed on Dave's titanic struggle. The first they knew of Frank's arrival was the implosion of a dozen fragile skulls, as the intuitively aimed bullets tore through them. Reaping time had come, but it wasn't human anxiety which was the crop; the Watchers and their spindly servants fell before a scythe of inescapable lead shot. Frank passed through them like a grim-faced angel of death, leaving nothing but smoking carrion in his bloody wake.

Somehow the group's hostess ducked outside this withering field of fire. Now she turned to Grendel and his kind, fury twisting her face into a haggard reflection of her personality. 'Stop him, you fools! STOP HIM RIGHT NOW!'

Grendel's Lurkers surged forward, fangs and talons at the ready. They meant to rend and kill, and their target would surely fall beneath their numbers. With a sense of timing worthy of a washed-up comedian both Frank's guns fell silent, firing pins clicking dryly on empty chambers.

* * *

Dave didn't just sit back and passively let the brain-hub suck his fears from him, he pushed them forward with all his mental might.

But his own growing paranoia wasn't all that he forced across the overloaded terminal's bio-circuits – he bombarded the half-sentient device with every ounce of his sane and rational nature, showered it with empathic love and understanding. It was a potent mental cocktail the Watcher siphon was never meant to channel. Not once before had a mere human fought back in such a way. Centuries of unvarying one-way traffic had cauterized rigid pathways through its brittle neutral networks. Now they were smashed asunder. With a sickening creaking its vein-riddled skin began to give way. The Watchers' preening midwife whipped round in stupefied disbelief.

'NOOOOO!' she cried, as thick black smoke poured from it and the stench of burning cabbage filled the chamber.

As one the dancing fronds sprouting from the summit stiffened and went rigid, moments before the hellish thing exploded in a blinding flash of unnaturally purple light. Its detonation showered those around it with its still-cooking innards, its vast bulk unleashing a reservoir of repulsive stagnant stew. Dave was almost drowned by the sweeping tidal flow, his wide-eyed companions blown backwards in a skidding tumble. Gasping for air they spat the thick brew from noses and mouths, and frantically prepared to meet their fate.

But the effects on the Watchers' servants were more dramatic still, though at first less apparent. Slowly Grendel sank to his knees, his huge paws groping for where his head should have been. To a Lurker his nest-mates did the same; being creatures of very little brain they relied on the group mind for instruction. Their link to this pool of collective thought was the hub Dave had just popped like a pus-filled balloon. It was safe to say the violent disconnection came as a nasty shock.

Moments later they were a seething mass of unco-ordinated limbs and spiky tentacles thrashing madly on the floor – cutting themselves to pieces, the maimed survivors of a slipshod abattoir. The consequences for the distraught hostess and her harem of Grey slaves was equally decisive. In unison they dropped to the ground, cold eyes rolling back in deformed skulls and blood-flecked spittle foaming from their lipless mouths. Their piercing shrieks of mental agony filled the cave in an ear-splitting crescendo.

The terrified captives saw their moment for escape had arrived. Just how long it might last was another matter. Kate and Noroco dived towards Dave, brushing staggering Greys aside. When they reached him he was already clambering to his knees, the tentacle which had skewered his forehead nothing but a withered creeper. Kate's voice was thick above the terrible din.

'Dave! Are you OK?'

'I've got one hell of a headache. And I never want to see another vegetable again.'

Frank was instantly at their elbow, dextrously changing both clips simultaneously. 'That was a nice move, soldier, but let's not hang around. I don't figure we've got time for tearful reunions.'

Already Grendel's howling Lurkers were showing the first spasmodic signs of recovery. The other brain-hubs were no doubt picking up the telepathic slack left by their nerve-centre's explosive demise – patching into the Watchers' reeling command system one by one. Just as during their initial penetration Frank unnervingly seemed to know the route they must take, bounding off towards a dark tunnel mouth with long strides.

The others rushed after him, all that is except the grim-faced Becker. The Dark Man dropped to the floor and swung around the armoured briefcase he still carried across his shoulders. Inside his trembling fingers danced in a bewildering series of complex motions, well aware that this might be his last chance to pull off what he had in mind. But Grendel was recovering faster than the other Watcher minions. As the clouds of pain-filled confusion parted he staggered dizzily to his hoofed feet, fearful claws scouring across the deck.

Becker saw the monstrous shadow fall across him and fumbled to repack his demolition charge. Scrambling upright he turned to run, but Grendel was far too quick. Lashing out with one massive paw he made contact with a stretching hamstring, tearing Becker's leg open from groin to calf. The Dark Man went down with a horrifying scream, his briefcase bomb skidding across the slime-veneered floor. Becker's companions raced on unknowing, his agonized thrashings lost amidst the tumultuous din behind them. Grendel fared little better. As the beast towered above, the Dark Man reached inside his bloody suit, grimacing against the inferno of agony engulfing his lower limbs. With practised ease he drew his faithful .45 and blindly emptied the gun's magazine into Grendel's heaving chest. On full auto the power was terrific.

The force of the shots hammered the creature backwards off its feet, but this wasn't the only misfortune to befall the Lurker pack-leader. The grey mists of chaos emanating from the place where instruction had once come threw out a swirling tendril once again and dragged him back into a twitching spasm of oblivion. But the damage had been done. Becker was going nowhere.

Sensing they were a man down Frank turned back, carbine at the ready. Instinctively, he trapped the spinning briefcase underfoot and looked up for its owner. His eyes instantly locked with Becker's, his CO already thirty paces behind and huddled in a blood-drenched heap. Momentarily an unspoken understanding passed between them, then Frank kicked the case back to his commander's groping arms. Despite his intense pain Becker's voice held all its usual sledgehammer authority.

'Ten minutes. That's how long I'll take.'

For the ex-Black Beret insubordination was not an option. For a moment their gazes remained fixed, the knowledge of half a century of squandered power passing between them. Soon Frank turned after the others and was gone, racing into the black, twisting caverns.

62. Premature Detonation

Even allowing for his insider knowledge of the layout of the Watcher craft Frank decided it was going to be very close indeed. There was only one means of escape he knew would get them clear of ground zero fast enough to matter; the trick was going to be getting there in time. Shouting encouragement like a frenzied drill sergeant he urged his stumbling charges onwards.

His cajoling was not strictly necessary. Dave and Kate were more than eager to leave the horrors of the central cortex far behind, while Yajik and Noroco had the racing motor of superstitious dread to power their short stumpy legs. The pace they set along the dim corridor would have done an Olympic athlete proud. That's why, when they burst into the Poke-It-On hatching-chamber, it took them twenty yards to skid to a halt, stunned terror carved on each and every face. The sunken floor was a seething mass of Poke-It-On hatchlings, beyond a raised lip the wide room ankle-deep in the wriggling spider-like forms.

'What the hell are they?' yelled Dave, his voice rising by several frantic octaves.

Frank held up a restraining hand as he cautiously edged back towards the chamber's doorway one step at a time. 'They're more dangerous than the rest of the Watchers' creations put together. The Poke-It-Ons are the final part of the plan, the means by which they'll harvest fresh paranoia from an unwitting human race. Their touch means life-long mental slavery – look.'

The others peered upwards towards the low ceiling. From it hung a multitude of slowly writhing forms. They had once been human, of that there was little doubt, but what they were now was open to debate. They were deathly pale and dead-eyed, sucked dry of every natural emotion. Dave had seen that living-dead look once before. He'd had a summer holiday job at a telephone call centre.

'*Kill us,*' one of the nearest victims seemed to moan, as an adolescent Poke-It-On scurried up slime-stained clothing to attach itself limpet-like to an abused forehead. Eagerly the squirming animal began to suck the thoroughly appropriate terror from its host's imprisoned mind, swelling as it transmitted its ill-gotten cargo. The fugitives looked on transfixed, the squirming sea of hostless parasites forgotten for the moment as they steadily drew in round their feet.

Dave recognized many who made up the Watchers' living power-cell. He was no expert on the business world but even he knew some of those vacant faces. What was left of the Committee of 300 served the Watchers in waking death as surely as they'd served their cause in life. Perhaps there was such a thing as natural justice. Even so, this aberration went several strides too far.

Frank was the first to break their hypnotic spell. 'Don't let the little bastards near you,' he spat, backing away from the remorseless wriggling tide.

Kate's voice was on the point of breaking as she continued to gaze upwards. 'Christ, but they're . . . people.'

'*Were* people,' corrected Frank. 'Now they're nothing but the batteries for the Watchers' rebirth. That's what we can all expect if they get their way.'

Meanwhile, Dave had noticed the recent reduction in their numbers. 'Where the hell's Becker?'

Frank looked him straight in the eye. 'Becker took a hit. He's down injured back at the central cortex.'

'We've got to go back. We can't just leave him to those fiends!'

Frank shook his head. 'He knows what he's gotta do. He's initiating the detonation sequence as we speak.'

Noroco kicked out at an over-eager Poke-It-On that had scampered towards his leg. 'By all the gods . . . how long have we left?'

Frank remounted the single step that would keep the Poke-It-Ons temporarily at bay. 'About six minutes, and counting.'

Dave's voice wavered. 'We've got to get as far from here as we can! Just how big is this bloody ship?'

Frank looked sick to his ground-down back teeth. 'It's not as simple as that. This whole craft is basically a capacitor of psychic energy, currently gearing up to receive its final charge. As soon as that bomb detonates it will set off a chain reaction that's likely to take this mountain range with it. We've got to get miles away if we're going to live to tell the tale.'

'Then we're done for.' It was Yajik's cheerful tones which chirped up now.

Frank slung his machine-gun tight across his chest. 'You're with me now, asshole, and I ain't a quitter. See that doorway on the other side? We've got to get there fast.'

'But how?' Dave backed away from yet more of the over-eager Poke-It-Ons. 'They cover the entire floor.'

Behind them a bellow of awesome rage echoed off the tunnel walls.

'That's it,' sobbed Yajik, 'the Old One's beasts come for us! Who wants to go first?'

Meanwhile Frank was quickly estimating the distance between the tunnel mouth behind them and the fast gathering sea of Poke-It-Ons beyond. 'Into the shadows. I might just have a plan.'

*　　*　　*

As Becker's delirious brain swam upwards through a sea of tortured pain he momentarily broke the surface back into conscious thought. With this ascent came the dizzy recollection of initiating the detonation sequence, and of re-strapping the briefcase to his mangled chest. Neither of these memories kindled much emotion.

How long had it been since he'd thrown that last switch? Not long, he felt sure. The process was reversible but it would take his opponents time, time he was going to have to kill, before they did the same to him.

Weakly he pulled himself over to where MJ13 had come to rest, the weighty volume exercising a compulsive draw even at his moment of terminal stress. Wearily, he ran his hands over its inlaid surface, its familiar texture some small comfort in his hour of need. No sooner had be dragged it under his head like a makeshift pillow than once more a hulking shadow slid across him. But this time there was no hope of a lead and cordite salvation, his weapon having long since clicked dry. But just when the deadly shadow seemed ready to fall the grating female voice which haunted Becker's dreams croaked up once again.

'Not him, you fool, his balls belong to me. Get the others. We can't have them running loose.'

The shadow snorted and seemed to shrug its shoulders, but within a straining heartbeat it was gone. Becker's blood-caked eyes creaked open for one final time. Weakly, he beheld the Chairman of the Committee.

It was safe to say she'd seen better days. The sudden destruction of the master brain-hub had taken its toll on her as well as on her minions. Her face was a mask of crazed dismay, her hair a blue-rinsed electrified mane. In her mad eyes burned a light of insane hatred for Becker and all his kind. Grimacing like a short plump gargoyle, she staggered towards him and grabbed hold of his shattered leg.

'We've got much to discuss Becker, you and I. Many old wounds to reopen before you die.'

*   *   *

Grendel was not dead. Despite gunshot wounds you could put a fist in, he was still a functioning creature – but only just. The Lurker leader had been through a lot just lately, and psychologically perhaps more than physically he was beginning to show the scars.

He was not only *not dead*, he was currently monumentally pissed off, and that was a new sensation for the previously all-conquering Lurker. He was also furiously following the trail of the cause of all his frustrations. When he caught up with them Grendel promised himself their reunion was going to be as bloody as he could make it – and that was very bloody indeed.

*　　*　　*

When Grendel rounded the last corner and charged down the gentle incline towards the mouth of the Poke-It-On hatchery, it took all of Dave's courage to stand his ground. Not much of a foundation on which to build a final desperate plan, but then Dave's soul was currently a building site undergoing a rapid and radical expansion – hard hats to be worn at all times. As his gaze locked on the avalanche of reformed blubber bearing down upon him the young man discovered he possessed fresh reservoirs of that previously scarce commodity.

It wasn't just the thought of the imminent nuclear explosion he seemed destined to become a part of, nor the faith his friends had placed in him, which egged him on. Just like a rickety old bridge reinforced by iron pins, a new steel ran through Dave's weary veins, holding him fast and steady. It was a disconcerting feeling, as if a wild-eyed newcomer were suddenly in control. It was a sensation Frank could have told only too much about.

When Grendel was thirty yards away Dave watched the beast's flailing arms and foam-flecked tusks draw near with detached curiosity, if with a slightly tighter than normal bladder.

Twenty yards away and he could smell the monster's putrid breath break over him in a crashing wave.

Ten yards and he could almost taste its pent-up rage. Feel the thing's fearsome momentum which threatened to crush him like a hammer-blow.

With just five yards to spare those thrashing claws lunged for him greedily for one final time.

Functioning on auto-pilot Dave flung himself from Grendel's remorseless path and flew through the air with the greatest of unease. As he dived for cover his self-control finally gave way. Dave began to laugh hysterically as if having a fit – ludicrous as it seemed, he was beginning to enjoy this. His shuddering impact with the unyielding floor did little to lessen his soaring adrenaline high.

Grendel surged forward, maiming nothing but thin air, his fearsome talons rending the green-tinged darkness. Howling with redoubled rage his vast bulk teetered on the brink of the chamber's lip for a heart-stopping instant as he scrambled to a slithering halt. This was the moment Frank had been waiting for. Charging from the shadows he gave the others his harsh signal. As one they sprang from their hiding places and converged on the swaying monster. Along with Kate, Noroco and Yajik, Frank hit Grendel's foul-smelling behind and pushed with all his might.

It was easier than would have seemed possible, but Grendel had not once come to a halt, his momentum had been ever onwards. It would have taken the merest nudge to topple him into the swathe of baying Poke-It-Ons, not the Herculean heave which he now received. Grendel swayed at the chamber-mouth for a further precarious second, like a giant redwood waiting to fall. Then, with gravity-defying slowness, he tumbled forward to crash headlong into the mass of waiting Poke-It-Ons – his last sound a bemused and terrified shriek.

Chirping in frenzied delight the little creatures washed

over him, smothering Grendel in a seething, inescapable tide.

*   *   *

'Go!' screamed Frank, hoisting his Sterling to his shoulder and cocking its firing mechanism.

He'd intended to blast a trail clear through any scuttling arachnids that didn't converge on the Lurker, but he needn't have worried. Each and every Poke-It-On made a beeline for the Grendel's stricken form, as if sensing the fresh reserves of paranoia the monstrosity held on tap. Within seconds Grendel was covered with thousands of the milling parasites, his vast bulk squashing untold numbers pancake-flat as he thrashed around in the mercifully concealing darkness. For their part the Poke-It-Ons seemed no less agitated. They were not used to locating such a ready supply of the Watchers' life-juice in one of their fellow creations and were having more than a spot of difficulty with Grendel's lack of a forehead.

Just one of the hand-sized creatures seemed to have no desire to become involved in the riotous fray. It sat up on its stumpy rear legs and regarded the stunned humans inquisitively with obscene puppy-dog eyes. That was its misfortune. Frank dispatched it with a controlled burst of automatic gunfire, the Poke-It-On exploding in a shower of green blood and steaming bile. The deafening boom of the 9mm's echoes took an age to fade.

'GO GO GO!' he yelled, shoving the general forwards onto the momentarily clear floor.

The others were not far behind, Frank bringing up the rear ready to lift any unlucky enough to fall. The going was far from easy. They had to stoop low to avoid the twitching feet of the Poke-It-Ons' previous victims, and the floor was uneven and slick with the viscous birth-juices of the creatures. In less than half a minute they'd traversed the nestling chamber, reaching the relative safety of the far wall and its welcoming retaining lip. Dave hurtled up the metre-high step as if his life depended on it. But there was one more nasty surprise waiting for them here: there was no beckoning tunnel leading from that hellish chamber, no flashing door marked 'Exit' – just what looked like a row of large tightly closed sphincters embedded in the vein-riddled wall.

'What now?' demanded Dave, turning to cover their rear. 'I want to *kick some arse*, but this is ridiculous!' Sadly for him there was no sign of any pursuit, just the eerie jerks and twitches of the undead psychic battery hanging behind them.

'We've got to get in,' panted Frank, 'otherwise it's us who'll do the dying.' Vainly thumping at the opening, he searched furiously for the control stud he knew must open it.

Kate was not convinced. 'In there? Is that a good idea? Looks like something big and nasty's waste-disposal chute to me.'

'Close, but no cigar,' said Frank, triumphantly punching a discoloured membrane to the side of the nauseously pulsating hole. With a rancid blast of methane gas an iris valve swelled and then dilated.

'It's what passes for an elevator around here. And unless you want to glow in the dark in many, many pieces, I suggest you climb inside. We've got three minutes left!'

As soon as the five had filled the tiny padded space a sudden surge of acceleration hit them. Seconds later a familiar sense of weightlessness sent their intestines on an upward trajectory. For these travellers this sensation was down to more than just their over-fast arrival. They were disgorged into yet another chamber, this one far longer than it was wide. To their right the corridor stretched towards an archway of unmistakably familiar light – a snow-covered helicopter just visible on the landing pad outside. Yajik took off in this direction like an excited greyhound – or at least he did until Frank caught him by the collar, almost throttling him as he did so.

'No time for that. Climb into one of those, two of you to a pod.'

Opposite them a long row of wide vertical tubes covered the entire wall, marching off into the dim and dusty distance. Broad slots were cut into the bottom of each – empty as if once holding some long-forgotten cargo. At least most of them stood empty. Jammed into two of the nearest tubes were some of the strangest objects Dave had ever seen. They were dumpy elliptical capsules – like giant vein-riddled eggs six feet high and maybe four feet wide. What's more they were fronted by clear hatchways which currently hung ajar, each device covered with arcane runes and symbols.

'What are they?' clamoured Kate, instantly regretting it. Nuclear oblivion was suddenly looking more appealing by the minute. She had no desire to become the first meal of some gluttonous alien hive. At least the bomb offered a good clean simple death.

Frank pushed all four onwards. 'Shut up and get in. No time for explanations.'

Dave feared this fact would soon become self-evident; he was already half-wincing against the expected blinding flash and skin-flaying surge of heat. By his best reckoning the three minutes were already up – their goose well and truly flambéed. He wasn't afraid, just strangely elated. If he was going to meet his maker he was looking forward to *popping him a good one* right between the eyes – after first asking him why he'd bothered giving men nipples.

Frantically, Frank crowded them towards the pods, Kate and Dave into one, Noroco and Yajik into the other.

'I still want to know what they are,' demanded Kate, pulling Dave in beside her.

Frank leant all his weight against the creaking hatch. 'This is a space ship, remember. These are its lifeboats.'

Her face went as white as a liver fluke. 'But the pods have been here for thousands of years. Are they going to work? How do they land?'

Frank did a fair job of shrugging as he endeavoured to lock them in. 'If they don't you can console yourselves with one thought.'

'What's that?'

'It's gonna be one hell of a way to die. Hold on for the ride of your lives.'

Dave and Kate seemed to have plenty further to say, but their words were lost as the semi-transparent carapace locked into place. The young man looked almost keen to partake of this exhilarating ride, the screaming girl jammed beside him somewhat less eager.

Frank fell backwards as the capsule was sucked fully into the launch tube, the automatic ejection sequence taking over. Before his weary eyes, with a hearty pneumatic *whomph*, the capsule disappeared from view, leaving nothing but a swirling tendril of violet smoke to mark its passing. Frank was thankful to discover Noroco and Yajik had climbed into their pod with less debate.

'Do not tarry, my friend,' called the general, pulling their own hatchway into place. 'You have done much to aid us in our hour of need. Now look to your own survival.'

As the Urgistanis' pod was pulled backwards into the second launch chamber, Frank dedicated himself to taking Noroco's advice. Would there be other operational capsules to hand? He was going to have to move fast if he was going to find one.

*   *   *

Becker counted down slowly in his head, trying hard not to let his panic, or the excruciating pain which wracked his lower body, rush the familiarly comforting rhythm. It wasn't easy; each second seemed to stretch for an agonizing

417

lifetime, but these painful moments at least gave him the chance to reflect on some of the things he'd done during his own long and troubled existence.

He knew full well he'd pulled some fast ones in his time – more than that, he'd orchestrated them, printed the sheet-music in fact. There were hundreds of thousands of people dead today because of the covert agendas he'd helped further. He'd had a job to do, not always a pleasant one, but a necessary one all the same – it was a job he'd done well. It hadn't all been about furthering the ends of the evil psychotic harridan who now stood before him, it had been about being a pro – and he had been, right up until the bitter, twisted end.

When you played fast and loose with the lives of others the least you could do was be prepared to do the same with your own. Well, now his time had come. He wasn't looking for forgiveness, he wasn't entirely sure he wouldn't do those same things again. Everything he'd ever done had been motivated by a sense of duty, not malice for its own sake. Right or wrong he'd at least been consistent. Maybe that was some sort of salvation, maybe not. He wasn't entirely sure anymore. The knowledge of what he was about to do, as long as he could keep this soulless harpy distracted long enough, brought its own comforting tranquillity. For the first time in more decades than he cared to remember Becker was at peace with himself.

Which was more than could be said for his reeling hostess. From out of the verdant darkness she towered above him like a nightmare wraith, her voice as shrill and mesmerizing as ever.

'There is no need to thank *One* for saving you from Grendel, no need to thank *One* at all.' She malevolently reached for his ruined leg and snapped it backwards with a loud crack of breaking bone.

Stifling a scream Becker refrained from pointing out

that he'd rather eat his own intestines than thank her for anything, considering it less than wise in his present helpless situation. Though perhaps some good old-fashioned name-calling would help stretch the time.

'You're such a humanitarian,' he rasped, shuddering against the pain. 'And there was me thinking you were nothing but an emotionally-repressed inbred Kraut, who'd never done an honest day's work in her life. What a fool I've been.'

Madame Chairman threw her head back and laughed like she never meant to stop. 'It would be better for your snivelling race if that's all I was.' She paused only to beat him round the face with such force it spun him around. Several of his teeth didn't survive her next playful slap. But suddenly something caught her eye and her merriment cut off as suddenly as it began.

'What's that strapped to your chest?' Her voice held its customary tone of assumed command. 'Show me this instant. *One* orders it to be done!'

Their gazes locked as Becker's lips seemed to move imperceptibly, as if counting under his breath. The Dark Man chuckled happily despite his pain. 'I'll show you, all right, but first you'll have to step closer. You'll have to forgive me, I'm not as mobile as I once was.'

The Watchers' midwife seemed genuinely unnerved by his cheerful manner, but nonetheless bowed to get a better look. 'What do you have in there – additions to your farcical notes? One has a mind to be amused by more of your laughable conclusions.'

Becker's smile was joyous to behold. 'Not quite, you mad old Teutonic witch. Though you are just about to receive something you've long deserved.'

Spittle leapt from her bloodless lips and her pale eyes tinkled madly. 'A curse on you and all your riddles. Hand it over RIGHT NOW!'

As her grasping hands fumbled with the clasp, Becker's

world suddenly turned a blinding white, then slowly faded to a welcoming numbing black.

*   *   *

'I don't like this one bit,' muttered Kate with Herculean understatement, as the capsule was subjected to a bewildering series of mechanical shunts and shudders. Laying side by side it was hard to escape the conclusion they were encased in some padded alien coffin.

Next to her in the cramped compartment Dave was experiencing a strange set of conflicting emotions. On one level he was as petrified as his companion, but on another he was strangely exhilarated. His devil-may-care mood had started soon after he'd destroyed the Watcher brain-hub, and then cranked up a notch by the part he'd played in Grendel's horrific demise.

'Loosen up, babe.' He took Kate's trembling hand. 'This is going to be fun – or a one-way trip to Valhalla. Yaaa-hooooo!'

She opened her mouth as if to reply but all the air was driven from her lungs by the stunning force of the eye-bulging acceleration that hit them. Dave guessed that, just as in their earlier black triangle ride, they were cocooned in some sort of inertialess field – but the rate of their take-off was awesome nonetheless. Just as he thought their ascent could not get any faster they were rocked by another monstrous hammer-blow from behind – a wave of unnatural heat passing through them. An instant later they were surrounded by a blood-curdling muffled rumble. Dave tried to turn to comfort his friend, but found any movement out of the question. Judging by her breathing he needn't have worried; Kate had passed out into merciful oblivion.

As suddenly as it had set in, the acceleration subsided, though the sensation of immense speed remained, the banshee howl of hypersonic air all around them. Dave was able to turn his head sufficiently to see out of the frosted capsule window. What he saw filled even his newly bullish soul with nausea and dismay. Below them the topmost clouds receded like tiny falling snowflakes, the ultramarine glint of some unknown sea clearly visible far beneath. Off at an insane angle the brooding mass of the cold grey Himalayas retreated into the distance, to slip over the gentle curve of the uncaring Earth.

'H-h-high up,' Dave stammered, promptly slumping back to the relative comfort of his oddly contoured couch. They stayed that way for what seemed like hours, with nothing but the swirling complexity of the interior of the Watcher pod to fill his mind. At some point Kate came groggily awake, but drifted back to sleep when Dave told her not to worry. He didn't say why he thought that good advice; there was little they could do to help themselves, their fate was out of their hands. Suddenly there came a sense of momentary weightlessness, then a subtle change of direction, and a slowly snowballing motion on a worrying fresh course. Unmistakably, they were falling back to earth.

When the sky outside the window turned from an unwelcoming black to a frigid azure, Dave heard a series of grating mechanical sounds, not unlike a temperamental old banger being coaxed into life. These noises were followed by a rapid unfurling, then the loud crack of a wide expanse of fabric suddenly coming under tension. Moments later, the capsule experienced a sharp jolt of deceleration.

After a long period of pendulous drifting, both passengers were awakened by a sudden jarring impact, the force of the collision burying them deep in the protective confines of the capsule's padded walls. Dave was overcome with a confusing new sensation. With relief he realized there was no longer any sense of speed. Within seconds the capsule's windowed hatchway had sprung open and bright daylight came flooding in. Dizzily, Dave pulled himself into a sitting position and gathered the folds of the silky parachute away from the hatch.

'What is it, what do you see?' Kate was not far behind. Dave had to raise his hand to shield his eyes from the fierce sunlight encroaching from outside.

'Don't know. Got no idea.'

From out of the distance, across a sea of thorny scrub little different in colour from the sandy soil from which it sprouted, a lone figure was riding towards them. Behind him a vast herd of sheep wheeled and mingled, as several dusty sheepdogs stalked them through the bush.

Presently the rider reined in his mount and peered at Dave and Kate from under a wide-brimmed hat.

'Jesus Christ. Where the 'ell did you spring from?'

Dave thought it time to impress all present with his in-depth knowledge of distant customs and traditions. 'Gooday, cobber,' he replied. 'You wouldna believe us if we told ya.'

63. Did the Earth Move?

Shakily, Kate lifted the tumbler of neat scotch to her cracked and calloused lips, downing its burning contents in one gulp. She wasn't accustomed to drinking this way and had only been doing so since her and Dave's low-profile return home.

Around her the flat was an awful mess, the combined result of an uninvited visit by Special Branch while they'd been away, and a week's worth of careless living since their return. Housework seemed to have lost its relevance after what they'd been through. Nothing was missing, she could be certain of that fact since the entire accumulated clutter of a life was strewn across the floor. What 'the Met's Finest' had been looking for she could only guess at – some clue to her involvement in the bizarre massacre at the TV studios no doubt. They must have been satisfied there was no evidence linking her to that messy slaughter – she'd made no secret of her presence and they hadn't been back in over a week. At least that was something; the last thing she needed right now was a jaded policeman incredulously picking over her story. She didn't think they'd find it any easier to believe than she did herself.

Over in one corner, half-buried beneath a mound of empty bottles and pizza boxes, Kate's television continued to spew forth its never-ending stream of meaningless drivel – at least some things never changed. The device provided the only light in the dingy room. The curtains were drawn, even though around them the first stark traces of grey dawn were clearly visible. The TV was tuned to a 24-hour news channel, as it had been ever since they'd got back, but it wasn't what was on the box that depressed her, it was what wasn't.

Nothing about their recent Himalayan adventures, at all.

She hadn't wanted a ticker tape parade, nor any sort of medal, least of all a telegram from the Queen. She didn't want the personal recognition, quite the opposite in fact. Kate was a private person and intended to keep it that way. All she was looking for was some small acknowledgement of what they'd done had meant to the human race – some token recognition that what they'd been through had indeed taken place. To date she had drawn a complete blank, leaving her despondent and baffled – and thirsty for alcoholic relief.

Of course for the first few days the news had been filled with nothing but Urgistan, but then it had been for the past four months, ever since the UN passed its first solemn edict regarding that previously unheard-of nation. The military build-up, the inevitably lopsided war and the sudden ceasefire had all in turn exerted a predictable hold over news editors around the globe – but only until the next big story broke, and what had come next had indeed been a biggie. As far as Kate could see Urgistan was fading back into insignificance. The Geneva Peace Talks were going well, so well in fact they were no longer even front-page news, pushed back to a brief mention in the midst of the bulletins by the unprecedented Royal revelations.

This was the crux of what had Kate baffled. If you watched the reports a certain way, in a suspicious frame of mind, there were *indirect* repercussions aplenty, you could spot them in every carefully scripted word. There was just no mention of the momentous events in which she and Dave had played so crucial a part. You could almost sense the newsreaders straining at the bit to tell the full terrible tale – a knowing smile here, a pregnant pause there. She didn't have to be a lip-reader to know what they were saying to one another as the closing credits rolled.

It was almost enough to drive Kate mad with frustration. In fact she'd found herself chewing her fingernails almost down to the knuckle whilst listening to reports of the wild roller-coaster ride the global stock market had taken over those recent turbulent days. Were these events linked to what had gone on in that hellish glacier in Urgistan? She didn't think so, but who knew for sure. These paranoid day-dreams had drawn her mind back to Frank and his unknown fate. Then she'd started drinking again, and all reason had left her.

As far as Kate could tell, these were the facts as GNN and the rest of the world saw them.

Eight days ago a massive volcanic eruption had rocked the central Himalayas. This had been followed up by the sort of earthquake that made whole continents tremble, and fundamentalist God-botherers head for the hills with shotguns and ten-year supplies of baked beans. After this tremor the Richter Scale was in drastic need of re-calibration. After-shocks had been felt thousands of miles away – there were even reports that Balmoral's chandeliers had been heard to tinkle. The epicentre had been a forbidding peak never before scaled by man in a remote area of northern Urgistan – the desolate Kara-Kuri region, so inaccessible even the recent war had largely passed it by.

Overcome with compassion for this plucky little nation, which only days before had been the pariah of the world, the 'International Community' sprang to Urgistan's aid. The army of spin doctors running the military operation hadn't needed an opinion poll to tell them which way the public mood would swing – right back in their sun-tanned, over-made-up faces if they weren't careful. The bombing had come to an abrupt and immediate end – the Urgi war machine judged to be halted in its tracks for the time being. Food parcels and medical supplies had replaced cluster bombs and napalm, with just the same minimal effect. Suddenly, far away in Switzerland, the moribund peace process had sparked back into life like a haywire cuckoo clock poked with a very long stick. Few of the world's elected politicians could recall why the bombing had started in the first place, if indeed they'd ever known at all.

As far as the rest of the planet was concerned the frenetic pace of events hadn't slackened for a minute – some unprecedented changes were taking place in fact. The Queen of England and the upper reaches of her family had all gone missing simultaneously. Under highly suspicious circumstances they'd disappeared without a trace. The Monarch's top aides and equerries claimed they'd been told nothing of any secret plans, but few of her former subjects believed these newly unemployed retainers. Since no terrorist ransom note had been received it was now widely assumed their disappearance represented a total and unannounced abdication of the family's power. Judging by the House of Windsor's publicity in recent years few begrudged them their withdrawal from the spotlight's intrusive glare.

In Britain's ensuing constitutional crisis many drastic options had been considered. In a frenzy of national self-recrimination the leaderless English did what they always did in a situation like this – they looked to contract out their monarching requirements. But they quickly discovered times had changed. All the usual suspects were considered, but the Houses of Tudor and Stewart were no more. Hanover was now nothing more than a major autobahn intersection overlooking a new Toyota plant. The net would have to be cast further afield. More than one under-employed monarch from Europe's dented tin-pot states had been interviewed with an eye to filling the role, but none could agree personal terms – abolishing income tax was not an option. To the intense relief of Middle England roulette tables and croupiers would not be making an appearance at Buck House after all. But the nation was no closer to finding a sovereign. The final straw came when Dame Edna turned Parliament down.

In the absence of an acceptable candidate the maniacally grinning PM volunteered to double up as Head of State. With what some considered undue haste he was measured up for a new set of ceremonial robes he'd designed himself. It was hard to escape the conclusion he'd had these locked away in a desk drawer all along. A small but vociferous protest movement sprang up overnight demanding police pathologists go through the garden behind Number Ten with a fine-toothed comb, but their pleas seemed likely to end in vain. As far as presidential candidates went the boyish PM was at least a better option than wheeling out the mummified remains of Ted Heath for one last chance to go out in a blaze of boredom.

The head of the Commonwealth was not the only high-profile VIP to have been lost in recent days. Many of the planet's top multinational corporations were recruiting new CEOs. To lose one looked like carelessness, to lose so many at the same time looked like extreme good fortune. The usual breed of internet cranks even went so far as to suggest the disappearances were linked by some sort of conspiracy. A whole host of fresh cranks sprang up overnight claiming the first group of internet cranks were in on the scam, and were cutting the corporate heads in on the proceeds from the vastly increased sponsorship deals they'd secured for their newly popular sites. During this chaotic period several of the most hysterical conspiracy .coms floated on the bucking stock market, only to sink Titanic-like without a trace. What with the widespread consumer unrest over the non-appearance of the long-awaited Poke-It-On toys, the commercial sector was in the midst of a deepening crisis. The business community could be certain of only one thing – in an unexpected bonanza for City recruitment firms the job market for corpulent felines seemed to have become more fluent than it had been in living memory. It might take years to fill all the roles. In that time corporate mergers, multi-million-dollar road schemes, cyclopean Third World dams and new brands of decaffeinated freeze-dried low-fat coffee would just have to be put on ice. What a shame.

Some of the other stories hitting the headlines sent a chill running down Kate's spine. There had been a surge of cult activity in recent months, peaking late last week. Kate found these reports easier to understand – the memories of Jackson's organization's fiery departure still all too fresh in her mind. A string of mass suicides were soon discovered around the globe, in more than one instance accompanied by explosions and all-consuming flames. In case of discovery the Watchers had laid careful plans to plug every potential leak; now their leaderless followers took their only way out. As bemused firefighters picked through the wreckage of cult HQs in a score of major cities, they were once again prompted to ask what drove people to such lengths. Few could come up with satisfactory answers. Kate could hazard a guess.

As she reached to pour herself another drink the doorbell chimed discordantly. Kate let it ring five more times before summoning the energy to stagger to her feet. She didn't need to check the security peephole to know who was there, and it wasn't MI6 come to break her thumbs. Dave was showing a disconcerting tendency to get up far too early just recently. With a tired mumbled hello, and a sinking spirit, Kate let him in.

'Morning, sleeping beauty. Weren't you up yet?'

'Actually I didn't go to bed.'

Dave looked at his old friend for a long while, finally tugging the empty bottle from her fingers. Judging by the state she was in he could well believe her claim. She was in the midst of a ferocious bad-hair week and had the sort of red-rimmed eyes that would have made an insomniac bloodhound wince. The girl staggered back into the lounge cradling her throbbing head in her hands.

'Don't look at me that way, I've been through a lot just lately. You've got your way of dealing with it, I've got mine.'

Dave shook his head. 'But this isn't *dealing with it*. You'll find no answers in here.' He waved the bottle in her face. 'The world has moved on, and so must we. I know it's not easy, but we've got to put what we went through behind us.'

His swaying best friend scoffed in disbelief. 'No one else seems all that bothered. You wouldn't have thought we'd achieved a thing.'

'What were you expecting, an invite from the production team of *Emergency 999*? Our enemies existed in the shadows, and they died that way too. Be thankful no more people know how close they came to winning.'

If Kate was depressed then Dave was just the reverse. In fact recently his perpetual high-energy enthusiasm binge was becoming quite a bore. Since their return it seemed he had not stopped moving for a minute. Having been exposed to the more violent side of life, perhaps the Kung Fu lessons were understandable, but the base-jumping really would have to stop, and looked likely to now that the Canary Wharf security staff knew his face – there were only so many ways you could smuggle a parachute past them.

Kate's haggard face broke into a hollow laugh. 'You're no good at taking your own advice, chum. You've gone from *Conan the Librarian* to *Conan the Suicidal* in one foul swoop. That's a mighty destructive monkey on your back – and it's demanding more than just bananas, in case you hadn't noticed.'

Dave felt his face flush. He hadn't entirely lost all trace of his old persona. He knew Kate's appraisal was correct. Scouring the night sky with binoculars and a flask of weak lemony drink might seem dull these days but at least it wasn't hazardous to your health. Relatively few of Britain's overcrowded hospital A&E departments had to regularly clear space for moon-blindness cases.

'Maybe you've got a point. That's why I've come to see you today.'

Recently Kate had become alarmed and slightly scared by her friend's change of character. She felt she'd lost a soulmate and gained a hyperactive student PE teacher in his stead. Was this the first sign he was coming down? 'I'm glad to hear it,' she said tentatively.

He nodded and lowered his eyes. 'Listen, I've been thinking.'

He pulled a package from his jacket. Triumphantly he slapped the colourful bundle of holiday brochures on her cluttered coffee table.

'Take a look at these. Tell me what you think. I reckon we need a break.'

She drowsily leafed through the book on top of the pile. 'After what we've been through, don't you think hiking across the Kalahari is a little excessive?'

Dave's face broke into his familiar lopsided smile. 'Perhaps you're right. But I still think we should get away somewhere. But *not* Las Vegas this time.'

Kate smiled to herself. It was the first time Dave had seen her do that in weeks. But then a shadow seemed to fall across her eyes. 'I'm sorry, I was forgetting he was your dad.'

Kate waved her hand in front of her face. 'We were never close. It was only last year I learned our true relationship. Up until then I only thought of him as my commanding officer – a voice at the end of the phone line who told me what to do. It was hard to think of Becker any other way.'

'I can imagine it was. He was quite a guy.'

'You can say that again. But at least he died doing what he would have wished – fighting the rising tide, helping to put right some of the wrongs he'd been tricked into perpetuating.'

Dave nodded. He knew Kate well enough, could tell just by looking at her in fact, that it wasn't her father's explosive demise that had her troubled. It was what had become of their other companion. He reached over and took her hand.

'You know, you could say the same thing about Frank. He was doing what he wanted right up to the very end. He wouldn't have wanted it any other way.'

She looked at him bleakly, in a way that wasn't just down to the early morning alcohol. 'Do you think he . . . made it out alive?'

Dave sighed. 'I'd be lying if I said I knew for sure, but I do know this. Frank was a fighter, in his own way just like your dad. He wouldn't have given up just because the odds were stacked against him. If anyone could have made it out of there alive, it was him.'

She turned to gaze back at the incessant TV. 'I hope you're right.'

*   *   *

Eight thousand miles from where Dave and Kate were beginning to put their lives back together, conditions were showing the first tentative signs of getting back to what passed for normality. In light of what Urgistan had been through that past year any normality was strictly relative – and this was an immediate family that consisted of Uncle Mayhem, two brothers Confusion and second cousin Mindless Slaughter.

As stunned Urgis were helped from bunkers and cellars by the joint Red Cross/Red Crescent rescue teams, they were bemused more than anything else by the world's sudden change of heart. To have blankets raining down from the sky instead of bombs came as a welcome relief, though at times an equally destructive shock.

Honest J's Rug Emporium, which had somehow escaped the Americans' valiant attempts to level it with their most up-to-date laser-guided munitions, was taken out by a surgical strike of powered baby-milk pushed from the back of a transport plane. The harrowed proprietor had returned home, with his wailing family in tow, to find a rain-filled crater where his shop had once stood surrounded by an extensive assembly of local cats.

These Outlanders were crazy, the Urgis concluded. The whole sorry war did nothing but confirm a host of long-standing local prejudices about those two-faced sea-level dwellers. Many of them were little better than amphibians. Gladly, they would encourage you to buy armaments one minute, with talk of regional stability and trade-aid schemes, only the next to spend millions of their own destroying what you'd bought when they thought you'd stepped over some invisible line. Surely some scheme could be worked out in future whereby the arms were destroyed back in their country of origin, with decreased expenses all round. GNN would just have to find some other way to boost its ratings – topless ladies' tennis, perhaps. An impossible dream, but a pleasant one nonetheless.

When Noroco had arrived unannounced at the Geneva Peace Conference he'd been more surprised than many by the warm welcome he'd received. How he had got there remained a mystery, but most international commentators agreed his timely arrival had helped swing the day in favour of the cause of peace. There were rumours of a spectacular entrance involving a blatant publicity stunt – parachuting into the Swiss Alps in some sort of capsule – but such trivia was soon lost amidst the scenes of general magnanimous good faith. There was talk of a Nobel Peace Prize in the offing, both for him and his taciturn sidekick Yajik, who seemed to do little but sit in the corner and whimper loudly for no apparent reason.

Back at home Noroco's people were content with more mundane rewards. At the moment they knew little of how the ancient curse had been lifted from their land, but their distant leaders would soon come to tell them the full heroic tale. For the moment they were simply grateful to be able to return to their quiet way of life, away from the unpredictable glare of the outside world.

Ten years later, when the statue of Dave, Kate, Becker and Frank finally went up in the rebuilt town square, the locals held a modest celebration at which President Noroco gave a rousing speech. Few others of the world's leaders found the time to attend, or for that matter were invited. The Urgistanis liked it just fine that way.

64. On the Beach

As the blazing sun sank lazily far out to sea, throwing a molten highway across the dappled waves, the newcomer lay back on his beach-lounger and took another sip of his unfeasibly large electric-blue cocktail. Once the annoying paper parasol had been discarded he came to the conclusion it wasn't half bad after all. He'd tasted better, but that had been far off and long ago. Since then the world had moved on.

Not far away, at the high-tide line, an egg-shaped capsule rocked on the gentle breakers. It was still attached to its parachute, which threatened to drag it out to sea some time in the near future – but not any time soon, very little seemed rushed in these idyllic tropical surroundings.

The capsule's erstwhile passenger didn't care one way or the other. The pod represented the last link to his former life, a life of ceaseless toil and nerve-frying danger – not to mention unending paranoia and an alarming expenditure of explosive ammunition. Now he calculated he deserved a break. Nothing too excessive, just ten or fifteen years in this most agreeable of spots would do.

His extended vacation was looking increasingly like a viable proposition. The island's bunkers held enough provisions to last a hundred years. Some time before he'd arrived the handful of Grey guards had elected to take the quickest route to that great saucer trailer-park in the sky, their frail bodies long since turned to ash on their makeshift funeral pyre. With this development the rest of the inhabitants had apparently chosen to make a long-overdue bid for freedom. By all accounts the raft hadn't made a pretty sight, but then neither had its strange cargo of bickering human flotsam. It was truly amazing how resourceful clapped-out 'dead' celebrities could be when they put their minds to it. The newcomer just hoped they didn't run into any tropical storms before they reached the safety of the nearest press conference or booze-fuelled film junket.

That was one consignment of Boat People who wouldn't find it difficult obtaining a new home. That's if the assembled press didn't mug them when they stumbled up the beach. The stranger realized, with a rueful smile, that he wasn't interested in watching the sensational news reports which were bound to follow – that was one monkey he'd shaken off his scarred and sunburnt back. Perhaps he really was a changed man after all.

Beside him his blonde companion kicked off her pom-pom slippers and stretched out her far from youthful legs. It seemed that in the final reckoning the Watchers' rejuvenation therapies were as half-baked as their bid for power had been. She was older than him by several decades, her golden locks long since turned to an ashen grey, but her playful sparkling eyes still held some of that innocence which had lit up the cinema screen. Norma's voice was still a silkily suggestive baritone, like candyfloss licked from a nipple.

'You won't leave me, not like all the others, will you Franky baby? I always get left the fuzzy end of the lollipop.'

Her companion slowly shook his weary head, and half turned to look back up the beach. Through the palm trees the remains of the administration bunker were slowly burning. 'We won't be leaving anytime soon, my dear. Shouldn't receive any unwanted visitors, neither. There's nothing here an outsider could want any more.'

At least he could be sure of this one point. He'd set the colony's last remaining black triangle on auto-pilot and sent it hovering out to sea not three hours ago – there to crash into the ocean's mysterious all-concealing depths.

There were some things man was better off not knowing, for the time being at least.

It was hard to escape the conclusion his new friend was a living, breathing embodiment of this statement. As she drained her own drink her big dark eyes took on a distant look.

'This whole business has been so confusing. Sometimes just thinking about it made my head spin. What's a simple girl supposed to do?'

The old soldier couldn't have agreed more. 'Don't worry about it, my dear. Make mine another large one.' Frank had every intention of enjoying his retirement.

PUBLIC SERVICE ANNOUNCEMENT

Now that you have been exposed to details of the Watcher Conspiracy – to make us believe all conspiracy theories are true (including this one) – your mind is in a dangerous state of paranoid turmoil and confusion. Your will to resist has been sapped, and you are ripe for the Ancient Masters' long-planned 'harvesting'. Along with the 'author' of this book you must be taken into protective custody for your own good, and for the future benefit of the rest of mankind. Please hand yourself in to the nearest police station with a note reading: 'I am a slave of the Watchers, a 42nd Level Royal Freemason and disciple of the Temple of Planet Love. Please lock me up and throw away the key.' The forces of law and order will know what to do with you.

Thanking you in anticipation of your co-operation.

Becker.

P.S. Of course, that's not my real name.

P.P.S. Time for my medication.

Only Forward
Michael Marshall Smith

A truly stunning debut from a young author. Extremely original, satirical and poignant, a marriage of numerous genres brilliantly executed to produce something entirely new.

Stark is a troubleshooter. He lives in The City - a massive conglomeration of self-governing Neighbourhoods, each with their own peculiarity. Stark lives in Colour, where computers co-ordinate the tone of the street lights to match the clothes that people wear. Close by is Sound where noise is strictly forbidden, and Ffnaph where people spend their whole lives leaping on trampolines and trying to touch the sky. Then there is Red, where anything goes, and all too often does.

At the heart of them all is the Centre - a back-stabbing community of 'Actioneers' intent only on achieving - divided into areas like 'The Results are what Counts sub-section' which boasts 43 grades of monorail attendant. Fell Alkland, Actioneer extraordinaire has been kidapped. It is up to Stark to find him. But in doing so he is forced to confront the terrible secrets of his past. A life he has blocked out for too long.

'Michael Marshall Smith's *Only Forward* is a dark labyrinth of a book: shocking, moving and surreal. Violent, outrageous and witty - sometimes simultaneously - it offers us a journey from which we return both shaken and exhilarated. An extraordinary debut.'
Clive Barker

ISBN 0 586 21774 6

Philip K. Dick

The Collected Stories

In five sumptuous volumes, the best short fiction of Philip K. Dick, the founding father of modern science fiction.

'A fitting tribute to a great philosophical writer who found science fiction the ideal form for the expression of his ideas'   *Independent*

'A stunning composite portrait of our times'   *Observer*

'The funniest writer of his time, and perhaps the most terrifying'   *Encyclopaedia of Science Fiction*

Volume 1: BEYOND LIES THE WUB   0 586 20764 3
Volume 2: SECOND VARIETY   0 586 20765 1
Volume 3: THE FATHER THING   0 586 20767 8
Volume 4: THE DAYS OF PERKY PAT   0 586 20768 6
Volume 5: WE CAN REMEMBER IT FOR YOU WHOLESALE   0 586 20769 4